BRONZEVILLE'S BOOTSTRAPS

The Revealing Story of African-American Entrepreneurs
Who Made History with Timeless Lessons for Today

A NOVEL
inspired by real
people and events

WALLACE S. HALL

Bronzeville's Bootstraps
Copyright © 2022 by Wallace S. Hall

ISBN
978-1-956161-78-6 (Paperback)
978-1-956161-77-9 (eBook)

DEDICATION

This novel was inspired by and is dedicated to America's mid-twentieth Century African-American entrepreneurs with whom I met, knew, lived and worked. In spite of segregation and prejudices, they economically overcame. Other successful Black businessmen and women whose accomplishments I have only read about are also included. The colorful characters Bronzeville produced have also been added to flavor and add excitement to this story. My devoted family, whose love, cash, patience and commitment, turned my dream of over 20 years, into a reality, deserve a deep measure of appreciation.

Bronzeville's Bootstraps (BB) is dedicated to Charlie Moore, whose significant participation in editing, constructive contributions and positive comments made (BB) a better novel, and me a better writer.

Live and in living color, forever.

ACKNOWLEDGEMENT

Without Writer's Retreat Worksshop, wrw40@netscape.net the formula and process of writing a novel would have never been learned. Charles (Charlie) L. Moore's charliemoore@hotmail.com, two year commitment as my literary mentor, struggled with me tirelessly. BB would never have reached a level of literary acceptance without his involvement. Mary Huckstep, yorkhouse@dslextreme.com, persuaded me to significantly revise BB, which has improved the story and readability. Richard (Rico) Gregg, rgregg719, has been my writing partner for over two years, which has made both of us better writers. Cheryl Leonhardt, 719-265-1003, professor and editor, brought BB to its present level of grammatical correctness. Thank you all. Here's hoping your efforts bear fruit.

Copies of this book may be purchased at the CreateSpace eStore: https://www.createspace.com/5811800

A BIT ABOUT BRONZEVILLE

Bronzeville's Bootstraps is dedicated to the people who made Bronzeville, through the 1970's, this nation's most prosperous Black ghetto.

Bronzeville's business-oriented destiny was forged when Jean Baptiste Point DuSable, a dark, West Indian, in the 1780's, established a fur trading business along what is now the Chicago River. A number of free Black people made an integrated Chicago home.

More than a century later, after the Civil War, many Negroes trekked to Chicago looking for a better life. They were forced to settle south of Chicago's downtown district, which became known as the South Side. The stock yards, railroad and bus line hubs, steel mills, hotels, downtown office buildings and scores of businesses hired unskilled, energetic Negroes.

Because Bronzeville was the most segregated neighborhood in the nation, many Negro entrepreneurs started enterprises. By 1917 there were 731 thriving businesses owned and supported by Negroes. Arriving, African American professionals found Bronzeville a captive, fruitful market.

The name Bronzeville was formally introduced in 1930 by James J. Gentry, a journalist. He persuaded a Negro newspaper to promote a contest electing the 'Mayor of Bronzeville'. WW II's factories sparked the second great migration to Bronzeville, also known as, "The Black Belt" and, because of employment opportunities, "The Promised Land."

During the forties, 47th Street was the main drag, saturated by lounges and bars. The elegant Regal Theatre, a stop on the "chittlin circuit," presented nationally known entertainers including Duke Ellington, Cab Calloway, Buddy Rich, Stan Kenton, and Sarah Vaughn, for week-long engagements, during the fall months. The Savoy Ballroom featured roller skating, and professional boxing matches. The Pershing Hotel promoted jazz musicians in their lounge, and, "Battle of the Bands" dances in their ballroom. The Parkway hosted elite, invitation only, social events. Club Delagado, (*Club Delisia*) was a popular night club, which along with the Rumboogie, offered floor shows with chorus girls. The Main Drag moved to 63rd Street in the 50's as Bronzeville expanded. Live jazz and blues prevailed.

City politicians allowed Bronzeville to manage its affairs; vice and corruption, including Policy, reined.

Many nationally renowned Negroes called Bronzeville home; Nat "King" Cole, among them. Gwendolyn Brooks' "Raisin in the Sun" was set in Bronzeville. Today a statue honoring the Bronzeville Businessman, named, Monument to the Great Northern Migration, stands between 25th and 26th streets, on Martin Luther King Jr. Drive. There is a Bronzeville Historical Society.

There are many residents of this exciting and once prosperous community who inspired ***Bronzeville's Bootstraps.***

TABLE OF CONTENTS

Dedication iii
Acknowledgement vii
A bit about Bronzeville ix

Chapter One 1
Chapter Two 18
Chapter Three.. 46
Chapter Four... 57
Chapter Five.. 79
Chapter Six 101
Chapter Seven 118
Chapter Eight.. 140
Chapter Nine 154
Chapter Ten 172
Chapter Eleven..196
Chapter Twelve 213
Chapter Thirteen 238
Chapter Fourteen.. 266
Chapter Fifteen 289
Chapter Sixteen.. 297
Chapter Seventeen.. 308
Chapter Eighteen 325
Chapter Nineteen.. 340
Chapter Twenty 353

CHAPTER ONE

"What the hell do I have to do to get a job? Drink Clorox until I turn white!" Jerome Gerard said aloud, more to himself than to his wife Gail, while he was dressing. Showering in a Kansas City, Missouri, For Colored Only cheap motel's pee stained stall had refreshed him, but because of the August heat, he continued to perspire. Gail balanced her daughters Michelle and Dana on the commode, rinsed them off, and then applied calamine lotion to their itching bedbug bites. *Driving through the South is a bitch*; thought Gail.

The burden of rejected pharmacists' jobs had weighed heavily on Jerome. Earlier, some Caucasian Texans had threatened his well-being for even asking for a White Man's job. Now, they were motoring East from Los Angeles to Cleveland, Ohio; Jerome's last hope for employment assistance from one of his six siblings.

"Remember, Mr. High and Mighty, being white wasn't one of my daddy's requirements," Gail said as she rolled her dark green eyes with disdain. "He offered you a good-paying executive position, black as you are, but no, that wasn't good enough for my uppity, headstrong, husband!" Gail was thoroughly shaking out each garment as she packed. "There's another one!" Gail shouted as she crushed a roach under her sandal.

The travel weary family had tossed and turned all night on one bare, full-size, spring-free, mattress. Disturbing them further were transient couples banging headboards against card board-thin walls all night. Three years old Michelle, had asked, "Mommy, why are they sounding like monkeys jumping up and down on their bed?"

After Captain Jerome Gerard was discharged from the Army last April, '54, having completed a four year hitch he had vainly sought employment near his widowed mother who lived in Beaumont, Texas; his six older siblings had moved away. Most sent Momma money regularly to subsidize her Social Security checks, but Jerome thought at least one of her children should be close… just in case.

One thing was certain: because of his earlier confrontations with his father-in-law, Jerome was not going to work for the narcissistic, egomaniac, Conrad Beauregard, no matter his economic plight. *I would rather shovel shit in a hurricane,* Jerome had decided.

"We need a break," Jerome said, more frustrated than tired, "so we're going to stop in Chicago and look up Namon Stewart," Gail's anticipated, negative response was immediate.

"Oh, I see," Gail said with one hand on her shapely hip as she bounced slightly, flashing glaring eyes, "now we're going to look for some Army reject you haven't even talked to in several years to party with, instead of job hunting!" Gail slammed her suitcase shut.

"We're going to Chicago, woman, no matter what you say!"

Jerome's trek continued with an angry wife, and his daughters Michelle and eighteen month-old Dana, who were sitting on the back seat, squinting; their eyes were being assaulted by the hot wind entering the car through slightly opened windows. They remained silent because of the obvious friction between their parents. The Gerards knew that Jerome's brother, architect Bryan, in Cleveland was the end of their cross-country job quest. Without finding employment Jerome would have to return to New Orleans and Conrad, "Daddy Beau," Beauregard, humiliated, with downcast eyes and bowed head, accepting whatever the 'Nigger rich', affluent, "Daddy Beau," would offer.

Gail had enjoyed a pampered lifestyle. Nothing was too good for Daddy Beau's little girl, that is until she got pregnant before marriage. Leaving her New Orleans home in a fourteen year-old car without a final destination, with an unemployed husband and two babies was extremely hazardous and appalling. But if Jerome couldn't be persuaded to stay, Gail's parents insisted she leave with her man. The Beauregards' would not allow a daughter with two children and no visible husband, make them peer and church members gossip fodder.

"You ugly, uppity, ignorant, no count, dumb-ass Nigger; mark my words, you take my baby and my granddaughters away from me and your life will be ruined forever!" *Daddy Beau's parting curse haunts me each time I leave one sibling, frustrated, heading for another. Maybe he was right,* thought Jerome as he drove along two-lane state highways reading Burma Shave signs, with 90 degree turns, dividing fields of produce. He paid special attention to his speed when driving through small towns, recalling his horrific encounter in Corsicana Texas. Jerome regretted their wild dinner party three weeks ago. *I sure hope Bryan has something for me.*

Ten hours later, the setting sun forced Jerome to squint as he poked along Chicago's busy avenues, straining and stretching to read street signs. He blinked twice, and then wiped the sweat from his tired eyes with his soaked and smelly T shirt. Suddenly a burst of energy surged through his weary body. "There it is!" Jerome made a U turn on the six lane thoroughfare. When Jerome parked his 1940 Chevy, the exhausted auto trembled and belched several bursts of smoke. Taut, six foot two Jerome stretched as he thought, *Namon said it was big, but I didn't think it was this big. It even has a doorman!*

Gail shouted, "At last!" She bounded out of the car, peeling her screaming daughters from the vinyl-covered back seat; she had to pee. Gail, through desperate eyes, asked the doorman for directions to the nearest ladies room. She scurried with Michelle in tow and Dana in her arms; Gail's purse and diaper bag elevated in her wake.

The huge canopy with hundreds of small, dazzling lights that extended to the curb brightened a darkening promenade. A forty by four foot neon sign attached to the eight-story structure pulsated, "Pershing Hotel."

The sidewalk was sprinkled with dapper Negroes in bright summer suits and feathered, wide-brimmed straw hats strolling as only citified hipsters could. Fine, sensual, high-heeled women in luminous, body-hugging dresses emphasizing shapely butts locked arms with their men, prancing, heads held high, proud to be out on a Thursday night.

Several dudes cast knowing smirks, and tilted their heads toward each other, ridiculing the dark, sweat-stained, square, according to his license plates, from Texas. They were heading towards Sixty-Third Street, a place to party, a block away. "*Damn!*" Jerome thought, he was physically aroused by the sistah procession.

The paunchy, five-foot six-inch doorman, standing inside because of the hotel's air-conditioning, an unusual accommodation in '54, observed Jerome's once white car, noted his dingy, T shirt, wrinkled kakis and military oxfords. Because of his appearance, the doorman presumed Jerome had only stopped for his family to use the facilities.

The perturbed doorman stepped through one of the four double-door entrances and shouted, "Hey boy! You stop just so's your woman could change her babies' stinky diapers? 'Cause if you ain't staying here, you sure as hell cain't park there!" He wore cocoa brown pants with wide gold seams, a white, short sleeve shirt with gold epaulets, a military cap, and a cab whistle that dangled around his neck.

"We're staying until Monday morning, Lewis," Jerome answered over a wide grin after reading the doorman's name pin, ignoring his negative remarks.

"Then welcome to Bronzeville and the fabulous Pershing Hotel, Sir" Lewis said, smiling broadly. He raised two fingers to the bill of his gold braided cap, saluted, and then pointed Jerome toward registration. Jerome handed him a generous dollar tip. Jerome's mustering out pay plus Gail's allotment checks, which she had saved over the four years, gave them a considerable bankroll.

The trip had been burdensome but for one bright spot; the life-altering stop-over with the McGhees' on their way to Los Angeles, from Dallas, two weeks earlier.

Because Negroes couldn't stay in for-white-only facilities in many parts of the country, Willie McGhee provided clean, spacious rooms and delicious meals for Negroes travelling to or from segregated Las Vegas and Los Angeles. The McGhees' owned a large, three story brick house, set on fifteen acres, ten miles east of Gallup, New Mexico, adjacent to the main east-west highway, Route 66. The McGhee's' had earned the top rating of four stars in the Negro travel directory.

It was almost midnight. Jerome noticed the dark driveway. "W. McGhee, Ph.D." was painted on the mailbox. "This must be the place," Jerome said, pleased to be ending a long day of driving.

"Who's there?" a hostile male voice shouted.

Jerome slowed as his tires crushed gravel. His headlights fell on an image in a multi-colored cotton robe with a hood that hid his face. Jerome slowed even more when he saw a 20 gauge double barreled shotgun under the figure's right arm pointed toward him. *Looks like the Grim Reaper with a shotgun instead of a scythe,* Jerome thought.

"We're the Gerards who called several days ago. Mr. Lonnie Blackman recommended us," Jerome said, slowly and clearly as he exited his car.

"Well, why didn't you say so," the little man with the big gun said through a laugh. "Come on in! Everything's OK Naomi; it's the Gerard's." The porch and house lights instantly brightened. Naomi stepped out wearing a light blue robe and matching hairnet. She and Dr. McGhee were both about five and a half feet.

There wasn't much law in the northwestern part of McKinley County. Mexican border jumpers, wayward Indians from nearby reservations, or drunken White men mad at Negroes who were doing well, caused McGhee to be consistently cautious.

By the time Jerome reached the steps, the hood had been thrown back; a dark, wiry, partially bald, Black man greeted Jerome with a broad smile and an energetic handshake. Jerome, while holding Michelle and Dana who were asleep, felt the gnarled knuckles on McGhee's small hand and shook it gently. *It almost feels like a chicken foot,* Jerome thought. Gail pulled their overnight bag from the trunk.

"Welcome. Let me fix you young'uns something to eat;" Naomi said cheerfully. She knew the only way they could have eaten anywhere within hours of her house was to accept sandwiches in brown paper bags through the back, screen door after all Caucasian customers had been served and then eat while driving. Naomi looked at the girls, realized they were sleeping, and then covered her mouth with her hand and said, over a broad smile, "Lawd, have mercy," apologizing for talking too loud.

"Please, Mrs. McGhee," Gail said, "don't bother. It's already past midnight. All we really need is a bed."

"Nonsense," Willie McGhee said, "our only fun is when folks visit. Nobody's come through in over a month since the Four Step Brothers. We stayed up all night drinking and dancing. They taught us some fancy steps, a couple I can do even with my bad leg. Lots of musicians stay with us; are either of you musically inclined?"

"Gail plays a pretty mean piano," Jerome said, embarrassing Gail.

McGhee moved toward the threshold dragging his left side, gave the screen door a practiced kick with his good foot, and caught it with his right hand. "Take the children upstairs, second room on the right. Your bedroom is directly opposite," Naomi said.

When Jerome returned downstairs, Naomi handed him a bowl of ice, "Just in case you need to, ah, clear the dust from your throat," she said. "I'll make some ham sandwiches right away."

"Please, Mrs. McGhee, let me help," Gail said, following her to the kitchen.

"Only if you call me Naomi," she smiled.

"Mr. Blackman wanted you to know he'll be coming through in September. He has a big deal fermenting with Golden City Mutual Insurance in Los Angeles." Jerome had met Lonnie Blackman at Conrad Beauregard's estate the evening of their tumultuous dinner. "This is an excellent scotch and water. What is this, single malt?" Jerome followed Dr. McGhee from the portable bar in the hallway into the living room and sat on the ottoman. McGhee sat in his chair, put his Jack Daniels and Coke on the end table, and then packed one of his pipes as he held it between his teeth.

"I suggested Lonnie start his business over fifteen years ago. Let's see, that was in '39." McGhee enthusiastically elucidated, "After Lonnie finished NYU with a Business under-graduate degree in '35, he worked for a North Carolina furniture manufacturer, doing a hell of a job. He sold to Black and White businesses in the North and Blacks in the South, but as his sales increased, the company kept cutting his clients, thereby limiting his income. He asked me for advice. He said, 'My sales manager told me straight up, "You're making more than most of my white salesmen, and that's too much for a Negro."

"I asked, 'Lonnie have you learned the technical end of the business, like the advantages of using certain woods and padding with specific upholstery fabrics?' He said, 'Of course. I have to know that stuff in order to sell my customers the correct furniture.' And then I asked if he could support his family for six months without income. He told me he could because his wife was a teacher, and that he had some savings and no bills. I suggested he hire an accountant and a lawyer, and then become a manufacturer's representative; Lonnie had no idea what a manufacturer's representative was. I explained he would be selling for a number of manufacturers, but strictly on commission. I further explained that he would have more choices for his customers and could sell anywhere in the United States."

"Now Lonnie sells primarily to Negro colleges, hospitals, insurance companies and hotels; of course, he still has White clients up North. Lonnie currently has offices in Dallas, Atlanta, and New York City, with an aggregate staff of thirty, and represents over a hundred manufacturers who don't know or care what color he is; now how about that!" McGhee took a drink and then smiled. "That was quite a risk back in the 30's, but he made it work; he is one of my major contributions to Negro economic equality."

Jerome knew Mr. Blackman sold furniture, that's why he was visiting Mr. Beauregard, but had never considered the size of his company. *I had never thought about all of the substantial businesses we own. They never taught us about Black owned businesses in college or offered any economic courses; probably because I went to a Catholic college for Negroes, which stressed religion, loyalty and humility, instead of entrepreneurship.* Jerome's eyelids were getting heavy.

"Tell me Son, what's in California?" McGhee wanted Jerome to become more alert and involved in the conversation.

"My brother-in-law, who is a successful dentist, said he would help me find a pharmacist job."

"That's it? You're traveling halfway across the country just for a job? You could go to work in Harlem any day of the week."

"I have to provide for my family, I have looked all over Texas without success, so I'm going to LA; what's wrong with that?"

"I'm surprised your well-to-do brother-in-law isn't offering to help you open your own drugstore. Obviously he's not a visionary. What you should be looking for is an opportunity Son, not just a job."

Jerome thought *I'm not ready to own a drugstore; I've never even worked in one. Damn, I'm sleepy.*

"First, it is critical that we take charge of our destiny and stop waiting for some unknown spiritual being to wipe racism from the face of the earth. If we can believe in the Second Coming, which I consider nothing more than a deep rooted superstition, we can certainly believe in ourselves."

I think he just said he was an atheist. Jerome became alert.

"Our biggest problem is a lack of self-esteem, not racism. Too many of us believe being colored is a permanent liability. And as long as we feel that way the perception becomes reality." McGhee took a couple of puffs on his pipe, a sip of his drink, and continued. Dr. McGhee's animated delivery indicated he was enjoying lecturing.

"White folks don't have to worry about us being constructive or productive because we persecute ourselves. Our individual economic success stories are rare; less than 1% earn over $50,000 a year. So few of us are educated or ambitious, that trying a substantial business venture isn't probable, and most of us are deep in debt. Continuously, we perpetuate the big lie whitey has brainwashed us with in movies, books, and advertisements: that Negroes are lazy, stupid, dishonest, and inferior."

Professor McGhee pulled out a full-color metal advertisement 18" by 3'. It was a picture of a black boy with wide eyes and big red lips, smiling broadly, holding a bottle of branded, chocolate milk, saying, "This sho is good!" McGhee continued, "And white folks, twenty years ago, thought this ad would cause us to buy their product!" McGhee laughed.

Jerome understood. He was raised in a southern, segregated town, where every Caucasian he encountered, from the age of reasoning through adult-hood, was assumed superior. But, for four years in a recently integrated Army Jerome had developed self-esteem and a sense of equality. Before, during, and after Officer Candidate School he successfully dealt with prejudiced underlings and superiors. Based on his rapid promotions, he had become quite good at it. Jerome had never heard anyone analyze the race problem so candidly. He took a sip of his drink, leaned forward and continued listening.

"Of course," continued McGhee, "education is the path to financial security. If you are fortunate enough to accumulate capital, keeping it will be difficult without economic intelligence."

"I'm missing something," Jerome said. "I'm educated and can't find a job, let alone save money."

"First, your formal education isn't complete. An undergraduate degree is merely a first step in today's competitive society; you must earn at least a Masters. Secondly, in time you will find what you are looking for because you haven't settled for less. The real question is what will you do after you become gainfully employed?"

"Pay my bills; buy a decent car and then a home. You know, the normal things people do."

"Therein lays the problem, Son!" McGhee slammed his right fist on the arm of the chair, increasing Jerome's alertness. "Don't buy into Whitey's world; making high interest-bearing loans, buying a home, a car and then a better home, a better car, in a better neighborhood, believing the closer you get to Whitey the more equal you are. Stay debt free! Don't pay high interest on money you didn't need to borrow in the first place. You have to think ahead, Son! You need a permanent place to live, but don't buy just a home."

"I don't understand. How do I get a permanent place to live without buying a home?"

Buy real estate where you can rent to tenants, like a two flat or a home plus Mother-in-law quarters, where someone will help you pay your mortgage."

"I had never thought about that," Jerome said.

"After you have accumulated some cash and can put half down without selling your first parcel, then you can buy a bigger, nicer, home and rent out your first residence. Your second parcel will cost you half as much with a large down payment. You will then be a property owner with income you don't have to work for and become mortgage-free a lot faster. No matter what you make, invest some of your discretionary income in mutual funds, or land. Not a pair of Florsheims, a Cadillac, or a White woman, all of which are overpriced and unproductive."

"You didn't quit teaching, Dr. McGhee; you just reduced your class size."

The sandwiches were ready; potato chips and Gershen pickles were stacked on paper plates. Naomi and Gail, at least 30 years apart, were laughing heartily while discussing their husbands' idiosyncrasies.

"I was one of his students," Naomi had confessed. He had a wandering eye until I kept his attention. Getting married was the reason I went to college, so I never finished," Naomi said with a mischievous twinkle in her eye. Naomi then asked, "You look whipped darlin', and not from traveling. Is something deep down troubling you?

"We left his sister in Beaumont, Louisiana to get help from his brother who is a high school principal in Dallas. While there, Jerome was considered arrogant, even by his brother, when he wouldn't take a porter's job in a White drugstore; we were asked to leave——in a hurry. Now we are heading for Los Angeles, and probably more rejection. I guess I am just tired of travelling, both physically and mentally. I told him to stay in New Orleans where my daddy, who offered Jerome a good paying job, said we belonged." Gail began to weep.

"You must believe in your man, young lady, even though you married slightly down," Naomi said while firmly holding Gail's hand with both of hers, "and that means your love and respect is unrequited. It's easy to be critical, especially during tough times, which reduces our men's self-esteem. Without a wife's support, the easiest thing for husbands to do is become permanently disheartened, and to accept the inferior status Caucasians have established. That's when they abuse their families——or desert them."

"Naomi, bring the food down to the den!" Willie called out from the living room. He then said to Jerome, "Come on, I want to show you something."

"We'll be down in just a few minutes dear," Naomi answered while widening her eyes and smiling at Gail; a few more exchanges and they still weren't finished. "We'll talk more later," Naomi whispered as she and Gail gathered the plates.

"Gooood night!" Jerome said as he reached the bottom of the stairs. Stained, gold-leaf mirrored tiles backed the wet bar which had four leather stools. An eighteenth century pool table with leather pockets was centered in the lower part of the L-shaped den. A teak poker table, covered with green felt, and eight leather upholstered arm chairs with side trays under a Tiffany chandelier sat in a corner. Dr. McGhee's den could easily have been featured in Home Beautiful magazine. *This is certainly not affordable on a retired professor's income; Daddy Beau's game room doesn't look this good,* Jerome thought.

Willie said, "While living in New York City I invested in the stock market and made a few bucks; I still do. A portion of my profits go into this house. Some of our guests really believe they can shoot pool or play poker. Then there are some neighbors who, fortunately for me, consider poker a way to relax. Even with one arm I can beat the pants off most of them!" Willie asked with a hopeful look in his eye, "Do you play either?"

Jerome very quickly said no.

"Since this house was built as a commercial bed and breakfast, its cost and improvements are tax deductible. Most of my stock market profits go into first mortgages with a Jewish friend who still teaches economics at New York University. We only make loans to Negroes with good credit that have been turned down, or redlined by traditional lending institutions. That's my ongoing contribution to racial equality.

"First mortgage profits are much more predictable than the stock market. I have been pretty successful at making money with money." Jerome was astounded. His father-in-law was wealthy, but he only invested in businesses he could manage. McGhee's investments required little supervision, an entirely new concept to Jerome.

The ladies joined Jerome and Willie in the den. They ate, talked and laughed like family. Naomi insisted Gail play something on the piano. When none of them could properly focus or complete a sentence without losing their thought, they went to bed; it was 4 a.m.

Naomi had been up since seven; it was 9:00 a.m. "Breakfast is almost ready!" she yelled from the bottom of the stairs.

Twenty minutes later, after an invigorating shower, Jerome looked out the kitchen window into the huge backyard as he sipped his first cup of coffee. Michelle and Dana, who had been awake for hours, were playing tag with "Uncle" Willie.

"He's having a ball!" Naomi said. "We have grandchildren in Detroit, but we don't see them often enough. Our son has a Master's in chemical engineering from Stanford; he works on a Ford assembly line." Willie McGhee's professorship reduced his tuition at Stanford. "His wife, who has a law degree, teaches at a high school. *Uh, huh,* thought Jerome, *no matter what you achieve, compatible employment can remain out of reach.*

Naomi's breakfast included: homemade, sage-spiced sausages; hash brown potatoes with onions; buttermilk biscuits; scrambled eggs with cheese and scallions; and fresh squeezed orange juice, with milk and coffee. Gail and the girls ate heartedly; Jerome and Willie stuffed themselves. Naomi beamed. Nothing pleased her more than to see hungry men enjoying her cooking.

"Glad you folks stopped over," Willie smiled after biting into his third biscuit, laden with butter and plum jam. "The only time Naomi puts her foot in her cooking is when we have guests." Angling for another delicious meal, Willie asked, "Sure you can't stay for dinner?"

While Gail and Naomi were cleaning up the kitchen, Naomi said, "From what I have gleaned from our conversations, your daddy tried to bribe Jerome with a job to keep you and the children underfoot. Because yours was a forced marriage, as was mine, your daddy would have never treated Jerome with respect or been fair in their business relationships. It would have been disastrous for you, your marriage, and your children. Your husband did the right thing; you'll see in the by and by. One other thing, you and your family don't *belong* anywhere, no matter what your daddy says. Your husband should decide where you *belong* and where he's going to start his business career," Naomi said.

"When did I tell you all of that?"

"Oh, sometimes we say a lot through body language, or by not saying anything," Naomi said through a knowing smile.

"Son, remember this as you go forward in life," Willie said when they reached the living room, "ego, more than drugs, drinking, gambling or womanizing, causes more business failures than anything else." Willie looked over his shoulder toward the kitchen to make sure their conversation was private, and then said, "Of course womanizing can be fatal too. Over a decade ago, I was screwing a young, sexy student when I had this stroke."

The Gerards left the McGhee stop-over rested and much wiser. Jerome had been enlightened regarding race relations, and money management. Gail had learned the thought processes of men and fathers and how women should relate to both.

* * * *

Lucille, the Pershing Hotel receptionist, said after removing her head set, "May we help you?"

"We would like two adjoining bedrooms for four nights," Jerome said to the friendly, well-groomed woman.

"With air conditioning," Gail added, who was now standing beside Jerome, enjoying the luxurious coolness.

"That will cost extra."

The cool lobby, an empty bladder and two quiet children had improved Gail's disposition. "We'll gladly pay what's required."

"Where can I park and who can help me find a friend?" Jerome asked as he filled out the 8x5 registration card.

"Hold tight; I'll call The Man," Lucille said while staring at Jerome. She plugged in the manager's phone through the switchboard, while continuing to stare.

"Look at me! No! Don't look at me," Gail said to Jerome. She was embarrassed by her compact's reflection of the red lines on the whites of her eyes and no makeup. *I hadn't planned on meeting anyone until I had an opportunity to repair the road damage,* Gail thought. She finger-combed her naturally straight, shoulder-length, auburn hair and then patted the few remaining curls in place. Gail straightened her size 4 dress over her curvaceous body, and then applied lipstick to her full lips and pinched her pink cheeks, adding color.

Jerome observed the lobby with wide eyes and an open mouth. Cordovan-colored, leather loveseats with matching chairs were set in several groupings on oriental rugs. A uniformed porter was screening ash stands and gathering abandoned newspapers. Everything was spotless. *This is more like it!* Jerome mused, comparing the Pershing with their horrid accommodations last night.

"Babe, they have a night club and a ballroom in this hotel," Gail said as she pointed to a wall-mounted, encased placard announcing that Ahmad Jamal was playing in the Pershing Hotel's Beige Room lounge. An arrow pointed toward the ballroom.

"We're definitely in Namon's part of town," Jerome said as he recalled the two of them being stationed in Suwon, Korea.

During their twelve months together, they enjoyed listening to Namon's cherished collection of 78's, among them: Dinah Washington, Lester Young, Jazz at the Philharmonic, and Ahmad Jamal. Namon's colorful commentary regarding his personal encounters with many of the stars enhanced their musical interludes. Jerome didn't believe Namon's tales, especially the ones about his making out with beautiful chorus girls, but his stories were entertaining. They became good friends and promised to stay in touch after returning stateside. They meant it when they said it, but didn't. Jerome had decided the first thing he would mention to Namon is please don't mention Yokohama, Japan.

While scanning the lobby, Jerome noticed a thin, middle-aged, cocoa-colored man, dressed in a dark green matching short-sleeved shirt and pants ensemble, wearing green alligator shoes and green, ribbed socks. He was sitting in a large leather chair, legs crossed, reading the *Racing Form* and smoking a crooked cigar. Several men, one at a time, sat near him, observed their surroundings to be sure no one was paying attention, and then slipped him a folded piece of paper wrapped in money. Green Ensemble ran his hand over his wavy hair, pocketed their hand-offs and continued reading the paper.

After observing several transfers and watching him separate the money from the paper, read and destroy the note, then scope the room for strangers, Jerome realized Green Ensemble was booking horses. *Namon told me things like this happened here, including fast women being picked up in the lobby, but I didn't believe him. Humm, maybe his stories were true.*

"What it be like?" The guttural voice and terrible grammar unsettled Gail. She, who graduated with a Liberal Arts degree and an English major, imagined it being amplified through the throat of an illiterate oaf. Gail turned toward the voice and again was startled. The Man resembled Jerome! He was thicker, and at least a generation older, but they could have been brothers. The Man's conked hair, double breasted royal blue suit, and blue and white wing tip shoes made him as sharp as a straight razor. His cologne was overwhelming.

His skin was velvet black with a slight sheen, as if he had just covered his face with beeswax. His stylish appearance was marred by a cut that ran from his ear to the bottom of his chin. It had healed without medical attention and left an ugly scar. The two men shook hands and were mutually surprised at their physical similarities; they were even the same height.

"The ambience of your hotel is enhanced by its courteous staff sir. Are you the owner?" Jerome asked.

Gail was annoyed by Jerome's elitist language. *My goodness, all we need is two rooms and a telephone book.*

"Naw," The Man blushed by lowering his eyelids. "I'm Lester Stevens, the manager." Lester didn't understand ambience or enhanced, but he knew what owner meant. He adjusted his suit coat on his broad shoulders then straightened his tie with both hands. With a wide stare, he said, "We own it and I run it!" His gaze became intense. Lester wanted to be sure his guests knew he was in charge.

"I see," Jerome said as he and Gail nodded slowly. *This hotel must have 400 rooms and it's owned by us? It has to be worth… what, ten million dollars?* Jerome asked, "Are there other hotels of this quality and size owned by Negroes?"

"Oooh yeah," Lester said with a fervor. "Other bloods own a couple on the West Side; then there's Detroit, Atlanta, Birmingham, Tuskegee, Harlem, Baton Rouge, and a few others in towns I can't name off my cuff. But The Pershing is the biggest and the baddest."

A moment passed, "Damn that––where you from Little Brother?" Lester's smile revealed an ivory star formed by a gold casing on one of his front teeth.

"Beaumont, Texas. My father was born in Alabama in 1885, as a freeman. His sharecropping family escaped to Beaumont in 1900 for a fresh start, leaving behind a lot of debt and angry, white landowners. He died when I was fourteen."

"That ain't nothin', my mother bought me to Chicago from Biloxi, Mississippi in the twenties', she got sick of that Jim Crow crap," Lester said. "We got a lot in common; I grew up without a father too. A lot of men in and out of my house, but no father, dig? I'm a Stevens and you're ….?

"A Gerard, Jerome Gerard." Jerome mused. *I didn't grow up without a father; he shaped my value system during those fourteen years. He taught me honesty, integrity, and a strong work ethic. Mr. Stevens has no idea how important those early years were. One valid point he makes perhaps without knowing it; mothers also make a difference. My mother instilled in me and my siblings Catholic morals and the importance of an education. She had to regularly clean the church because of my basketball scholarship. Wonder where and what I'd be if my mother had just slept around?*

"But back then names didn't mean nothin'; shiiit, they still don't. We're related somehow, we must be," Lester said.

"I'm sure you're right," Jerome smiled.

"Well you're here and I'm here to help. So what's u-up?"

"Two things. Where can I park, and how can I find an old Army sidekick?"

"Parking's done," Lester held out his hand for Jerome's keys.

"Maybe I had better park Gertie, sometimes she's hard to start."

"Gertie? What a lame name for a car!"

"She was named by my Army buddies after decrepit Gravel Gertie, one of Dick Tracy's comic strip characters. And believe me, she's getting older and uglier," Jerome smiled.

"I can dig it, 'cause ain't nothin' uglier than an old-ass white woman."

Jerome and Gail laughed out loud; the disrespect to White people was refreshing. Lester said to Lucille, "Have Lewis park Gertie in our garage, with the tenderness of a mother's love. Now little brother, let's find your ace boon coon."

"The Pershing was Namon's hangout, so I guess he lived near here in Bronzeville." Jerome recalled the doorman welcoming him to Bronzeville.

Lester laughed loudly and then said, "Aw Man, Bronzeville ain't no neighborhood––it's a way of life, an attitude, a great feeling you git partyin' the night away when O'Fays ain't watchin'. Bronzeville means night club hoppin' without stoppin' on the Black Hand side of Chi Town."

Jerome looked puzzled. Lester took Jerome's very dark hand, back side up and said, "Black Hand side," then he turned Jerome's hand over and revealed his light palm, "White Hand side; dig?" Jerome understood, everyone laughed.

"Bronzeville means one, big, never-ending party. It means after-hour clubs that don't open till three in the mornin'; it means down-home blues and ribs so sweet you don't need teeth to eat, you just suck the meat right off the bone. During the winter months you might be lucky enough to grab a plate of chittlins sprinkled with hot sauce. It means rent-raising bashes that last for days, with boogying down in the front room, gamblin' and home brew in the kitchen and wall-to-wall friendly ladies, all while gut-bucket blues is fillin up' the place." Lester looked at Gail, who was staring at him with contempt. He stuttered and then said, "Uh, uh, let's try the telephone book Youngblood; maybe your main man is listed."

Namon Stewart wasn't listed and there were too many Stewarts on the South Side to start calling. Lester asked, "Is he legit or does he make his living under cover?"

"He's probably legit. In the Army he was an administrative officer in a medical unit. Oh," recalled Jerome, "he graduated from Roosevelt College in the mid forties."

"Now we're gettin' to the nitty gritty. He's probably bourgeois, degreed, prim n' proper, you know, a square john, knotted up and all, five out of seven. Likely he's a Felix and Bea's disciple. It's where the brainy bunch hangs out. Tomorrow's Friday, Felix's fills up on Fridays, you know Eagles and all."

Jerome only understood half of what Turkey had said; he asked, "Eagles?"

"Payday man, the Eagle flies on Friday! Where you been?" Once again, the Gerards laughed. "I'm going by for lunch tomorrow; couple of them dudes owes me some lettuce, so why don't you two tag along?"

"You're very gracious Mr. Stevens," Gail said. "Here we are, a couple of strangers…"

"Mr. Stevens died from aged whiskey and under-aged women. My name is Lester, but," as he smoothed his lapels with his palms and grinned, widening his large mouth, "My friends call me Turkey 'cause I'm always dressed."

"The name sure fits when you think of it that way," Gail said. She also knew turkeys were the only animal dumb enough to stand in the rain with their mouths open until they drowned.

"Listen, tomorrow's in the pocket, but what's up tonight?"

Jerome looked at Gail, who looked blank, and then said, "Not a thing."

"Well now, how 'bout us hangin' out? One of the maids will stay with your girls. I mean we might even pin your main man." Turkey looked Jerome over. "I can see you been hoofin' it all day. Get cleaned up. You better put some cocoa butter on that scar," Turkey said, noticing the three week old burn on Jerome's face.

"Great, that's why we're here, to relax, right Babe?"

"Yeah, right." Gail said sarcastically; she was hungry and tired. Going out, God only knows where, with some flashy illiterate, did not sound inviting.

End of Chapter One

CHAPTER TWO

"This is responsive," Jerome said as he bounced on the full-sized bed. The chenille spread's nubs had been worn thin. He pulled back the sheets; there were no bedbugs. The chest's varnished top was worn and the drawers had no rollers. The 13" black and white televisions with five channels, in both rooms worked. Jerome noticed a radio that required quarters to play sitting on the night stand. *Haven't seen one of these before.* The bathrooms were clean with face cloths, wrapped, small bars of soap, and white and blue towels emblazoned with "Pershing Hotel." Clothes hooks on the back of the doors served as closets. The Gerard's were pleased that their accommodations were far superior to Kansas City.

A warm bath refreshed Gail. She sucked in her stomach as she zipped up her size four, black, brocade dress. *O.K., a little more dieting and exercise and I'll be back in my size two,* she thought while looking in the full-length mirror on the bathroom door. She stepped into her pumps, inserted her pierced-ear pearl earrings and put on her matching necklace. As Gail straightened her stockings' seams on her perfectly shaped legs, fluffed her knee-length hemline, and smoothed her dress over her small waist and round butt, she recalled an earlier time when she was looking even better: on her wedding day.

The wealthy Beauregards lived in New Orleans, but wanted Gail to stay on St. Barbara's campus, a local, prestigious, Negro, Catholic college, to be socially available. "Unless you are engaged by graduation, you have wasted four years," Sylvia had repeatedly said. "Becoming a spinster or a loose woman may be your destiny, if marriage is not a part of your immediate future." St. Barbara's demographics were twenty-five percent males, from middle and upper-class families, seventy-five percent beautiful, husband-hunting women. Gail would not 'put out,' she could see through shallow come-ons from handsome, glib, young men as though she were peering through a fish net. For four years Gail, while dating occasionally, remained unattached and a virgin.

Jerome's basketball scholarship required him to serve meals, and wash fellow students' dishes. His shabby appearance made him the butt of "he's so broke …" jokes from most students; Gail was an exception. Jerome never flirted with any of the girls; dating was expensive. Besides, learning was his passion. He knew one day his intense study habits would be rewarded. Jerome was determined to get a degree in Pharmacology. It was a family tradition; since 1934, all of his six siblings had earned at least an undergraduate degree, mostly in land-grant colleges established after the Civil War. Jerome's father, Joshua, knew the path out of poverty and second-class citizenship was a good education. Although he was penniless, he persuaded his children to do what was necessary to get at least an undergraduate degree; some exceeded his expectations.

Neither Jerome nor Gail pledged Greek. Jerome wasn't invited nor could he afford it. Gail was begged to join every sorority on campus, but never agreed with the conditions of having to be insulted, blatantly embarrassed, and amenable to frat brothers' desires, before being accepted. Gail and Jerome were platonic friends, voracious readers and excellent students. As members of the debate team, they prided themselves on being able to take either side of an issue and win. When they were on opposite sides, it was always close.

At a Senior Social someone poured 180 proof grain alcohol into the punch. Jerome and Gail, after several drinks and having melded their bodies while dancing, became intimate on smelly, gray, tufted floor mats under the roll-out stands in the gym. They were several months away from graduation; *what the hell,* Gail decided, *I'm probably the only virgin here.* Jerome's partial penetration and premature climax left them both regretting the hurried, unpleasant experience, they vowed never to repeat.

"Oh, mercy me!" Sylvia said when a mortified Gail revealed her pregnancy during a private meeting at home. "Will he marry you?"

"Yes, of course. He too feels badly about this, but said he will stand by me."

"Well, that's good news." Sylvia knew of several marriages resulting from unwanted pregnancies that had lasted for years. "Who is this Lothario that has stolen my daughter's heart?" A light touch was in order; after all, marriage was imminent.

"Jerome Gerard from Beaumont Texas; we've been friends since our freshman year, but this was the first time …"

"Yeah, sure baby, everyone gets knocked up their first time," Sylvia said as she patted Gail's face. "What does his father do?"

"His father was killed in a cotton gin accident several years ago. His mother lives on Social Security."

"Oh! Sweet Jesus!" Sylvia threw her head back on the sofa, put her hand over her left breast and gasped for air while turning ghostly white.

"I didn't send you to college," Daddy Beau shouted as he rushed into their "private" meeting from his listening post just outside the parlor, "to get knocked up by some poor-ass Nigger. You could have done better hanging out in the French Quarter!" Conrad was wearing his Mandarin embroidered dinner jacket, over a white, silk ascot, carrying his ever-present Beefeater's gin and tonic, and puffing on a Cuban cigar. His rotund belly shook as he berated his only child.

Conrad demanded a meeting with this no-count boy who probably purposely impregnated his daughter. Several weeks later, Jerome reluctantly appeared. Conrad was in his study wearing a silk, light blue summer suit with contrasting tie over a white-on-white, French cuffed summer shirt. He was sitting behind his desk and remained so when Jerome entered wearing a clean, white T shirt with worn, creased pants and Keds gym shoes.

"My beautiful daughter," Conrad began, "wouldn't have chosen someone as homely as you for a husband if you hadn't purposely impregnated her. Even you, as dumb and poor as you are, must agree with that!" An hour later, without allowing Jerome to sit or speak, Conrad closed with, "All of my life I have anticipated turning over my holdings to my son-in-law because there is no way a woman could manage my businesses, and she brings a poor, black-ass, fortune-seeking, good-for-nothing, into our family. What a waste!"

"I understand——" Jerome was rudely interrupted.

"You don't understand a damn thing. Before I let you near my fortune, I'll disown my daughter. Now, get out!" Jerome rushed from the parlor, humiliated, insulted and bewildered, wondering whether the wedding should occur.

They were married in the college chapel on graduation day, along with five other couples. The Beauregards did not invite any of their friends to either of the day's events. As soon as both ceremonies were completed, Sylvia and Conrad left without congratulating their daughter or sharing cursory greetings with Jerome's mother or his relatives. Jerome's six siblings and their families had come long distances to celebrate both auspicious occasions.

Martha was wearing a beautiful dress over her large frame she had taken a month to make. Sylvia was embarrassed by her husband's rudeness, but followed his lead and did not speak to Jerome's relatives, for fear of being reprimanded by Conrad.

The Beauregards would have chosen, under honorable circumstances, a high-toned, terribly expensive wedding at their beautiful estate, and an exotic honeymoon on some exclusive Caribbean island. Without her parents' blessings, Gail and Jerome spent their post-nuptials at Jerome's mother's house in Shreveport. Martha stayed with friends, allowing the newlyweds to enjoy their wedded ecstasy, unfettered. The Beauregard's opulence was not missed.

During their first encounter under the bleachers, Jerome barely penetrated Gail before orgasming. However, on their honeymoon, Jerome, after several unions, gave his bride all he had—and it was substantial. On their third night, for the first time in her life, Gail experienced an orgasm. Bells rang, whistles blew; her body took her mind on a celestial trip through worlds she had never imagined. There were screams of ecstasy! Her body trembled and tingled like never before. Sex was beautiful, all encompassing. It was the ultimate pleasure times infinity. Jerome became the deliverer of the most unique, feeling; her emotional liberator; someone she would adore, respect, and love always.

Late in their first week, she became a willing partner every time Jerome suggested making love; each event brought with it new discoveries. During their second week she persuaded Jerome to partake as much as three times a day by snuggling whenever he sat down, or lounging about scantily clad. They didn't sleep much.

Between encounters Jerome and Gail enjoyed playing Scrabble, engaged in intellectual trivia games and discussed books they had both read. Gail couldn't cook, but that wasn't a problem. Cold cereal and fruit for breakfast was easy. When they were hungry, the newlyweds, his arm around her waist, her hand in his jean's back pocket, walked to a nearby Colored, family restaurant.

During their third week, Jerome began looking for a job, in vain. That Friday Conrad called and demanded a meeting. After the call Conrad mentally intruded, especially whenever Jerome and Gail were intimate. Gail said, "He probably wants to give you a job." Jerome agreed with Gail's assumption, but knew working for Daddy Beau would be impossible. *I would have to ask permission to breathe.* Jerome avoided the unpleasant encounter by joining the Army. Gail and Jerome had their first argument. She returned to the Beauregard estate unhappy and pregnant.

College ROTC training resulted in Jerome being commissioned as a second lieutenant after two months basic training and three months Officer's Training School. Jerome called and asked Gail to join him at his first permanent assignment: Fort Dix in Central New Jersey.

"She'll stay here!" Sylvia injected; as she listened on an extension. "It's too close to the baby being born for Gail to be living on somebody's miserable, Army post." Gail didn't object to her mother eavesdropping, or her declaration, so neither did Jerome.

Maybe this marriage is over before it has begun, thought Jerome. *But she's entitled to an allotment and child support, even though she doesn't need it.* He filled out the necessary paperwork.

Michelle Myrtle Gerard was born January 13, 1951, at 6:00 a.m. Sylvia, as an afterthought, called Jerome at 10:00 a.m. "I named her Michelle, after my mother." Before Jerome could bask in the glow of being a first-time father by asking the most basic questions, Sylvia hung up.

After arriving on the first military plane to New Orleans, Jerome and Gail shared their amazement at the miracle of birth, as only new parents can——until Sylvia interrupted. "Gail, you should stay home with us," Sylvia said. Again, Gail did not object and Jerome, now deeply in love with his wife and baby, knew Gail would get better care at home than on the post.

Six months later, Michelle and Gail joined Jerome at Fort Dix. They were good Catholics and practiced the rhythm method to avoid a second pregnancy. Their desire for each other made the calendar moot; Gail was soon pregnant again. Jerome returned from a three-day field maneuver three months into Gail's pregnancy—she was gone. The note read, "Call me at home." *Home is here, damn it!*

"Mommy, everything's terrible here," Gail had complained to her mother over the phone. Sylvia immediately made arrangements for Gail and Michelle to fly home on American Airlines.

"Gail's okay," Sylvia told Jerome when he called, "considering her horrible living conditions with you. She's asleep and shouldn't be disturbed. I'll tell her you'll call back tomorrow."

After Dana's birth, the first words Gail said to Jerome, as instructed by Sylvia, was, "No more babies, please!" Gail's decision troubled Jerome. Practicing birth control violated their faith, but, once again, he said nothing.

"I'm shipping out to Korea, Babe," Jerome said during one of their phone conversations. Jerome was granted a two-week leave. At his insistence, Gail agreed to spend his furlough at his mom's.

Jerome and Gail enjoyed playing with their daughters, but their fantastic sex life had vanished because Gail was deathly afraid of a third pregnancy. She refused to try diaphragms, sponges and gels, fearful the contraceptives might not work. Jerome tried condoms, but they were too tight. They settled on his withdrawing seconds before climax, which was one step above masturbation.

The "cold showers" that chilled their sexual encounters was Gail always reminding Jerome to "be careful." Seconds before climax, Gail would stiffen like a corpse and push Jerome out. Then she would catapult out of bed, grab her red bag, and while cleansing herself with vinegar and warm water, yell, "Please tell me you pulled out in time!" Sex became a biological exercise, and Catholicism, much to Jerome's disappointment, was ignored. Gail's response to Jerome regarding their living in a state of mortal sin was, "God understands."

After putting their girls to bed, Jerome bathed, shaved and put on his only suit, which after four years, still fit. He asked, "You ready for a night on the town in Bronzeville, Babe?"

"Do we have to? I'm tired," Gail said.

"We won't be out late, I promise. I'm tired too, but we just can't ignore the manager's invitation." Jerome checked his generic watch; they were in the lobby at 8:15 p.m. Jerome had promised Turkey they would be ready at 8:30; he had told Gail their appointed time was 8:00.

Minutes later, Turkey appeared in a tan suit, hand tailored from tropical weight virgin wool. He wore a dark blue shirt with a Billy Eckstine high-rolled collar. A two-karat diamond stickpin held his white and blue tie in place. Diamond cuff links peeked from under his coat sleeve. Turkey wore a large diamond pinkie ring. Tan and white, wing tip Florsheims; a Panama hat with a matching tan band and feather, completed his flashy ensemble. The Man was an all-the-way-live, after five, Negro fashion statement.

Turkey's left leg is shorter than his right, Jerome noticed as their host walked toward him. *He sure has had a rough life: the scar, the gimp,* thought Jerome.

"Hey Momma, you look good enough to eat," Turkey said to Gail. She threw him a look that would stop a train. Turkey then said to Jerome, "You clean up pretty good Brother Man. 'Course that vine is strictly from Hicksville."

"Is something wrong?" Jerome inspected his suit expecting to find his zipper undone or a tear.

"Let's go up to my place and get you a better looking outfit; we're 'bout the same size. Miss Gail, sit over here near the receptionist till we get back, so's nobody gets froggy." Turkey signaled the night clerk who understood.

Several minutes later Jerome returned wearing a summer-wool, light grey pinstripe suit with a matching tie, and panama straw hat. It was a tad loose in the shoulders; the coat covered the vastly too wide waist. Jerome was smiling broadly. Gail thought he and Turkey, with matching hats, looked like a vaudeville act.

"Let's roll. My hog's out front."

The doorman helped Gail and Jerome into the front seat of a tan '54 Eldorado "Fishtail" convertible Cadillac. Several strings of Mardi-Gras beads along with a large pair of fluffy, white dice were hanging from the rearview mirror. A miniature pig had replaced the Cadillac's hood emblem.

"This is a hog?" Gail asked.

"Yeah, 'cause it swills gas like a hog swills slop. Hey now!" Turkey snapped his fingers in the air. Gas was 37 cents a gallon.

"And I suppose you have a different Cadillac for every suit, huh?"

"Hey, you pretty sharp for a broad," Turkey laughed. Without checking traffic or signaling, he sped away from the curb and made a mid-block U turn on screeching tires. Cars in both directions slammed on brakes while drivers cursed and made obscene gestures. Gail shut her eyes, stiffened and grabbed Jerome's leg, relaxing only after Turkey had completed his turn, which seemed to take forever. He drove one block to the main drag, Sixty-Third Street, and turned west, under the el tracks. The only parking space was near a fireplug––he took it.

Sidewalks were filled with happy people entering and leaving the many store-front businesses. Several couples were strolling in step with interlocked arms. Even though there wasn't a breeze, dudes held onto the brims of their hats. A group of four boys and a girl doing a reasonable imitation of the Platters were singing, hustling change on a corner. Turkey crumpled a five-dollar bill and threw it into their crinkled top-hat, tip taker. He said, "Buy yourselves a joint." They sang a practiced, elongated, thank you.

Each block housed single store-front take-out eateries with hand painted paper window signs advertising, southern fried chicken, deep fried shrimp, fried catfish, open-pit barbecued ribs, and hot links. All dinners included White bread, French fries and/or cole slaw; sandwiches, without the sides, were available for a dollar less. Bottled 16 ounce strawberry pop was the drink of choice. The Chinese eatery, which was the busiest, released the strongest fumes. All orders from all food stores were sold to go.

The incense shop window confused Gail. She had never seen the odd shaped pipes and strange-looking marijuana paraphernalia on display. A record store with colorful 9" LP jackets attached to the window and The Ravens' *Sixty Minute Man* blaring over a loud speaker, invited patrons. A brightly lit double store-front beauty salon with a large sign, advertising "No Appointment Necessary," had five beauticians and two shampoo girls working.

An open door barroom playing Muddy Waters' recording *Baby Please Don't Go*, was filled with the Brogans and coverall crowd. Singles were seated on barstools; couples at small, square, unbalanced wooden tables; most were drinking bottled beer. Lounges with protruding canopies, elaborate neon signs, and artistically painted, one way windows welcomed the carriage trade. The scene reminded Gail of Bourbon Street: happy people and changing venues every twenty feet. But no one had a drink outside.

The threesome entered Danny's Show Lounge, whose rectangular, umbrella-type canopy extended to the curb. "House, my main man,"

Turkey said to the tall, heavy, doorman/bouncer, who filled the entrance with his 300 plus pound physique, "Got any room in the back?"

"If we don't, we'll stretch the place for you," House smiled. "Is this your little brother?" House placed a velvet, circular passage barrier across the door, which stopped anyone from entering or leaving before he returned.

"Naw, Man," Turkey smiled. "'Course you know we's all related somehow." Gail saw Turkey pass a folded ten dollar bill as he and House shook hands.

"It's so nice and cool, and everybody's friendly," Gail commented as House slowly wedged them through the crowd in the softly lit room. "It's like a huge private party." Gail wasn't sure Jerome, who was one step behind, heard her over the live music and loud voices.

A thin, short man in a Hawaiian sport shirt and a baseball-like straw cap moved between tables with a large, square cornered satchel. When Gail was close, she peeped in and saw premium brand fragrances. Straw Cap sold his goods for fives and tens, which was far less than retail. He repeatedly glanced over both shoulders.

They navigated through the sea of beautiful people. Rows of men in suits, ties, and straw hats were entertaining attractive ladies seated at the bar. Turkey slapped extended palms and yelled to those he couldn't reach, "What it be like?" Over an exaggerated pointed finger, in his distinctive, gravel-sounding voice, Turkey shouted, "Hey Eighty-Eight, my place next week, right?" The pianist nodded his agreement as his trio, elevated over the back bar, played Fats Waller's *E Flat Blues,* up tempo. A well dressed Caucasian was selling single roses to romantically intentioned men.

"Oops, pardon me," Gail said as she bumped inebriated people while dodging darting cigarettes and tilted drinks. She was determined to stay close to Turkey and avoid getting spilled on or burned. A young woman, wearing a shiny, tight, short red dress, too-high heels, and dark glasses stepped between House and Turkey. Gail was shoved to Turkey's right when Miss Shapely forced Turkey to stop. Gail wondered why she was wearing dark glasses in such a dimly lit room.

Miss Shapely pressed her stomach against Turkey, gyrated to the music and said, "Hi Daddy. It's been forever and a day since we hooked up." She peeped over her shades at Gail, pushed them back over her eyes, and added, "I see you're outfitted, but maybe your baby brother needs a playmate."

"That really ain't your bi'ness, now is it?" Turkey's violent stare shocked Gail; Miss Shapely said, "Sorry if I misspoke," stepping away fast. Gail thought, *she was worried about getting hit. Obviously Turkey has a violent reputation.*

When they reached the rear, House opened a heavy, insulated steel door, took three steps and opened a similar door which led to another world.

The laughter and music ceased as the second door closed. The secluded chamber was first class, colored mauve. Gail adjusted her steps to the plush carpet. They were seated at a table with lavender linen by the tuxedoed maître d', who said while bowing slightly, "Welcome to the Papagayo Room. Good to see you Mr. Stevens; you've been missed; dinner tonight?"

"Naw, just drinks, Hamilton." Turkey slipped him ten dollars. He turned to Jerome, "We'll eat at Killer's; I owe him a play." A violinist, playing romantic ballads and singing softly, added to the ambiance and elegance of the room. A waiter served Turkey a double Gordon's gin and tonic as soon as he sat down. Turkey ordered Gail a frozen daiquiri. Jerome ordered a scotch and water; Turkey changed Jerome's drink to a Rusty Nail.

"This room is so chic," Gail said. There were fifteen couples and several foursomes dining. Some were enjoying various cuts of steak; others were eating lobsters or barbecued ribs. Several pairs, romantically inclined, were holding hands, whispering over martinis and manhattans. The ladies, who looked much younger than their escorts, were stunning in their designer dresses. Gail didn't see any wedding rings on the women, only on the men who wore tailored suits, expensive ties, and gold-banded watches. Turkey and Jerome's suits were a bit strident. "Violins and everything. My father owns a small lounge in Baton Rouge, but nothing like this."

"Who's your daddy?"

"Conrad Beauregard, but I'm sure you don't know…"

"I knew you folks had class! Shiiit, everybody knows Brother Beau. Why he used to book Ray Charles before he was THE Ray Charles!"

Jerome sipped his pleasant tasting drink and reluctantly recalled his last encounter with his nationally known father-in-law.

After reigniting the flame in Gail's heart, with her imposed limitations, and enjoying his mom's home cooking, former Captain Jerome Gerard began his job search. He approached white owned drugstore owners in Negro neighborhoods and was ridiculed; sometimes threatened. Jerome quickly learned Southern Whites had not adopted the military policy of racial equality. There were very few black-owned drug stores; none needed a pharmacist.

During an interview at Houston's Negro Hospital, Jerome mentioned his father-in-law was Conrad Beauregard. The administrator, before hiring Jerome, called Mr. Beauregard, anticipating accolades, perhaps even a sizeable contribution to their well-publicized out-patient clinic.

"I won't have my boy passing out pills to charity cases." An insulted administrator eliminated Jerome from consideration. After three months of frustrating job searches, Jerome told his mother and wife he would have to go further afield to find a pharmacist's position.

When Conrad heard the news he became disturbed, he realized torpedoing that Houston job offer might have been a mistake. He decided to have a special dinner to resolve the problem.

Two of Conrad's executives, Leon "White Gloves" Franks, and Archie "Stick" Hogan, were invited, along with their wives, to their first dinner at the Beauregard Estate. Conrad gave clear instructions. "Jerome must decide to work in one of my businesses; the manager that makes that happen will receive a generous bonus."

When Jerome and Gail arrived, Pompeii, the Beauregard's head servant, ushered them into the parlor where cocktails and hors D'oeuvres were being served. Lonnie Blackman, interior designer, was the Beauregards' houseguest. Through casual conversation Jerome learned the source of their nicknames: Leon's, because he wore white gloves most of the time, even when eating. He washed his hands ten times a day, ostensibly, to avoid infection. Leon was waiter turned manager of the Baton Rouge complex. It included a banquet/meeting/dance hall, a restaurant that could seat fifty, a four-lane bowling alley, a night club that could accommodate a hundred, and a fifty room motel. *Beau's Place* was the only upper class entertainment and dining facility for Negroes in Baton Rouge.

"I shoot a pretty good game of eight ball," Archie bragged. He was originally a top salesman and then promoted to agency vice president of Conrad's primary holding, United Mission Insurance Company.

Several drinks and jokes later, Pompeii announced to those relaxing, "Dinner is ready." He then said, after reaching Conrad's closed bedroom door, "Everybody's where you want 'em Mastah Beau, and jest like you said, they's been gettin' to know each other."

Conrad Beauregard, aka Brother Beau to his peers and friends; Daddy Beau to his only child and wife, Granddaddy Beau to Michelle and Dana, Mr. Beau to his employees, and Mastah Beau to his servants, sauntered in. His guests quieted. He was wearing an almond-colored linen suit that matched his complexion. His coat hung perfectly; a quarter-inch of sleeve peaked out. A smooth back with buttons comfortably holding his coat together manifested the optimum fit. The creases in Conrad's pants were blade sharp; he hadn't sat down since putting on his trousers. His naturally straight, partially grey hair held a slight wave. Conrad at 59 was still quite handsome. His handmade ostrich-skin shoes with lifts added two inches to his short stature.

The children had been seated; Dana was next to Gail. Michelle, according to Conrad's instructions, was seated aside him at the head of the table. Everyone else was standing.

The twelve-foot, triple pedestal, hand carved, solid mahogany table covered with embroidered lace was set with gold-trimmed, wafer-thin dishes, gold-plated silverware, and monogrammed Steuben wine glasses, for eleven. The ornate chandelier with obscure bulbs, hidden by reflective etched crystal designed in an inverted pyramid, hung six feet above the table. Conrad inspected the table settings looking for the proverbial gnat on a bee's back, through piercing light brown eyes. He picked up a wine glass with a smudge, frowned, and then handed it to Pompeii who instantly replaced it with one from the silent butler.

Because this was their first invitation to the Beauregard Estate, Leon's and Archie's pretty wives had bought new dresses for the occasion. Both wore bare shouldered, tight-waisted, flare bottomed, bright, flowery frocks that hung just below the knee. Their short hair was freshly hot-combed. The gay colored frocks contrasted beautifully with their dark skin. Gail wore a lime-colored, double layered chiffon dress her mother's seamstress had made, which accented her eyes. The inner layer clung just enough to show her svelte figure.

The gown Sylvia wore was a hideous multi-colored, monstrosity. Her deeply powdered, highly rouged cheeks and heavy eyeliner reminded

Jerome of the clowns on a Mardi gras float. *She's trying to look twenty-five at forty-five; that high-yellow Creole skin sure ages fast,* thought Jerome.

After Conrad took his seat at the head of the table, he then said over a chuckle; "Y'all can't eat standing up; sit down!" Everyone knew Conrad had to be seated first.

Conrad, born in 1895, was the bastard son of Homer Beauregard, a rich Frenchman, who owned a lucrative import business, which included slave trading. He had a carnal relationship with his beautiful, young Negro maid and mistress, Lucy, Conrad's mother. To satisfy Conrad's sexual desires, Lucy had been given a bedroom in Homer's large home in the French Quarter. Matilda, Conrad's wife, tolerated the arrangement; complaining may have worsened the situation. Besides, Matilda decided, she could use the help keeping her husband's libido satisfied.

"Mastah," Lucy asked while massaging Homer's hairy chest as they lay in her four-poster bed after an unusually pleasing, wild, tryst, "Would it be too much to ask that our son be schooled with your other chillen? After all, he has your blood and good sense, and he looks just like the rest of 'em." Homer agreed.

Ten years later, Homer was shot and killed while playing poker in an upscale New Orleans brothel. Matilda kicked Lucy and fifteen year-old Conrad into the street before Homer was put into the ground.

Middle aged Lucy Beauregard washed clothes and scrubbed floors to survive. Five years of living hand-to-mouth took its toll. "Ain't sure what killed her, Son," the doctor said to Conrad. "Sometimes life's pitfalls are just too burdensome to bear."

"If you had one of them burial policies," a fellow teacher said as she handed Conrad a dime to bury his mother, "you wouldn't have to beg so hard." The Colored Burial Insurance Company in Louisiana was based in Shreveport and had no representation in New Orleans. After considerable thought, instead of representing the Shreveport-based company, 20 year-old Conrad decided to start his own company in 1915 while he continued his teaching job. With legal assistance, he adopted the successful Atlanta Life Insurance Company's policies and rates. He offered his teacher friends burial plans of $200, $500, and $1,000. Most bought the $200 plan to end Conrad's pestering, and paid him fifteen cents a week, or fifty cents a month. Conrad visited other Negro schools in Louisiana and sold insurance to their teachers.

Six months into his side business, he solicited the support of a well known preacher who told his congregation that "Coming Home" with a United Mission Burial Plan would get you closer to the Pearly Gates because you had paid your own way. The preacher received the first month's premiums.

A year after Conrad had begun his business Sister Rosina Ware died. She had a $200 policy; Conrad, through a stroke of genius, announced she had his $1,000 plan. The mortician made her look 20 years younger. She was laid to rest in a copper coffin, lined with white fluffed satin for all to admire. The preacher, Conrad's cohort, was grabbed by "The Spirit" in church and at the gravesite.

"That was some Coming Home service Sister Rosina had. She went to meet her Jesus the way I want to go," Rosina's friends said to each other. Conrad and the preacher announced at every opportunity that Sister Rosina's $1,000 policy was named the Pearly Gates Plan. Church members rushed to buy the best burial plan available at the bargain price of fifty cents a week, or $1.75 a month. Street women and high rollers, after a persuasive conversation with Conrad "saw the light." They became Conrad's clients … just in case.

After two years of hard selling, Conrad's insurance business demanded he quit teaching. He also realized he had to increase his business knowledge. Conrad audited accounting, commercial law, and actuarial science classes at Dillard University, a New Orleans Negro Christian college, without receiving credits or grades. It was less expensive to pay to listen to lectures and read appropriate texts than to be enrolled and receive college credits. Conrad also audited classes at Louisiana University, not available at Dillard, while passing for White. He learned economics, marketing, sales, sales management, and finance. White professors taught him how to invest wisely and avoid paying taxes and interest.

To increase business, Conrad hired commission-only representatives and taught them how to sell. In 1920 he introduced a $2,500 life insurance policy that would give the surviving family "a leg up" when and if the breadwinner unexpectedly passed on; it cost $5 a week, or $18.50 a month. He changed the company name to United Mission Insurance Company.

By 1925 burying clients had become a sizeable expense, so Conrad built a funeral home and bought significant acreage he converted into a Negro cemetery. Before Conrad's cemetery, Negroes were buried behind their church or in a special plot on the plantation where they worked as freemen. His mortician prepared and buried all Negroes, which increased his profits. After funeral services for a client, Conrad elaborately presented the beneficiaries their check in front of relatives and friends, which created new customers. After burying a non-client he gave the surviving family members a special "beneficiaries price" if they immediately bought a policy. Conrad expanded throughout Louisiana, Alabama, and south eastern Texas, adding more salesmen and funeral homes.

As surplus cash increased, Conrad bought a fleet of taxis and kept them rolling 24 hours a day in party-oriented New Orleans. Maintenance from White garages was expensive and slow because they only serviced Conrad's cars when there was no other work, and at higher prices. Conrad bought a four-bay garage, hired a mechanic, and installed a gas pump out front. Gas sales and car repairs to New Orleans Negroes increased profits.

Some abandoned acreage in Colored Town was being sold at auction as part of an estate settlement in Baton Rouge. Because Caucasians weren't interested, Conrad bought it for almost nothing. He built his entertainment complex on his newly acquired property, one business at a time.

"I can't afford your Pearly Gates policy on my teacher's salary," cooed petite, cute, twenty-year old Sylvia when thirty-five year old Conrad pitched the benefits of insurance to her in 1929.

"You marry me and I'll insure your happiness for the rest of your life, darling," Conrad promised. Sylvia got the whole package. Gail was born a year later.

In 1950, 20 years later, when the Beauregards stopped by his garage, Sylvia noticed the cabs. She asked, "What are you doing to these taxis? I have never seen anything like that!"

"This is what fleet owners are doing up North," Conrad smiled. On each cab Conrad had placed three advertisements; "Come home with United Mission Insurance." "Quality Car Service keeps your car rolling," and, "Visit Beau's Place ––Baton Rouge's only Negro entertainment center." Other companies wanted to buy ads on Conrad's cabs, but space was not available at any price. The advertisements significantly increased business for Conrad's mini-conglomerate.

Conrad never confronted Caucasians. He sought business opportunities they weren't interested in. On those rare occasions when he interacted with

Whites, he smiled, grinned and spoke incorrect English as expected. New Orleans Caucasians had no idea the amount of money Conrad was making. He kept an account in one of New Orleans' banks that always had a small balance. Most of Conrad's money was kept in Atlanta's Negro bank. In 1954, the year Jerome was discharged, Conrad's net worth exceeded a million dollars: a rare accomplishment among Negroes.

"That prime rib smells delicious, Pompeii," Gail said, as he held the sterling silver tray close. Boiled Okra, golden brown, sugared sweet potatoes, mixed greens, and corn-on-the-cob saturated with butter, were offered by Pompeii's staff. The corn bread, baked with kernel corn and sugar, had a strong bouquet which wafted from the warmers.

"You're stuffing your mouth like I cain't cook at all," Mrs. Franks whispered angrily as she kicked Leon under the table. Leon slowed his consumption rate. He was wearing a new pair of white stitched, Stacey-Adams knob-toed shoes, which were a size too small, that were killing him. He kept flexing his toes in his shoes for relief, but it didn't help.

Conrad continuously bragged about the success of his many businesses. Droopy eyed, slow-talking Leon embellished every statement his guru made. "The Baton Rouge businesses I manage, Mr. Gerard, serves the best home cooking in Louisiana." Leon looked at Mrs. Beauregard and quickly added, "Present meal excluded, Maam. Why I could find you a nice home nearby in nothing flat... Uh, with Mr. Beau's OK, of course."

"Just a cotton-pickin' minute," Archie said, waving both hands over his heavily pomaded hair as he exaggerated being insulted. He flashed his best Satchimo smile through thick lips and a dark Cheshire face. Looking directly at Jerome, he said, "United sells life and burial insurance in four states. Why Mr. Blackman is in town to furnish our brand new office building, and he'll outfit your office anyway you want if you just give him the word. That is, after Mr. Beau decides that's where you're best suited to work, won't you Mr. Blackman?"

Lonnie Blackman just smiled. He wanted to avoid becoming a part of these obvious high pressure tactics aimed at Jerome, but he was enjoying the evening's mental sparring. He was impressed by Jerome's ability to remain noncommittal. Lonnie wore a dark blue cashmere sports coat with a large thin maroon pattern, beige pants, and a yellow, open collar sports shirt. He was the only man at the table without a tie.

These dudes act as if Daddy Beau can turn grits into granulated gold, Jerome thought. *I had expected a job offer or two, but nothing quite so blatant.* He continued to smile politely when making eye contact.

After dinner, Conrad motioned to Pompeii to bring him a Beefeater's gin and tonic. He then pulled out a thick, black cigar and said, "Nothing like a fine cigar after a delicious meal." He suggested the men join him; Leon and Archie accepted; Jerome and Lonnie refused. Conrad ceremoniously clipped the tip, rolled the Rum-Havana between his thin, wet lips and lit it with his special gold plated cigar lighter. Leon and Archie, without a cigar clip or a special lighter, fumbled through the cigar-lighting process. The smoke aggravated the ladies and children; some coughed, but no one objected. The presence of the cigars signaled Conrad wanted everyone's attention.

Pompeii and his staff cleared away the dishes and took orders for dessert and after dinner drinks. Lonnie started to speak to Sylvia seated next to him, but she put her forefinger across her lips.

"Another delicious dessert, please," Jerome whispered to a server. *No drinks while I'm in the trenches.* Moments passed. Everyone had stopped eating except Jerome, who was enjoying his second peach cobbler.

Contemplating his cigar as if it were a work of art, Conrad said, "So Jerome, when you going to decide your life's work?"

"I've decided Daddy Beau," *I almost choke every time I'm forced to call him Daddy Beau. Maybe another mouth full of this delicious cobbler followed by a sip of coffee will loosen the constriction.* "I'm going to work as a pharmacist and eventually own a chain of drugstores."

"Can't you stop eating, Boy?" Jerome smiled shamefacedly and put down his fork as he hurriedly swallowed the cobbler then dabbed the corners of his mouth.

"Why haven't you asked me for a job, Son? I can pay you twice what you'd make as a drugstore stooge for half the work. Why, you'd be the highest paid young buck in the South," Conrad said over a chortle. Leon and Archie roared as they slapped the table and leaned back in their chairs. The ladies, all except Gail, giggled. She didn't appreciate her husband being called a "young buck;" it suggested his sleeping around. "Didn't Archie and Leon tell you what they make?"

"Yes sir, they did, and without my asking, but money isn't my only concern, and hard work plus my ability to…"

"Listen Boy, forget pushing pills; go to work in my insurance business. In no time you'll be running the place." Conrad pointed his cigar toward Archie. "How many agents do we have?"

"Fifty-two in four states," Archie said proudly, "The highest paid…"

"And ten funeral parlors that need managing, right Archie?" To avoid being interrupted again, Archie just smiled and nodded. "Boy, you'll get a good salary and as a bonus a brand new Buick. You can junk that old Chevy that barely got you here." Conrad drove a current Cadillac sedan.

"Jerome's car is so old it runs on Geritol," Archie said, looking around the table, hoping others found his comment funny.

Most laughed. Jerome smiled and then said, "We may have to move elsewhere because I can't find a pharmacist's job nearby. I'd like to stay near my mother, but …"

I knew I should have given Houston more consideration, thought Conrad. "What about my Zanzibar complex in Baton Rouge?" Conrad said. "Why Leon can show you how to run those businesses in nothing flat, can't you Leon?" Leon looked embarrassed as he agreed.

Jerome noticed Conrad silently apologizing to Leon and Archie; if Jerome can learn to manage the Zanzibar Complex in "nothing flat" and the insurance business in "no time," what would Leon and Archie do?

Because Jerome had avoided him, Conrad incorrectly assessed Jerome as being timid, submissive, indecisive, mentally dull, and controllable. Jerome's military experience had turned the young, guilt-ridden, college student into an intelligent, confident individual, therefore difficult to influence. *I had better come at this colored boy from another direction.*

"Daddy Beau," Jerome said, "I appreciate your interest in our future and your willingness to help, but I worked hard to graduate as a pharmacist and while in the Army, was fortunate enough to gain three years pharmaceutical experience, so my career plans are set."

"I see, I see," Conrad nodded. "Okay then, suppose I open a drugstore and let you run it?" Conrad noted Jerome's eyes reflected surprise; he presumed progress was being made. "There's a boarded up store front on Canal and Spruce that would make an excellent location." Conrad put down his cigar, leaned toward Jerome and said, "You know I just remembered; I didn't give you kids a wedding present. Sylvia, how could I have been so thoughtless?"

Sylvia blinked twice, looked at Conrad through wide eyes, and started to remind him of his negative attitude before, during, and after the graduation and wedding ceremonies, but didn't.

Conrad reached over Michelle, caressed Gail's fingers and said, "Gail, how about that house on Chestnut Street you have always loved as a wedding present? Why, I'll even furnish it!"

Gail turned toward Jerome, then toward her mother, beaming. "Oh Daddy Beau, that would be wonderful! Our own drugstore and living in that beautiful house is more than…"

"Mr. Beauregard," Jerome said, aggravated by Conrad's barefaced bribery attempt, "as wealthy as you are, I wouldn't ask even you to make such an unwise investment." Jerome placed his hand over Gail's to quiet her. "Right now, I don't know the first thing about running a drugstore and you know even less. It would be foolish for us to anticipate being successful." Jerome slowly took a sip of his coffee.

Leon and Archie had never heard anyone tell Mr. Beau what he didn't know, that he was considering an unwise investment, or that his suggestion was foolish. They sat frozen, awaiting the thunder clap after the lightning. The only sound in the room was the ticking of the grandfather clock.

"Now Son," Conrad said laboriously, "we might have started off on a bad footing, but that's the past. You're part of the family now and we should stay together. You are the son I never had." Conrad's eyes reflected an emotion no one in the room had ever seen.

"You talk about going somewhere, looking for a job. That's just plain stupid." Conrad caught himself; drink was usurping his diplomacy. "I didn't mean you were stupid, Son. What I meant was your best opportunity for growth, wealth, and security is right here. No matter where you go you are not going to find any better offer. I have invested 30 years in building my businesses. All you have to do is join me. In five years you'll be ready to take over my entire operation; hell, I need to retire anyway." A desperate Conrad had offered Jerome everything.

Jerome stared at Conrad, whose arms were on the table, awaiting Jerome's response. *I don't believe even <u>you</u> believe what you're saying old man. I'm getting out of here before I become another Leon or Archie,* thought Jerome.

"You thinking about going up North?" asked Conrad trying a new approach. "There are twenty Negroes with degrees in line for every position a Negro can fill in those overcrowded, rat infested towns. Wherever you go you are still going to be a Nigger!"

"President Eisenhower," Jerome said, "during his first year in office, passed an equal economic opportunity edict requiring all federal agencies to eliminate discriminatory hiring practices; that means VA hospitals…"

"That don't mean sh… nothing," Conrad countered, laboring to keep his language clean. "So did President Roosevelt in '41 and Truman in '48. All executive orders to integrate have been ignored because Southern Congressmen and Senators aren't going to allow federal department heads to hire educated Negroes who may eventually supervise White folks."

Conrad took a deep breath, as he lowered his voice and urgency level, he said, "The only government agency that is hiring us is the Post Office, and that's where ambitious, college educated Negroes bury their dreams, in the Dead Letter rooms, as they work for peanuts and are by-passed for promotions. Integration isn't happening anywhere except in the military. We are still catching hell all over the country. The only Negroes doing well are taking advantage of segregation like me and Lonnie." Conrad gulped down his second drink; Pompeii gave him a fresh one. "Tell him, Lonnie, how rough it is out there." *I need time to think.*

Lonnie bowed his head momentarily, and then through a smile said, "Your father-in-law is right Jerome, about those presidential orders being ignored. A lot of us had hope after three presidents signed equal employment opportunity bills, but nobody has paid any attention. Just like after the Civil War, there was no penalty for practicing Jim Crow, so southerners continued doing what they had always done; mistreat Negroes. Why none of our presidents, from Andrew Jackson forward, would even declare lynching a federal offense!

"The only reason I am doing well," continued Lonnie, "is that Southern Governors are trying to keep their state colleges segregated. They had anticipated Equal Rights laws passed by the Supreme Court last May, so they have been pumping hundreds of thousands of dollars into Negro land grant colleges, desperately trying to make them appear equal, and the Negro college presidents are buying most of their furnishings through me."

"There, you see? And Lonnie knows what he's talking about. He travels from coast to coast," Conrad thought; *thank you Lonnie.*

"But Brother Beau," Lonnie added, "you know how young folks are; you can't tell em anything. If we had listened to most of our mentors when we made our moves we wouldn't be where we are today. And as much as you may hate to admit it, we are now in the Old Folk category."

Gail's sobbing in her hands drew Conrad's attention. "What's wrong with you, girl?" Conrad asked.

"All of my life, all I have ever wanted was a nice home, a couple of kids, a loving husband, and no money worries. Daddy Beau, you have offered us that and more and Jerome doesn't have sense enough to accept it. He is just being asinine!"

Conrad and Sylvia knew Gail had crossed the wife-to-husband respect line when she publicly called her husband asinine. "I know you have family all over and most of them are well off, but if they can't give you a good paying job, they can't help you. The man with the jobs has the power, and I have over 200 jobs!" Conrad said.

When he finished he was out of his seat, eyeball to eyeball with Jerome, who remained stoic. Conrad relaxed back into his seat believing he had won the debate. He took a long drink and said in his most paternalistic voice, "I know what I'm talking about, Son. You'll do best here, so pick one; the insurance business, your own drugstore, or the Baton Rouge complex. Whatever you choose, the new car and a completely furnished house are yours." Conrad smiled at Jerome, cigar held by his teeth, hanging from his mouth, looking victorious.

All eyes were on Jerome. Gail, with eyes closed and hands folded, was silently praying he would choose one. Jerome said, "Neither."

Gail screamed, "Oh no!" and bolted from the table; Sylvia went after her.

Conrad opened his mouth; Jerome raised the palm of his hand toward him and said, "Please?" Conrad reluctantly remained silent. Jerome said, "I apologize for Gail's outbursts. I'm sure you realize better than me how prone she is to temper tantrums, and name calling." Jerome paused while gathering his next thought. "At the risk of being redundant, I know my objectives. I will not rest until I am working as a registered pharmacist, hopefully in a drugstore."

"Then you don't know where in hell you're going to end up. It might be in Tupelo, Mississippi, or Podunk, Iowa. And no matter what I say or do, you're going to take my only child and my grandbabies away and not give a damn if I ever see them again!"

"We won't end up in Tupelo, Mississippi. I don't think employment…"

Conrad ripped his napkin from his shirt collar and shouted, "You stubborn, dumb…"

"Brother Beau," interrupted Lonnie, "You're frightening your granddaughters." Dana had started crying and Michelle had gotten up from the table searching for her mother.

Conrad glanced around the room; the servants had disappeared. Everyone avoided his wild stare. Conrad tried to shake the liquor out of his head. "Well," he whined, "if you're so set on going, God only knows where, you'll need some money. So how much do you want to borrow?"

"None," Jerome said as he strained to smile and remain calm. "Gail has saved her allotment checks, and we don't have any bills. My car is old but it's paid for."

Conrad paused while Gail, Sylvia, and Michelle returned to the table.

"That's admirable Son. How much did you save?" Conrad was prepared to demonstrate, no matter the amount, Jerome's savings were insufficient.

"Enough." Jerome said over a confident smile. Four years of allotment checks plus his mustering–out pay was a significant sum.

"In all my years!" Conrad shouted as he pounded his fist on the table, tipping over his wine glass, "I have never!" Conrad jumped up, knocking over his chair, stumbling. He righted himself and glared around the table. All eyes were watching him warily as if he had lost his mind.

Conrad shook his fist in Jerome's face and began yelling, "Who do you think you are? You uppity, ignorant, ugly, no-count, dumb-ass Nigger! Mark my words, you take my baby and grandchildren away from me and your life will be ruined forever." Conrad turned and left the room shouting words no one understood.

"Now Baby," Sylvia had said as she held a sobbing Gail in her arms as they once again moved from the dining room to a couch in the parlor, "Men are sometimes difficult to understand. Your daddy, no matter how righteous, is sort of bossy, and Jerome isn't ready to submit to his father-in-law; not yet." Gail stopped crying, sat up and looked her mother in the eyes.

"After your inexperienced husband learns how cruel segregation and racism can be, he'll see your daddy's offer as being the best he can do, and will be eager to return; you'll see," Sylvia said while patting Gail's hands.

"But Momma, I don't want to go——wherever he's going."

"You must dear, so you can bring him back home after he fails; and he will fail. If you aren't with Jerome we may never see him again, and you don't want to raise two beautiful girls without a father. I don't know why I haven't said this before, but you can't publicly embarrass him, ever."

That was the last time Jerome had seen Conrad; twenty-seven days, five cities and over 4,000 miles ago.

"When did you meet my daddy?" Gail asked Turkey as she sipped her frozen daiquiri in the elegant Papagayo Room.

"Some time ago. He probably wouldn't remember me." Turkey picked up his drink and digressed. "There are over twenty first class lounges within five blocks of here. On a Saturday night you can't get in any of 'em, that's unless you know somebody. Yes sir, Sixty-Third Street is where it's at!"

Gail accepted her question being ignored. She remembered her mother whispering when Gail was a teenager and her daddy came home while they were having breakfast one Saturday morning, "There are some things about husbands wives aren't supposed to know." Gail was sure that womanly advice included fathers too.

The violinist serenaded the threesome with Hoagie Carmichael's *Stardust*. Turkey tipped him and ordered another round. They laughed; about Chicago, the Army, and New Orleans; interruptions were frequent. Turkey seemed to know everybody in the room.

"These Rusty Nails are potent," Jerome said as he concentrated on standing. Turkey smiled at Jerome's unsteadiness as he signed their bill. Their drinks would become a hotel expense.

"Put this in the glove compartment," Turkey said to Gail handing her a parking ticket he pulled off his windshield. Gail opened the unit, saw numerous citations, shoved in the additional one and quickly shut the compartment.

Killer Jackson's Mood Indigo Restaurant and Lounge was five minutes away. "This is larger than the Papagayo Room——I think," Gail said. The smoked glass partitions and subdued lighting made people two tables away unrecognizable. In a far corner a trio played jazz arrangements of standard tunes.

"They'll play and sing anything you want to hear," Turkey said to Gail. Turkey put a ten dollar bill in the giant brandy sniffer on the piano, while pointing an exaggerated finger at the pianist.

"This here's Brother Beau's little girl and her husband, Jerome Gerard," Turkey said to Killer Jackson through a proud smile. Turkey was presenting the Gerards to royalty. Killer had a boxer's face: slightly enlarged cheeks, sunken eyes, and flattened ears. Several scars were laced through his eyebrows. Killer wore an expensive dark blue, subtly patterned suit. His pinky ring was at least a four karat diamond.

"Brother Beau and I have been tight for years," Killer clasped Gail's fingers. Jerome had trouble encircling Killer's hand; he hid the pain from Killer's grip. "Last time I stayed with your daddy was during Mardi Gras in '46. You were graduating high school that spring. Staying in town long?"

"Just through Sunday; I'm looking for an Army buddy named Namon Stewart."

"I don't know him, but if he's here, Turkey'll dig him up. Listen man," Killer said to Turkey, "I know this was to be your treat, but if Brother Beau found out his kids ate here and I didn't pick up the tab, I'll be on his sh… On his list until Hell freezes over." Killer summoned the maître d' and gave instructions.

A battery of waiters served five gourmet courses. Entrees were ribeye steaks; inch-thick, grilled pork chops; and prime rib. Jerome had never eaten a steak so tender, nor had he been served with such grace and aplomb. Coffee laced with cognac completed the delicious meal. Turkey and his guests said good night to Killer. As Turkey generously tipped the maître d' he said, "Give the waiters some."

"Don't ding it." Turkey warned the valet as he left the keys in the ignition in front of Club Delgado, the hottest show room in Bronzeville.

"I have never seen anything like that!" Gail said, bending her head back. Curved stick figures of musicians, men in top hats, and dancing girls were moving in jerky motions in multi-colored neon tubes atop the club which covered a quarter-block.

Their table was right down front. During the floor show, a nearly nude dancer, to a boogie beat came very close to Jerome's face; he became wide eyed as he put his hand between his face and the dancer. The sensuous dancer laughed at Jerome's gesture and moved on to other front row VIP's.

Turkey folded a five spot into her G string. Gail looked at Jerome and then at the dancer and shook her head, flabbergasted at both performances.

The star of the show, comedian Redd Foxx, made Gail blush with his risqué jokes. After the show, Gail was amazed to see White and Black couples dancing on the same floor. Gail noticed an attractive, middle-aged woman in a red pillbox hat and gloves, several tables away, discreetly waving at Turkey. He ignored her gesture.

"One more stop before we head back," Turkey said. Outside, the threesome walked left then turned into a narrow, dark gangway. Halfway in, a light came on and illuminated the entire tight passage.

"How you doin' Mr. Turkey?" A burly man said standing at the top of a long flight of wooden stairs. His taped right hand remained in his bulging suit coat pocket while he opened the door. Normally, Burly would pat-down visitors, but not celebrities like Turkey or his guests.

Gail covered her eyes as bright, naked, 200 watt light bulbs and smoke-filled air assaulted her. Seven men with various stacks of bills in front of them were playing five-card-stud poker in a converted bedroom on a padded, sheet-covered table. Several eyeballed Gail as she passed, then quickly turned their attention to their cards.

"Hit me," one of the six men in another room, standing at a half-circle table said to the black-jack dealer.

"I wish the hell he would win, lose or do something," an obviously impatient, sleepy woman sitting with several others, said, waiting in what used to be the dining room. She had slipped off her high-heels, exposing holes in her nylon stockings, and was sipping a dark drink from a six ounce glass. Gail noticed a large floor fan in the corner. The welcomed breeze kept the funk moving. Unpleasant aromas piqued Gail's senses.

Turkey walked into the living room where a crap game was underway. The tall, heavyset stickman looked up, spotted Turkey and said, "All right crap shooters, big money's in the house. The price of dice just went up, give The Man some room." Space was cleared for Turkey and his party. A pool table with cardboard cut outs covering the six pockets and a string across the center to trip rolling dice served as a crap table. Heavy, black drapes covered the windows.

Turkey waited for the shooter to complete his roll, and then threw a crumpled $100 bill on the table, shouting, "The dice win!" His gravel voice drew immediate attention.

"Who's he?" a player asked.

"That's Turkey Stevens from the Pershing," his friend answered. It took six gamblers to cover Turkey's bet. The shooter wagering five dollars rolled an eight. A waitress handed Turkey a Gordon's gin and tonic. He motioned to Gail and Jerome indicating the waitress should bring them drinks while handing her a ten spot.

"I'll have a frozen daiquiri please," Gail said.

"We serve drinks here Missy, not snow cones." The waitress gave Gail a super-critical up-and-down look.

Turkey snatched the ten dollars and said, "Give her rum and Coke and him a premium scotch and water, none of that no-name watered down shit. This joint can use some classier drinks and some classier waitresses. Incidentally, Miss Smart Ass, you buy this round. If you don't like it, let's talk to Mike!" The waitress dropped her head and moved on without comment.

"Think he'll make his eight?" Turkey asked Gail.

"I guess so," Gail answered. Turkey continued to stare. "Sure, why not?"

"Another yard the dice win!" Turkey shouted as he tossed another crumpled hundred dollar bill onto the felt.

"Oh my goodness, Turkey," Gail exclaimed. "I don't know a thing about shooting dice!"

"Hell, I know that." Turkey smiled.

"Eight is the point. Turkey believes they will, who believes they won't?" the stickman announced. Only half of the second hundred was faded. Turkey picked up his change. The shooter rolled a nine, a six, and then two fours. "Eight, the hard way, Turkey and the dice win!" The stickman handed a laughing Turkey a fistful of bills. Turkey tipped him ten. The shooter grabbed his five dollar winnings and prepared to shoot for another five dollars.

"Them that gots gets," a loser moaned.

Turkey shouted, "If I had gotten my second C note faded, I might have hung around and put some real money in the game. See you sissies when I see you."

Turkey backed away from the table and began smoothing his bills. He whispered to Jerome, "I covered all tonight's expenses and then some without even touching the dice." Jerome sipped his drink and smiled. Turkey continued, "Action's light tonight. On weekends, White folks come here to match bankrolls with us. Mike Turco, just like I do, runs a straight up game. Only cuts half of craps and two dollars each time the dice change hands; a buck on a slow night like tonight. Anybody slips in loaded dice gets their wrists broke." They were in and out in less than twenty minutes.

"A lot of people out here," Turkey said as he joined the crowd in front of Club DeLago awaiting their cars. "Too many," he decided. Turkey approached the valet manager, gave him his ticket and a five spot; the manager ran off.

"Who's crying?" Gail asked as she turned her head toward the sound of slaps and a woman's sobs. A man had collared Miss Red Pillbox with his left hand, while slapping her repeatedly with his right.

"You," he bitch slapped her twice, "don't wave at nobody," another two slaps, "when you out with me," followed by an extra hard slap, "dig it?" He loosened his grip around her neck. Miss Red Pillbox, with her head bowed, handkerchief in hand, stayed next to her man. She was still obligated to serve him sexually.

The crowd shifted to give them room. Turkey looked at the couple then looked away. "Don't worry 'bout her, Miss Gail; she's woman enough to take it."

Gail moved closer to Jerome, she whispered in Jerome's ear, "Woman enough to take it. What on earth does that mean?" Jerome wrapped his arm around Gail's shoulders, pulled her close and put a finger over his lips, suggesting Gail remain quiet.

"Turkey, isn't gambling illegal in Chicago?" Gail asked as they rode through Washington Park with the top down.

"Ain't nothin' illegal if you're connected," Turkey laughed. "Ahmad hits at 2:30 for his last set, we'll just make it."

"Look!" Gail yelled. "Over in the grass. Stop the car!" Gail saw a Caucasian-looking man in a white dress shirt and dark pants lying still, face down, arms stretched over his head. His right leg was bent as if he had been crawling. He looked immobile——or dead.

Turkey glanced toward the grass, slowed, saw the man, and then accelerated. "Let him be," Turkey growled. "Fuzz drive through here all the time. They's paid to help. If he's dead nobody can help. One thing you do in this town is mind your own bi'ness. And he ain't none of our bi'ness."

"But, but…" Gail started to argue. Jerome pressured her left shoulder while whispering, "We're strangers here, Babe; be quiet, please?" Jerome, inebriated, was having the time of his life. In college his social life was limited to the generosity of his classmates in Downtown New Orleans, in the military he and his fellow officers visited officers clubs and local bars, once even in Atlantic City, but he had never had the VIP treatment in such erotic, sophisticated, Negro drinking establishments as he had experienced tonight. Jerome couldn't wait to see what was going to happen next.

End of Chapter Two

CHAPTER THREE

"This spiral staircase is as dark as a bad attitude," Jerome said.

"The lights are low 'cause the Genius is playin'," Turkey whispered. Smooth jazz sounds increased as they descended. The Pershing Hotel's Beige Room was moments away.

The high-back, leather, semi-circular booths, tablecloths, and drapes along the wall were dark chocolate to beige. The Ahmad Jamal Trio was playing their signature number, *Poinciana*. The maître d' squeezed in a table near the stage for Turkey's party. The enthralled audience of 150 was enjoying avant-garde jazz.

"Is this seat taken?" asked a tall, sensuous woman with a smoky voice. Her tight, light blue silk dress with varying sizes of white circles exhibited a deep cleavage.

"This is Faye, my main squeeze," Turkey said, just loud enough for the Gerards to hear. Turkey wrapped his arms around Faye's small waist and fondled her firm butt as she glided toward her seat. Turkey's eyes widened as he realized she wasn't wearing undergarments. Faye encouraged Turkey's roving hand by slightly shaking her ample derriere.

Gail thought the axiom main squeeze would have insulted Faye, but it didn't. She was fair skinned with long, brown hair, closer to Gail's age than Turkey's. Her face could have graced a magazine cover sans her heavy eyelids and jaundice-infected whites surrounding her beautiful, auburn eyes, indicating drug use. Ahmad's next number, the romantic, *Autumn Leaves,* received a thunderous applause as it concluded.

Turkey leaned backward and conversed with several ladies at another table; Faye whispered to Jerome and Gail, "Did you have fun tonight?" The excited couple interrupted each other describing their evening. Faye pulled out a cigarette, glanced toward Turkey, who was still engaged, shrugged, and then lit it herself.

Minutes later, Faye whispered to Gail, "Here's how you get a stray dog's attention." Faye reached under the table and yanked Turkey's testicles through his pants. Turkey's head snapped forward; his eyes were as wide as a caught carp. His mouth flew open as he swallowed a cry of pain. Faye said, "<u>Your</u> woman is over here, Daddy." She then said to the startled ladies, "Tonight he's with me!"

"That wasn't funny you high yellow bitch! Wait till I get you alone," Turkey whispered while massaging his crotch with both hands.

"Promises, promises, promises," Faye responded. As Turkey's pain and embarrassment subsided, Faye whispered into Turkey's ear, with her tongue emphasizing sexual remarks. Turkey was mollified. Ahmad ended the set with his own composition, *Ahmad's Blues.*

"Let's grab some vittles and then hit the after-hour spots," Turkey said as he downed his drink.

"Its 3:45," Gail said. "More? You mean there's still more?"

"Oh Yeaah! The swinginest party places start jammin' right about now. Sometimes they cook till noon; that's when the musicians really get down, playing for themselves," Turkey said while summoning their waiter.

"Turkey," Jerome pleaded, "tonight has been a blast and you have been the perfect host, but we need some sleep, man."

"I can dig it little brother," Turkey chortled. "See you at 11:30 in the a.m. C'mon babe, let's go party. You still got somethin' comin'."

"Yes, Daddy," Faye said submissively, as she switched her hips and waved her small purse toward Gail with a twinkle in her eyes.

After Gail relieved the babysitter, she slurred, "Did you shee how Turkey tipped, like his money was counterfeit. This shtopover idea was shimply marvelous," Gail giggled, "and the women here are so sassy! Irritating their men seems to be the norm."

"What a town!" Jerome said, as he turned up the window air conditioner and let the forced breeze blow over his chest's knotted hairs. "We couldn't have had more fun, even with Namon. I wonder…."

Gail watched Jerome undress as he leaned into the cool air. She became aroused while staring at his muscular shoulder blades, trim waist, and tight, dimpled behind. She knew he was talking but had no idea what he was saying. *I should start behaving like a brazen, Bronzeville broad instead of a spoiled wife.*

"You know, it's amazing to me…" Jerome said, as he, completely naked, turned from the A/C. He began picking up Turkey's borrowed clothes. Jerome stopped mid-bend.

Gail's dark brown hair, normally in rollers at bedtime, fell loosely about her intense face. Her hands caressed her shapely hips; her beautiful legs were slightly apart, one in front of the other. She posed nude and proud, barefoot, staring at Jerome through hot green eyes overflowing with desire. Her flat stomach and stiff nipples accented by a tucked chin, met Jerome's passionate look. In a low, sultry voice Gail said, "Make love to me Babe."

Gail moved toward Jerome, placed the palms of her hands on his chest and kissed him, full. As their kiss smoldered, Gail stood on her toes and wrapped her arms around Jerome's neck. He grabbed her butt and lifted her from the carpet. She placed her legs around his hips. Their tongues fought for access; Gail won. Jerome countered by engulfing Gail's lips with his. The turbulent kissing continued, saliva escaped; Gail broke away, breathing heavily. Jerome, with Gail suspended, tongued the base of her neck, breathed over the wet spot and bit lightly. Gail, on fire, leaned forward pushing Jerome onto the bed. They landed with his mouth on her large breast, nibbling. The pain was pleasurable.

"Do me, Babe, until I beg you to stop," Gail said as she rolled over, centered herself and dug her heels into the spread.

"Umm hmm," Jerome mumbled through a full mouth; incensed by Gail's newfound, carnal wildness. Gail bit down on her lip slightly anticipating the huge penetration. After adjusting, Gail tied their bodies together with her legs and arms leaving her toes pointed upward. Jerome, encouraged by Gail's aggressive actions climaxed quickly; his head fell over her shoulder. Jerome was disappointed with his performance. The end had come before he had begun.

"That's all right Honey, I understand. It's been awhile, just lay still." Gail cupped Jerome's face, tongued his lips and neck, and then lightly scratched his back. Jerome's phallus enlarged a second time. Even during their most sexually active days, they had never reached climax twice during a single session. "Give it to me babe, all of it." Feelings she hadn't felt since their honeymoon emerged.

Gail reached over her shoulders and grabbed the top of the mattress and pointed her toes sideways, spreading her womb and flexing her stomach muscles. Their pace increased, gradually, then faster until rhythmic strokes were replaced with breakneck speed. The springs creaked as the headboard banged against the wall. The sweat on their stomachs popped when they slightly pulled apart then slapped themselves together.

Jerome shifted his bodyweight to his elbows and knees. She tossed her head from side to side, transformed her beautiful face into a determined frown that joined her eyebrows. Gail's nose flared, and her eyes, which were ablaze, focused on Jerome's face which was just inches away. Gail braced herself and threw her butt upward. "Aw give it to me, Babe, harder, harder!" Her words and moves invited Jerome to plumb her deepest passages. Jerome grunted like a football linesman on the snap. They fell into a surreal ecstasy, oblivious to sound and time.

"Oh babe, oh, oooh Babe, that's it, yes! The implosion started in Gail's toes and continued upward until it reached her brain. It was Gail's longest and best orgasm ever; she passed out momentarily from the pleasurable impact. For the first time in two years Gail didn't give a damn about pregnancy. Several moments later, after their breathing returned to a manageable level, the spent couple fell asleep, intertwined.

Jerome grabbed the phone seconds before it shattered his eardrums. "Mr. Gerard, its 10:30." Gail was still asleep; he shook her gently.

"Uh uhh," Gail said into her pillow. Her melodious negative, mumble manifested an afterglow. "You go on; I couldn't make it through the lobby." Gail's earlier trip to the bathroom had made it clear she would have trouble walking.

"Maybe I should stay too," Jerome whispered into Gail's ear, snuggling. His daughters were playing in the next room; Jerome realized a repeat performance was impossible.

It was a typical August day in Chicago: sunny, hot and humid by midmorning. "Hey, hot sauce," Turkey yelled, standing on the driver's side in the No Parking zone, "Let's go!" *I wonder what time he and Faye got to sleep; what an endurance level!*

Turkey was wearing a beige hound's tooth sports-coat, a gold colored silk shirt with an overlapping collar, brown pants, and beige and white wingtip shoes. His pinkie diamond ring was glistening.

"Should I take off my tie?" Jerome was wearing his only suit over a fresh, white, short sleeve shirt.

"Naw, man, you're cool. I'm the one out of step, but that's just my nature."

Felix and Bea's, located on 39th Street just west of South Park Blvd., occupied three storefronts under a hand-painted sign; it could accommodate seventy five people. Their restaurant had been a fixture in Bronzeville for over twenty years, since the Great Depression. Felix and Beatrice Long initially opened a single storefront restaurant on 31st Street. Felix financed it with profits from his illegal policy wheel, affording them the best equipment available; success forced them into larger quarters. Their restaurant had always served delicious soul food and decadent, home-made desserts. Bea was an excellent cook and Felix managed the ever-expanding staff and liked to talk; he made their customers feel at home. Bea died from breast cancer in '49. The soul food tradition has been carried on by Felix's staff.

The restaurant was spotless. Florescent lights beamed from the ceiling. The walls were imitation bamboo with occasional mirrors. A four-seat bar was obscure. Most of the tables with blue linen and napkins sat four. A centered, round banquet table for ten covered with white tablecloths caught Jerome's eye.

"The high class Negroes sit there," Turkey said. "They used to talk between tables or pull 'em together and block the aisles. Finally, Felix gave 'em their own table." Jerome and Turkey sat at a table for two against the wall. "There's Felix; I'll be right back," Turkey said as he disappeared through the swinging doors into the kitchen.

"You drinkin' or just eatin'?" A bored voice asked; a strong perfume which assailed Jerome's nostrils accompanied the question. Jerome looked into a dark, smooth face with a wide nose and thick lips. She was about five feet, nine inches, perfectly proportioned with a flat stomach. The clear whites of her eyes accented her jet black pupils.

"I'm waiting for Mr. Stevens, ma'am." *I don't know why I called her ma'am, she couldn't be more than 25, but she sounds so old.*

"You with Turkey Stevens? I know what he's drinkin'. You want somethin' from the bar?" The voice softened. "Where you from anyway?"

"Beaumont, Texas."

"I knew you were from somewhere. Folks 'round here call me a lot of things but never ma'am——not that I mind you understand. You staying at the Pershing?"

"Yes, uh, uh..."

"I'm Rowena."

"OK, Rowena," Jerome smiled. "We're heading for Cleveland. I'm trying to find an Army buddy named Namon Stewart. He's lighter than me, two years older, nicer looking."

"You mean he looks better than you?" Rowena's thick lips broke into a huge smile which flashed large, white teeth. "How do you spell we, W-I-F-E?"

"And C-H-I-L-D-R-E-N," Jerome smiled. He blushed when Rowena said he was handsome, especially with his month old facial burn.

"Hey, you're in the right place, especially if he's somebody. And he must be somebody if'n you came all the way from Texas to find him. Anyway, it's nice to meet you good looking. Oh, what you drinkin'?"

"I'll have a scotch and water, please."

"It's on me." As Rowena walked away her tight, blue uniform shifted over her small waist, shapely hips, and low-slung behind, which quivered as if two cantaloupe halves were loose in her panties. Jerome was embarrassed when Rowena glanced over her shoulder and caught him leaning out of his seat, eyeballing her "cantaloupes." Rowena had increased the quiver. She gave Jerome an inviting glance.

"Hey, little brother, com'n over," Turkey called. "Meet Attorney Samuel Stovall. He's a big-time criminal lawyer; even if you've confessed, he'll get you off!" Turkey, who was sitting, laughed, threw his head back, kicked up a leg and clapped his hands once. Samuel smiled tolerantly at Turkey's antics.

The thirtyish, handsome lawyer had distinguished himself early on by winning a not-guilty verdict in a jury trial for a prominent Negro physician accused of a double murder. He had admitted shooting and killing his wife and her lover when he caught them in his bed. A fervent, thirty-minute temporary insanity closing argument set the physician free. Afterwards, every Negro charged with a serious crime beseeched Samuel to defend them. He only represented those who could afford him; he never lost a case. Samuel graduated from John Marshall Law School; for eight years he attended part-time while working at the post office. Samuel only took the State Bar once which was unusual.

Samuel wore a tan, custom tailored tropical suit over a white-on-white, translucent, summer-weight French cuffed shirt. His hand-painted, expensive tie, matched perfectly. Jerome shook Samuel's firm, soft hand. His nails were manicured but unpolished. Jerome, because his suit was substandard, felt uneasy under Samuel's subtle but intense observation.

"Thank you, but won't we be taking others' seats?" Jerome asked.

"No one has reservations at the Bull Shit Table," Samuel said. "Some stop for a drink or coffee and conversation, others have a quick lunch, a few spend the afternoon. Lester says you're looking for a friend?" Samuel asked, "You sure you two aren't related?

"No sir, I just arrived yesterday." As Jerome perused the carbon copied, handwritten menu, attached by rubber bands to a hard back holder, he overheard Samuel talking to Lester.

"Have you heard about the attacks on the Negro families moving into Englewood?" Samuel asked. The question signaled to those seated not to discuss confidential topics with a stranger present. The Caucasian political establishment was continuously trying to identify militants in Bronzeville.

Since the Supreme Court had outlawed segregated schools three months earlier, scores of affluent Negroes were expressing anger with Chicago's segregated, unequal school system, as well as their segregated police districts. Outspoken dissidents were being harassed by police who were enforcing rare, misdemeanor violations, like dirty license plates and writing tickets for driving 36 MPH in a 35 MPH zone.

"Naw, sure haven't," Turkey said as he raised his drink. Jerome noticed how little Turkey had to say today, as opposed to last night.

"What's happening?" a tall, thin, ruddy complexioned, handsome gentleman asked as he sat down. The greeting was rhetorical. His thick, grey, nicotine-stained moustache was neatly trimmed. Leo Lafarge was in Remington Rand's (manufacturers of the new, room-sized computer called Univac), Special Markets division.

When Negroes were empowered to make major buying decisions, the Fortune 500 companies' Special Markets people, AKA "Spooks who sit by the door," socialized with their kindred. Caucasian sales specialists managed the technical presentations. Spooks' salaries were respectable by Negro standards; lucrative commissions though, were nonexistent. Spooks also worked national conventions where influential Negroes were expected to attend.

"Leo," Samuel said, "meet Jerome Gerard. Of course, you already know Brother Lester."

"Everybody knows Lester," Leo said as he stretched across the table and shook Jerome's hand, "But I also know Jerome Gerard, at least I know of him. Aren't you from Beaumont, Texas?"

"Why, yes," Jerome answered.

"I was at Xavier College with Lucius and Mildred, your older siblings, graduated with Lucius in '39. One of your brothers became a priest, didn't he?"

"Yes, that's Eddie. He's now Father Francis in a Savannah, Georgia parish."

"Let's see now," Leo said glancing upward. "You're the youngest of seven who married Gail Beauregard, Brother Beau's daughter, from New Orleans."

"I'm Fred Hawkins," a man seated on Jerome's right said. "Your father-in-law and I have played poker on occasion. He keeps telling me how poorly he plays, but he always wins. Brother Beau has been a great host whenever I have visited New Orleans." Fred was light skinned had naturally wavy hair with a deep bass voice––and a glass left eye.

"Leo, can you co-sign for this young brother, Samuel?"

"Of course I can; why he's almost family."

"Then welcome to the controversial and provocative center of What's Happening Now," Samuel said. Everyone at the table extended more genuine salutations. "We didn't know what your real agenda was. You never know who may be wearing false colors with rising racial tensions and all."

"But I came in with Turkey," Jerome said. No one responded, indicating Turkey's endorsement carried no weight.

"Jerome," Fred said, "meet Baxter Bridges, our most prominent real estate broker. He makes so much money selling scared White folks homes to us, he doesn't file taxes. At the end of the year he just calls Uncle Sam and asks 'how much do you need this time'?" A light chuckle followed the quip. Baxter extended a hand to Jerome as he took a seat. Arthritis, or in the Negro vernacular, rheumatism, had disfigured Baxter's hands.

Baxter was in his late fifties, clearly the senior at the table. He was dark plum colored, with a brilliant smile. He removed his hard brim straw hat. Baxter began selling real estate over twenty years ago; in 1933, when Negros could only buy homes in Negro neighborhoods.

Jerome gave Baxter a little of Namon Stewart's background then asked if he knew him. "Well now, let me see," Baxter glanced upward, toward Samuel, and then procrastinated.

"He's cool," Samuel said, "Leo co-signed for him."

Baxter then said firmly, "I don't know him but a number of customers here are alumni of Roosevelt University; I'll introduce you if any come in."

Brother Bridges," Samuel asked, "what do we have to do to allow Negroes to move into their newly purchased homes in Englewood without being vandalized or torched? Why do we have to put up with the mistreatment?"

"Well," Baxter smiled, as he put down his menu, "it's not as bad as it used to be with Restricted Covenants. At least now we can at least buy a home in Englewood, even if we can't get the proper insurance. Of course nobody ever gets arrested for the vandalism." Baxter's practiced smile lingered long after he had finished speaking.

"Segregation isn't as visible or as humiliating here as it is down South, Mr. Gerard," Buddy Laws, legislative assistant to Democratic Congressman William L. Dawson said, responding to Jerome's puzzled look. "But we are definitely second-class citizens. Racial prejudice prevails when we try to move into, or work, or even walk through, a White neighborhood." Buddy silently asked Jerome to give him a minute while he finished a mouth full of food and then continued, "Here, Jim Crow laws don't exist, but down South separate water fountains are required by White folks. From their perspective, if you're not better than a Nigger, who are you better than?" Thin, short, Buddy Laws returned to his lunch with gusto.

A tall, comely lady wearing a straight line, red linen suit with white accessories took the last seat. Fred Hawkins whispered to Jerome, "That's Attorney Rachael Piernas, a stone, cold, power house."

Rachael commented on Baxter's remark while resting her purse on the floor. "To effect change, city officials must recognize federal law. A good example is the Supreme Court's decision regarding schools, which can no longer be segregated legally."

Buddy always debated Rachael; Bronzeville's most prominent, but rare, republican. "You think that's going to make a difference?" Buddy countered. "Chicago schools are just as segregated as those in Mississippi!" When Buddy was angry, as he was now, his Van Dyke beard and goatee gave him a satanic appearance.

"Then let's take the city to Federal Court and see what happens, regarding home vandalism and the schools," Rachael rejoined, staring Buddy into silence.

Fred laughed under his breath, and then whispered to Jerome, "She's third generation Oberlin grad, second generation lawyer. She specializes in divorce, but only represents women; she kicks husbands' asses daily. Even Congressman Dawson won't mess with her."

"Who's Congressman Dawson?"

"Oh nobody, just the second Black man elected to the U.S. Congress since Reconstruction," Fred said.

"Who was the first?" asked Jerome.

"Adam Clayton Powell from Harlem, but history lessons cost extra." Fred said as he waved to Rowena; he was drinking his lunch. "Gentlemen, and ladies, who is going to challenge Republican Mayor Kennelly next year," Fred asked. He was enjoying the political banter.

"You can bet somebody will," Buddy answered after swallowing another mouthful of food. "The congressman and Kennelly don't get along at all. He told the congressman to his face, 'I don't want to see you in city hall again as long as I'm mayor.'"

"Oh my goodness," Samuel said, validating that such a blatant insult would have certainly upset Congressman Dawson.

"Does anybody know a county clerk named Michael O'Malley," Buddy asked. Glances were exchanged, but no one answered.

As the lunch hours preceded, B. S. Table regulars came and went. Jerome, Turkey, and Fred stayed. Jerome nursed his second scotch when he noticed that only he, Fred, and Turkey were drinking; Turkey was having his fourth.

"Damn, its 2:30. I'm late for an appointment, again," Fred said. He turned to Jerome, "If you need anything while you're in town, call me; I owe Brother Beau a favor." Fred's card read, Able Accountants and Tax Consultants, Fred Hawkins, CPA, CEO.

"Do you have Roosevelt University's phone number?" Jerome called to the departing Fred Hawkins.

"Hell, it's in the telephone directory, Boy." Jerome felt stupid. During the two plus hours, Jerome had attentively listened; he mentally organized his observations.

Most of Felix's customers wore coats and ties, but were not as sartorially dressed or well groomed as those at the B.S. Table. All of the 20 plus men and women who had lunched at the ten seat table were informed and articulate. None used slang as much as Turkey did. The majority was college graduates; several had masters or law degrees. Several were officers in WW II. At least four were self-employed. A few were professionals; dentists, physicians, and lawyers. All were between 30 and 55, ambitious, independent, financially solvent, and political activists. The apparent leaders were; Attorney Stovall, Leo LaFarge, Buddy Laws, and Fred Hawkins. Jerome had never seen so many successful, educated Negroes. Turkey, who had said very little, was not a regular at the B.S. Table.

"You and Mr. Turkey don't have one," Rowena answered when Jerome requested their bill. Turkey had gone to the rest room. "Turkey and his guests eat here free; Mr. Long and his guests drink––or whatever––at the Pershing, free." Rowena smiled impishly and tilted her head as she fingered her short, pressed hair. Jerome tipped her five dollars.

While walking toward the car, Turkey slurred, "You want some of that? She used to manage our office, but she makes more in tips daily than what we paid her in a week. Rowena ain't a bi'ness woman, but she owes me a favor. Besides, little brother, the lady has eyes for you." Turkey grinned as he nudged Jerome in the side with his elbow. Jerome noticed Turkey wide-stepping as they left Felix and Bea's. *Turkey is too drunk to drive. I'd ask him for his keys but I have no idea how to get back to the hotel.*

End of Chapter Three

CHAPTER FOUR

Turkey hung his arm over the door's window channel and thumped with his thumb in time with the blues radio station as he drove south on South Parkway Boulevard. When his sport coat pulled back while moving in his seat he revealed a holstered gun clipped to his left inside pocket. "Guess we'll go shopping, get a good night's sleep and leave for Cleveland Saturday instead of Monday. We've already unwound and had a great time, thanks to you."

"What's in Cleveland?" Turkey asked, looking directly at Jerome. His unsteady eyes were dancing under his narrow, dark green sun-glasses.

"Possibly a job, hell I don't know." Jerome's frankness frightened him. His recent conversations with his brother Bryan regarding employment had not been encouraging.

"If all you want is a job, little brother, you might as well stay here. Those dudes we just left put up with me 'cause I see 'em with their pants down, but with your pedigree you fit right in. Most of them can get you a gig overnight; hell, even I could do that! What kind of work you lookin' for?"

"Why, as a registered pharmacist." Jerome realized he hadn't mentioned needing a job since arriving in Chicago. *How stupid can I be; you never know who can help.*

"Hell, Harold Oldham owns five drug stores. He'll put you to work tomorrow; he's always looking for good help. Walgreens Drug Store Chain hires Negro pharmacists all the time because White boys are scared to work in Bronzeville after dark." Turkey stared at Jerome, smiling; it took him forever to look forward.

"When can you make the call?"

"As soon as you say you're staying my brother."

Jerome exhaled when Turkey looked straight ahead. He was speeding around cars, taking ambers, and crisscrossing lanes. Jerome questioned Turkey to keep him awake. "How did Negroes here get so many good jobs? We aren't' doing this well in Dallas or Los Angeles."

"Sure you're right Little Brother; Bronzeville is in a class by itself. We been comin' here since the early 1900's takin' all kinds of jobs; from stinky stock yards work, to red caps and railroad porters, or workin' in the steel mills." Turkey accelerated and changed lanes on screeching tires; several horns blared. He looked through his rearview mirror at the disruption and laughed.

"Newcomers went from fifty cents a day; pickin' cotton, tending White folks chillen, doin' wash, or shuckin' shrimp, to fifty cents an hour. The word was, 'if you can get here, you can get work here.' Then the swells came: doctors, lawyers, preachers, and teachers, even pharmacists like you, heh, heh, heh. Back then our town was called 'The Promised Land'. 'Course sportin' ladies and hustlers has always followed the action." Turkey laughed softly; his head bobbed.

"Hey Turkey," Jerome shouted, "Where did Negroes get the money to start their own businesses?" *Please stay awake!*

"Policy, brother man, policy; tens of thousands was bet every day in nickels and dimes." Turkey sped through a red light and swerved to avoid crashing. He laughed, "Man I stole that light like a thief in the night."

Jerome anticipated a serious accident. Maybe I should ask Turkey to pull over and give me directions back to the hotel. "What's policy?" Jerome asked as he braced himself in the passenger seat.

"Heh, heh," Turkey laughed, "Policy was a dream maker, an earthshaker, an answer to a prayer. Some called it the Black Jesus. Here's how it worked. You picked two to ten numbers between one and eighty, and then bet with your favorite wheel. They had funny names like **Juicy Lucy** and **Major Moto**. The more numbers you picked that hit the more you won. Numbers were drawn from bingo barrels every evening and printed on policy slips the size of dollar bills. If you were lucky enough to walk in the rain without getting wet, you could win $100 on a nickel bet."

A police car with a wailing siren and a flashing red dome light, pulled in behind Turkey. "Aw shiiit," Turkey whined as he stopped.

A White policeman, over six feet tall with a beer gut, strolled up to the driver's side with ticket book in hand. His equipment belt was hanging beneath his girth.

Turkey, with both hands on the steering wheel, gave him a Satchimo grin and said, "Officer, I's so sorry. I know I ran that light but I was runnin' my big mouth so, I didn't even see it." The gold star on his front tooth reflected the sunlight. Turkey batted his eye lids rapidly. Jerome knew Turkey's breath reeked of liquor. *We are in serious trouble now.*

"Hand over your driver's license, boy, and you sure as hell better have one, or else you're going to jail; out here driving like a damn fool," the officer barked as he peered though his aviator sunglasses and stood with his empty hand on his pistol.

Turkey, after receiving permission, slowly leaned, opened the glove compartment and removed his wallet; several traffic tickets fell to the floor. Jerome stepped on them, trying in vain to hide the repeated violations evidence. When Turkey straightened up he adjusted his coat, exposing his pistol. Jerome's hands nervously raced from his cheeks to his lap.

"You better be still boy, don't know what you niggers are up to," the policeman warned Jerome. *What are we going to do now,* thought Jerome, *if we get arrested, Gail would never forgive me*!

Turkey opened his wallet and handed it to the officer; the exposed insert held a folded fifty-dollar bill. The officer palmed the bill and glanced at the driver's license underneath. He then handed Turkey his wallet and said while smiling, "Take it easy, hear; we don't want you having an accident and getting hurt, now do we. And Sir, have your license renewed; it expired two months ago."

Damn, Jerome thought, *Turkey is driving drunk and erratic, carrying a concealed weapon, has a glove box full of traffic tickets, ran a red light, has an expired license, and the policeman politely sends him on his way. What kind of town is this*!

"Well," Turkey said moving back into traffic, "they've got to make a living too. Now where was I? Oh yeah, talkin' 'bout policy." Turkey's driving had improved. "The policy lords were filthy rich. They paid out about fifty percent of the handle which was enough to keep the suckers playing. Policy bosses supported charities, churches, police captains, politicians and hundreds of employees, which gave them plenty of clout, 'specially at election time. They also loaned money to friends to start businesses.

"Hell, little brother, Felix is part owner of the Pershing, which several policy kings bought to launder their take. Damned if that didn't make money too. Now he's clean as a cooked chittlin'. His income from the Pershing is in shoeboxes. Danny's Lounge was financed with policy money, so was my tailor." Turkey's facial expression changed to a frown, his voice dropped. "Then in the early 40's, the trouble started."

"What trouble? Things look great to me."

"The Diegos' wanted in on our good thing. What they couldn't buy they killed to get. Felix, the Douglas Brothers, and others took the relatively tiny tokens that were offered." Driving with one hand, Turkey pulled out a gold cigarette case, offered Jerome a Camel, lit both from his gold pocket lighter, and continued.

"That wasn't bad enough; they introduced dope which made policy profits look like poor box contributions. Weed used to be sold like roasted peanuts. When Forty-Seventh St. was the main drag, there would be twenty to thirty pusher men in one block, hanging back in darkened storefront entrances, selling reefers, three for fifty cents." Turkey was moving with the traffic. *I think we'll reach the hotel alive; thank you Jesus.*

"Pot smokers graduated to Heroin. I've found too many junkies with rubber tubes wrapped around their arms, needles still in their veins, their eyeballs out of sight. I quit renting them and their women rooms, too much police paper work when they wind up dead. Those that don't waste themselves kill others. They will steal anything from family, friends and stores that could be sold. Jail, with three hots and a cot, ain't nothin' but a rest-stop. Another thing that's missin' is the Policy Lord's support. No more clubs for kids, teen-age sports teams, or gifts to widows, all the real cash leaves with the spaghetti eaters, leavin' only bitter herbs behind. Streets ain't safe no more."

"They seem pretty safe to me."

"That's 'cause you been runnin' with me, Blood," Turkey grinned. "Remember that John in the park last night? He might have been offed by a desperate dope addict." A soft, pleasant look crept into Turkey's voice, "You know, back in the day, during the war when ever'body was workin', we had fun. Prostitution and gambling didn't hurt nobody. Sure, you might lose your rent or catch a dose of clap while cuttin' up, but dope, man, that's as serious as the electric chair. Lots of innocent people get hooked, 'specially young people."

"Sure, I book horses, hook sportin' ladies up with out-of-towners, run poker and crap games, fence jewelry, make loans to losers, and rent locals rooms off the books, but I don't mess with drugs," Turkey confessed.

Selling stolen jewelry, pimping, or stealing from your bosses is all illegal activities, Jerome thought.

"Why won't the police do something about the drug problem?" Jerome asked as they parked in front of the hotel.

"Drug payoffs go way up. Same law that took my half a C note takes dope dollars. But don't blame the cop; he probably bribed his way onto the force and kicks in to his sergeant. Guess Bronzeville is a pretty messed up place to live, huh? You still want me to make that call?"

"Probably, but let me think on it."

The Gerards caught the Jackson Park el at Sixty-Third and Cottage Grove and marveled as the elevated train went underground. They were fascinated by the variety of stores in The Loop, Chicago's central shopping district. Gail bought a silk scarf in Marshall Fields; Jerome purchased a Cross pen and pencil set with personalized engravings. They were surprised by the courteous service they received from Caucasian clerks.

While absent-mindedly answering his wife's bland comments, several thoughts occurred: Turkey mentioning Walgreens hired Negro pharmacists, Turkey's declaration of immediate, gainful employment, and Fred Hawkins' offer of assistance. *I have probably found a job. Now I have to choose the right one.*

The Gerards enjoyed a delicious dinner at George Diamond's Steakhouse, and were surprised when they were seated next to a Caucasian couple. They enjoyed *On the Waterfront* at the magnificent Chicago Theatre, and were impressed with all the enormous photos of stars hanging on the walls that had appeared in person: Frank Sinatra, Ertha Kitt, Billy Eckstine, and others. Caucasian ushers led them to their integrated seats. They returned to the hotel just before midnight.

After putting their daughters to bed, Gail re-gained her negative perspective and asked, "What time are we leaving tomorrow; we have relaxed enough, and you still haven't found Namon or a job!"

"I have no idea, Babe," Jerome said pensively.

"What kind of answer is that? The highways should be empty Saturday morning."

"I need to check out a few things first."

"I hope you're still not trying to find Namon. Gail had recognized an unusual, somber disposition in Jerome while they were in The Loop; it had intensified since they returned to their hotel.

"My finding Namon is no longer important––I'm trying to find us, damn it! Jerome said while starring at Gail.

"Well, let me know when you find whatever in God's name you're looking for." She considered insisting on leaving early but didn't. Reflecting on Naomi's advice, Gail decided to let Jerome manage things, at least tomorrow.

Gail hurried into her nightie and feigned falling asleep. Last night was too beautiful an event for Jerome to enjoy an encore; especially without a job.

After bathing and putting on his pajama bottoms, Jerome leaned back in the corner chair and flipped Fred Hawkins' business card over and over. The outside, pulsating light allowed him to flash-read the card. Fred's home and business numbers were printed on the card.

Turkey offered a pharmacist's job, but probably, because of his under-the-radar lifestyle, it may have unethical if not illegal obligations, and I don't want to risk losing my license, or going to jail. Mr. Hawkins had offered help. I'll call and hope for the best. One thing is for sure, I'm not leaving here until I exhaust every employment opportunity, including Walgreens.

It was 12:45 A.M. "This better be good," a sleepy Fred Hawkins said after two rings. Jerome identified himself, Fred became cordial. Jerome apologized effusively for awakening him and spoke for several minutes in vague sentences.

"Listen man, do you play golf?" Fred asked.

"No, I don't."

"Well, regardless, I'll pick you up at 5:00 a.m. Will what you called me about keep till then?"

"Yes Sir, of course."

"Great! Now can I please get some sleep?"

"Get in," Fred said as he leaned to push open the passenger door of his '52 Buick, 225. "I'm surprised you're on time, especially since you're on vacation."

Vacation! Yeah, I wish, but how would he know any different? "Why do you and your friends start so early? I thought golf was played around lunch."

Unlike our Caucasian counterparts, who belong to expensive country clubs, we play early on a public course and still get in a full day's work. And yes, we work on Saturdays." Fred glanced at Jerome's face and asked, "How's that burn healing?"

I should explain; my employment inquiry will have to wait. Jerome began. "We were stopped by local police about fifty miles south of Dallas. In Corsicanna, Texas the cops approached our car as if we were bank robbers. The officer on my side of the car yelled from a crouched position, with gun drawn, 'Get out of that car nigger, with your fingers spread.' I complied hurriedly. The officer on Gail's side helped her out, asking, 'you alright lady?'

"My cop, who was six feet tall and obese, shouted, 'Get on the ground in a hurry!' He handcuffed me and forced my face into the gravel with his knee, scaring my cheek. 'Where you goin' with this here white woman, boy?'

"Suh," I said, sounding ignorant because I knew crackers despised educated Negroes almost as much as they hated seeing Negro men with White women, "She ain't white, dis here's my wife. She's Creole, check our I.D.'s, and them's our chillen'. The officer tore my pants snatching my wallet out of my back pocket."

'This is a military I.D., you a captain in our Army, boy?' "Not waiting for an answer, he mumbled to himself, 'I guess we got two armies, 'cause if I was a soldier, ain't no darkie gonna give me orders.' He shouted across the car, 'What you got Wilbur? Gerard for a last name?'"

"After seeing Michelle and Dana, and realizing Gail wasn't White, Wilbur snatched Gail's purse off her arm, emptied its contents on the ground and picked up her wallet. 'Yep, sure do.' Wilbur was thinner, younger, and dumber than Jethro; who said, 'Shoulda knowd you weren't no pimp, cars too raggedy.'"

Fred muffled a laugh, without interrupting.

'Can I go first boss?' "Wilbur asked. He wanted to rape Gail." 'Always did want some o' that Creole poon tang and this shor is a dress full!' "Wilbur grabbed one of Gail's butt cheeks through her thin dress and squeezed. Gail screamed.

"That's when I started kicking and squirming while lying on the ground, grinding more gravel into my face.

"Jethro laughed, 'You want to get up boy so's you can see?' He lifted me by the handcuffs, and slammed my face onto the hood of our car. Then he placed his forearm on my neck. That hood was hot enough to fry fish. My facial rawness created by the rocks increased the depth of the pain and burn. All I could do was gnash my teeth and grunt.

"When I opened my eyes, I saw Wilbur pulling Gail toward a tree by her arm. Through tears I looked into the car and saw outlines of my daughters sitting on the back seat, hugging each other. I knew what they were about to witness. Desperate, I shouted, 'Mastah officer, suh, please don't hurt her, she's ailing enough already.'"

'I ain't goin' to hurt her boy,' "Wilbur laughed." 'Colored girls cain't be hurt by White men, our gonads ain't big enough, don' cha know.' "Wilbur tied Gail's neck against the tree with his belt and unzipped his pants. He pulled the bottom of Gail's dress over her panties. I said as calmly as possible, 'What I meant suh was she's been under medical care and she's tender down there. We's on our way to Dallas to see a special kind o' doctor. She's got some female disease Colored doctors in Beaumont cain't figure out.'

"Well, Jethro's hand fell away from Gail as if she were a leper. He unleashed his belt, rushed back to the road, holding up and zipping his pants while running. Wilbur, after freeing me, bent over laughing at Jethro's antics. A speeding car passed; they took off after it.

"We sat on the back seat, hugging and crying; I have no idea how long the four of us embraced. It was over ninety degrees in the shade, but we were shaking as if we were naked in an ice house. Gail pleaded to go back home, but I convinced her we were too close to Dallas to turn back."

"That's a hell of a story Youngblood," Fred chuckled, "You think pretty fast on your feet-I mean your face." Fred, because of his relationship with Jerome's father-in-law, already felt a rapport, now Fred respected Jerome's mental agility and aptitude.

Moments later they turned into Jackson Park's public golf course. As Fred pulled his clubs and golf cart from his trunk, he waved to three players taking warm-up swings in the practice area. "Good gawd almighty, Fred as a caddy," yelled the biggest! He looked White and sounded southern.

"That won't help, he still won't win a hole!" teased the shortest and heaviest waiting player.

Changing his shoes while sitting on his bumper, Fred said, "The big guy is Daniel Quibble, our only stock broker; his father is a physician. Daniel attended the University of Chicago prep school and then went to their university where he majored in finance and received a Masters degree. I'm not sure if his brokerage firm knows he's Colored. I don't think they care as long as he produces. Most of his clients don't know his ethnicity because he contacts them by phone. With his practiced accent, I'm sure they assume he's a Southern cracker." Jerome thought, he received a first class education and now has an executive position in a large corporation; and he's Negro. It can happen!

"The fat fellow is Eugene Burns," Fred continued. "He and his daddy own a Gusto Beer distributorship. The third is Kenneth Appling, second generation funeral director and city alderman. He has a law degree."

After introductions, Kenneth asked Jerome, "Do you know what LSMFT stands for?"

Jerome was familiar with the cigarette commercial, "lucky Strike Means Fine Tobacco," but assumed Kenneth had another definition. "Well, I'm not sure."

"Lord, save me from Texas!" Everyone laughed.

"What do most White folks call a Negro who has a degree in pharmacology?" asked Daniel. Before Jerome could answer, Daniel blurted, "nigger!"

After several humorous one liners, Fred said, "All right, lighten up." Jerome welcomed the amusing jabs; he felt accepted. Jerome inhaled the fresh smells of morning: moist grass and camaraderie which produced a delightful fragrance.

The eastern side of the golf course abutted Lake Michigan. Jerome watched the sun rise, gradually turning dawn into a bright new day, seconds at a time; it was breathtaking. As Jerome walked the dew capped grass with the foursome, he kept wondering, *how and when should I ask about a job?*

After each hole the players fussed over stroke counts and then settled their bets. As Jerome and Fred hiked toward his hooked tee shot, Jerome asked, "How did Eugene and his dad get a premium beer distributorship?"

"Eugene Burns, Sr.," Fred explained, "was given the gold mine when prohibition ended in '33, about 20 years ago. He had risen from office clerk to Al Capone's chief accountant because he never stole a dime and exposed anyone who did. The Mob who owned the brewery gave Mr. Burns, Sr., CPA, Chicago's Black Belt as an exclusive territory because he was the only executive without a criminal record. Eugene Senior's white and Jewish clients knew complaining would be unwise."

"The Appling's and the Burns' parents," Fred continued, "because they could afford it, insisted their children graduate from college. They didn't know specifically what the future held, but knew their children would be better equipped with at least an under graduate degree. They are the trailblazers in our economic struggle." Fred continued looking for his ball. "Eugene Burns Jr. and Kenneth Appling do not take their good fortune lightly; that's why they play golf so early." Fred had walked into the rough and shouted, "Where the hell is my ball!"

While Fred studied its lie, Jerome said, "And what about Leo Lafarge and the others I met yesterday? How did they get such good jobs?"

"Like me, they are first generation college graduates. We too were persuaded by our parents to prepare ourselves with a good education to compete in a racist, segregated society." Fred looked around, saw that none of his foursome was watching, and then tossed his ball into a clearing. On his fourth swing Fred hit more grass than ball. "Damn it!" After recovering he said, "The major corporations hire Negroes like Leo because of competition between big businesses, not out of altruism. They realized it was an advantage to have a Negro at the table when Negroes were the decision-makers."

"Would you please hit your damn ball, Fred? The whole golf course is waiting!" Daniel yelled. Fred hurriedly hit his fifth shot.

"Who among us are signing major contracts?" Jerome asked while walking with Fred.

"Your father-in-law owns an insurance company plus a number of other businesses; he should be interested in modern data-processing equipment that cost, maybe a hundred thousand dollars. It will greatly improve his total business acumen.

"Incidentally, the first Negro-owned insurance company was in Philadelphia in 1810, over fifty years before Emancipation," Fred digressed. "There are forty-seven Negro-owned insurance companies; five are headquartered here. All of them need this new business equipment called computers. There are 120 Negro colleges and universities and we own at least 25 hospitals. There were over a hundred Negro banks before the crash in '29, at least 50 survived. Several state governments have Negroes responsible for making multi-million dollar decisions. Pennsylvania is one; bet you didn't know that." Fred struck his ball; it stopped on the green, 25 feet from the hole.

"But Turkey, ah Lester," Jerome said, "is living quite well and I'm sure he isn't college educated." *Why does Mr. Hawkins have all this Negro historical knowledge?*

While walking toward the green, they stopped to allow Kenneth to play. Fred whispered so he wouldn't interfere with Kenneth's shot, "Lester is what most White folks consider us all to be: a low-life, illegitimate, hustler. His opulent lifestyle is temporary at best. He and people like him usually wind up dead or in jail at an early age. We tolerate Lester because the Pershing Hotel is our Las Vegas where gambling and prostitution flourish." Fred decided to keep his personal life private and then continued. "Lester is one arrest away from going back to prison." *Back to prison, which means he has done time. I made the right decision last night, even if Fred doesn't find me a job,* Jerome decided.

The group had reached the seventh green. Fred lied about his stroke count which caused an argument; he finally acquiesced. After paying the winner, they moved on to the eighth tee; a five stroke hole.

"Now that's the way you drive a ball!" Fred bragged as he watched his ball land 250 plus yards in the fairway. He and Jerome, because Fred was last to drive, started walking. "You and your friends who are self-employed are trail-blazers, right?" Jerome asked, building on Fred's comment, keeping their conversation alive.

"You learn fast, Jerome; we are the hope and the future. Owning your own business is the ultimate objective. Not only does it create jobs; it's the beginning of a new legacy. Negro, W.E.B.DuBois, who earned a doctorate from Harvard in 1895, dubbed the more educated and fortunate among us the Talented Tenth; his equation was generous. Of the million plus Negroes in Chicago, only three percent are middle class or better.

We who are twenty-five percent of Chicago's population, control less than one percent of the city's wealth. Home ownership is atypical. We are consumers, not producers or investors.

"On the low end of the economic pole are 97% of Bronzeville's Negroes. Our public school system is way below par. Because city officials underfund our primary and secondary education systems and our graduation requirements are lower, half of Negro high school graduates are unable to complete an employment application. We are not encouraged to attend college so college graduates are as rare as hens' teeth. Those who do graduate from high school, educated, with college aspirations owe it to their parents.

"As adults we are overworked, underpaid, and excluded from most middle-class jobs like semi-skilled factory positions, or management. Our police and fire departments are segregated; black policemen do not arrest white folks. Negroes in management positions in Caucasian companies do not exist. And we are always the last hired and the first fired. And remember, Negroes in Bronzeville are better off than Negroes in other cities." Fred had upset himself; he quit talking and concentrated on his next stroke.

"I need to sell some tables to next month's NAACP luncheon," Alderman and Funeral Director Kenneth Appling said. "Freedom isn't free you know. Now let's not all commit at once," he said sarcastically.

"I'll buy a table and hit on Reginald Benjamin and Sidney Reis," Fred said as he smacked another long drive straight down the fairway, over 300 yards.

"Even the worst of us are sometimes blessed by golf angels," beer baron Eugene Burns said, commenting on Fred's long, "lucky" drive.

Stock broker Daniel committed his company to purchase one table, "Even though I won't be able to get anyone from my firm to attend. My wife and I will be there; I'll donate the remaining seats to the NAACP and they can fill them with whomever they wish."

"Are Reginald and Sidney friends of yours?" Jerome asked. *That was dumb, of course they are his friends, but I'd rather say something dumb than nothing at all.*

"Reginald is an M.D. with offices next to mine. Sidney Reis, our Jewish landlord, owns the corner drugstore and most of the damn block.

Reginald will buy at least one table and let the NAACP invite ten college students; two, if he and his friends plan to attend. But Sidney, who makes a fortune off the neighborhood will have to be begged to take two tickets and there is no way he will attend. He's so tight; he'll probably make a Negro delivery man reimburse him."

"How big is Mr. Reis' store?" Jerome asked.

"Not big but very profitable, thanks to Reginald who phones in his prescriptions. Sidney is a two-faced leech who takes our money and runs. We had to harass him before he would make a deposit in our new savings and loan, which is also his tenant."

"Does he have any Negro pharmacists?"

"No, but he should," Fred chuckled, "Last week his White pharmacist disappeared before Sidney could have him arrested for selling barbiturates illegally and pocketing the cash." Fred approached his ball for his second shot on the par five hole.

"Do you think Mr. Reis would hire me?" Jerome asked after taking a deep breath. Jerome looked at the ground and with his hands thrust into his pockets, dragged the toe of his shoe through the wet grass. It took forever for Fred to answer.

"What, you staying here?" Fred spoke without looking up. He hit his third stroke 150 yards onto the ninth green; it rolled into the hole. "Hot damn! That's the first eagle I've made this summer!"

After the excitement subsided, Jerome answered Fred's question, hoping he remembered asking it. "I'd like to, that's why I called last night, to ask if you would help me find a job." Jerome waited; Fred was silent while staring at Jerome. An eternity passed, Jerome said, "Well, will you?"

"Yesterday at lunch there were several people who could have helped you find employment; why didn't you say something then?" Jerome remained silent with a blank look. Fred said, "You do have a degree in pharmacology and I think I heard you say you practiced pharmacy in the Army for three years, right?"

"Yes sir."

"And you were honorably discharged, right?" Jerome nodded yes. "Then you deserve the position. Sidney will hire you instantly if Reginald asks him." Fred waited for Daniel to complete his shot, and then said, "I know, Reginald will tell Sidney you are his cousin from Texas. That was easy. Fred counted his winnings, and then pulled his longest driver from his bag as they moved toward the tenth tee. Because of Fred's eagle he was first to strike.

That's it? I have been travelling forever, repeatedly being told that I should have accepted my father-in-law's offer, and after Fred solves my life's greatest enigma, he says, 'that was easy.' Jerome waited until Fred swatted his ball, "Now all I need to do is move out of the Pershing; forty dollars a day plus meals for four is expensive."

"Where is my mind? Of course you'll need a place to live. There are hundreds of vacant apartments on the South Side owned by us, but we'll find you a home. We'll talk to Ted Thomas; he manages our S&L. They have foreclosed on several VA financed homes which have accumulated some equity. We'll ask Leo Lafarge to write a reference letter. You'll be employed and you're a veteran, so you're eligible for a VA mortgage which requires a small down payment."

"Do you think I need a lawyer? Buying a house is a pretty big deal."

"We'll ask Samuel to look over the paperwork as a favor; you couldn't afford to pay him." Fred asked, "How are we doing?"

"So far so good, but I need an Illinois license, and what will be my starting salary? I turned down a drugstore job in Los Angeles for a non-professional wage. The Negro owner was insulted. He called me a greedy colored boy who didn't know his place. My wife, my sister and her dentist-husband agreed."

"That's the difference between Watts Negroes and Bronzeville Negroes, we help each other. Reginald will insist your salary is the same as Sidney's White pharmacists. We'll get your state license through Buddy Laws; anything else?"

Jerome's eyes filled, a lump developed in his throat. After regaining his composure, he said, "Not a thing!" *I can't believe it; I have finally found a job and a home, on a golf course! We are no longer nomads travelling between relatives being pitied and misunderstood. We will no longer be living out of suitcases. My wife will have her own kitchen and my children will play in their own back yard!*

On the tenth tee, Fred announced, "Jerome is staying in Bronzeville!" Congratulations were extended.

"Now," Daniel said to Jerome, "you should seriously consider buying a block of these new-issue penny stocks…."

Jerome said to Fred, "Thank you so much. You have no idea what this means to me and my family. We have been…"

"Need to keep you around my young brother; being educated and young makes you an asset, besides, you bring me luck," Fred smiled. "Seriously, all we're doing is priming the pump for a brother in need, which will hopefully increase Bronzeville's net worth. It becomes your responsibility to keep the water flowing by doing an excellent job so Bronzeville continues to grow."

"You can count on me Fred, I won't let you down."

"And, years from now, when you get a call in the middle of the night from a sincere, young brother who's making no sense at all, perhaps you'll tolerate his naiveté and encourage him by passing the favor on."

After golf, while Jerome and Fred were having breakfast, Jerome said, "Thanks again, my relatives…"

"Your relationship with your father-in-law has been a recurring conundrum. Why didn't you go to work him? He must have offered you a job."

"We don't get along," Jerome answered.

"That's too bad. He's one of our most respected pioneers. Back when Negroes' developing new businesses was most difficult, he succeeded. I heard he is starting a mortgage company, another first."

"And we still don't get along," Jerome said burying his face in his menu.

Fred said, "That's a shame. One of the greatest achievements every parent looks forward to is having his legacy perpetuated." Jerome's face stayed buried in his menu. "One more personal intrusion and then I'll shut up.

"Your father-in-law delivered a speech to the National Insurance Association convention several years ago, part of which I will always remember. He said, 'the reason Negro businesses are successful is the arrogance and ignorance of White folks. Arrogant because most refuse to do business with us, ignorant because they have never bothered to learn our aggregate, gross incomes. As long as they are asleep at the switch, Negro businesses will continue to prosper; but once Whitey wakes up, look out!' Fred added, "Soon, the economic invasion will begin and we will be reduced to fighting over chump change."

"By the time Caucasians invade, perhaps Negroes will be able to compete in the General Market," Jerome said.

"What am I missing?" Fred asked.

"From what I have learned yesterday at Felix and Bea's, and today, we are presently involved in insurance, hospitals, hotels, supermarkets, restaurants and lounges, taxi chains, mortgages, burial services, stock investments, real estate landlords and brokers, beer, bakery and dairy commodities distribution, auto dealerships, banks, retail stores, manufacturing Negro hair care and cosmetics, and saving and loans. Turkey mentioned Harold Oldham owning five drug stores; he's already competing with Walgreens. We're just a major marketing step away from soliciting Caucasians as customers; why we might even start a mini P&G, and begin manufacturing soap and toothpaste."

"That is extremely profound," Fred was impressed. Yesterday at lunch, and at golf, scores of persons representing all of the business disciplines Jerome had mentioned joined the BS table for lunch, but Fred had never realized how many different enterprises were represented. He certainly didn't expect a stranger to process, categorize, and memorize all those businesses. Attempting to regain a one-upmanship posture, Fred asked, "Did you know Chicago's first settler was a Black fur-trader from Haiti named Jean Baptiste Pointe DuSable?" Jerome nodded no. "Of course not; very few people do."

After swallowing a mouthful of breakfast chased with coffee, Fred asked, "Did you know Negro Dr. Daniel Hale Williams, performed the first successful heart surgery in his own hospital in 1893, right here in Chicago, because he couldn't practice at any of the White hospitals?" Once again Jerome shook his head.

"Of course you don't. The reason is White historians leave out our achievements when writing history books. The truth is history is neither an objective nor accurate record of the past. History is really Whitey's story, his story equals history. Get it?"

"What I'm beginning to understand," Jerome said, "is what a waste prejudice and racism have been––for both races."

"Now what are you talking about, man?" Fred had lost his authoritative position again.

"If Doctor Williams didn't open his own hospital where he could perform surgical procedures, how many more years would have passed before successful open heart surgery would have become a reality? And how many more lives, probably more White than Negro, would have been lost over that period of time?"

Fred studied Jerome, amazed at the depth of his thought processes. After a long moment, Fred asked, "OK who was it that said, 'History is a set of lies agreed upon.'"

"Napoleon," Jerome answered.

"Well, excuse me."

While Fred placed a coffee pot on a hot plate, Jerome perused the plaques and certificates on Fred's office walls. Jerome noticed a post graduate degree from the University of Chicago, awarding Fred CPA credentials. "That's an expensive and prestigious school," Jerome said.

"The G.I. Bill paid my tuition, my disability checks helped support me. I majored in history at Morgan State Negro College before the war. Wasn't much we could do then but teach and preach."

That's why he is a Negro historical expert, Jerome realized.

"I wasn't smart enough to be a lawyer," Fred said, "besides federal and state governments weren't hiring Negro lawyers. Hell they still aren't. I volunteered for the Army Air Corp Negro pilot program during WW II." Fred proudly pointed to a photo of him in front of his single engine P-51 plane. He was wearing a stiff leather flight jacket with a bright, yellow, lamb's wool collar, first lieutenant bars and a long white scarf flung about his neck.

"We were the Negro 332nd fighter group, 450 strong, better known as the Red Tailed Tuskegee Airmen. We escorted more than 200 bombers over Europe and never lost a single plane, but a lot of us lost our lives achieving that stellar accomplishment. I caught a piece of shrapnel in my left eye over Germany."

As the blue-speckled coffee pot with a glass dome perked, Fred pointed out to Jerome his Distinguished Flying Cross and the Purple Heart. "I returned home in 1946 and applied several times for a commercial pilot's job. They all sang the same hypocritical song. 'We would hire you, but the pilots' union has to accept you first.' The union said, 'An airline has to hire you first.'" Fred grinned, but his good right eye still reflected the pain of rejection.

"Most of the new hires were former Air Corp pilots, all White, few if any were recipients of the Distinguished Flying Cross. That's when I decided to let the G.I. Bill pay for my career change."

(The first African-American pilot was hired by American Airlines in 1964, following landmark, Civil Rights legislation.)

"But…" A knock on the door interrupted Jerome. He was about to ask how Fred could expect to be a commercial pilot with only one good eye.

"I got your message," Dr. Reginald Benjamin said as he entered.

"Doc, meet your long lost cousin."

"He doesn't look like anyone in my family," Reginald giggled as he shook Jerome's hand and touched his muscular upper arm; "Oh my." Reginald was six inches shorter than Jerome, thin framed, thirty-ish, light skinned with a pencil moustache. His expensive ensemble was a cream-colored Izod golf shirt and matching slacks with tasseled, matching Cole Haan loafers, sans socks. The three had coffee as Fred explained his plan. "You know," Dr. Benjamin said as he stared at Jerome while talking to Fred, "the only thing worse than co-signing for a brother, is his quitting or getting fired before the ink dries on his application."

"A amen," Fred said, "But Jerome is certified, qualified and has been battle tested; he can handle Sid. I've observed him closely over the last couple of days. He's educated, intelligent, a quick and deep thinker, and controls his emotions under pressure." Jerome now realized Fred had been evaluating him while they were together.

"Does he know Sidney will try everything his little mind can conjure to make him quit?" Dr. Benjamin continued staring at Jerome, determining whether he was worth the effort, risk, and potential embarrassment. Not since his officer review for Captain, by field grade officers had Jerome been under such intense analysis; he managed it with calm and poise.

"He does now," Fred said.

"If you're co-signing for this young brother," Dr. Benjamin said, "after knowing him for only two days, so will I, he must be extraordinary. Mr. Gerard, show up for work Monday morning; you'll be hired immediately or Sidney will have to find a new meal ticket." He then said, "Oh, stop by my office before you leave and let me treat that burn." He touched Jerome's facial scar. "Luckily it's only a surface wound. I'll write a prescription that will make you look and feel better." Jerome felt unshackled; life was beautiful. *Halleluiah,* he thought.

At Freedman's Savings and Loan, Fred explained his, Dr. Benjamin's, Samuel Stovall's, Leo Lafarge's, and Buddy Laws', involvement. He also mentioned Jerome was a veteran. Ted said to Jerome, "With this impressive posse behind you, you're automatically in! Here is a packet and two sets of keys with addresses. Monday, return the completed forms, your 214 discharge certification, and the keys to the house you don't want. Move into your new home at your convenience; leave the rest to us."

"Girls, turn off the television, we've got get into our uncomfortable car and start traveling again." Gail said, when Jerome entered their hotel room. She walked toward their luggage, grumbling, "It sure took you long enough; we have lost the morning's driving advantage."

"Wait till you hear what's happened!" Jerome said.

"Let's see, you've learned how to play golf, now isn't that special. Maybe you have forgotten, but what you need is a job; and another thing…"

"I didn't learn golf, but I did find a JOB! And," Jerome pulled the house keys from his pocket, held them over his head and shouted, "and A HOME!"

Gail's mouth flew open momentarily, she then threw her arms around Jerome's neck; tears of joy flowed mightily. "You didn't, you didn't, you did!" Gail privately thanked Naomi McGhee.

The Gerard family hugged and danced around the room. Jerome thought, *improbable meetings with influential people who helped a stranger without obligation or reward; concerned Negroes who improve their community by helping others, one person at a time. Bronzeville is unique.*

"I told you I was going to find a job; didn't know where or when, but I knew it was going to happen!" Jerome said, between shortened breaths.

"Yes, you did, Babe, yes, you did! You'll have to tell me how all of this happened as soon as time permits." Gail heard the restored confidence and self-esteem in Jerome's voice. His eyes were bright and confident. They would plant their family tree in Bronzeville.

"Well, it all started at lunch yesterday…" Jerome spurted out names, titles, places, and events until he was tongue-tied. He laughed out loud, grabbed Gail in a big hug and squeezed her too tight. Being able to provide for his family and to have Gail's confidence was intoxicating. He felt omnipotent, ten feet tall, strong as Sampson, and wise as Solomon.

As they left to select their new home, Jerome said to the operator/desk clerk, "We'll be staying here till Monday, that's when we'll be moving. I said that's when we move into our new home!" The young lady smiled and gave Jerome two thumbs up. Others in the lobby applauded.

Their chosen home was a brick bungalow in a middle-class neighborhood called Park Manor. It had one bath, living and dining rooms, and three bedrooms, on one level. There was an unfinished, cement floored, basement. The master bedroom was less than half the size of Gail's bedroom in New Orleans. An old, one car frame garage covered half the small yard with an entrance from the alley. There was about ten feet between houses. The palatial Beauregard house in New Orleans sat on 10 acres. "It's nice." Gail said.

"This is our first home Babe, not our last, but it's ours!" Jerome said as he pulled Gail close while standing in the kitchen.

"You're right honey." Gail erased memories of her previous home, the large house on Chestnut Street, and accepted a new beginning. She recalled her mother saying, "And he will fail." She thought, *so much for mother's projections.* They prepared a floor chart and headed for the Negro-owned furniture store Fred had recommended.

Ten years ago, during The War, Dennis Peterson, a top salesman for one of the larger, Jewish-owned furniture stores in Bronzeville, was encouraged by two policy lords to explore opening his own store by visiting Chicago's Merchandise Mart. He learned that top-of-the-line furniture manufacturers, in spite of doing very little business in Bronzeville, would only sell to Dennis for a 100% payment, in cash, prior to delivery. Economy furniture manufacturers also required up-front payment, and added a delivery fee. Dennis' silent partners accepted the stringent terms. They decided, "Who needs credit? Our accountants will make this another money-laundering venture; if we're wrong; it ain't nothin' but money."

Dennis' landlord required six months' rent in advance, and gave him no remodeling allowance; again, unusually stringent terms. Dennis employed two experienced salesmen, bought a truck, hired a delivery team, retained an attractive, ebullient, receptionist/bookkeeper, and opened his large store with a wide range of furniture at competitive prices, courteous professional service, and the word-of-mouth endorsement of the policy kingdom.

Quality Furniture offered one price for single pieces and a discounted price for multiple-piece packages. Banks, as advised by their Caucasian furniture store owner clients, would not extend credit to Negroes or Caucasians who purchased furniture from Dennis. He required a 20% down payment from customers who wanted to finance for one year at 15% interest.

With additional profits from financing, Dennis paid off his backers in three years with nominal interest. Five years into his venture banks and manufacturers, after being made aware of Dennis' cash flow, customer demographics, and profitability, got in line for Dennis' business. He was looking for his third location.

"Mr. Hawkins told me you would be in," Dennis said to the Gerard family. "Make your selections. We'll deliver and set up Monday morning. Gail was pleased with the style and quality but noted the high prices with apprehension.

"Don't let those tags frighten you," Dennis said. "Mr. Hawkins told me to give you our deepest discount and discuss payment terms with him; I think he's going to fold your furniture costs into your mortgage, which will eliminate the need for a down payment and make your furniture costs tax deductible. So be sure to furnish your house completely"

Rinnng! Jerome answered the hotel room phone. "I heard the word Little Brother," Turkey said. "Congrats! Since you're not leaving we can hang out tonight, right? We still haven't found your bosom buddy, then there's Rowena."

"Wrong Turkey on both counts," Jerome laughed. "I don't womanize and we have partied enough, besides I'll have all the time necessary to find Namon. But I do want to talk to you. Meet me in the bar in fifteen minutes."

Over drinks, with blues tunes from a juke box playing seven inch, 45 RPM's, Jerome told Turkey all that had transpired. He summarized by saying, "Thanks to you, in two days my life has been completely transformed."

"Damn Man, stickin' it with the swells, gettin' a good gig and a pad full o' fine stuff in a classy hood, that's shur' nuff TCB. You went from nothin' to mutton in one day."

"What?" Jerome answered.

"I keep forgettin' you don't speak Negroease, but don't sweat it, brother man, you will."

"Here man," Jerome handed Turkey a gift-wrapped package. "This was supposed to be a going-away present."

"Aw man," Turkey said after examining the walnut Cross writing set, "and my name's on' em. Ain't nobody ever gave me nothin' like this." Turkey wiped his nose with his sleeve and squeezed the corners of his tear-filled eyes.

"Think about me every time you write a check, or sign a restaurant tab," Jerome said, his hand was on Turkey's shoulder.

"'Course you know I don't use checks or banks," Turkey said. They laughed and then drank in silence for a long moment. "We'll stay hooked up," Turkey said. "Faye and I will give you a play at your new gig and you know where to get a decent drink." Several more moments passed, then Turkey added, "Oh, don't worry 'bout your hotel bill. Bronzeville dudes have ninety days to settle, same as cash."

Turkey and Jerome toasted. "To good times," Turkey said.

"And to the best of times which are yet to come," Jerome added.

End of Chapter Four

CHAPTER FIVE

Truck drivers, some double parked, were making deliveries; business owners were cleaning their outside turf by sweeping away the gathered debris, preparing for another day of commerce. Several men stood in front of a vacant store, sharing yesterday's, Sunday morning newspapers' classified ads. Boys shod in worn, black Keds chased each other between adults. Jerome walked amidst a mosaic of Negroes, most scurrying to catch the next El headed downtown. He reached Tailors Drugs at 7:30 a.m., 30 minutes early.

Fifteen minutes passed. Jerome's short sleeve, white shirt collar and armpits under his dark blue suit, were moist; partly from the heat and humidity, mostly from anxiety. Occasionally, he wiped his forehead with his small handkerchief. His dark, narrow tie was flush against his neck, causing more discomfort and perspiration. As Jerome waited, he shined the toes of his black shoes on the back of his pant-legs, while evaluating each approaching White man. *I must make an excellent, first impression.*

At 7:50, a short, potbellied, bow-legged man with his head down waddled passed Jerome; his pants crotch reached mid-thigh. The partially bald, middle-aged, overweight, male fumbled with a large ring of keys until he stood opposite the iron, diamond-shaped, retractable gate. His frown seemed permanent.

"Good morning Mr. Reis, my name is…" Jerome transferred his manila envelope to his left hand, wiped his sweaty, right palm on his suit coat, smiled and reached out.

"Your name I know already, and it's obvious you know mine." Reis jerked his head up, glaring at Jerome as if he were accosting him. "Please, can I open my fucking store before you start telling me how to run my God damn business!" Reis slammed the accordion iron gate into itself, and then rushed inside.

A tall, shapely, honey-colored woman in high heels and a translucent blouse suddenly appeared and entered with them. Reis disappeared in the rear; Jerome, given no direction or instruction, halted after entering. The woman stopped beside him, smoothed her flared, colorful cotton skirt and said, "Can't stand this August heat; naps my hair in minutes." Both were facing forward. She produced a collapsible church fan and stirred the air around her.

"That's why I wait across the street in the air conditioned cleaners until Sid gets here." Louise placed a hand on her indented waist, looked Jerome over and said, "Saw you standing outside, thought you were a knotted up stud with a V.D. problem." Louise whispered, "Never would have put you in Dr. Ben's family."

"Louise!" yelled Reis. "Quit jabbering and get to work so we can open the damn store!"

"He got here twenty minutes late 'cause he knew you would be waiting. Guess he thought you might vanish or somethin'. He's hollering for your benefit, darling, not mine. If he had been on time we would have opened on time."

She's a spunky lady, must be at least 40, Jerome thought as he watched Louise casually walk away. Her skirt, which was slightly heightened by her broad behind, swished. Louise turned on the lights and the air conditioner, counted her change drawer, cleaned her counter with Windex, and then invited in waiting customers.

While growing up in Beaumont, Texas there was a drugstore Jerome could make purchases from over the back half-door, but only when there were no White customers. At college there was a small store on campus; in the Army there were enormous post exchanges. Jerome had never been in a Negro neighborhood drugstore. He sighed deeply after feeling the cool breeze from the air conditioner.

Three, eight by five foot gondolas were paralleled and angled, each was three feet wide. All were filed with merchandise from school supplies to aluminum skillets. Jerome counted the 9" floor tiles and estimated there was about two thousand square feet of display space.

Most of the early customers bought pints of wine or packs of cigarettes for fifty cents, or half-pints of liquor; Louise's register was near the front door. Opposite her counter were a radio/television tube tester and two waist-high ice cream freezers with plastic, rollback tops, which were shut most of the time. Bic cigarette lighters, ball-point pens, sun glasses and car perfumers with bikini-clad White women, all on display cards, hung on a wire over Louise's station. None were priced over two dollars. Further into the store, a lighted, Timex watch display on top of one of the two glass cases rotated. The Pharmacy counter was in the rear with a variety of medical supplies encased and locked. The store had been opened 20 minutes; Jerome waited.

Through his peripheral vision, Jerome noticed Mr. Reis often peeping from behind his seven foot, smoked, decorated glass counter. Finally, Reis said, "Hey what-cha-name, you here to work or watch? Get back here——now!"

Jerome's legs had grown stiff from standing for over forty-five minutes. He walked toward Prescriptions with eager eyes and a practiced smile, still carrying his tan envelope.

"You ever work in a drugstore before?" Reis asked without looking up. He was wearing a white, waist-length coat over a pale, generic, blue golf shirt, sitting on a stool, making entries in a ledger on the prescription counter.

"No sir, but I…"

"I didn't think so. If you had you wouldn't need your cousin to get you a job." Reis eyed Jerome with obvious contempt. "Cousin, yeah, I'll bet. You must be from the dark, homely side of the family. You do have an Illinois pharmacist license, right?"

"No sir, but it's being processed, here's my military license, my certificate from St. Barbara's College, as well as a letter of recommendation from my Army commander. My Illinois license should be…"

"God dammit," Reis shouted, "you can't fill one damn prescription until your license is hanging on my wall!" Reis again refused Jerome's documents. "If a state inspector comes in and catches you, there'd be hell to pay. Then what's your "cousin" going to do? Did you tell Dr. Ben you didn't have a license? I can't wait till he gets here. I knew this was a mistake from the beginning!" The two men stared at each other for a long moment.

Well, I was warned, thought Jerome, *if I get fired I might lose our home and down payment before we've unpacked. What will I tell Gail?*

"Until Dr. Ben arrives, go up front; maybe Louise can put your worthless ass to work." Jerome had taken several steps when Reis yelled, "And I suppose you expect to be paid White pharmacist's wages for selling cigarettes, already."

White pharmacists' wages are obviously different from Negroes' pharmacist's wages. Jerome turned, stopped less than a foot in front of Reis, and said respectfully, "No sir, I'll work for nothing until my license is in place if that's acceptable."

"Nothing is all you're worth right now. Besides, everything might change when Dr. Ben gets in," Reis chuckled to himself as he resumed his bookkeeping. Jerome anticipated Dr. Ben withdrawing his support when he arrived; neither he nor Fred had mentioned a license.

"Where can I hang my coat, Mr. Reis?" He ignored Jerome, he spotted a nail near the basement door and hung his coat on it. *I know the government moves at a snail's pace, but I'll work without pay no matter how long it takes. I'll stay employed, without wages; at least until Dr. Ben arrives.*

Low-playing R&B music on the radio behind Louise's counter camouflaged their conversation. "Don't let him frighten you sugar; he's just selling wolf tickets, hoping you'll quit. When Dr. Ben told Sid about you Saturday, he was chinnin' and grinnin' all up in Doc's face. Excuse me." Louise waited on several customers, and then resumed talking. "Soon as Doc left, Sid turned bitter as a dose of quinine. Guess he didn't like a nigger––even if it was Dr. Ben, telling him who to hire; this license thing changes ever thing; looks like White Folk wins again."

Louise serviced customers; Jerome bagged their purchases. "I've been here ten years; you're his first Negro pharmacist. Let's break you in right so you won't get fired. 'Course, White folk fire us for breathing to fast––or to slow. But you got a Black angel watching *your* back."

The top of Louise's teased hair reached Jerome's chin; she had slipped on a pair of scuffs. Louise said, "This is the liquor key, the cigarette key, the sundries key and the over-the-counter drugs key. Each represents a different profit margin, that's why it's important to ring up items correctly." Between customers Jerome selected items and named the correct key. Louise said, "You pretty smart for a Colored boy."

They bumped often while moving within the tiny space behind the counter. Jerome inhaled to squeeze past Louise, occasionally scraping his back against the shelves. Jerome felt Louise's ample breasts press against his chest as he reached for items behind her. After Jerome and Louise experienced a serious bump, Jerome jumped as if he had been hit with an electric cattle prod, knocking over merchandise. "I'm sorry; I just can't seem to…"

"Relax sugar, don't worry 'bout it. Besides," Louise smiled through full lips and sparkling eyes, "I don't bruise that easy." In two hours Jerome was able to find any brand of cigarettes or bottle of liquor.

"Thank you and come back soon," Jerome said as he gave customers their purchases and change. Some were surprised at his politeness; Louise picked up the habit.

"Jerome, get back here, right now!" Reis bellowed. Jerome rushed to the pharmacist's counter; Reis said while shaking the phone in Jerome's face, "Now you listen boy, no personal calls already, do you understand me! You haven't been here long enough to piss and already you're tying up by business line. You can get your damn calls at home!" Reis pushed the phone towards Jerome, but remained between him and the wall mounted cradle, eliminating privacy.

"Mr. Reis, I have no idea who this is," Jerome said. "I don't even know your phone number, so I couldn't have asked anyone to call. I'll be off in less than a minute."

"You had better be!" Reis scowled, crossed his arms and stood glaring at Jerome.

"Is this Jerome Gerard," asked a stern, male voice.

"Yes?"

"This is your first day on the job, right?"

"Why yes. Who is this?"

A friendlier voice said, "This is Roscoe Black, secretary of licensing and registration, calling from Springfield, IL, the state capital. I'm about to inform Mr. Reis that you are in fact an Illinois registered pharmacist and should be treated as such. I just talked with our mutual friend in Washington, D.C."

"Thank you, you have really made my day!" *And thank God for Negroes in high government positions.*

"Now give Mr. 'no personal calls, already,' the friggin phone. Before I'm through he'll develop a new respect for us or I will close him down instantly. Let's see how big his balls really are."

"He wants to talk to you," Jerome said as he handed a surprised Reis the phone.

Reis' frown vanished. "Yes… Yes sir… Oh no sir, I recognize your voice from seeing you on television… Oh yes sir, I know my congressman… I understand and agree… Let me write that number down… No questions sir, none at all, everything is clear… Thank you for calling Mr. Black, sir."

Jerome had returned to the front counter before Reis turned a dark pink. Each time he glanced towards prescriptions, Reis was watching him.

An hour later, Reis said in an exaggerated polite voice, "As soon as it's convenient Mr. Gerard, please come to the pharmacist's counter," Reis' face was contorted. Staring at Jerome, Reis said, "Let's see now, Dr. Ben is your cousin, Secretary Black is your uncle, Congressman Dawson is your daddy, and I'm your new girlfriend about to be screwed, right!" Jerome made eye contact but said nothing. "Here, since you're so damn official, put this on." Reis began slamming drawers and grumbling. Jerome stepped into a corner, removed his shirt and tie, and put on a heavily starched pharmacist's smock. *It's too small, but feels oh, so good.*

"You work six days a week, ten hours a day, and there's no lunch breaks; you eat between customers. All cash and welfare prescriptions are rung up on this key; OTC drugs on this one. You may be connected, but you haven't done a damn thing until you increase my sales, understand! The capsules and tablets are kept alphabetically…"

"Mr. Reis," Jerome interrupted, "thank you." He paused, waited until eye contact was made, and then repeated the phrase, "Thank you. I appreciate this opportunity. I realize I have much to learn, but you taking the time and energy to teach me will be rewarded. I take criticism well, so don't hesitate to correct me. Within two weeks, I hope to be worth more than any of your previous pharmacists." Jerome extended his hand. Reis hesitated and then shook it as he looked up at Jerome.

"Call me Sid." A smile emerged as he noticed Jerome's smock's tight fit, "You can leave the top unbuttoned. I'll get your size with the next laundry delivery. Incidentally, there's a coat rack behind that screen." Sid was impressed with Jerome's attitude; maybe Dr. Ben had done him a favor.

Between customers, Sid showed Jerome pharmaceutical cost codes and how to mark them up 200% or more. "When you fill welfare prescriptions, use generics, which cost less, but charge the government as if you had used name brands."

Under intense scrutiny, Jerome wrote out Dr. Ben's phoned-in prescriptions correctly, located medications, touched-typed labels, and with experienced professionalism, poured precise amounts of elixirs. He correctly determined the price on each prescription. After welfare patients signed their forms, he always said over a genuine smile, "Thank you; hope you feel better."

"It's seven o'clock; you should have left at six," Sid said, "You did OK today; your hours tomorrow are noon till closing, and you're off on Wednesday."

It's seven already? I didn't even stop to eat. "Glad you're pleased

Sid, see you tomorrow." Jerome floated out the door, thrilled to be leaving his job, knowing he will be welcomed back.

"What it be like?" a gravelly voice said.

Without turning around, Jerome thought, *that has to be Turkey.* Jerome was creating room for more merchandise on one of the gondolas.

"Came by two Wednesdays ago to buy some stuff, didn't see you so I split; wanted you to get the credit, boon." Turkey's order exceeded $200. It was Jerome's biggest sale during the month he had been working.

"I'll do this 'bout once a week until my liquor manager starts to cuss n fuss." Turkey whispered, "Where's the boss?"

"He's been leaving me alone lately. He had a couple of his stooges validate my honesty, so he's beginning to trust me——as much as he can trust anybody."

"Word is he's a bitch to work for. Rich as cream, but carries a KKK card close to his heart."

"He's pleased with me; that's all I'm concerned about."

"Told Faye to check out your cosmetics; she spends a fortune on that junk. Has she been by?"

"Oh yes. She and two girlfriends spent almost seventy-five dollars two weeks ago. They even placed special orders for up-scale merchandise we don't stock. Thanks a lot Turkey, its order like yours and Faye's that make me look good."

"When you comin' by my place little brother? We still serve a decent drink, don't cha know."

"Between working long hours and getting settled at home, I just haven't had time man, but I'll make it by soon."

"Cool, see you when I see you––Mr. Medicine Man," Turkey said lyrically while leaving.

Every other Wednesday Jerome had lunch with Fred, sans cocktails, at Felix and Bea's, converting acquaintances into friends. He always collected business cards of those he hadn't met before. After several meetings he called his new acquaintances, invited them by Tailor's drugstore any day but Wednesday, and offered them a 10% introductory discount. Jerome was getting to know Bronzeville's elite; Fred and Jerome were becoming fast friends.

Once a month, on his early Fridays he would have a drink or two at Scotty's, Fred's regular hangout, before going home. In order to eliminate an inflated bar bill, Jerome would buy he and Fred their first drink and pay for it immediately. *Fred's bill from Scotty's must be enormous. I have no idea about his expenses at the Pershing,* Jerome surmised. Jerome brown bagged his lunch daily instead of ordering a hot plate from the restaurant across the street, with Louise. Sid never ate lunch. Jerome also realized that spending time with Turkey, because of his reputation and lifestyle, should be avoided. 'Associate with people you admire,' was one of Jerome's edicts he had learned from Dr. McGhee.

"But how can I compete if you have no-competition contracts with my competitors?" A middle-aged Negro man was pleading with Sid as Jerome entered. "Anson ice cream is as good as anyone's and our prices are competitive. I've offered you volume rebates, advertising allowances, and interest-free, extended payment terms, but no matter how much I cut my profits you won't carry my products. Your customers are ninety-nine percent Negro. If I can't get distribution here, where can I get it? Without added distribution Mr. Reis, I can't grow!"

"That's your problem, boy, not mine. You shouldn't even be making ice cream, that's a White man's business. Look, I've told you a dozen times there's nothing I can do. If you're going to keep trespassing, see my assistant manager." Jerome watched Sid disappear behind the pharmacist's counter while the Anson representative was still talking.

"Every damn day some strange-looking colored boy tries to sell me stuff," Sid griped to Jerome constantly. "I can't buy from every peddler that comes through the door, that's why we have wholesalers." During Jerome's second month, Sid said, "From now on, you handle all new sales reps, especially the Colored ones, but don't buy anything unless I OK it."

Handle; that means reject. "Sure Sid, I understand."

During one of Fred's visits, always when Sid was away so they could talk freely, Jerome described the Anson ice cream incident. "That was Neal Anson, an entrepreneur. He encounters that same sorry story wherever he goes. Chain stores are even worse. Katz Drugs, with 20 stores in Chicago, told him he isn't big enough to service their stores. Quality Foods won't even talk to him."

"But how does he grow without…?"

"I know, I know. He owns two successful ice cream parlors; they validate the quality of his products by staying busy. Even Harold Oldham can't give Anson any space because he also has a no-competition contract."

"Will you give Anson space in one of your freezers?" Jerome asked Ralph, the Plenty Good Ice Cream representative.

"I can't go against company policy Jer and shame on you for asking. I thought you had more sense than that," Ralph said, pointing his finger in Jerome's face, as he ate an ice cream bar without paying for it. Overweight Ralph playfully rubbed Jerome's hair for good luck and consistently shortened his name. *White people disrespect us blatantly, I've never seen Ralph touch Sid, outside of a handshake, or call him anything but Mr. Reis.*

When Jerome politely asked the potato chip company driver to give a Negro who manufactured a snack named Soul Skins, space, which was fried pork rinds, he refused. "We're not prejudiced, just competitive. We place racks free of charge with that understanding."

Soul Skins, per Jerome's suggestion, made smaller packets. They then stapled them to cards which Jerome could hang on the outside of the potato chip racks. The driver let the product remain because it didn't cost him any space. "Besides, they aren't moving any product, anyway," the driver concluded. He didn't know Jerome placed a full card on his rack every potato chip delivery day. With their smaller display cards, Soul Skins increased distribution, profits and sales throughout Bronzeville. Soon Soul Skins began installing their own racks. Because of customer requests, they acquired distribution in super markets, all but Quality Foods.

Jerome suggested to drug and sundry wholesalers' representatives they inventory Negro manufactured items. "Gee, we'd like to, Jer, but Negro products don't move fast enough, and they don't have the required product liability insurance."

"That's what cow pastures are full of; bull shit," John T. Williamson answered when Jerome sought confirmation. John was the only Negro drug wholesaler in Chicago. He worked for Leonard and Strauss, aka, L&S Distributors. "But you are the first Negro to raise the question; most believe the misinformation.

"White companies that manufacture Negro hair products don't have liability insurance; they don't need any. All of them are made from petroleum jelly, food coloring, water, and fragrances; all natural ingredients that don't require insurance."

"What about turnover?"

"Negro products made by Whitey, like Magic Shave, Nadinola Bleaching Cream, pressing combs, make-up, and scores of hair products move fast enough to justify warehouse space, so why wouldn't those that *we* manufacturer? Now don't quote me or I'll be fired."

"It's like Willie McGhee said," Jerome concluded, 'In a capitalistic society, economics is one of the keys to equality. As long as White folk control our economic growth, we will remain second class citizens.' *I have got to help these struggling pioneers,* Jerome decided. For those who would leave product on consignment, Jerome made space.

"Who's paying for all this new merchandise, Jer?" Sid asked, as he examined a new Negro invented product; leatherized shoe strings.

"I'm not buying anything and we only pay for product after it's sold, which increases our ROI percentages."

Sid was pleased with consignments and impressed with Jerome's grasping the finer points of inventory control, like Return-on-Investment, or, ROI. Jerome and Louise encouraged the other cashiers to push the Negro-manufactured items.

One of the hair care manufacturers was Richard Thompson. He manufactured a new, technical breakthrough product, called Easy Wave that would straighten Negro's hair. He also manufactured several companion items and a superior line of hair conditioners.

"I don't want to sell you anything," Richard said, surprising Jerome. "I need an order from you and other druggists to take to L&S to persuade them to warehouse my products. Once drugstores can buy from a wholesaler, I can advertise, creating a greater demand. My products' quality will guarantee repeat sales. With consumer demand, chains will want to stock my items." Jerome was happy to give Richard an order; who further explained, "Because we have a harsh chemical in our hair straightener, we also have the proper insurance." When a plethora of Thompson's products were delivered, Jerome quickly pointed out that they came from L&S Distributors.

Customers, old and new, flocked to Tailors Drugs because it stocked the hard-to-find items. Sales, profits, and customer loyalty increased. In mid-November Sid said, "Jer, you're doing a great job! Several customers have thanked me for hiring you. Keep up the good work; you'll be getting a raise before you know it."

"It's been a long day; I'm almost too tired to eat," Jerome said as he collapsed in his recliner around midnight. Gail purposely looked unattractive in her college jersey and loose-fitting sweat pants. Her hair was pulled back and she was without make-up. Gail was sitting on the sofa, pouting, her sock-covered feet tucked under her butt. Gail was protesting Jerome's order to set the thermostat no higher than sixty-eight to reduce heating costs.

"I kept re-warming your dinner until it was no longer edible, so I pitched it. I don't care whether you eat or not. Where in the world have you been? Doesn't the store close at ten?"

"I had to write an order that needed to be placed tomorrow morning, so I stayed late."

"If you're hungry, you can make yourself a sandwich; I'm tired." Several fallen leaves had stuck to Jerome's shoe, reminding him, and Gail, he had yard work to do.

In addition to often working late, Jerome read *Drug Store Age* and other trade journals at home, well into the night. On some early days, after work, he visited larger stores and talked business concepts and new product introductions with the managers. Hard work and self-development wasn't sufficient; following Dr. McGhee's advice, Jerome took University of Chicago's home study post-graduate business courses.

He had no time for mundane television shows, which Gail enjoyed, or even sports, which he enjoyed.

Jerome awakened at 4:00 a.m., five days a week, to read for two hours. He understood knowledge was the key to success. He also learned from W.E.B. DuBois' writings he had to work harder and be smarter than his Caucasian counterparts.

With a ham and cheese sandwich and a glass of milk, Jerome returned to the living room to watch the late news on their only television which was a second hand color set. Gail complained, "I don't know how I'm going to buy Christmas gifts with the little money you gave me. I can barely get the girls something nice, and we still have a lot of family left."

Whenever Gail mentioned being tired to her mother, as she had done today, her mother preached, "There's no way you can manage a household and two children by yourself. Make Jerome get you some help or better yet, all of you should just come on home."

Oh no, not again, her mother must have called, Jerome thought. He tried to listen to both the news and Gail; she won. He answered her consistent gripe, "Babe, we agreed to buy only those younger than ten presents. Don't worry about our girls; I'll get them something nice."

During the commercials Gail was silent. When the news returned, she whined, "When are we going out? All I do is cook and clean, without help, I might add."

"We don't go out because we can't spend and save simultaneously; we severely reduced our savings when we bought this place, and no matter how much you complain I am going to continue to save at least ten percent of my take-home pay," Jerome said with less patience. "As hard as I work, if I can pay all these damn taxes I can certainly pay us. That's how my daddy helped his seven children get through college, by saving some of what he earned, no matter how little it was. What's left of our income after taxes and savings barely covers our expenses. I'll probably get a raise after Christmas, then we can spend a little more, but not before the raise." Jerome turned up the television to hear the sports report, and then sat back down.

As soon as the announcer began, Gail whined, "We don't have drapes, carpeting or dining room furniture. We don't even have a piano, and you know how much I enjoy playing. Besides it's time for Michelle to begin lessons. All you care about is that damn drugstore!"

Jerome got back up, turned the television down and said, "You're right Babe; we'll buy a good, used piano." Jerome took a bite of sandwich; he had missed the sports results.

"If we had stayed home I'd have friends, things to do, and help around the house. I wouldn't be so miserable."

"You did it again!" Jerome shouted. He slammed his fist on the TV tray; milk and sandwich remnants hit the hardwood floor. He caught the glass mid-air. "Home is here, dammit!"

A vintage movie had started. Gail glued her eyes to the TV; she didn't like vintage movies but was afraid to look anywhere else. Her mother had told her to nag until she got her way, but never mentioned how to finesse an angry husband.

"Babe, it's going to take a few years and some hard times, but I'm on the right track, you'll see." Jerome had returned from the kitchen with several paper towels and cleaned up his mess.

They retired. Gail curled on one edge of their full sized bed, Jerome on the other. Both folded their arms into themselves so they would not touch, even after falling asleep. They slept back to back, only inches apart, yet they could have been on different planets. The tension was palpable. "I love you," was a foreign phrase. They were intimate only when Jerome insisted, and he rarely did. The withdrawal method, accompanied by hostile inquiry, reprimand and what-if-I'm pregnant scenarios, left much to be desired. They shared a deep love for their daughters, but little else.

"Tailor's Pharmacy, how may we help you," Jerome said answering the phone.

"Honey; guess who's in town?"

"Tell me Gail, I need some good news, who?" Jerome was hoping a college fellow or one of his six siblings had surprised them.

"Daddy Beau and Momma; isn't that great!"

"Damn!" Jerome clenched his fist and put it in his mouth. Recovering, Jerome lied, "Excuse me Babe; I just messed up a compound prescription."

"I wonder why?" Gail looked into the receiver; she could almost see Jerome lying.

That evening, the Gerards met the Beauregards at the diminutive, elegant, Negro owned Manor House Hotel, located on 47th Street. A huge Murano crystal chandelier lit the elegant reception area. The registration counter had a marble top. The fifty rooms had color televisions and combination bathtubs deep enough for soaking and showers; no transients were allowed. The Gerards arrived ten minutes early, sat on an embroidered silk, almond colored French provincial sofa——and waited. Conrad and Sylvia were forty-five minutes late.

"We've been waiting an hour, Daddy Beau," Gail said, "the least you could have done was call the front desk to let us know what to expect!"

"What could be more important than waiting on your parents, girl?" Conrad continued, "Boy, you still wearing that same cheap suit you had on the last time I saw you?"

"Well, Daddy Beau, I just can't throw it away because you've seen me in it, now can I?" Gail smiled at Jerome's retort. Jerome had only added work clothes to his wardrobe.

Conrad wore a brown tweed Hickey-Freeman suit with matching outer coat, and lizard-skin and suede shoes——with lifts. "I'm surprised this heap still runs," Conrad said as he helped Sylvia and Gail into the back seat of Jerome's two-door auto.

"I bought it just before being discharged; the motor pool mechanics installed an engine with only 40,000 miles, salvaged from an accident, so it's good for at least another three years."

"Humph," Conrad muttered. "It's still the ugliest car I've ever seen. Take us to Killer Jackson's Steak House, I'll give you directions." He continually adjusted his bottom to the vinyl seat.

I know the way, you conceited, overbearing, old fart. Jerome looked at Gail through the rearview mirror; she winked. She too remembered having eaten at killer Jackson's their first night in Bronzeville, with Turkey. "I sure hope none of my friends see me in this clap-trap. I knew I should have rented a car," Conrad said.

"Why didn't you call, moth… man?" Killer Jackson said as the two heavyset men attempted to embrace. "I could have gotten some of the fellas together to win some of your New Orleans money."

"You'll get enough when I pay my check," Conrad laughed. "Besides, I'm booked tonight. The president of Glory Mutual has invited me to the Royal Reprobates Club. You want to play poker with the big boys?"

"No thanks; that's only for members and visiting muckity mucks like you; besides, most of the Reprobates are fags anyway," Killer laughed.

"Good evening Mr. and Mrs… Gerard, right?" Killer said as he and Jerome shook hands. "It's been awhile since you've been in; welcome back."

Conrad's jaw dropped, his eyes widened. Killer Jackson's was the most expensive supper club in Bronzeville, and his poor-ass children had eaten there——at least once! Killer sat next to Conrad; he gifted Conrad's party with Dom Perignon champagne. It was poured into gold-trimmed flutes. Several times Conrad asked Killer how often the Gerards had dined there. Each time Killer politely avoided answering. Finally he said, "Don't ask me anymore; ask them."

Each time Gail turned to talk to Jerome, Sylvia literally pulled her back for more inane conversation. Conrad and Killer talked, mostly in whispers, followed by outbursts of laughter. Jerome was ignored. He ate his salad, huge baked potato properly seasoned, steamed asparagus, and delicious prime rib as he watched the staff rush by.

When the check arrived on a silver tray, Conrad waved it at Jerome. "This is what you can do when you make real money, boy. But you've been here before; you must be stealing to afford this place." Jerome stared at Conrad, Gail seethed at her daddy for calling Jerome a thief. Conrad pulled out his bankroll, peeled off two, one hundred dollar bills and told the headwaiter, "Buy something warm and mushy with the change." The ladies blushed.

"Take me by your job, boy." Jerome parked across the street. "Looks mighty small, much smaller than the drugstore I was going to open. How much they pay you?"

Jerome answered Conrad's impolite question; "Two hundred a week."

"And you work how many hours?"

"Around sixty, six days a week; I usually go in on my off day if I need to catch up."

"Hell, that's way less than I pay Leon and Frank. They only work eight hours a day, five days a week——when they feel like it, and money goes a lot further at home. You're working like a slave; introduce me to your Jew-boss." Jerome pulled off, Conrad laughed. "I didn't think you were that stupid."

Again Gail fumed at her husband being called first a thief, now stupid and a slave.

While they rode, Conrad complained about the traffic lights, the pot holes and the cold weather. Jerome's stomach was gurgling like a pot of oatmeal as he parked in front of his home.

After climbing out of the back seat, Sylvia elaborately brushed out the wrinkles. "Just look at my dress," she complained. She looked up and down the block. "This is quaint; all the houses are alike." Sylvia walked between the two houses toward the Gerards' side, front door. She extended her fingers and said, "Why these houses almost touch." Sylvia walked past the side entrance to the rear, "And this yard is almost big enough for Michelle and Dana to play in—-if they don't have any friends over."

"Young man, your yard needs your attention," Sylvia said as she pointed her finger in Jerome's face while walking back to the entrance. "It's amazing a yard as tiny as yours could accumulate so many leaves—-and you don't even have a tree!" Conrad laughed.

During the brief inside tour, Conrad constantly frowned and grumbled, Sylvia sighed. Every time she caught Jerome or Gail's eyes, she rolled her own. In the living room Conrad sat in Jerome's recliner and complained about a draft coming through a rotted chink in the nearby window frame. He ran his fingers over the space as if he could stop the cold air flow. Gail dismissed the baby sitter and then joined Jerome on the couch. She rubbed his back, symbolically removing the pain from her parents' rudeness.

"Now that you have established your independence Son, when the hell are you coming home? The quality of your furniture indicates you are deep in debt. You can't afford a new car; you never take your wife out to dinner, well not often enough. And as small as this, this sharecropper's shack is you still have a burdensome mortgage. What's it going to take for you to realize leaving me was a mistake?" Conrad asked while lighting his cigar.

"We're making ends meet and are managing to save a little," Jerome said. He and Gail exchanged confidential glances.

"Damn that, you still need to come home. It will take you at least twenty years to get out of debt, if ever. White folk, especially Jews, don't pay their help any more than they have to!" Puffing on his cigar, Conrad stood up, paced within the small living room, bent slightly over while looking through the house, shook his head and said, "My granddaughters will have to marry up to get a decent place to live. You don't have carpet or dining room furniture, you got holes in your window frames large enough to drive a Mack truck through, and you think you can save enough money to buy your own business. Boy, I thought even you were smarter than that."

Gail was fighting back tears, sharing Jerome's tongue-lashing.

"My offers still stand, but damn Boy, one day I'm going to run out of generosity and patience." Conrad shook his head in disgust and then said, "Nigger, just what are you trying to prove!"

I haven't heard that word used seriously since I left Conrad's home. He must really be upset. Jerome steeled his emotions and said, "Conrad," Jerome knew calling him Conrad was insulting, "My objectives haven't changed. I now have the job I told you I would get, and this might be difficult for you to accept, but I'm working with someone who respects me. One day Sid and I might form a partnership. One thing that's not going to happen is my <u>ever</u> working for you." Sid had not mentioned a partnership, but it sounded good.

"I've had about as much of your impudence as I can stand. Gail, take us back to our hotel."

Gail took about an hour to make the round trip. Jerome was sitting in his recliner, holding a glass half-filled with scotch and water, steaming. Gail took a seat on the couch, crossed her ankles and said, "Please forgive my most recent behavior. It took me far too long to understand what you have been trying to tell me all of our marriage. I was proud of you this evening for maintaining your self-control, and saw my daddy, with all of his infirmities, for the very first time. I now know we are moving forward on the course you have set. I don't know the milestones or timetables, but I'll be patient.

"I can't tell my daddy what to think any more than you––probably less, because no matter how old I get or wise I become, I'm still his little girl––and a woman. We'll have to live with his attitude until he sees things differently." Gail reached over to Jerome's chair and caressed his hand.

"I don't have to do a damn thing; he has the problem, not me!" Jerome had heard Gail's sincere apology but could not erase being angry as quickly as he wanted.

"You're right," Gail said, "and before Momma leaves town I'm going to have a long talk with her. She'll make Daddy Beau understand; she has that ability." Gail knew better, but it sounded good.

"Did you tell your daddy how you feel?" Jerome asked, appreciating Gail's new posture.

"No, I didn't, but I told him he couldn't smoke cigars in our house because it was bad for the girls." Jerome and Gail smiled. She remembered Naomi McGhee saying, 'You have to show your man you have confidence in him, every day.' Gail left the room. Jerome believed something had been gained from Conrad's offensive behavior. He and Gail were closer; after a few more sips he decided to retire.

Their bedroom was lit by candle glow. Jerome saw Gail stretched out on the bed facing him, smiling, hip turned upward; her legs were slightly crossed, the cover was thrown back; she was wearing only a fragrance Jerome liked.

After getting into bed, Jerome felt the smoothness of Gail's body, first with his hand, then his leg. They kissed and fondled as their urges increased. Gail said, "I love you Babe." As Jerome mounted Gail she asked softly, "Please, don't make me pregnant." Jerome thought; *push-pull sex with love and respect is tolerable.* Their carnal interlude was mutually pleasurable.

Conrad, Sylvia, Gail, and the girls were standing in front of the Manor House Hotel. A strong, cold wind, known nationally as The Hawk, hurried them along. After receiving hugs and kisses from his granddaughters, Conrad said, "Those were great hugs, worth at least five dollars each. Now when I talk to you young ladies again, I hope to hear when you are coming home."

"Yes Granddaddy Beau," they sang together.

"Now Darling," Conrad said to Gail, "Don't let me down. You know you belong at home, don't you?"

"Well Daddy Beau, maybe we need to…"

"Then convince your bull-headed husband. Fine as you are, use your, ah, influence girl. Make that horny fool sleep on the sofa until he sees things your way." Conrad emitted a dirty laugh.

Pain filled Gail's eyes. She had not enjoyed a sexual encounter for the first time since their first night in Bronzeville. Besides, her sex life was none of her Daddy's business.

"You ladies have fun in the Loop. Sylvia, see you around six for dinner."

Conrad walked up a wide, spiral staircase to the entrance of the Parkway complex. He was helped out of his grey, mink collared Chesterfield coat, matching cashmere scarf and his $100 Knox hat by an attractive hostess wearing an after-five, knee-length dress and corsage. She patted his grey suit-collar into place, and then escorted him past the ballroom to the Blue Room.

Pleasant gloved waiters poured fresh coffee into bone china cups from insulated, sterling vessels. They served orange and tomato juice from iced carafes, and offered warm, fruit Danish from covered bread warmers. With refreshments in hand, Conrad chatted with friends, some of whom he had beaten at five-card stud last night. They laughed at worn stories and relived practical jokes played over the last twenty-five years until all twelve members of the National Insurance Association Board of Directors had gathered.

"Gentlemen," the chairman asked, "May we get started?"

"This place is just like downtown, only not so crowded," Conrad whispered to his friend Carl Harrison, president of Chicago based Glory Mutual Insurance Company. He was Impressed with the Parkway's elegant, new, appearance.

"First," the chairman said, "Let me thank and congratulate our host. This recently renovated multi-complex is truly first class." Applause validated his evaluation. "Secondly, thank you all for rearranging busy schedules. Your time, input, and presence are appreciated.

"Last August, during our annual convention, Brother Mack, Tennessee Agriculture and Industrial College, and other Nashville Negro businesses were excellent hosts. We had 787 attendees from forty-seven insurance companies. Did everyone enjoy themselves?"

All applauded and nodded affirmations toward last year's host. "Next year," the chairman continued, "our host city is Chicago. With five home offices we should expect even better accommodations and outstanding entertainment." The applause was louder. Shouts of "A college campus won't do," and "We're meeting up North now," accompanied the ovation. "Carl, our convention chairman, has some exciting news."

Two hostesses, on cue, unfolded a five by two foot oil cloth banner which read, 'Strive to Win in 55'. "We go first class in '55, and that's no jive," chanted Carl! "If convention trips motivate our sales forces, then new business should skyrocket. We have booked the Conrad Hilton, the nation's largest hotel, located on prestigious North Michigan Avenue. We will be the first Negro convention held in a major hotel in the country."

"Amen!" said Atlanta Life's president.

"It's about time," Detroit Mutual's chief executive added.

"We're going in the front door, up the private elevator, straight to the Presidential Suite, which our Board Chairman will occupy, gratis. We'll have hospitality suites, private breakfast meetings, a display area for exhibitors, and a twenty-four piece Negro orchestra playing in the Conrad Hilton's magnificent ballroom for our dancing pleasure––wearing white tie and tails, no less! So tell your sales forces where contest winners will reside in '55!" Carl signaled the hostesses to pass out convention packets to each member, which included a banner, hotel amenities brochures, and a things-to-do events calendar for Downtown Chicago. The racial breakthrough was enthusiastically applauded by all.

The Chair thanked Carl and continued with the agenda. Minutes and budgets were approved; there were no serious problems. All member companies were growing and profitable. The competition between companies licensed in the same states was aggressive, but no serious infractions had been reported. The golden rule of never suggesting a competitor's policy be canceled had not been violated.

During the break, while walking toward the twenty-five foot oblong bar behind the ballroom, Carl said to Conrad, "We lost one of our best salesmen recently––to New York Life."

"What! When did _they_ start hiring us?"

"Mercer is their first, but don't worry, New York Life doesn't sell industrial insurance, only ordinary."

"That's going to make selling easier for, what's his name, Mercer," Conrad said. "He won't have to make collections; his clients will pay by mail."

"So you think he'll make it?"

"Oh, he'll make it big time!" Conrad Answered. "Their premiums are probably less because of lower collection costs, their enormous size, and Caucasian actuarial tables, which, for the first time, will apply to _us_." Conrad took a long drink from his Beefeaters gin and tonic. "Another thing, if he's successful, other major Caucasian insurance companies will follow suit."

"But what about his loyalty; he wouldn't even be in the insurance business if it wasn't for Glory Mutual."

"Whoa Hoss," Conrad said, "You, just moments ago, proudly announced that we were taking hundreds of thousands of dollars from Bronzeville's businesses. How many insured do we have working at the Conrad Hilton?"

"Well, some of the maids…"

"Cut the bull Carl, you know what I'm saying. Chicago will be the first city to host a Negro convention where Negro businesses will be virtually eliminated from the economic equation. Our agents will need a Negro Geiger counter to find Bronzeville; that is if our staying Downtown, and giving them a damn events calendar doesn't persuade them to stay downtown."

"I get the message. We rush to integrate and call it an accomplishment, yet yell foul when those who work for us do the same."

"That's right. We can't blame Mercer for stepping up in class and probably doubling his earnings," Conrad said.

"I see. We want the benefits of integration without the liabilities." Carl ordered another drink.

"What benefits?" Conrad asked. "We didn't need the Conrad Hilton. It's bigger but their rooms aren't any more comfortable than the Manor House. The food won't taste as good as Felix and Bea's or Killer Jackson's, and will probably cost twice as much. There are enough Negro hotels in Bronzeville to accommodate our attendees and we could have held our meetings here. Another question; what is this splendid facility going to do when White hotels offer us accommodations for our formal affairs?"

"Oh, we'll continue to support the Parkway," Carl said apprehensively.

"Carl, you know as well as I, we believe the White man's coal burns hotter and his ice melts slower. When the downtown hotels open up to us, we will trample each other going in their front doors."

"Well," Carl said, "Let's wait and see how well Mercer does before we start making adjustments."

"Don't you realize what is happening right now?" Conrad became frustrated that Carl missed his point. "Because of integration, Negro businesses can no longer count on <u>us</u> for support. Caucasian businesses, with our help, are cherry-picking <u>our</u> economy. We are robbing Black Peter to pay White Paul. Within a year or two we can forecast formidable Caucasian competition in *our* industry. And you say, 'let's wait?'"

"But I thought integration was a good thing," Carl said. The two chief executives stared at each other.

"Lunch is being served," announced the maitre d'. Ambitious male executives and attractive female staffers from the five Chicago home offices swarmed in to make lasting impressions on the twelve opulent, influential presidents. Carl and Conrad proceeded toward lunch, somewhat confused, leaving Integration unsolved.

End of Chapter Five

CHAPTER SIX

The young women customers blatantly flirted with Jerome, the newest professional Negro in the neighborhood. Their trip was worthwhile if Jerome rang up their inexpensive purchases. To the more aggressive pursuers Jerome said, as he pointed to his ring, "I'm flattered, but I'm married." Some asked Louise about Jerome's personal habits; they received no usable information. Louise watched Jerome politely ignore their advances; this made him even more desirable.

It's 6:15; if Gail doesn't get here soon, I might freeze to death! Chicago's frigid, November wind penetrated Jerome's unlined poplin jacket, chilling him to the bone. Breathing was accomplished in short, cold, spurts. He peered into every old, white car for his tardy wife through frosted eyes. Louise saw Gail drop Jerome off this morning. She had decided tonight was worth another gamble, especially with Gail's parents in town. After work Louise went home and applied fresh make-up and combed her hair without changing clothes.

Parked, Louise watched Jerome as long as she dared. He was hunched over, bare hands shoved into his pockets, lifting one foot at a time off the cold pavement. "Hey bro; need a lift?" She was leaning over the passenger seat, speaking through the slightly opened window of her toasty, late model Ford.

"Only if I can buy us a drink," Jerome answered, rushing toward Louise's car.

That's exactly what I wanted to hear. "Where's Gail?" Louise asked, as Jerome settled in her car; she knew the answer. Tonight, unlike other nights, she had rolled a seven.

"Hell, I don't know; she's probably with her parents. Why are you still hanging around?"

"Oh, just doing some shopping," Louise said sounding blasé.

"Lucky for me," Jerome said, blowing on his cold hands then rubbing them together.

"Another day, another dollar," Louise said.

"Soon it will be a dollar and a half when I get a raise after the New Year."

"You deserve it. Customers are always telling Sid how polite you are and how you always remember their names. He's happier than a Jew at a welfare convention." Louise added, "Listen, there's a hip little lounge off Fifty-Eighth Street that has…"

"If it has heat, it qualifies," Jerome said as they drove south.

The Vintage Lounge's lights were low, the juke box was playing Lionel Hampton's classic, *Stardust*. The Vintage's major attraction was its straight-up jazz vendor venue. Four middle-aged men and a woman were leaning on the bar's leather rail, obviously bored, smoking cigarettes. The men wore coats and ties which were superfluous, considering their environment. The bar's regulars' challenge was sipping drinks without emptying their glasses to avoid buying another drink. Vacant seats separated them, emphasizing their availability. Sports or jazz trivia occupied the men. The woman, when given the opportunity, exaggerated past romances.

These were the downtrodden, those who had been defeated by racism, the lack of ambition, and mediocrity. Each had a reason for having failed, which was a poor excuse at best. Entrepreneurial opportunities or advanced education were no longer objectives. They worked only to pay their bills. Promotions were not anticipated. Increasing their skill levels, motivating their children, being good providers, or saving for the future, were, to extrapolate a phrase from poet, Langston Hughes, "dreams deferred." They were one paycheck away from being in dire straits. Going home, generally an unhappy place, was an option only when their bar bucks ran out or the Vintage closed. Getting laid, a fleeting accomplishment at best, was their facade.

As Louise and Jerome entered, the bar flies snapped their heads toward the door. They were hoping for a friend who would confirm their relevance back in the day––alas, it was only Louise.

"Hey, lucky." (Being with someone, especially a young someone, made her tonight's winner).

"What's the word?"

"Glad to see you lady L."

"There she is, the hostess with the mostest."

Louise smiled and fluttered her fingers. Normally she would have joined their reverie, but not tonight.

The habitués twisted their sullen faces with weighted eyes back toward their glasses and resumed meaningless, mundane, mindless, intermittent chatter. Louise directed Jerome to one of the vinyl, burgundy booths, marred with black veins and slight tears from decades of wear, opposite the bar as she visited the ladies room. "Here girl thanks a lot," Louise said as she returned Emma, the barmaid's, cologne. Louise touched each person seated at the bar as she exchanged pleasantries. While Louise was talking to the woman, Jerome overheard something about pig meat.

"Dark Bacardi and Coke, Louise?" Emma asked as she approached the couple's booth. She was Louise's age but a little heavier.

"Oh, make that with a dash of Rose's Lime, please," Louise added.

"Tonight, I need special instructions, huh? I been fixin' your drinks since Prohibition ended, but this evening, for some reason you need to be sure I don't fuck up; I get it."

"Aw girl, don't go off on me. You know how tight we are." Both women laughed. They were friends since high school; forty years ago.

"I'll have a scotch and water please." Jerome didn't see any Drambuie, so ordering a Rusty Nail may have been embarrassing.

Between sips Louise said, "It's amazing how predictable most of our customers are. They come in about the same time every day and buy the same smokes or booze."

"Then there are the hypochondriacs," Jerome added, "who, after I diagnose what ails them, will gladly pay an inflated price for placebos." Hypochondriacs or placebos were unfamiliar words, so Louise just smiled. Moments later Jerome said, "You've been with Sid since forever. How have you put up with him for so long?"

"I was his first Negro cashier when the neighborhood started changing, 15 years ago." Louise bit her lip, stared and then said, "He kept putting his hands where they didn't belong, so I gave him some; I was thirty pounds lighter then." Jerome lowered his eyelids, hiding his surprise.

"We had a thing for several years; he paid me and my rent. He would stop by two or three nights a week, have a drink out of his own bottle, spend five or ten minutes in the sack, which was the extent of his Johnson's attention position. It was a wham, bam, thank you maam. I could have read a magazine while he was doin his business, but that would have been rude." Louise laughed and then continued. "Anyway, afterward he headed for the suburbs, his wife, and four kids." Louise added, "Probably had help with them."

She lit another cigarette, took a long swallow of her second drink and said, "Then several young, fast-ass hussies started flat-backing for a few bucks and a bottle of cheap cologne. Sid stopped paying my rent, so I changed my door locks. Ever since, he's been jumping from one young heifer to another. Sid loves him some brown good thing; hell, they're younger, so what can I do? This rum has me talking too much." Louise took a pull from her cigarette and another long drink as she stared into the bottom of her glass.

Jerome, noticing her embarrassment said, "Younger isn't always better."

"Maybe that's why he keeps jumping," Louise said as her smile returned. She then asked, "How well do you know Dr. Ben?"

"Not well. I've noticed he gets everything he wants, free."

"And he doesn't pay any rent. He throws some wild parties, but I've never been invited. Guess I'm too old, the wrong sex, or both," Louise said. "I didn't think you were related."

"No one else does either. He humiliates me every time he loudly proclaims, 'Hi Cuz'." Jerome rolled his eyes, extended his tongue, and waved a limp wrist while raising his voice an octave with an exaggerated lisp.

While laughing hysterically, Louise said, "You better watch your backside Sugar, or hemorrhoids will be the least of your worries." Jovial conversation enhanced their evening. Louise taught Jerome how to dance the be-bop. Lester Young's *Lester Leaps In* and Duke Ellington's *A Train*, with Louise's riffing, added to their fun. Louise's bar-mates sent over drinks. They really couldn't afford to, but it was required to validate Louise's cachet. Three hours flew by.

"How tight are you and Turkey Stevens?" Louise asked.

"He's the reason I'm here."

"You know he did time for murder?"

"Why, no! Who did he kill?"

"He did the time, but not the crime. Word was, one of the Pershing's owners shot and killed a jealous husband when he was caught in bed with his wife. Turkey took the fall; pulled ten, did three. You don't do much time for killing one of us, especially if you spread enough green. Attorney Samuel Stovall defended him. Turkey's been on easy street since he got out five years ago."

After his fourth drink, Jerome stood, leaned on the table, and said, "Can you drive me home or should I call a livery?"

"Depends on whose home you're talking about. I live 'round the corner."

"Waash a minute," Jerome slurred, "I'm not…"

"Naw, you wait a minute." Louise was stone sober. "I know I'm drifting into middle age, and that I date married, dumb men, older than dirt, but working near you the last several months has made me remember being young. Having someone as fit and fine as you in my bed would be a thrill I haven't had in 20 years!"

"But Louise…"

"Relax Sugar," Louise stood, put Jerome's hands on her hips, and looked into his dancing eyes. "I don't expect nothing to come of it and I know we don't think alike. I just want to mean something to you for a little while." Louise pressed Jerome's hands and gyrated her waist. Her eyes intensified as she said, "Come home with me, please; just for an hour. If I don't introduce you to new worlds I'll appreciate your kindness and never mention it again. But if I do," Louise's eyes twinkled, she stepped closer, moved Jerome's hands over her curvaceous body and continued, "You can have me whenever you want any way you want, without strings." Louise's eyes were pleading. The drinks plus Louise's enticing invitation had aroused Jerome's libido and put his conscience to sleep.

"Let's go."

After an erotic and exciting three hours of lovemaking, Jerome ate two pieces of cold fried chicken, sprinkled with hot sauce, a slice of white bread and drank a glass of milk as he dressed.

It was 1:45 a.m., his neighborhood was asleep. Louise pulled a half-pint of scotch from her purse. "Pat this on your face, Sugar, then take a swig, but swish it in your mouth before swallowing." She took several pulls from her cigarette and blew smoke into Jerome's shirt and jacket. "There, now you smell like you've been out drinking with the boys. The smoke and scotch will kill any trace of perfume."

As Jerome walked a half block to his house, euphoria was replaced by reality, followed by guilt. "Damn," Jerome whispered at the noise his key made in the lock. He eased off his shoes, tiptoed through the house undressing and then entered his bedroom, clothes in hand. He eased into bed naked, without awakening Gail.

"You smelled like a distillery this morning. How much did you drink last night?" Gail asked when Jerome joined her and the girls for breakfast.

"Not much." *Oh man, that was lame.* Jerome picked up his fork, almost dropped it, started to reach for his coffee cup but thought better of it. "Turkey was in the store when I got off. We stopped by his place for a few. Since I wasn't driving I had to wait until Turkey was ready to leave, and you know how involved he gets." *There, that's better.*

"I started to call Scotty's, but didn't. Wouldn't want the world to know I can't keep up with my husband."

"If you had picked me up on time, you would have known where your husband was."

"I called the store a little after six; Sid said you were gone, so I couldn't pick you up. The girls and I had dinner with my parents at the train station. We got home after nine, what time did you get in?"

"Oh, I don't know. Hell, I made enough noise stumbling around to wake the dead."

"I guess I was more tired than I realized. Daddy Beau said he's not angry with you and that his offer still stands, but not forever." Gail hurried through her message. She picked up her orange juice, which washed the glass' sides before it got to her lips.

Michelle and Dana said together, "Daddy, when are we going home?" Michelle continued, "Granddaddy Beau said he misses us and if we…"

"Shut the… just, shut up!" Instantly regretting his words and tone, Jerome reached out and apologetically patted his girls' hands.

"Gail," Jerome said over a stony stare, "Do you think we should return to New Orleans?"

"No. Oh no! Certainly not!" Gail was afraid to touch anything, so she laced her fingers in front of her. She did not want to go through the home identification issue again. "The girls and I are just messengers, passing on what Daddy Beau said."

"Are you sure?"

"Absolutely; I told you," Gail said under her breath while widening her eyes, "and showed you, how I felt the other night. I definitely do not agree with the message." Gail looked down at her plate, then into her juice glass as she took a sip. She looked everywhere but across the table.

"Home is unique," Jerome said to his daughters as he gained their attention. "The word 'home' is very personal because it means so much, yet it means different places to different people." Jerome engaged his daughters' eyes and glanced in Gail's direction.

"When Granddaddy Beau says home he means New Orleans because that's where he has lived all of his life, and where he and Granny Beau raised Mommy. When we say home we mean Chicago because that's where we live, where Mommy and I work and where we will raise the two of you as all of us build pleasant memories." Jerome had his family's undivided attention. "Home describes where we have pleasant dreams, where we are comfortable, and where our most precious possessions are safe. Home is where you make friends and have parties. Home is where we feel protected. We may have many homes during a lifetime, but only one at a time. Your home is with your parents, not your grandparents. This house is our home, so we can't go <u>back</u> home, because we're already <u>at</u> home. Do you ladies understand?"

"Yes, Daddy," the girls said in unison. Their expressions were wide eyed and serious.

"Isn't this our home dear?" Jerome asked Gail.

"You're right honey. Oh yes; no doubt about it, this-is-our-home, our only home!" Gail found Jerome's discourse moving. She committed to calling Chicago home forever more. Jerome believed Gail was sincere. He knew his daughters didn't understand everything, but that was all right. For the first time he likened himself to his father, who would, with all the time required, explain life's complexities, like why we couldn't drink from the more desirable fountain that had a "Whites Only" sign above it, when Jerome was too young to understand.

"Thanks again for getting us invited to Samuel Stovall's birthday party," Jerome said. They were in Fred's Buick. Jerome had purchased a blue blazer, grey pants, a matching long sleeve sport shirt, and his first pair of tasseled loafers. He encouraged Gail to get a new outfit.

"No biggee," Fred said. "Last February his party lasted until…"

"Hey Esther, it's good to see you girl. You're looking mighty foxy," Jerome said, turning his head toward the rear seat. Esther feigned a weak smile. Jerome looked forward as he listened to Gail and Esther.

"That's a pretty dress Esther," Gail said, "and I really like your mink jacket. Jerome told me this was a casual affair, so I bought this waistcoat and slacks." Esther was wearing a bright red, flared dress, two inches above the knee, with a pinched waist, red stockings and red high heels.

Esther answered, "This old thing? I just threw it on at the last minute. I had completely forgotten about Sam and Charlotte's––I mean Paula's party; so many social events, so little time. Your colors are so, so dark, so morbid. Anything would have looked better than what you're wearing. Next time call me and I'll suggest something more appropriate."

Jesus, thought Jerome, *Esther is being downright insulting.*

"About time you got here!" Samuel said after opening his fifteen foot double door and inviting the arriving couples into his grand, glistening marble floored foyer. The Stovall's lived in Hyde Park, a prestigious community which was protected from blight and residential abandonment by the nationally renowned University of Chicago. Although adjacent to Bronzeville, Hyde Park had virtually no crime, no corruption, and, because of the university's teacher's demographics, was a montage of ethnicity; it had its own police force. A butler took the couples' outer garments.

"Jerome and Gail meet my lovely bride, Paula." Samuel placed his arm around Paula's small waist and pulled her close to him. Gail noted she was wearing dark grey slacks with two-inch heels; similar to her's. *So much for Esther's clothing evaluation*, thought Gail. The top of Paula's attractive beehive hairdo with interlaced pearls, reached Samuel's chin. Samuel and Jerome had grown close during his Wednesday visits to Felix and Bea's, and at Scotty's.

"Welcome," Paula smiled as she hugged Gail, touching faces on both sides while puckering. She shared a sincere, firm handshake with Jerome. Her smile, which revealed perfect teeth, along with the warmth in her light brown eyes, was rapturous. Paula's skin was flawless; the color of creamed coffee. She was about fifteen years younger than Samuel.

"How are you doing, stranger?" Paula grasped both of Fred's hands, pulled him toward her and kissed him on his cheek; she quickly wiped off the smudge. Fred was the best man at the Stovall's wedding 18 months ago; Esther would not attend. Paula's warm glow instantly became a frigid stare, her voice hardened as she said, "Hello Esther, surprised you found the time. Your baby doll dress is cute; a little tight and out of place, but cute; and your fake fur piece is rather dated."

"Fred didn't tell me this was a casual affair," Esther said as she looked away. Her voice was as unfriendly as Paula's.

"All our parties are casual dear. We know who we are without having to dress to impress––or do we?" Esther looked toward Fred, expecting him to chastise Paula. Fred returned her glance, but remained silent.

"Are we bopping tonight?" Fred whispered to Samuel.

"Hell, yes! It's my birthday, Man, so we're really getting down."

"Aw man, what a combo," Fred said as he leaned back slightly and pointed both forefingers toward Paula and Samuel's perfectly fitted, tailored black tops with muted stripes and yellow slugs validating the superb quality of the silk. "Where did you get those?"

"They were cut from the same bolt on Kowloon Island when we visited Hong Kong last summer. They tailored them in about an hour."

"You like?" Paula asked while doing a slow spin with arms outstretched; she had an exquisite shape.

"OK," Samuel said, "drinks are being served by waiters, food is in the dining room and kitchen, and folks are partying on all three levels, so enjoy." Samuel and Paula welcomed their next guests.

The foursome turned right into an enormous sunken living room. A baby grand piano occupied a far corner. There were four French antique furniture arrangements in various lengths covered with the same expensive fabric, including several ottomans. The flexibility allowed Paula to arrange her formal reception area in countless ways. The sculptured, plush, beige carpet enhanced the fabric. Scores of people were fashionably dressed in sophisticated casual wear, lounging and laughing, with drinks in hand.

While walking beside Gail in front of Fred and Jerome, Esther, without warning, bolted in the opposite direction. Gail, startled, smiled awkwardly at the husbands and then hurried after Esther. She sauntered into the parlor on the other side of the foyer, ignoring Gail who was close behind.

"Our problem is we don't do business with each other," Jerome overheard Rudolph "Tiny" Frazier lecturing three men sitting on a sofa. Tiny was jabbing his finger just above their heads, wearing a grave expression. The trio looked intimidated by their six foot six, over 300 pound captor. "I sell prime and choice meats, carry name brands and offer sales better than my competitors, but you can't tell it by my traffic patterns. All my stores are open twenty four-seven, but I do most of my business after the competition closes. And here is the worst part; some of our competitors, like Quality Foods, don't have any Negroes in responsible positions!"

"You think you have problems," a dentist, who was one of Tiny's captives, said. "Less than twenty percent of us professionals, present company included, use Negro doctors and dentists. They think their medical history would become cocktail party gossip. Hell, we're as professional as they are. We would starve to death if it wasn't for the colored union members and postal employees with good insurance."

Fred stopped a waiter, took two pea pickers, a potent lime juice and vodka drink off his tray, passed one to Jerome and whispered, "Tiny has three progressive franchised supermarkets. He's our biggest, but not our only, super mart store owner. He complains about business, but is doing very well. He's one of my clients."

We support our brethren, thought Jerome. *Glad we have been shopping at one of Tiny's supermarkets, Fred has identified a pediatrician, a gynecologist, and a dentist. Dr. Benjamin is already our general practitioner.*

Jerome and Fred meandered about the first floor, through the Florida Room and kitchen. They sipped their drinks, dipped in and out of small groups, and ingested finger food. Fred introduced Jerome when appropriate. He was impressed with all the titles and mentally photographed the faces. "What's bopping?" Jerome asked, remembering Fred's confidential question to Samuel when they arrived.

"It's a brother's only party, a BOP. We realize more deals are hatched at social events and on golf courses than in business meetings, so normally, we invite one or two O'Fays, hoping they will introduce some business opportunities, but when it's a real party, like tonight, we exclude them. They exclude us most of the time."

Eddie Williams, advertising manager for nationally distributed *Ebony Magazine* was playing bridge in the breakfast nook. Jerome overheard him say, "My primary job is to persuade Caucasian manufacturers to compete for the fourteen billion dollars Negroes earn each year." Eddie took the book, laughed and said, "You dudes thought I wasn't paying attention." Afterward he said, "Check this out, we're only eleven percent of the national population, yet we consume eighty percent of the scotch, but ad agencies won't place premium scotch ads in *Ebony.* They say their brands' prestige will drop among Negroes——and they're right!

"You know how it goes," Williams said after the surprised expressions subsided, "Once it's offered to all of <u>us</u>, it's not good enough for some of <u>us</u>. For instance, Cadillac has never advertised with <u>us</u>, and you know how many of <u>us</u> buy Cadillacs. Sometimes we have to sleep in 'em but we still buy 'em." Laughter followed Williams' witticism.

"Eddie makes $14 billion sound like something," Fred said as they moved on. "Actually it's less than three percent of America's gross income, which was $550 billion last year. Our earned percentage should be over $55 billion. That would be our fair share, but who said anything was fair?" Jerome and Fred laughed. "This is a test," Fred said, "What makes the publisher of *Ebony* a Super Trailblazer?" Jerome shrugged his shoulders.

"Most of <u>us</u> make money off <u>us</u>; insurance, retail, real estate, professional services, but *Ebony* gets most of their income from Caucasian companies whose products Negroes consume in high percentages like Riceland rice, Alaga syrup, record producers, plus cigarette and beer companies. His magazine brings hundreds of thousands of dollars into our community through his annual payroll.

"Walk ahead, I'll catch up," Fred said as he eased over to an attractive young lady, bent his head and patted the back of his neck. The lady laid her left hand in the bend of her right arm and spread her fingers over her mouth. Both looked away while having a very private conversation.

Hmm, thought Jerome, *she might be the reason Esther's mad.* An older distinguished gentleman wearing a rust-colored suede coat over a thick white turtleneck sweater was standing aside a glowing fireplace in the library, expounding to a male audience.

"Our problem is that we are too complacent. A big black ass in some Johnson grass is often our ultimate objective. Hell, we can't make any serious money until we can control our testosterone." Everyone smiled or chortled. Mr. Suede puffed on his curved pipe, noticed Jerome and asked,

"Will you share with us seasoned lions your thoughts young man?" Mr. Suede backed away from the fireplace and, with a gesture, gave Jerome his audience.

"Well," Jerome said nervously, "I'm amazed at both your accomplishments and your dissatisfactions, but without the latter perhaps you wouldn't have the former." Jerome sipped his drink, then, encouraged by a few affirmative nods, continued. "W.E.B. DuBois hoped the 'talented tenth'––that's those who are here, would lead the underclass––that's those who are not here, from the valley, full of ignorance, criminal activity, drug usage, and deprivation, to a plateau of education, prosperity and self-worth. Imagine what Bronzeville would become if each of us lifted one of us, and then each lifted person would lift another. What a positive impact on racial progress that would have over a generation or two." Several voiced their agreement and urged Jerome to continue.

"I've visited several cities recently, and have found Bronzeville to be exceptional. My opinion is shared by *Time Magazine*, who named Bronzeville "The Black U.S. economic capital," as its cover story in March 1938, almost a generation ago." Jerome's audience silently asked each other, did you know that? The silent response was, no. Jerome discovered the article in the Bronzeville library's archives while preparing himself for future discussions with Fred Hawkins.

"And what will be your drummer's beat?" someone asked.

"To master the drugstore business, and over time, develop a chain with Sidney Reis, my boss."

"You think Sid will offer you a partnership, even with a significant investment?" another asked.

"The value is in the mutual respect and synergism, not in the investment."

"There's not a successful salt-and-pepper business team in the country," Mr. Suede said, "but don't let us bust your bubble. A lot of things happen here before happening elsewhere. What would make more sense is your partnering with Harold Oldham. He already has five stores and can always use someone of your apparent aptitude and intelligence."

The provocative conversation flowed from one subject to another. Fred rested his hand on Jerome's shoulder and eased him out of the conclave. "Hope you didn't embarrass me by saying something stupid. That was Criminal Court Justice Vernon Grantham leading the discussion."

"Damn," Jerome said softly as they walked away, "he asked me my name and wrote it down."

While going up the spiral staircase, Fred said to a dark, well-dressed gentleman coming down, "Well, if it isn't Bronzeville's drugstore tycoon."

"You calling me a coon, man?" Harold Oldham teased. After introductions, Harold said, "So you're the new pill-pusher Turkey mentioned. How are you and Slippery Sid getting along?" Harold was south of six feet. His apparel was conservative and expensive. He could have been a Brooks Brothers clothing store ad for *Ebony*, if their ads ever appeared in *Ebony*––which they didn't.

"Great! He's taught me a lot already, but I still have much more to learn. Every day I work at being worth more than I was the day before."

"Man, that's a beautiful attitude. Damn Fred, why didn't you point Jerome in my direction when he hit town?"

"We'll talk later man; right now we've got to find our women." Harold shook Jerome's hand with a sincere smile. Harold's large diamond ring interfered with the handshake. Fred and Jerome continued up the stairs.

"Harold's bad news," Fred said. "Very few people know that Harold has a lifetime contract with his partners."

"What kind of contract?"

"If he breaks his contract with the mob, it may cost him his life. He wanted me to handle his books. I took a look, didn't like what I saw and refused."

"How do you know that only a few people know about Harold's business affiliations?" Jerome asked.

"Because if it were known, he wouldn't be here; you don't see Turkey do you? 'Nuff said."

"Speaking of missing people, I haven't seen Doctor Benjamin."

"Fags and heterosexuals don't mix my brother."

"Hello, excuse my incursion," Fred said politely as he interrupted conversations, exchanged pleasantries and discreetly passed out business cards. Several minutes later, with fresh drinks, Fred and Jerome went back downstairs heading for the lower level. Jerome glanced into the parlor and saw Gail sitting on a huge pillow among a group of older women. He waved; Gail smiled.

"Who has that ruggedly handsome man's attention?" a heavyset woman asked; she was sharing a love seat.

"That's my husband," Gail said proudly. Gail had been sitting at Esther's feet for almost an hour. Esther was in a chair and talking to everyone. She had not introduced Gail when they joined the group; consequently, Gail had been ignored.

"My compliments," Mrs. Heavyset said.

"Thank you——I think. My name is Gail Gerard."

"I'm Geneva Grantham. Your husband's like prime steak dear, with just enough fat to add flavor. There are scores of women in Bronzeville who would like to screw that hunk." Gail was startled. She looked quizzically at Mrs. Grantham, who sipped her special ordered Manhattan cocktail, and then said, "Pretty young pepper, don't get upset, over the decades we older women have weathered the whorish hurricanes that have tried to suck, or blow, our husbands out of our homes. Now, our men are settled——not faithful, you understand, but mature and disciplined enough to sleep around and not get fidgety, which leaves us with a small measure of dignity." Several of the group endorsed Mrs. Grantham's comments with jibes regarding their husbands' philandering ways and the obvious mistakes they had made trying to cover their tracks.

"Incidentally," Geneva said, "the first Mrs. Stovall didn't survive the hurricanes. Paula met Samuel at Scotty's, you know, where our boys bond? As our hostess manifests, there's much more than men bonding going on at Scotty's." The gaggle agreed.

"The tragedy is," Geneva continued, "Charlotte Stovall couldn't hire Attorney Rachael Piernas because of her relationship with Samuel, so she received the smallest of settlements without child custody and was forced to leave town. That's why what's-her-name was able to afford that new living room." Geneva Grantham rolled her eyes in disgust.

"Well, maybe men will stray from time to time; what's the big deal?" Gail said, shocking her audience with an insincere expression at best. Gail adjusted her pillow and looked down.

"Yeah," Geneva responded, "and what do you say when goo-goo eyed chippies, like that skinny, sexpot over there, with the artificial boobs, flaunt their affairs with our husbands? Those floozies hope we, who have paid our dues in spades, split!" Gail looked where Geneva motioned; she continued, "Well, that's my husband's current plaything, and I'm going to let her know I know what's going on before this party ends!" The woman was Andrea, Paula's close friend.

"You mentioned spades, do you play bridge?" Gail asked. Their exchange was becoming argumentative and Gail wanted out.

"You keep on being naïve, Ms. Baby Face, and a tender sender, even younger and prettier than you, will have your man and gone!" Geneva turned away, took a sip of her drink, and began another conversation.

"Shhh, here she comes," and "Be quiet girl," grabbed Gail's attention; everyone fell silent. Paula was standing among the group. She called each wife by their last name, smiled and awaited their "polite" responses. They all were friends of the former Mrs. Stovall and had reluctantly attended the party because of their husbands. After the stilted greetings, Paula extended her hand to Gail and said, "Come on girl, let's get you something to eat. You're the only one here who can afford to gain a pound or two." Gail smiled and accepted the lift. The wives smothered their hisses with pouted lips and scornful eyes.

"Yes, I am famished," Esther said as she stood, smoothed her dress and followed Paula and Gail. Paula exchanged glances with Gail, silently asking who invited her. Gail instantly liked Paula and was pleased to have Esther tagging along.

"Your buffet looks delicious. I haven't had okra since I left ho… New Orleans." The buffet included deviled eggs, potato salad, and fried chicken, three of Jerome's favorites. Gail also placed small portions of green beans with almonds, collard greens laced with shallots, and apple cobbler on Jerome's plate.

"Sorry, I can't take credit," Paula said, as she spooned several of the tasty offerings onto two plates, "We used caterers. You and Jerome should come by for dinner, then you'll see what happens when I'm let loose in the kitchen."

"Why yes," Esther, chimed in, "That sounds like a…"

"Not this time, Esther. Let's be clear, the invitation was to Gail and Jerome."

As the three women proceeded to the lower level, Gail and Paula carrying two plates, Esther carrying one, they spotted Fred next to Andrea with Jerome at the bar. Esther seethed, "How could he sit next to that vixen? He knows the real deal."

Before the ladies could move down the steps and through the crowd, Fred, with Jerome in tow, moved to a table for four, leaving Andrea at the bar. Paula handed Fred one of her plates, saying, "I thought you might be hungry, others weren't hardly concerned," and then took a seat next to Andrea.

"Sit here," Fred smiled, offering Esther a seat at his table. Gail had sat next to Jerome, and Fred was standing aside his seat with the plate Paula had given him. Esther was prepared to raise holy hell at Fred's previous sitting arrangement, but it no longer existed.

"Thank you Babe, I was starving," Jerome said to Gail between mouthfuls. The younger people, including Gail and Jerome, filled the dance area. Jerome surprised Gail by be-bopping; she had trouble keeping in sync. She wondered where Jerome had learned the new dance steps, but didn't ask. Esther and Fred sat, ignoring each other.

The disk jockey shouted, "IT'S DO THE GRIND TIME!" which was the current rage and the most explicit dance in years. A chant swelled, "PARTAY! PARTAY! PARTAY!" The music volume increased, people upstairs came down, including Judge and Mrs. Grantham.

Gail and Jerome, who had returned to their seats, were shocked to see refined, sophisticated ladies make such lewd moves in the name of dance. Andrea, with hands clasped behind her head and knees slightly bent, threw her hips like a belly dancer, moving as if her perfectly shaped body was boneless. "Aw churn that butter, baby," her dance partner said. Other dancers formed a semi-circle, and clapped in time with the music. Andrea lifted her already short, black dress, bent her knees further, and danced even more explicitly.

"See how this fits, home-wrecker," Geneva Grantham said as she poured her iced drink down Andrea's back. Esther shrieked joyously at Mrs. Grantham's action. A surprised Judge Grantham disappeared.

Andrea whirled and spotted the empty glass in Geneva's hand. Without missing a beat, Andrea backed her wet butt into Geneva until she stumbled off the dance floor. The crowd roared.

"We better leave before this party turns ugly," Fred leaned across the table and said to Jerome. "Half the wives here are mad anyway." Gail smiled; she knew Esther was in the mad half.

"Tanks for a wunnerful evening, your gracious hospitality is only exceeded…" Jerome was leaning forward and delivering an elaborate farewell to the Stovall's at their front door. Gail smiled at Samuel and

Paula as she gently pulled Jerome away; he was still elucidating. The Stovall's laughed.

"Mercenary leeches!" Esther declared as the two couples walked into the cold night air. Esther was walking independent of Fred, stumbling a bit. Gail held Jerome's arm and snuggled.

"And she wonders why I don't take her out more," Fred turned to Esther and added, "we may be heading in the wrong direction, wife of mine, but I'm taking you home."

"If you men spent half the time with your wives that you do with the streetwalkers who magically show up at these affairs, we wouldn't be so damn angry!" Esther shouted.

"See what I mean?" Fred laughed. "She thinks we're magicians." Esther continued to complain. Fred interrupted, "And if you wives wouldn't isolate yourselves, whining to each other, making yourselves angry, maybe we would magically appear and enjoy your company."

"Yeah, ah dere's ah, ah, magic in de air," Jerome said imitating *Amos 'n Andy*, "Ah yeah dat's what it are, ah magic." Jerome laughed out loud and looked at Gail, who tugged on Jerome's arm as if he were her mischievous little boy.

That night Jerome and Gail made love, using the removal-in-the-nick-of-time method. Both were fulfilled, but Gail thought she and Jerome deserved better. She imagined several scenarios under which Jerome had learned how to be-bop. As she drifted off with her head on Jerome's chest, she decided to talk to her gynecologist about having her fallopian tubes tied. She realized the surgery was against Catholic doctrine, but with Jerome's approval she would have the operation performed.

End of Chapter Six

CHAPTER SEVEN

Since Samuel's birthday party, Paula had invited Jerome and Gail to dinner several times. During their first visit Gail suggested playing bridge. Paula learned bridge easily, especially under Gail's delicate, fun filled tutelage. Paula gave Gail cooking tips and recipes. Samuel suggested Jerome take golf lessons. The two couples became good friends.

"Do you know why I rescued you from those stuffy, old, prudes at our party?" Paula asked. She and Gail were having lunch in an up-scale café on North Michigan Boulevard after shopping. (Paula shopped, Gail shopped vicariously).

"No, girl, and I've wondered about that."

"Because I didn't like the way they were treating you. Those dried up hussies, who probably haven't been laid in years, have 'young bitch' paranoia."

"Is that a serious condition?" Gail laughed.

"Oh, yes," Paula said as she swallowed a mouthful of Waldorf salad, "Serious enough to cost some of them their marriages! Every time their man comes home late, they nag, 'you've probably been screwing some young bitch again,' which becomes a self-fulfilling prophecy."

"How do you know what wives say to their husbands?" Gail was having crab salad garnished with boiled egg.

"Because unhappy husbands tell all, especially after a few drinks; Samuel used to complain like crazy," Paula said over a sly expression, "that's when I decided he was eligible."

The two gorgeous women finished their lunch while ignoring flirtatious remarks from leering White men. On other occasions, more serious womanizers had picked up the lovely twosome's checks after sending a bottle of champagne to their table which, after being poured by the Maître d', went untouched.

"Is it okay if I go to lunch with Fred? Jerome asked Sid."

"Don't stay too long."

"Alphonso Major," Fred said at the B.S. Table, "recently started an ad agency targeting Caucasian-owned companies who wanted an edge in influencing Negroes; he calls his print and electronic commercials, 'special invitations.'"

"Is there anything we can't do?" Samuel asked.

"A brother to watch, that's all I'm saying. He used to work for *Ebony*, now he's self-employed. OK, who knows how Thomas H. Jackson, publisher of *Ebony*, got his start?" Fred was the self-appointed B.S. Table's historian. Without waiting for an answer, he continued, "In order to help Tommy finance his first publication, his mother hocked her furniture for a $500 loan; now how many of your mothers would do that?" Fred smiled.

"My mother wouldn't buy me lunch," Buddy said, while buttering his third corn muffin.

"Here's another little known fact," Fred continued. "Several years ago Richard Thompson, manufacturer of Easy Wave products, went downtown to Second National Bank, asked the loan officer for $250. 'We don't loan Negroes money,' the loan officer said before Richard could sit down."

"I know that burned his buns," Buddy said, glaring.

"You're right," Fred continued, "but instead of getting angry he got smart. He asked, 'Sir, who does loan us money?' The banker was surprised by Richard's politeness and aggressiveness. He said, 'Courtesy Loans, our subsidiary. Their interest rate is a little higher but they will make you a loan if you have good credit.' When Richard mentioned starting a business to the Courtesy Loan officer, he became burnt toast."

"So where did the money come from?" Jerome asked. Most knew the answer, having heard Fred tell the story numerous times.

"He got it from another Courtesy Loan office. He flashed the banker's card and told the second manager he was going home to Mississippi on vacation. He got the money in a New York minute; the irony is Richard was born in Chicago."

"So," Jerome said, "tell the truth, get the boot; tell a lie, get the loot."

"A better lesson," Fred added, "tell Whitey what he wants to hear. I mean Whitey knows we take vacations, but he doesn't believe we understand business fundamentals, right?"

"The amazing thing is how little money was needed to launch businesses that now generate millions of dollars and hundreds of jobs." Jerome was greeted with stares and nods; no one had said that before.

When Jerome returned from the men's room, Fred said, "You just volunteered to work on the upcoming mayoral campaign."

"What, did I miss a meeting?" Jerome looked around the table. Everyone looked away; several choked while chuckling.

After swallowing a mouthful of smothered chicken with mashed potatoes and gravy, Buddy explained. "Congressman Dawson is backing some dude named Mark O'Malley to run against Kennelly. O'Malley is a supervisor in the county commissioner's office and has never held political office. He asked the congressman for his support before announcing his candidacy, which showed respect. If O'Malley wins, the congressman will be able to name high ranking officers in the police and fire departments––only in Bronzeville of course––plus appoint precinct captains to city jobs. The new mayor will ask Chicago based corporations to consider Negroes for mid-management positions. A loosening of nuisance laws in Bronzeville will also be forthcoming."

Buddy's right, thought Jerome, a number of my customers have menial jobs in spite of having college degrees. "I'll be happy to help the congressman; I owe him big time," Jerome said. *How does Buddy stay so thin while eating everything on the table?*

"Has anyone bought a New York Life policy from Mercer Woods?" asked Stuart Sykes, Vice President-Comptroller of Shoreline Insurance Company. "I hear he's targeting professionals."

"I haven't, but he has been asking," Leo Lafarge said, "and his presentations are very professional and convincing." Others made similar comments.

"Ladies and gentlemen, the economic invasion has begun," Fred said in a dramatic tone, while waving his finger in front of his face. "For years the Caucasian insurance industry has been monitoring the Negro Insurance industry's executives' tax returns. To test their assumptions, they hired Mercer Woods. The token Negro is doing better than expected; more hires will follow. In a few years Negro insurance companies will only be able to insure the underclass, those who can't afford to pay premiums in advance. Negro owned insurance companies will become an endangered species."

"How in hell can Caucasian insurance companies steal what it has taken us a century to develop?" Stuart asked.

"Ask the Indians," Buddy said as he reached for another muffin.

"Has your company considered selling insurance to Caucasians?" Jerome asked Stuart. The table awaited his answer; Stuart did not respond.

"Same thing happened in South Africa," Buddy said. "Six years ago, White folks interjected laws that disenfranchised native Africans. They call it Apartheid." When Buddy reached for Rachael's muffin; she slapped his hand.

"Jerome is right; Integration is the new direction," the radiant, cocoa-colored Rachael Piernas said. She was, as usual, sartorially splendid in a grey wool suit with a mink collar. Earlier, when Rachael entered, congratulations were extended. She had been recommended to President Eisenhower by Illinois republican governor William Stratton, for Deputy U.S. Solicitor General, whose responsibility included representing the United States before the U.S. Supreme Court. Helen Freeman, DDS, had extended her hand across the table; they touched fingers.

The Chicago Defender had Rachael's photo on the front page, above the fold. *The Chicago Chronicle*, Chicago's leading Caucasian newspaper, ran a one column, five-inch, no-photo story on page six. They used a small "n" when identifying her as Negro.

"Incidentally," Rachael said, "I bought a policy from Mercer and was pleased that he didn't suggest I cancel my existing policies, even though his premiums were less." She mouthed a small portion of her lunch, and then continued, "But I digress from the integration issue. The Supreme Court has recently outlawed segregated schools and restricted covenants. Next month, President Eisenhower's ICC secretary will ban segregation on interstate trains and busses. Airlines already integrate."

"Airlines integrate passengers on the plane, but Southern airports segregate waiting rooms, drinking fountains, and restaurants," Leo Lafarge, a frequent air traveler, said.

"Point taken," Rachael acquiesced, but stayed on message. "We should demonstrate our willingness to meld by inviting Caucasians to join our business organizations, even before we're asked to join theirs."

"If integration is a two way street," Felix said as he pulled up a chair, "why is all my traffic going one way? A lot of you are paying more for lunch in White-owned restaurants and enjoying it less just because you can, but nobody White eats here. Business has dropped off at the Pershing and the Manor House too because downtown hotels are now accommodating us. What we need are the benefits of integration, and the benefits of segregation."

"Felix is as right as rain," Fred said. "Less than one tenth of one percent of our discretionary income is spent with Negro businesses and, because of integration, even that's dwindling." Most of the B.S. Table regulars were guilty as charged.

"That's what I'm talking about," Felix said as he stretched his arm into the center of the table and touched it with his fore-finger. Felix then went back to work.

"Next Thursday evening," Sid said as he and Jerome filled prescriptions, "I'm taking you to the annual Chicago Druggist Association Smoker. We'll have Allen cover for us." Because business had increased, Sid had hired his second Negro pharmacist, Allen, to work part-time, which gave him and Jerome a little more time off, especially on weekends. His hourly compensation was half Jerome's.

"That sounds like something special Sid, I can hardly wait!" Jerome thought, *I knew this relationship was going in the right direction. A partnership may be just around the corner.* To prepare, Jerome read current trade journals. He memorized optimum square footage dollar volume yields by product category and researched display techniques for higher profit merchandise, like inexpensive foot and athletic wear.

The smoker was held in a softly lit parlor in the posh downtown Palmer House Hotel; about 200 Caucasian druggists were present. Jerome felt comfortable in his blue suit; not one druggist wore expensive clothes. *Looks like Willie McGhee was right again,* thought Jerome, *we do spend too much on clothes. Most of these druggists dress like paupers, but I'll bet, like Sid, each one has a significant stock portfolio. I haven't heard anybody at the B.S. Table mention stocks.*

As they walked toward the open bar, Sid paused and introduced Jerome to Erwin McKlosky. He was slightly stooped, 70-ish, with alert green eyes and a firm grip. Sid was pulled away by two of his fellows.

"Tell me m'boy," Erwin asked. Eagerness filled Jerome's eyes; anticipation caused his heart rate to increase, "What do you think of Ernie Banks, a Hall-of-Fame candidate already, eh?"

"Great shortstop," a deflated Jerome answered, "But I'm more interested in the new gondolas featured in last month's *Drug Store Age* that hold twenty percent more merchandise because of built-in extenders and more flexible shelf adjusters. Do you know if anyone on the South Side has them?"

Erwin looked at Jerome as if he were speaking a foreign language. Then he said, "Do you think Congressman Dawson will support mayoral candidate O'Malley?"

"Yes. Most Negroes support O'Malley because Kennelly has kept us out of Chicago's economic main stream and keeps our schools segregated. Incidentally Mr. McKlosky, do you get many prescriptions for the new antibiotic Abbott just introduced?"

"Excuse me Sonny; I have to see a man about a dog." Erwin shuffled off as if his shoelaces were tied together. He glanced back at Jerome over his half-moon glasses several times.

A chubby Negro, whose name tag read Peter Monroe, sidled up to Jerome and whispered, "Say, man, do you see Negro-ologist stamped on my forehead? How in hell do I know what Sugar Ray Robinson had for breakfast? I'm trying to learn the drugstore business."

"I've attended these affairs for years," said grey-goateed Negro, Edgar Rhodes, to Peter and Jerome, "And I have never seen any Negro drugstore owners, like Harold Oldham, here. For Caucasian druggist, this is, 'Show-off-your-Negro-Night.' Eat and drink all you want, smile a lot, talk politics and sports, and you may be invited back next year, but," Edgar lowered his voice, "mention opening your own store, and you might become unemployable within this clique. Have you noticed how they stop talking business when we might overhear?"

A couple of minutes later, a joke caused the three to laugh, which attracted attention. Edgar warned, "Oh, oh, they're watching us; we better split up before we are accused of taking over their association." They dispersed.

A familiar voice said, "What do you think of our smoker, Laddie?" Jerome recognized Sol Gitel, who owned four drugstores, including the largest in Bronzeville, which was part of the Certified Drugs franchise system, which allowed him to compete with Walgreens. Jerome had visited Sol's largest store often for merchandising ideas. He was considered a shoplifter until Jerome introduced himself. Afterwards Sol and Jerome discussed business trends.

"Well, your membership is very interested in our views regarding Negroes in sports and politics," Jerome answered. "I'm waiting for someone to ask me to do the Sammy Davis Jr. split."

"Sid just suggested our association buy a controlling block of apple futures so we can raise the price at harvest time and make a bundle. Now you wouldn't be interested in that, would you?" Sol said.

"Of course not, nor am I interested in my economic future or the education of my children." Jerome stared at Sol for a long moment.

During Jerome's visits Sol had decided Jerome was a serious-minded, intelligent Negro; the first one he had met. Their present conversation confirmed his opinion. "I apologize for my peers' behavior. The next time you visit, we'll talk seriously, I promise." Sol patted Jerome on the shoulder and said loudly, "I agree, Buddy Young is an outstanding running back," then walked away. Jerome was confused until he turned and saw Sid standing behind him.

"O'Malley kicked Kennelly's ass!" shouted Jerome as he entered the drugstore. O'Malley's victory meant Congressman Dawson's clout would return. It also meant leniency when a Negro had committed a misdemeanor such as traffic violations if co-signed by his precinct captain. Prostitution, gambling, after-hour clubs and "victimless" crimes, with the proper pay-offs, would once again flourish. A seasoned politician once said, "Chicago ain't ready for reform," that also included Bronzeville.

Full color brochures with photos of O'Malley and Dawson, arm in arm, with endorsements from Black preachers, entertainment and sports celebrities, had been mailed only to Bronzeville residents. Negro-sensitive collaterals had to be kept within the Negro community; they would cost O'Malley votes if seen by Caucasians.

Collections were made at every Negro church, barber shop, and pool hall. Election pundits knew people followed their money to the polls, no matter the amount given. A hand-written thank you note was signed by the candidate and the congressman and then mailed to large Negro contributors, like national entertainers and policy lords.

Voters had to be registered. Even though dead residents voted in Chicago elections, sometimes more than once, live, warm bodies were still essential. Hundreds of welfare recipients after promising to vote Democrat were given five dollars by precinct captains, supposedly, to cover baby-sitting costs while voting.

During the campaign, due to his significant fund raising from B.S. Table regulars, his intellect, and his public speaking skills, Jerome rose from envelope stuffer in a church basement to president of Bronzeville's Young Democrats for O'Malley, with an office and a phone in Bronzeville's headquarters. Jerome added significant strategies in late-night brainstorming sessions. He had asked that Alphonso Major be commissioned to produce Negro-oriented commercials and collaterals without success.

At many of the headquarters meetings, O'Malley publically expressed his undying gratitude to Jerome and repeatedly spoke of his unrequited loyalty to Congressman Dawson. Jerome and candidate O'Malley talked at length on occasion and developed a mutual respect. O'Malley and Jerome never socialized; their families photographed together would have been a liability among White voters.

The primary election followed predictions: the White vote split between O'Malley and Kennelly, the predictable Negro vote carried O'Malley to victory. In Chicago, winning the Democratic primary, was tantamount to winning the election.

"Good," responded Sid after hearing Jerome proclaim victory, "Now maybe you can get your work done. We still have spring and summer merchandise in the basement, already!" Sid had given Jerome time off to work in candidate O'Malley's campaign. "You never know," Sid had confided to a fellow Jewish drugstore owner, "the young, long shot Mick just might win, giving me some clout because I loaned him my boy."

"Damn! Would you look at that," Buddy said. He was commenting on the horrific photos in a September 1955 publication of *Jet Magazine* that was being passed around the B.S. Table. Emmett "Bobo" Till, a 14 year old Bronzeville boy, had been beaten savagely, one eyeball hung from its socket. He was shot in the head and then tossed in the Tallahatchie River. An exhaust fan was tied around his neck with barbed wire. He was so disfigured, dental records were the only way his mother could identify him. The tragedy had occurred while he was visiting relatives in Money, Mississippi.

Emmett had said "Hey, baby," to a white teen-age girl in front of a store.

"His mother," funeral director Kenneth Appling said, as the dreadful pictures were being viewed, "had insisted we leave his coffin open so the world could see 'the manifestation of hate in White men.'"

The two kidnappers were found not guilty on all charges, and later admitted having committed the crime.

"I wonder how much pain he endured before succumbing," Buddy asked, mostly of himself. The ghastly photos spoke volumes. Bronzeville's premier Negro radio commentator disparaged at length the inhumane White men who had done this. "It's enough to make a Negro turn Black," ended his radio oratory.

In December, 1955, Felix and Bea's topical conversation included Rosa Parks' arrest in Montgomery, Alabama for refusing to give up her bus seat in the adjustable "Negroes Only" section to a White man. Rosa Parks, remembering Emmett Till, had determined, "enough is enough." Because of her stellar reputation, the Negroes of Montgomery decided to "sit" with her by boycotting the bus line. An unknown preacher, Dr. Martin Luther King Junior, reluctantly assumed leadership of the economic protest. He was 26.

Nothing will come of it, was the consensus of the B.S. Table.

To prepare for his second Christmas, Jerome had been working extra hours since mid-November. He worked 84 hour weeks instead of the normal 60, without off-days. Sid had offered Jerome extra pay, but he had refused. Jerome considered himself an essential part of Tailor's Drugs and believed working extra hours without additional compensation would validate his commitment and positive attitude. Sid thanked him. "You will be handsomely rewarded in the not-too-distant future, Jer."

During Jerome's sixteen month tenure, he had become a master merchandiser. He moved product repeatedly to improve visibility, shelf capacity, and impulse purchases. He added a shelf of large two-by-fours to the gondolas during the Christmas shopping season. Sales had increased significantly. Every crevice was yielding profits.

"Merry Christmas, Baby," Jerome sang, imitating Charles Brown. He awakened Gail with a light kiss. "I've already started the coffee, the girls are dying to open their presents."

"What time did you get home?" Gail asked while stretching.

"Oh, I'm not sure," Jerome lied, "but it was after midnight." *About two and a half hours after midnight.* "Turkey called just before we closed and invited us to a VIP party at the Pershing. I didn't think you could get a baby-sitter, so I dropped by intending to stay only a few minutes. Celebrities were all over the place! I put the tricycle together after I came home. It's under the tree. C'mon, let's go up front."

"So there really is a Santa Claus, huh?" Gail said; her penetrating eyes and tight jaws attacked Jerome's conscience. Turkey had called last night to wish the Gerards a merry Christmas; he said he hadn't seen Jerome in quite awhile. Paula, while warning Gail about husbands' infidelity, had told her not to nag unless she wanted to push Jerome away, but to let him know she knew when he was lying.

Oh, oh, she knows something, and this isn't the first time I've had that impression. I'd better cool it. No side action is worth losing my family over, decided Jerome.

Two, three-foot dolls with long, blonde hair that could be lengthened and styled, plus several wardrobe changes, were gifts to Michelle and Dana from their grandparents. They opened other gifts, but after each one, the girls returned to the blue eyed blondes.

"Here's a present for you, Honey, from Daddy Beau," Gail said as she passed Jerome a gift-wrapped box. It was a bright colored, hand painted hula girl tie.

"Conrad knows I'll never wear this." Jerome tossed the tie and box into the Christmas wrap trash bag. Gail agreed with Jerome's assessment; she realized her daddy was insulting Jerome and she shared his affront.

"Look at what Santa Claus sent me!" exclaimed Gail as she pulled off her robe and slipped into a Ranch Mink coat from Daddy Beau. Her short night gown was hidden under the mid-length fur. Gail's legs looked perfect as she stood on her toes and modeled her new treasure.

Even though they had agreed not to exchange gifts, Jerome gave Gail an amethyst necklace and earring set, her birthstone, and she gave him an expensive ostrich-skin wallet. His current one was a high school graduation present from his mother.

The Christmas of 1955 was Jerome's first spent with his family. Last year, his first in Chicago, he had to work. For the first four Christmases of their marriage they had been separated by hundreds, sometimes thousands of miles.

Because sales had exceeded Sid's highest expectations, Jerome received a Christmas bonus. They had no bills except their mortgage, so it went straight into savings. The Gerards made and received long distance phone calls to and from family members. Jerome in jeans, white socks and a Polo shirt, rolled around the hardwood floor with his daughters as they ate chocolates and cookies. He exaggerated his pain when Michelle collected rent while playing Monopoly. Jerome thought, *next year I'm taking my family to midnight mass.* Gail began preparations for cooking her first Christmas dinner.

"Jer, your hard work is paying off," Sid said a couple of weeks into the New Year. "Even though you have been with me for less than two years, I want you as a partner."

"A partnership, wow!"

"Well, you've earned it. We'll draw up the paperwork soon, but you can begin sharing in the profits now. As you have probably noticed, I skim off some cash daily and bank it in a special savings account. Starting now, I'll set aside ten dollars a day for you as a tax-free Christmas bonus for next December, but don't tell anyone, not even Gail."

"I won't Sid, and thanks a lot. Incidentally, when will we put our partnership in writing?"

"Be patient with me Son," Sid said through a fatherly smile, as he patted Jerome on his back. "Just keep up the good work; I'll take care of you." He wanted to keep Jerome happy––at least for now.

"I know it's only June, Sid, but my in-laws may be visiting soon and I wanted to buy a dining room suite and make some repairs on my home," Jerome said during a slow period; Sid was grumbling while paying invoices. "Can I have an advance on my Christmas bonus?"

"We'll see, Son, we'll see. Now where was I?" Sid returned to his bookkeeping.

"My figures indicate I have about $2,000. A thousand would help me..."

"I said we'll see!" Sid slammed his palm on the counter as he shouted. Louise and her customer were startled. Sid's scornful stare carried the impact of an axe handle shoved into Jerome's gut. "Damn boy, I promised you a bonus in December and that's when you'll get it, not one day sooner. That's the trouble with you people, can't manage your money no matter how much you make. Now leave me the hell alone so I can pay these damn bills, or you won't get one red cent. You know, it's still MY money!"

"I'm sorry Sid, I just thought…"

"That's another thing. You think too damn much, instead of doing what I say. Now go up front and get some work done for a change!"

It was another blow to the gut. *Sid sounds like he hates me!*

From time to time, Sid yelled at Jerome, Louise, and the other employees, but it was more like an impatient father. This scolding sounded like the final step before getting fired. With his shoulders slumped, his head bowed, and his mind completely disoriented, Jerome went downstairs. He sat on a stack of empty Coca Cola cases, cupped his face in his hands and cried profusely. He hadn't cried so hard since he was fourteen when his father died. This was the worst tragedy of his adult life. Jerome was mentally shattered.

I worked for three weeks, from open to close, so he and his family could visit Israel. When they returned I told him any extra salary was my gift toward their vacation. A lot of people have told me, "Never trust a Jew." I told them they didn't know Sid. Hell, I don't know Sid! Jerome reviewed the confrontation. I think too much? Every idea of mine that we have tried, worked. You people…? When did I become a faceless, nameless part of the underclass? Can't manage my money? I didn't say I was broke, I just asked for a portion of what was promised.

"Where's Sid?" Jerome asked Louise after composing himself and returning upstairs.

"Oh, he won't be back until it's time to relieve you," Louise said. Their affair had cooled months ago. She begged for a trip to ecstasy-land often, but Jerome had refused. Initially Louise was hurt, but Jerome thought, based on their civility toward each other, time had healed the rejection. "And you ain't seen nothing yet," Louise added, wearing a smirk that looked as if she had solved the mystery of eternal life.

For several weeks Sid left immediately when Jerome arrived. He never mentioned their partnership or Jerome's bonus. Gradually normalcy returned.

In late September, Sid arrived with a young Jewish man in tow. His curly dark hair almost reached Jerome's shoulder. He was thin with dozens of facial zits. He was wearing a grey sweatshirt with University of Illinois emblazoned across the front. Khakis and saddle oxfords affirmed him being a college student.

"Here's your bonus, Boy. It's a damn shame you became so impatient," Sid handed Jerome a business size envelope. "It's not what you expected, some things came up. Meet my nephew, Joel Turner, and he is my nephew. Joel will receive his degree in pharmacology next spring. In the meantime he will supervise you and Allen while I manage the new store."

"Supervise me––wha, what new store!?" It was the axe handle to the gut once again.

"The one in South Shore; I mentioned it a couple of months ago, but as usual you forgot. Show Joel around while I'm gone. Remember, he's in charge." Sid hurried out. Joel stood behind the pharmacy counter grinning. He had never been in charge of anything.

Jerome rushed downstairs and opened the envelope. *Only five hundred dollars! It should have been $2,700!* Jerome's stomach soured; he ran to the bathroom, fell on his knees, hugged the commode and heaved until there was nothing coming out but bitter bile.

"Jer, where do we keep the prophylactics?" Joel yelled.

"I apologize for his indiscretion," Jerome said to the gentleman as he completed the sale. Joel stood nearby unaware of his gaffe.

"We have four departments," Jerome said as he began Joel's orientation. Joel's eyes glazed; he didn't even look at the register. Joel was there to watch the Negroes, not work. For several hours he followed Jerome, watching his every move but understanding nothing, nor did he bother to ask.

"Jerome, get back here, now," Sid bellowed; he had returned and found the safe ajar. Several hundred dollars were in the daily receipts pouch, the $500 change bank and prescription-only narcotics were also exposed. "You left the safe open, you forgetful prick! Do it again and you're fired!"

"I didn't do it the first time," Jerome said calmly. "I have never left the safe open since I've been here, you know that. Joel asked for the combination; I refused. Joel reminded me that you had said he was in charge, so I gave it to him."

"I left the safe open after getting a roll of quarters for Louise about a half-hour ago," Joel admitted, grinning sheepishly. He added, "But Jerome should have seen that it was open and closed it, right?" Sid walked away without comment.

I see; selective rule enforcement, Jerome realized. He watched each minute tick away until 6:00 p.m. As Jerome left, Louise said through a sneer, "I knew this was going to happen three months ago, you silly-dilly star fool."

"Well, little brother," Fred said after listening to Jerome's scenario over drinks at Scotty's, "You have just experienced a rude awakening. Our friends predicted this would happen. Obviously, your naiveté needed adjusting."

"You are so right, and believe me, I have made the adjustment; but what went wrong?" Jerome cried.

"We want things to go right so badly," Fred answered, "we believe they are going well even when indicators say otherwise. We become disillusioned idealists."

Disillusioned idealists, silly-dilly-star-fool; what's the difference? "But Sid lied to me!"

"Most bosses lie," Fred said. "Bosses make promises to secure loyalty, and then break them because of nepotism, unforeseen opportunities, economic downturns, or just plain greed—–and that's in businesses <u>we</u> own. Don't even think about White folks keeping promises to <u>us</u>, even when they put them in writing."

"His profits have soared because of me. I'm one of the best at what I do!"

"And Sidney agrees, Fred said. "He wouldn't have made you awesome promises if he wasn't afraid of losing you. Now, he no longer fears you're going to work for Sol Gitel; sales are up, the improvements are in place. His nephew's presence clearly indicates Sidney never intended to give you a partnership. And for what it's worth maybe you should check out the genetics between Sidney and Joel." Fred took a drink and reflected, "I used to work at Shoreline, the largest insurance company in town. They promised me vice-president, comptroller, and then gave it to Stuart Sykes. That's when I resigned and started my own business."

"Oh man, how I wish I could start my own business," Jerome said.

Friends asked in the form of a greeting, "What's happening my brothers?" Jerome tried to answer but had lost his ability to communicate. Most understood he was inebriated, ordered he and Fred another drink, made a sympathetic comment like, 'ain't that nothing,' or, 'aw man, what a drag,' and moved on, not really interested in the obvious, but unclear, calamity that had befallen Jerome.

"Take care of my buddy, Gail," Fred said as he poured Jerome into his home. "He's had a bad day."

Jerome, against Sid's instructions, had told Gail about the special account and Sid's refusal to give him an advance. The next morning, Jerome told Gail about the last incident, indicating he may be fired.

"I'll get a job in Baxter Bridges' office as a typist and start studying for a real estate license, just in case," Gail said.

Conrad was in town for an emergency winter NIA Board meeting. Negro agents were being employed by Caucasian insurance companies throughout the North, specifically to sell policies to Negroes. It was a threatening and growing issue; adjustments were needed within the Negro insurance industry.

"That was a fine meal, darling," Conrad said. The fried chicken, mashed potatoes, home-made rolls, and green beans with sliced almonds had turned out perfectly. When Michelle and Dana finished dinner, they politely asked to be excused and went into the empty dining room to play. Gail, after clearing away the dishes, adjourned to the living room.

After pulling a Havana from his inside coat pocket, Conrad remembered Gail's no smoking rule and only rolled it between his fingers. "So, Son, how's the job going?" Conrad said as he leaned his chair back and studied his cigar as if it were a kaleidoscope.

"Oh, I'm holding on." *I'm sure you know the whole story. Gail told her mother and she told you, so have at me.*

"I told you this wouldn't work, didn't I?" Conrad twirled and occasionally chewed his unlit cigar.

"*Here it comes.*" With his head down while sipping coffee, Jerome mentally stiffened for a verbal trip to the woodshed.

"Well, some good came from your running away after all. You should have learned how to run a drugstore over the last couple of years, even if you aren't the sharpest knife in the drawer." Conrad glared across the table, and with unbridled contempt, added, "That was one of your objections, wasn't it? You didn't know how to run a drugstore, and I knew even less!"

Ouch! I wondered how he was going to rub my nose in the manure; no mystery now. Jerome continued sipping his coffee without comment. His facial muscles tightened. He kept his eyes diverted, hoping to hide his embarrassment.

"Well Son, you'll be pleased to learn I've already secured our location. You can abandon this shotgun shack; I'll have my lawyers' dump this mess, probably with you declaring bankruptcy. We should be open in several months, let's say by March 15th."

That wasn't so bad. Thought I'd hear at least a half-hour of 'who did I think I was.' Maybe the old man has mellowed. I can sure use the change. "Daddy Beau, I need a little time…"

"Time! Boy, you crazy?" Conrad grimaced at losing control. He breathed deeply then continued. "Now I know we haven't gotten along in the past, and maybe I'm partly to blame, but I'll stand by my original offer. A fully furnished home, and a new car, and even though I'm putting up all the front money and assuming all the risk, we'll split the profits, fifty-fifty."

Conrad paused, anticipating a favorable comment; there was none. "Why I can see it now," Conrad formed a rectangular frame with his thumbs and forefingers and peered through it, "Beauregard and Gerard Drugstore. No, that's too long, how about B&G Drugs? Yeah, that'll fit." Conrad folded his arms victoriously.

I don't see any alternative. And Conrad is right; I now know how to manage a drugstore. Besides, I think he finally respects me. And wouldn't I enjoy going in tomorrow and telling Sid and Joel what to do with their job. I'll do it. "The bookkeeping system we use works perfectly…"

"Bookkeeping! The last thing you know anything about is how to keep books! My people will pay the bills, handle the money, control the inventory, and keep the books! I will personally sign all the checks." Conrad turned red, veins rose in his temples. He jumped up, came within inches of Jerome's face, and then shouted, "Your job, probably because you don't know what you are doing, has turned to shit, your house is falling apart, your car is a highway hazard, you work all the time and you have no money. And you're going to tell me how to count!"

Well, so much for respect. That was just one suggestion, which forecasts how our business meetings would be run—business meetings, that's a joke. I'd be just like his other stooges, and because of declaring bankruptcy, my credit rating would be shot. I would be totally dependent on Conrad. 50-50 profit-sharing, yeah right. Not in this life. "Daddy Beau, I will not accept slave quarters no matter how spacious, and having you vilify me whenever you feel like it would be unbearable. We just cannot work together!"

Gail had eased into the kitchen and was standing in the far corner facing the stove with her back to Conrad and Jerome, being as inconspicuous as possible.

"Who do you think you are, Jesus Christ?" Daddy Beau screamed as he paced the floor and pointed his unlit cigar in Jerome's face. "You'll have to walk on water to get out of this mess. If you aren't in New Orleans in a month, my offer is permanently withdrawn. Do you understand me!?"

"Daddy Beau," Gail pleaded, turning around, facing both men, "Why don't you give Jerome a little time to think things through, right, Honey?"

"Yeah, right," Jerome said, but his words sounded more like "your momma," than Jerome being willing to consider Conrad's proposal. Earlier, when he was interrupted when asking for time, his sentence would have ended with time to pack, but not now.

"What are you doing in here girl? This is men's talk. Go back up front, we'll be through directly." Conrad was planning on mentally whipping Jerome into submission.

"This isn't just you and Jerome's decision, Daddy Beau," Gail said as she stood in place, "This affects me and our daughters. Unlike you and Momma, Jerome and I discuss things other than what we're having for dinner, right Babe?"

"Damn right," Jerome said. Gail walked over to Jerome's chair and put her arm on his shoulder; he engulfed her waist. *Now deal with this Mr. Smart Ass.*

"Thinking, sure, that's what he's good at," Daddy Beau said. "Look where thinking has gotten him so far." He was speaking to Gail as if Jerome wasn't present. He then turned to Jerome, "I'll do all the thinking; you just follow my instructions and fill the damn prescriptions. I'll teach you how to run a business!"

"Thinking is the process that precedes purposeful action," Jerome said. Reading successful businessmen's biographies had produced that gem. *If Conrad and Sidney don't want me to think, neither do they want me to work for them.*

Conrad's mouth was ajar. Jerome saying something strange about thinking and Gail standing with her husband against him had left Conrad speechless. He sat back down, shook his head, and looked at his unlit cigar, then at Gail and Jerome, together. After a long moment he said, "You got any gin and tonic in this poor excuse for a home?"

"Here's your drink, Daddy Beau," Jerome said, as the tension slowly evaporated. "I read in the *Defender* about a bus boycott in Montgomery. Have you heard anything?"

"Yeah, a waste of time and shoe leather if you ask me. I'm surprised it lasted this long; started over a year ago. Dumb, poor-ass Negroes are still walking, trying to change the South. Lincoln's successor, Andrew Johnson kept us in our place. That young preacher just doesn't know the rules. White folk write the laws White folk enforce the laws, and Niggers live by em. That's the way it is, always has been and always will be."

Based on Caucasian propaganda, Conrad believed Negroes were shiftless, lazy and dishonest. He had always functioned within the parameters of segregation, appeasing "Mr. Charley" when required, and consistently disrespecting Negroes, especially those who worked for him. He thought anyone who challenged Jim Crow laws or the superiority of Caucasians was asking for trouble. Conrad's genius was having the ability to make money within the White man's burdensome restrictions.

After Gail and Jerome dropped Daddy Beau off at his hotel, they talked in their living room over drinks. "So what's it going to be, Babe?" Gail asked.

"I really don't know. I hate to start over with Walgreens where managing a store might be a couple of years away," Jerome said as he sipped from his glass.

"I know how hard you work," Gail said as she moved to Jerome's chair and perched on the arm. She pulled his head to her breast and continued, "And I share your pain. Take all the time you need to decide our future. The more time I spend away from my daddy, the more I understand how difficult he would be to work for or live around. I respect your judgment and know you will make what you believe is the right decision."

Gail, after putting the girls to bed, said, "Know this; whatever you decide will be our decision. I love you." And then they kissed.

What started as a tender kiss turned torrid. Jerome stood up, pulled Gail into him, wrapped his arms around her, and, with her head nestled on his broad shoulder said, "I love you back, Babe." They kissed again. It lasted forever, ending when Jerome's tongue and lips mauled Gail's neck. Jerome slipped his arms under Gail and carried her to their bedroom; they hurriedly undressed. Their emotions unleashed. Gail, naked, fell into bed, Jerome quickly followed. His tongue went everywhere. Soon, Gail was begging to be ravaged. They made love without fear of pregnancy, thanks to her recent tubal surgery. It was a beautiful end to a terrible evening.

Tailor's Drugs, which was once an exciting, challenging place to work, became a dismal dungeon. Sid came in twice daily, staying briefly. While there he was severely critical of Jerome's every move. Joel criticized Jerome too, without cause or credibility.

Christmas of '56 was in the air but not in Jerome's heart. Jerome eavesdropped on every conversation he could between Sid and others; it's clear. *When Joel graduates this spring, I'll be out of a job. Maybe I should talk to Sol Gitel. Not a good idea; he has four stores in Negro neighborhoods with no Negro managers. Harold Oldham clearly wants me on board, but I can't work there without knowing more about his silent partners.*

Jerome got along with Joel by not asking him to do anything. Sid was pleased with Jerome and Joel's relationship, but not with Joel. When he worked alone, sales dropped and customers complained; items were incorrectly rung up. Joel's drinking beer with fellow students became more important than keeping his work schedule. Joel repeatedly left early, leaving no manager on duty. Jerome had to be called to return to close, often. Most Saturday mornings Joel was hung over. Customers as well as Dr. Ben complained about his attitude. Joel filled a prescription incorrectly; it would have killed the patient had Jerome not caught the mistake.

Sid realized that his plan to force Jerome to quit was wrong; any Jew, Sid had learned, is not automatically more competent than any Negro. Sid decided Joel needed more time to develop.

"How's business Jerome?" Sid asked. Joel was off. Jerome looked at him silently saying, you already know the answer.

"My sister insisted I put Joel to work. I see now that was a big mistake. Not only is he a sorry excuse for a pharmacist, he's irresponsible and undependable. Can we get back to the way things were?"

"Well," Jerome said, "There's the matter of $2,200."

"Yeah, I know," Sid said with his head bent and his eyes cast downward. "I needed that to finance the new business and it's not going as well as projected. Can I owe you?"

Yeah, right. If you wanted me as a partner, the new business should have been included. "And then there's the partnership."

"That was also a mistake. I should have followed through as I had promised." Sid appeared remorseful as he looked askance at Jerome.

You ought to win an Oscar for this performance, but I'm going to use you until I have determined my new direction. "Sid," Jerome said, acting relieved, "I agree with your assessment of Joel, and it's obvious you can't run two stores by yourself. Can we change the rules a little?" Sid expressed an interest. "Going forward, pay me my base salary for forty hours a week instead of the original sixty, and time and a half for all additional hours. Since I'm working double shifts, that will increase my earnings to over $500 per week until you hire a new pharmacist or put our partnership in writing."

"Jerome I agree with everything you've said," Sid smiled. "We are going to have to keep Joel, temporarily at least; my sister would cause a family crisis if I didn't, but we both know how important he really is." Sid and Jerome shook hands.

Please don't rub my hair or call me boy; your lies have been insulting enough. Jerome returned Sid's smile. *I can act too.*

Felix and Bea's was tastefully decorated for the holidays. Large wreaths were strategically spaced. Aluminum 'Merry Christmas and Happy New Year' streamers hung between them. Each table held a burning candle in an oval red, smoked holder. A ten foot Balsam tree filled with scented cones, decorated with miniature white lights and Christmas ornaments, stood in a corner. Holiday tunes, sung by Nat King Cole, Charles Brown, Ella Fitzgerald and others, were playing through the intercom. Cocktails were being consumed at every table. Company parties, some with Caucasians in attendance, were held on extended lunch hours. Sounds of exaggerated silliness filled the restaurant.

"Don't let Whitey get to you, Honey," Rowena whispered to Jerome as he hung up his coat. "You're a stand-up dude who knows what to do when trouble gets in the mix."

Obviously she's been listening to private conversations. Jerome joined the B.S. Table. Rowena slipped a note in his coat pocket. It read, "If you need a place to be somebody, call me."

"A toast to Martin Luther King," Leo Lafarge said as he raised his glass, just as Jerome was sitting down, "And to the Negroes of Montgomery. The Supreme Court outlawed segregation in all public places!"

"Should have started their own bus company," Buddy Laws said, frowning.

"We couldn't start our own bus company here," Fred responded. "You remember, they forced our jitneys off the street to eliminate competition with city busses years ago."

"Still," Buddy said, "God bless the child that's got his own," reciting a Billy Holliday lyric.

"Sure wish I had my own," Jerome said, almost to himself.

"That's the second time you've said that; your own what?" Fred asked.

"Why, my own drugstore."

"Erwin McKlosky's store is for sale," John T. Williamson, L&S representative, said.

"I've met him, but I don't have any serious money."

"Negro," Williamson said, "Wish in one hand, spit in the other, watch which one gets wet fastest." The harsh simile hurt Jerome's feelings. Jerome stared at Williamson, hoping someone would change the subject.

"Boy," Williamson was disturbed by Jerome's silence, "Pull your head out of your ass and think about what you <u>can</u> do instead of what you <u>can't</u> do. Everyone here knows what you're going through, and it ain't anything new. We have all been gang-raped at least twice. You have prognosticated about what others should do; now it's on you."

The table agreed; Williamson continued, "Losers gripe about conditions and give up, causing them to accept mediocrity for life. Fools get angry and become violent, ending up in jail or dead. Strivers, that's us, work wonders with what we have; the Jacksons, the Thompsons, and others have proven that. Adversity builds character and ability, but only if you rise above it. So it's decision-time my brother. What are you; a loser, a fool, or a striver?"

"What the hell can I do, make McKlosky give me his store? I only have five grand."

"There you go, whining again." Williamson caught Jerome's eye. "One thing all strivers know is your financial condition is second to your mental attitude. Think about it, man. Doc McKlosky is as rich as Blue Valley butter; hell, he owns half the block. His wife died two years ago, and he and his store have been going downhill ever since. Go by and talk to him.

What's the risk? You might not need more than you have!" Williamson dropped his head and shook it.

"OK, ok, I'll do it! If Rosa Parks can eliminate public segregation, if Thomas H. Jackson and Richard Thompson can build multi-million dollar businesses with minimal investments, the least I can do is try to get my own store. I'll talk to Doc McKlosky. Like the man said, what's to lose?"

End of Chapter Seven

CHAPTER EIGHT

"It's 7:58 my brothahs and sistahs; a foot more of white fluffy stuff fell during the wee, wee hours and the temperature is minus ten, with a thirty-five mile-per-hour hawk, making it feel like twenty-five below nothing. That is as cold as my landlady's heart when my rent is late. So, if you don't have to meet The Man this morning why bother getting up my brothah, just stay between the sheets and under the covah," the disk jockey on WBEE rhythmically intoned.

After hearing the weather report, knowing traffic would be difficult and enjoying Dinah Washington's *Teach Me Tonight* between up-tempo wake-up tunes, Jerome's mission on his day off seemed unwarranted, unnecessary, and not nearly as pleasant as what he was contemplating. He wrapped his arms around Gail's curvaceous body and fondled her ample breasts through her silk, short nightie.

Feeling Jerome's growing member, Gail said, "Babe, I'm ready." Gail rolled toward Jerome, intertwined their bodies and said, "You know you're all that matters, so if you want me to be late, I'll be late. We can blame it on this ridiculous weather." They shared a passionate kiss.

"As much as I hate to say it, business must come before pleasure, especially during these uncertain times," Jerome said as he reluctantly rolled out of bed.

The drive to Forty-Seventh and Lake Park was treacherous. Cars had plowed into snow banks, had become involved in fender-benders, and stalled in the middle of streets. Every attempted stop included sliding forever. Two hours later, which should have taken twenty minutes, Jerome parked a half block from McKlosky's drugstore, three feet from the curb.

The piercing wind blew frozen needles into Jerome's face. He walked bent over, high-stepping through deep snow, gasping for air. *Ten minutes out here and I'd become a fudge cycle with nappy hair.*

Window signage indicated a bakery, a delicatessen, and a florist once occupied three of the vacant stores Jerome passed. *These businesses don't exist where <u>we</u> live.* A single store-front tavern that also sold package goods, a small grocery, a beauty salon/barber shop, and a combination dry cleaners/Laundromat, were closed. Above the stores were several windows with Milton E. Steinbaum, M.D., painted in black script edged in gold. Black and red cardboard posters indicated the remaining upstairs offices were, 'For Rent.'

What can I do to impress Mr. McKlosky? It's always easier to do business with someone when they like you; I chased him off with my questions the last time we met, thought Jerome as he pushed open the door with his cold, gloved hands. Three bells that a cat might wear jingled.

"Hurry up, boy; be sure you close that door behind you," ordered the obese White woman behind the front counter. She was wearing a purple and pink sweater with a white scarf and wool gloves with cut out fingers. Jerome stomped the snow from his galoshes; he ignored her insult. He loosened his garments, allowing the slight warmth of the store to penetrate.

After seeing that the door was closed, the cashier returned to her *True Romance* magazine, ignoring Jerome. He saw Doc McKlosky peeping through decorative pestles and jars from the pharmacy area. Jerome said loudly, "Good morning, Doc McKlosky, perhaps you remember me. We met…" He remembered Sid speaking loudly to the seventyish Doc McKlosky, intimating he was hard of hearing.

"Of course; you're Sidney Reis' boy, but I've forgotten your name."

"Jerome, Jerome Gerard." He headed towards McKlosky forcing a smile, inwardly bristling at being called boy a second time, especially Sid's after recent events.

"Yeah, Jerry, that's right. I remember now."

"How's business these days, Doc?" Jerome asked as he drew closer.

"Bad." McKlosky then said, "That's why you're here Sonny, on a day like this, to ask me how my business is?"

"No Sir, I heard your store is for sale."

"Well now, Mr. Money Bags, if it is, just what the hell are you going to do about it?" Jerome remained silent. McKlosky said, "Yep. Has been for quite a while, too long if you ask me." McKlosky stepped toward a waist-high counter; they were less than three feet apart. "Lots of lookers but no takers, the way Coloreds are moving in makes everything hard to sell. Most of my tenants just closed up and left, they couldn't sell either—at any price."

"How much square footage do you have?"

"You're looking at it, boy. What's the matter, can't you see? Nine hundred square feet and another six hundred in the basement." Jerome looked confused. "'Course you never count storage space when quoting store space, but I guess even you know that much." Doc looked at Jerome contemptuously, awaiting his next comment.

"What's your asking price, Doc?"

"Not much; only $15,000 for fixtures and good will, plus fifty percent for inventory."

And John said he didn't want any money. Jerome removed his gloves, blew over his freezing hands, rubbed them together and thought *that's way overpriced.* Realizing making a deal was unrealistic but wanting to delay returning to the cold, Jerome asked, "Doc McKlosky is that inventory price fifty percent of cost or off suggested retail?"

"Well now," McKlosky said, breaking into a smile, "looks like I've finally run into a real druggist, even if you are a nig... Colored. I've told others the same thing; they told me I was crazy and left. They didn't even know if the price was negotiable." *So the price is negotiable.* "That's fifty percent off cost, of course. Come on back; how about a cup of hot coffee to knock the chill off, m'boy?"

"Here, hold this." Doc poured a steaming, thick, black liquid in Jerome's mug from a pot off an electric hot plate. Cream and sugar were not visible. Jerome took a sip. He fought the impulse to spit it out and swallowed. It was at least three days old, hot as Hades, and bitter as a battered wife. Jerome forced a smile as he sat the cup down.

"You know little feller," McKlosky had perched himself on a stool. Jerome was standing. He loosened his coat further. "I knew it was going to drop below freezing several days ago, my joints..."

Jerome was an erect six foot two; McKlosky, a stooped five foot eight. Jerome thought, *which one of us is the little feller.* McKlosky began talking as if his vocal chords were a released spring. He complained about aches and pains, ungrateful, pilfering employees, strange-looking Negro customers, and old friends, tenants and residents, moving. He compared this weather with winters of yesteryear.

Jerome became an excellent, active listener; he made the appropriate remarks in a timely manner and maintained eye contact. Thirty minutes later, with obvious sadness, McKlosky recounted how his wife worked with him every day for forty-five years, and they never took a vacation or the time to have children, and with her passing two years ago, how meaningless his life had become. He ended saying, as he choked, "Now, going home is the worst part of my day."

"I have no idea how great the loss of a life-long loved one might be, Mr. McKlosky. I've only been married five years and I know how heartbroken I would be if I lost my wife or one of my daughters. My father died when I was very young, but that was a different loss. I hope she went painlessly and peacefully to her better place. Please accept my most sincere, but belated, condolences." Jerome grabbed McKlosky's hand with both of his as he looked directly into his eyes. McKlosky was moved by Jerome's remarks and thanked him.

When McKlosky went to help a customer, Jerome poured his coffee down the sink's drain and evaluated the store. Shelves, some with glass doors, were from floor to ceiling; all behind the counters. There were many vacant spaces, meaning sold items had not been replaced. Customers could only pick up magazines or use the booth-enclosed telephone. It reminded Jerome of the drugstore in the movie, *It's a Wonderful Life,* without the ice cream counter. Jerome estimated the upstairs inventory cost $20,000. *That's $10,000 I don't have, not to mention the $15,000 for fixtures, or what's in the basement. What the hell am I doing here?*

A middle aged Negro woman, who appeared to have put on everything she owned to keep from freezing, asked McKlosky for a swivel handled straightening comb. Obviously it was something she really needed. McKlosky had no idea what she wanted. He became impatient as she explained; she left angry. Jerome knew exactly what she wanted. *That's a $10 sale and a customer that's lost forever.*

"See what I mean, stupid nig … Negroes!" McKlosky said. *No wonder his business is dying. The hostile attitude of his cashier is also a contributing factor.* "Why do you want to leave Sidney, Boy?"

Well, at least he got Sid's name right. "Just thought it was time to do my own thing," Jerome lied.

"You're mighty kind, m'Boy, mighty kind, but I know that cheap Jew better than you. They think I'm hard-of-hearing. I hear better than most of em," McKlosky chuckled and then said, "Sid overheard Sol's conversation with you at our smoker. At our next meeting Sid scolded Sol for sharing business confidences with you."

"I don't understand," Jerome said. "The purpose of the gathering is to meet people with similar interests, isn't it?"

"Nobody wants to hear your ideas, Sonny. The purpose of our annual smoker is to identify 'The Negro Untouchables,' so the cost of Colored help doesn't rise. Once you darkies have been introduced, you can't be hired by another member. That's why Sid introduced us, thinking I might be hiring a colored back-up pharmacist, with my wife gone and all. Members don't steal Coons from each other; that's against the rules, y'know."

"I didn't know," Jerome was upset. "How could I know I was Sid's property within the association?"

"Come on, it's not that bad, Boy, you could always work for Walgreens. Anyway," continued McKlosky, "a couple of meetings later, Sid told Sol he couldn't pry you lose with a crowbar, said he had offered you a partnership. Sol laughed, knowing Sid would never give anyone a partnership. Recently, Sid told Sol he could have you because Sid had found your replacement; said you were too expensive anyway. Sid calls him his nephew, right?"

"You're right, Doc." Jerome was infuriated. He hid his feelings under downcast eyes and a slight chuckle.

"Sid wants you to quit so that, that octoroon doctor... what's his name?"

"Dr. Richard Benjamin," Jerome said.

"Yeah, that's him. He's what your people call High Yeller; see, I know a few things. Anyway, Sid didn't want him to get angry for firing you. If you quit and the Doc complained, Sid would just hire another nigger, probably a jack-leg pharmacist, at half the price. Sid never did like paying you a White registered pharmacist's salary. Allen gets half your salary and is paid off the books. Bet you didn't know that either did ya, Boy?"

Even though I have increased business more than any of his White pharmacists, I'm still not worth a White man's wage. Jerome thought.

"This used to be a nice neighborhood," McKlosky said, encouraged by Jerome's attentiveness. "But you people are moving large families into very small apartments, staying up late with loud music and all."

Probably at twice the rent, Jerome thought.

"And a lot of Colored families shop here on credit. You Coloreds just can't manage money very well, can you?"

I've been here over two hours, Jerome thought, *I'm wasting my time, and I'm sick of his insults.* Jerome stood up, pulled his coat together and said, "Doc McKlosky, I have enjoyed…"

"Call me Erwin, here have another cup of coffee," McKlosky suggested, clearly wanting Jerome to stay.

"No thank you," Jerome quickly covered his cup. *He's harmless, just too old to change. Besides, I think he likes me.* "Erwin, I am interested in your store, but before I can make a serious offer, I'd like to review your financial records."

"You got a lot of nerve, Boy, asking for my books, acting like you understand bookkeeping; and then what will you do?" McKlosky's contemptuous look returned.

"Negotiate a price including payment terms. I don't have much money," Jerome smiled broadly.

"Negotiate! I gave you the same price as everyone else. Anyway," McKlosky sounded impatient and frowned as he spoke, but Jerome noticed a twinkle in his eye, "how do you shop for a business without real money?" *John was right, money was not McKlosky's primary motivation.*

"Well," Jerome answered, "It won't take me but a minute or two to look your records over, and then I'll know whether I can afford your store." Once again Jerome smiled.

"Here," Erwin said as he handed Jerome a dogged daily cash flow ledger, his credit account pads, plus his latest quarterly P&L statement from his accountant, "a lot of good it'll do ya." Erwin had been manipulating his books for years to pay lower taxes.

Jerome pulled a stool up to the counter and became immersed. He made notes and calculations on his pad. His unusual ability to concentrate for extended times on specific tasks had put him at the top of his college and OCS classes. Jerome congratulated himself for having recently completed a home study accounting course from the University of Chicago.

The documents showed a good welfare prescription business from the physician upstairs, but McKlosky's payroll, with two part-time and two full-time people, was double what it should be. McKlosky's salary was the lowest. Jerome assumed he was probably skimming, as did Sid. McKlosky's Sundry purchases, which should have been 33% lower, were only 15% less than gross sales. Cigarette purchases were almost as high as sales. Which meant internal pilfering was a problem. His Good Will and Fixed Assets amount tripled when his drugstore went on the market for no apparent reason. McKlosky had added ten percent to all customers' credit sales. *His Negro customers are more interested in charging than what they are being charged.*

"Fortunately," Jerome said after his review, "we want the same things, Erwin, a business that charges fair prices and helps those in need when practical." McKlosky nodded his agreement, believing Jerome hadn't uncovered any helpful information.

"Your store is clean and well-stocked," Jerome lied. "It's the type of store that can afford my wife and me a good living. Of course our two daughters will have to spend a lot of time here as well." Jerome knew nothing would be gained by revealing his findings or asking embarrassing questions. He also thought suggesting that he and his wife, like McKlosky and his wife, would work in the store, may generate empathy.

"Tell you what Sonny, this neighborhood has changed. More Coloreds than I know what to do with. Besides, I like you. You are sensitive to my loss. You've got respect for an old geezer who talks too much and sometimes says the wrong thing. You are respectful, considerate, and a family man. Most of all, you didn't knock my business. I know it's not what it should be, but I just don't care anymore." Jerome remained silent. "Here's my final proposition. Pay me $10,000 now, $700 a month for ten months for the inventory, and the store is yours. Hell, these Chicago winters are too rough; I need to move somewhere warm."

Jerome pulled out his pad, wrote down some numbers, then said, "Erwin, your price is more than fair, but it's much more than I can afford. But I agree, you should move to a warmer climate; your waning years would be much more enjoyable. You should think about some place like Miami; its 75 degrees there today. If you could make the fixtures and good-will payment $8,000 and let me pay you $300 a month for ten months for inventory, interest free, and allow me to manage your attached real estate for fifteen percent of the rent, I'll find new tenants to fill your vacancies."

McKlosky peered over his spectacles, looked up at Jerome and said, "How did you know I own this building and the six adjoining stores?" McKlosky looked violated.

John T. Williamson had informed Jerome; he thought quickly, "You told me when I came in a number of <u>your tenants</u> had moved out without being able to sell their businesses. If they were your tenants, I assumed you owned the property. Wasn't I right, Doc?" Jerome again looked confused.

"I hadn't even considered my property. You listen pretty good Boy." McKlosky relaxed and said, "Mmmm, 75 degrees huh? OK, sonny, the store and the real estate management responsibilities are yours. You are a smart, polite, young feller who has children to raise; you deserve a break."

"Erwin, here is five thousand dollars to cement our deal," Jerome said with his head down while writing out the check. "I'll pay you the balance of three thousand by next Wednesday." He was proud he had saved his bonus and hadn't bought another car or any new furniture. The $5,000 was all Jerome had. "If I don't pay you the additional $3,000, no later than next Wednesday, I will forfeit the five."

"What just happened? This is not what I agreed to," McKlosky looked at Jerome's check while frowning, and then at him. "When you came in here I was looking for $15,000 for my business, now you say we have a deal when you give me a lousy five thousand dollar check!" The frown returned, but so did the twinkle. McKlosky waited for an explanation.

All Jerome did was smile. *He heard me.*

Finally, McKlosky said, "Tell you what Sonny, you've got a deal, but remember, if I don't have your three thousand by next Wednesday, you lose the five."

"I understand and agree. Just don't mention this to anyone."

"Don't worry, I would never admit to being finessed by a nig… Negro." McKlosky smiled, "Funny thing, I started not to come in today, the weather and all, but I've been here forty-five years and never missed opening on time. Can't break a record like that, now can I, Boy?"

"That's an outstanding record," Jerome smiled as he shook McKlosky's hand. As Jerome wrapped himself in his coat and scarf, he said, "I'm glad both of us disciplined ourselves this morning. It was difficult for me to get out of bed also." Jerome trudged into the frigid weather. *Let's see now, Colored, Coon, Darkie, Octoroon, Boy, Sonny, High Yeller, Little Feller, Jerry, Jer, You people, Youngun, and the N word, but never Jerome. Erwin McKlosky can call me anything he wants as long as he gives me a deal as sweet as this.* The Hawk was friendlier now.

"Sam," Jerome said after getting through three subordinates, "I've just bought a drugstore and I need you to make it legal." Jerome was calling from the gas station across the street. He had written down all the specifics.

"Congratulations! Give Joseph, my paralegal, the details; when's the closing?"

"My next stop is Ted Thomas at Community S&L to borrow three thousand dollars, and then we'll set the closing date, which has to be no later than next Wednesday."

"It will never happen. But just in case, I'll prepare the paperwork, even though I'm probably wasting my time," Samuel said, and then he was gone.

Jerome gave Joseph all of his contract stipulations. Joseph asked scores of questions Jerome had not considered. Before hanging up Jerome asked Joseph, "Why did Attorney Stovall say this deal would never happen?"

"You'll have to ask him," Joseph said. "He told me to have everything ready by Tuesday morning, and that's done."

"Damn Man," Ted said after Jerome explained his need for a loan. "Our charter limits us to only first mortgages for single family homes. We can't grant second mortgages. Even if we could you wouldn't qualify because of your limited equity."

"That's why Samuel said it wouldn't happen. I should have talked to you before writing that check." Jerome walked down to Fred's office.

"You really stepped into it this time," Fred said. He completed working on a file, and then said, "Statistically speaking, ninety-five percent of new businesses fail within the first five years. That's why banks don't loan

Whites non-collateralized start-up capital. If it was your second store I might consider investing, but this deal is too risky. And you better steer clear of Harold and his friends because if they get involved, what you think you own, you won't."

"Harold seems to be doing all right."

"Trust me. Stay away from the easy money and that includes Felix. You'll be better off losing the five grand than getting obligatory financing."

Jerome trusted Fred's judgment. "Do you think Dr. Ben would make me a loan?"

"He might," Fred smiled. Jerome anticipated a further explanation. Fred's secretary announced over the intercom, "Mr. Hawkins, line two." Fred picked up the phone; Jerome left.

Dr. Ben's private office was small, but contemporary. African ceremonial masks, a Chinese Buddha with jade eyes, and antique Egyptian urns were displayed on several glass shelves. The opposite wall was filled with certificates, validating advanced medical study. Meritorious awards from the NAACP, the UNCF, and the National Urban League were prominently displayed. A spotless white shag carpet covered the floor.

"Well, how's my favorite cousin?" Dr. Ben was immaculate under his white, knee-length coat, the proverbial stethoscope hung around his neck. He perched on the corner of his single-panel, oval desk with hands flat on both sides; his naked ankles were crossed.

"Not doing too well," Jerome answered. His voice tone and facial expression reflected his dilemma.

"Is Sid trying to fire you?" Dr. Ben said through an exaggerated pout. "I don't know who Joel is but I don't like him. He's too Jewish, know what I mean? Sid told me he was his nephew. I think he's offering the goose the same sauce that was served the gander, earlier."

Jerome explained how he had negotiated an excellent drugstore deal, his not being able to borrow the money from Community S&L and his needing three thousand dollars, lest he lose his life's savings.

"So you need the money to tell Sid to kiss you where the sun doesn't shine," Dr. Ben said as he moved to his high-back leather chair behind his desk. "You are already moving up. Good. That's how Bronzeville grows, one business at a time. That was our hope when we helped you get the job. Who should I make the check payable to?" Dr. Ben asked.

"To me," Jerome said, relieved. "How much time do I have to pay you back and what is your interest rate?"

"Take as much time as you need and there is no interest. Just consider me a very, very, silent partner."

This is better than I expected.

"It's a long shot, but you just might make it. You'll have difficulty establishing credit lines with some companies, especially if Sidney discourages them. And you won't have a prescription writer like me, but not to worry. If more capital is needed just let me know. Here you are," Dr. Ben said as he handed Jerome the $3,000 check. Dr. Ben watched Jerome's face brighten, and then said, "I'm having a party this Saturday night at my place. Would you come as my special guest?"

"I would be delighted and honored. Let me call Gail so she…"

"Not you and Gail, just you." Dr. Ben's eyes hardened, a leer crossed his face.

Jerome understood; he said, "Dr. Ben, I'm happily married with a beautiful wife and two lovely girls…"

"Cut the crap, Jerome, I know all about you and Louise so don't play holier than thou with me." Dr. Ben continued in a softer voice, "just because you spend an evening with the boys doesn't make you any less of a man, now does it; especially a buff, young man with a purple pole big enough to choke a snake." Dr. Ben's leer intensified. "I mean, Louise isn't the only one who can do fellatio. Our night together will lead to some new adventures, most of which you may even enjoy." Dr. Ben's eyes glistened as he ran his tongue over his lips. His inner thoughts were turning him on.

"You're right about me and Louise," Jerome said as he forced a pleasant expression, "but what you're suggesting is something I don't find attractive or interesting. Since we first met I have respected you and your lifestyle, but if your loan is based upon my attending your party, then I must refuse the loan."

"Well said; perhaps my approach was too crude or too sudden," Dr. Ben chuckled softly. "Keep the check. Think about it for a day or two, and then if you still feel the need to reject my offer, tear it up. After all, your losing five large <u>might</u> not mean the end of your world." Jerome studied the check, read the number over and over, and pocketed it.

"You are an excellent pharmacist, Jerome, but since I don't have a feel for your business acumen, investing $3,000 in a new business venture is too speculative, even for me; however, it's not too much for a new playmate. If you don't attend the party our partnership is over before it begins. However you proceed, your attempt at buying a drugstore is safe with me. I hope you will treat my indiscretions in a like manner."

"You've given me a lot to think about Dr. Ben, but whatever I decide I will never mention this encounter to anyone."

It was 2:00 p.m. when Jerome returned home. His successful negotiations with McKlosky, his information given to Samuel's paralegal, plus his meetings with Ted, Fred, and Dr. Ben had been a rapid, mental roller coaster ride that had left him exhausted. Jerome collapsed in his easy chair. He didn't know what to do. *I can't ask Samuel for a loan. He knew the S&L wouldn't make the loan and didn't offer an alternative. Obviously he doesn't believe me buying my own drugstore will work either.*

Before falling asleep Jerome had torn up the $3,000 check. *I will not prostitute myself; the assault on my dignity would be unbearable. And my first time with "the boys," would be just the beginning. I would be at Dr. Ben's beck and call; his male prostitute. My self-worth would be lost forever. My becoming self-employed, my own boss, the master of my fate, cannot begin with me abandoning my personal values.*

"Wake up Babe; how did it go?" Gail asked as she took off her coat and boots, still chilled.

Groggily, Jerome said, "My day was terrible!" He described each of his day's segments except the Dr. Ben encounter. "I have probably lost our life savings. I'll just have to begin again," Jerome sounded defeated.

Gail listened without interrupting. When Jerome finished, Gail went to the kitchen and returned with two cups of hot tea and lemon. She said, "Think you're going to be out of work soon?"

"Sid will probably fire me sometime in the spring, but I won't be unemployed long. I can always start over with Walgreens."

"Well," Gail said, "If we're not going to lose our home and are going to keep food on the table, how serious is the problem? We had anticipated some obstacles, that's why I'm working."

"Didn't you hear me? I said I have lost our life's savings because I didn't think ahead! All of our sacrificing has been for nothing. The cold nights, an unfurnished house, and driving a raggedy car didn't mean a damn thing! It will take me years to accumulate that much money again, but you don't even see the tragedy. Daddy Beau was right, all my decisions stink!" Jerome dropped his head into his hands and quietly sobbed.

Once again Gail recalled her conversations with Naomi McGhee. "Losing our money is one thing, losing your self-confidence is far worse," Gail said. She pulled Jerome from the easy chair, sat him on the couch next to her, and put his head in her lap.

"When I was a little girl," Gail said while stroking Jerome's head, "I used to sit on the floor next to Daddy Beau's big leather chair and listen to him, Lonnie Blackman, and other businessmen as they cited problem after problem in their struggle for economic independence. He ran his fingers through my hair as they talked for hours, got mad, swore, thought something up, determined it wouldn't work, and then came up with something else. You lost our savings while trying to grow; then what could be nobler? Only difference between you and them is… they didn't quit."

Jerome jerked his head from Gail's lap, and said, "Who the hell…" Gail quickly picked up their cups and rushed toward the kitchen. She stood at the sink for what seemed an eternity and washed each dish over and over, waiting for….

Ten long minutes passed. "Gail!" yelled Jerome; he came into the kitchen. Life had returned to Jerome's eyes. He held Gail by her arms and said, "You're right! The common dominator between the Beauregards and the Jacksons and the Blackmans is perseverance. Not intelligence, not ability, not money, not luck; but perseverance. If those pioneers couldn't get what they wanted one way, they tried another and another, for days, weeks, or years, until they achieved. They used their cunning, their wit, their shrewdness, until a path was possible through serious obstacles; that's what I have to do."

"What's that Honey?"

"Why persevere!" Jerome said, as if Gail should have known the answer. Jerome moved to the kitchen table, pulled out several pencils and a legal pad from a drawer and began writing.

An hour later Gail asked, "Want some tea, Babe?"

"Hell no; what I need is some strong coffee, with…"

"With perseverance added?" Gail said.

"Yeah, that's right. Keep the coffee coming Babe, with lots of perseverance!"

Later that evening, Gail put before Jerome another fresh, hot mug of black coffee. She looked over his shoulder and didn't understand anything on the page except $3,000, which had been written repeatedly. Gail checked back an hour later. The second cup was empty. Names of persons, phone numbers, and partial sentences had been scrawled. Several pages had been trashed. She wasn't sure if Jerome wanted more coffee; she bought some anyway—just in case. But what Gail realized was that Jerome was working intensely toward a solution.

It was after midnight. Jerome had reduced his strategies and tactics to one page without stopping for dinner. Gail and her daughters had eaten in the living room on T.V. trays. The one remaining page contained the essence of all the knowledge he had gathered since leaving Beaumont, Texas, including his University of Chicago studies and readings, all that other successful entrepreneurs had done and talked about doing to accomplish their goals. After an evening of concentrated study, research, and phone calls, Jerome had prepared a plan that had to be executed in six days. Tomorrow, Thursday, was Day One.

End of Chapter Eight

CHAPTER NINE

"Hey Joel, I'm glad to see you," Jerome said as Joel arrived late for the evening shift. It was Sunday, Day Four. Thursday through Saturday Jerome had worked at increasing sales.

"Hey man, what's going on?" Joel answered as he extended his open hand for a light brush; he was speaking and acting colored. Two hours later Joel said, "Jerome, there's a play at school I want to see, so I'm leaving early." Joel considered Jerome a subordinate. His position was secure with his "uncle."

"How's business?" Sid asked as he pulled out his register key and took an interim reading. Jerome had added to the purchases of his present customer. "I came back for my checkbook. Joel left early again?"

"Around five, said something was going on at school; I don't mind."

"You never mind, no matter Joel's irresponsible behavior. You know, your off-day is our slowest day. Joel hasn't learned much, especially how to increase sales as you just did."

Pleasant, idle chatter passed between Sid and Jerome until closing. Sid locked the front door, pulled two cans of Schlitz beer from the cooler, handed one to Jerome and said, "You know Jer, the new store is not doing well, and then there's Joel who treats this job like a bad cold." *Something's up* Jerome thought. He took a long swig and waited.

"I've been feeling rotten lately. My doctor says it may be ulcers or clogged arteries; he is giving me a complete physical. I'm going in Tuesday, might have to stay two days." Sid looked at Jerome and said, "What I'm trying to say is, we're a team and Joel isn't part of it."

"I understand Sid. I'll put in all the time needed until your diagnoses are completed." *His hospitalization improves my tactics,* Jerome thought.

"Stay close to me Jer, I'll look after you. Just let me get through this medical ordeal." Sid looked pitiful as he smiled and patted Jerome on his shoulder.

"You can always count on me Sid," Jerome lied.

It was Monday, 4:15 p.m. Day Five, only two days left. Sid was expected to stop by before his hospital internment Tuesday morning. Joel was off. Each time the front door opened, Jerome searched for Sid. Time was running out. *Come on Sid!*

At last; Sid finally entered. Jerome stooped down behind the counter and called Gail at work. Jerome whispered, "Now! Make the call now!" He sneaked downstairs, opened his handkerchief, placed black pepper pods under his lower eyelids, and waited.

After answering the phone, Sid yelled, "Jerome. It's a Dr. Spaulding's nurse from Beaumont, Texas."

Jerome looked perplexed while taking the phone. Sid started to leave, but Jerome raised a finger asking him to stay. "Yes, this is Jerome Gerard… What!… Oh no!… Yes doctor… no, no, you go ahead, I'll be there with the money in a couple of days… Yes… Yes… I'll have enough to pay all the bills… Guaranteed… Please take good care of her Dr. Spaulding… Thank you, Sir."

"Oh Lord. It's my Momma!" Jerome sobbed as he hung up the phone and laid his head on the counter. Through irregular breathing Jerome caused his complexion to blanch making him appear ill. Jerome kept his head down, crying until he heard his cue.

"What's the matter?" Sid asked as he patted Jerome's back after hearing Jerome's frantic side of the conversation and witnessing his reaction. Sid never questioned why Jerome suggested he stay within hearing range.

"Momma's appendix has erupted!" (Dr. Ben had helped Jerome determine the right medical emergency) Through flashing tear-filled reddened eyes, because of the pepper pods, Jerome said, "She needs surgery immediately. I authorized the operation and told him I would be there with the money in two days."

"I don't have much cash on hand," Sid said as he pulled out a wad of crumpled bills.

"Thank you Sid," Jerome said, as he pushed back Sid's hand. "But I don't know how much I will need. Can you spare me for a week, maybe two?"

"Of course we can; this is an emergency. Joel and Allen will cover this store. Joel will just have to work long hours for a change."

"I will need some money, though, probably as much as a thousand dollars, to cover the cost of travel, the operation, and I don't know what else. I know you would advance me the money, but I'd rather borrow it from your bank. That would allow me to repay the loan over time. I just don't know how much I'll need." Jerome paused a long moment and then asked the crucial question. "Would you cosign a loan for me?" Jerome peeked at his watch. It was 4:40. *They quit answering the phone at Avalon Bank in five minutes!*

"I'll do it, but only because it's for your mother. Besides, by telling this Dr. Spaulding you will guarantee him being paid legally obligates you, which means if you don't pay you can be sued for treble damages, then where would I be?" Sid said as he called the bank. Jerome continued sobbing, leaning on the counter and shaking his head. *He bought the verbal contract scenario that Samuel had suggested.*

"Manny Singleton please, Sidney Reis calling… Well catch him, this is important… Manny, Sidney Reis. Jerome has an emergency back home. He needs a loan… Hell, I don't know, perhaps as much as a thousand dollars… I know you don't normally, but he's obligated himself so what else can I do? Whatever it is I'll co-sign for it… Yes, use my special savings account as collateral… He'll be in tomorrow morning. I'll tell him to ask for you."

"Thank you so much, Boss," Jerome said smiling and crying simultaneously.

"You go on home now and pull yourself together," Sid said, "you can't handle customers crying all over the place." Jerome walked out of Tailor's Pharmacy for the very last time. The only thing he left was his Illinois license hanging on the wall, which he had replaced with a photocopy.

Tuesday morning was Day Six. Based on information from Daniel Quibble's bank specialist Jerome had decided that Mr. Singleton, because of his having only a high school education, would be more favorably influenced by an ignorant Negro than an intelligent one.

Jerome had visited the bank many times, for Sid, but was sure Mr. Singleton had never noticed him. Caucasians ignore Negroes. "How about those Bears," Manny said to himself; he was a day late reading Monday's

Chicago Chronicle. Manny was leaning back in his chair, one foot in a lower drawer, drinking coffee and smoking a Lucky Strike. His desk plate read, "M. Singleton, Vice President, Loans."

Daniel Quibble's bank specialist had also reported Manny Singleton had been passed over for promotion several times. His latest evaluation read, "Mr. Singleton has difficulty making decisions within his realm of responsibility."

"Suh, uh, did Mr. Reis say somethin' to you 'bout me yestiddy?" Jerome asked as he extended his neck and bucked his eyes, doing a Willie Best imitation which he had practiced for a week. Willie Best was a Negro movie actor, during the 40's and 50's that played a stereotypical, ignorant, subservient, colored man. Jerome was standing at Mr. Singleton's desk. He flashed his white teeth and held his cotton plaid cap in both hands. His back was slightly hunched and his course hair uncombed. Jerome was wearing worn gym shoes, kakis, a white tee shirt, and a thin poplin jacket. He was underdressed for the cold weather.

The buttons on Singleton's dark blue vest stretched their links over his protruding stomach. The first two fingers on his right hand were nicotine stained. Singleton pulled down his newspaper and said, "Mr. Reis said you needed a loan, Boy. So what else is new? You people never have learned to save."

"Naw Suh, we shor doesn't, but I's learned my lesson now, I truly has," Jerome grinned with his large teeth flashing.

"Don't you have sense enough to put on a coat on a day like this?" Singleton said paternalistically while shaking his head.

"Aw, it ain't dat cold, but thank you for carin', Suh, dat's mighty kind o' you, mighty kind. But I'll be headin' down south directly; where it's warm." Jerome's coal-like complexion, his left eye which never opened as wide as his right, his large nose and gargantuan mouth which he left slightly open, made it easy for him to appear ignorant. "It took me most o' de night ciphering, but I's finally figured it out. To pay for ever'thing including travel, de doctor, an de hospital, spec I'll need at least $3,000. See?" Jerome handed Singleton a torn piece of paper with illegible numbers and scribbled words.

Singleton crushed out his cigarette, put down his newspaper, and stared at Jerome through pig-like eyes as if he had expelled a loud fart. Singleton glanced at the ragged paper and threw it in the trash.

"Now I knows that's a heap 'o money, Suh, but my kin will hep me pay you back, yes dey will. My mammy is having an operation and I's already tol de doctor I'd be dere wit de money on account uh, Mr. Reis tol me to. He said he tol you he would co-sign… did he?"

"Sorry Boy, personal loans cap out at $1,000. Mr. Reis will have to withdraw the money if he wants you to have that much." Singleton picked up his paper, flipped the portion above the fold into an upright position and began reading again.

"But Suh, dis is a co-signed loan. Dat's what co-signing means; dat Mr. Reis is responsible, don't it?" As Jerome spoke he slowly raised his face above Singleton's newspaper making eye contact. "Why any one o' Mr. Reis' accounts has way mo dan $3,000, doesn't dey?" *How could Singleton have missed the portion of Sid's assuming responsibility*, Jerome thought?

"Well, yes," Singleton said as he lowered his newspaper, scratched his scalp with one finger and then patted his thinning hair back into place, "but I need to make sure Mr. Reis knows how much money you want."

'O course you does Suh. Here's his number right chere. He'll ok it jes like he did yestiddy. Boss Reis takes real good care 'o me." A broad smile covered Jerome's face. He turned to Singleton's assistants, displaying pride and confidence in his employer. Jerome had anticipated Singleton would call Sidney.

"Mr. Reis is unavailable for at least the rest of the day," Joel said per Sidney's instructions. He did not want anyone to know he was in the hospital.

"Well, Mr. Reis did say he would co-sign for any amount, using his special saving account as collateral," Singleton said to himself as he hung up.

"Yes Suh, he surly did. And I do has to leave town directly, my mammy bein' sick and all." Jerome presented Singleton with another broad smile.

"Well," Singleton said, as he played with the gold chain across his vest, "I'd better speak to the president about this sized loan, even if Mr. Reis is ultimately responsible."

Oh oh, thought Jerome, *I'm about to get fired. President Mosel might attempt to call Beaumont, Texas and discover my story is totally fictitious.*

I hadn't anticipated this. "Uh," Jerome said very slowly again looking confused. "Mr. Reis said you was in charge 'o loans and dis is a small loan, ain't it? Why your thing-a-majig don't even say small loans, it just say loans." Both men looked toward the president's office. The door was closed.

Last week, Singleton entered Mosel's office without knocking. The president had said, "my door is closed for a reason! Aren't you capable of making any decisions?" Alsip Knowles, the senior vice-president's, door was open; he was the last person Singleton would consult. Knowles was given the much sought after promotion instead of Singleton three months ago.

"I am," Singleton said as he recalled the comment in his last evaluation. He took a long pull on his cigarette and repeated, "You're right dammit, I am." Singleton pulled out a multi-copy contract, rolled it into his manual typewriter and, with two fingers, began filling in the blanks.

"Uh Suh, is it awright if I sits down?" Jerome asked. His seat, with an adjustment, allowed him to read Singleton's entries. When he reached the payment terms Jerome said, "Please make that a two year loan with the first payment due in 90 days, and with a no-penalty prepayment clause?" *Oh, oh, I forgot my dialect*, Jerome realized.

Singleton stopped typing and stared at Jerome, who said, "Uh, that will gib' me the uh time to uh work tings out wit' the rest 'o my family, you see." Jerome blinked repeatedly.

"Where did you learn so much about loan structures, Boy?"

"Uh, Mr. Reis tol' me to ax you to do it that a way. He made me repeat it ober and ober until he was sure I knowd ever word; uh, did I git it right?"

"Yes, you did," Singleton said, reflecting. He then decided, even though Jerome spoke correctly, it didn't mean he knew what he was saying. Singleton believed Negroes could memorize words without knowing their meaning as he had witnessed in Negro minstrel shows when he was a child, so he resumed typing. Ted Thomas had advised Jerome regarding favorable loan structures.

"Sign here Boy. You can write, can't you?" Singleton said loudly, attempting to embarrass Jerome. His subordinates snickered, Jerome smiled.

"Mr. Singleton, Suh," Jerome asked while inspecting the contract, "is it awright if'n I write in the date ob my fust payment, just so's I don't forget? They's a space for it right chere."

"Give me that damn contract." The date of April 15, 1957, should have been and was then typed in. Jerome signed above the space reserved for Sidney Reis' signature, which also held Sidney's skim account number.

"Here are your bank draft and your copy of the contract; not that you know anything about reading contracts. You're mighty lucky boy. There aren't many bosses who would co-sign for this size loan, especially for a nigger."

"I knows you right Suh." Singleton grabbed his newspaper, lit a cigarette, and returned to the sports page. Jerome went to the nearest teller and received a cashier's check for $3,000. He put on his overcoat as soon as he cleared the bank.

"Erwin, can we meet in my lawyers' offices tomorrow, Wednesday at 9:00 a.m.?" Erwin agreed; he was surprised that Jerome's lawyer's office was downtown, near the courthouse. Jerome was so happy he could hardly speak without laughing. Jerome called Samuel and gave him the details.

"I'll be in court, but everything's ready. Say, Man, how did you negotiate a personal loan with Avalon bank? They don't finance anything for us but cars, and only when they hold the titles."

"I persevered."

During the closing Joseph, the paralegal, agreed to place the legally required public newspaper notices without Erwin's involvement. Jerome flinched but said nothing. Irwin and Jerome knew that was supposed to be a seller's expense.

The published Change of Ownership notices appeared only in the *Chicago Defender* and the *Chicago Crusader*, both were Black owned, which technically met the legal requirements. The wholesalers' attorneys never checked Negro publications for anything, so McKlosky's credit lines stayed open.

Jerome and Erwin went to what was now Jerome's drugstore. "I'll give you a through orientation before leaving you on your own," Erwin said. All day Jerome asked questions; he wrote down anything he wanted to remember. Jerome filled a bucket with soapy water and began cleaning and merchandising shelves while listing out-of-stocks, like hot combs and curling irons. He called each customer Ma'am or Sir, when appropriate. They assumed Jerome was a new porter.

At closing time McKlosky put the day's receipts, the change bank, and the cash from each register drawer into his money pouch. McKlosky pilfered two hundred dollars' worth of controlled narcotics he had promised to sell a fellow druggist and put them in the pouch. After McKlosky locked the front door he handed Jerome the keys, tucked the pouch under his arm, and started to depart. Jerome said, "Erwin, since we closed our deal this morning, today's receipts are mine, aren't they?"

"So I was working for you today, eh?"

"I thought that was your intention; didn't you say this was a voluntary orientation session?

"But my change banks are in here. That's $300 separate from the day's receipts."

"We'll let that cover your employees' pay, your utility bills to date, and the public announcements." *And I'll get back the narcotics you didn't think I saw you steal.*

"You're a lot smarter than I thought, Sonny," McKlosky laughed as he handed Jerome the pouch. McKlosky pulled up his fleece-lined storm coat collar and shouted as he walked away, "Anyone asks where I am, tell 'em after I sold the store I went to Aruba," He took a few steps, stopped, looked back over his half-moon glasses and shouted, "but you've probably developed a reason for my not being here, already."

All Jerome had in the world was the pouch containing over $500. As soon as McKlosky drove away Jerome yelled to the stars with arms raised. "I'm in! I'm in!"

At home Jerome explained to Michelle and Dana that a life-altering event was taking place. "Are you going to be your own boss, Daddy?" Michelle asked. Being the boss sounded special.

"Well," Jerome smiled, "I'll be responsible for what happens in my business; however, many people will suggest what I should do. They are called customers. Keeping them satisfied will determine how well my business does." Jerome considered the difference between keeping customers satisfied and satisfying customers, which was in a University of Chicago, marketing home study course, but didn't introduce the complicated variance to his daughters.

"Mommy is going to help me get started, so, for a little while, we won't be with you as much, which means you must mind Aunt Allie even better than you usually do and continue to do well in school." Both girls agreed to put forth a special effort which they understood would help the family's new venture.

They were standing in front of his store on a cold Thursday, February morning at 7:00 a.m. Gail had reluctantly received a two-week unpaid leave-of-absence from Baxter Bridges. Jerome said to Gail, "So this is what it feels like."

"What? All I feel is sleepy and cold."

"Why to open your own store! It's amazing, like nothing else I have ever experienced; it's even better than sex!" Jerome savored the power as his key unlocked his store's door for the very first time. He knew he would be working twelve hour days seven days a week for––the Lord only knows how long––but that didn't matter.

It was two hours before the store would open. Jerome taught Gail how to departmentalize on her register, how to sell older cigarettes first, based on date codes, and where popular items like toothpastes, cold remedies, and aspirin were located. "Anything you can't find quickly ask me. We'll learn where things are together," Jerome said through an encouraging smile.

It was 8:55 a.m. Just before Jerome unlocked the front door; he took Gail's hands in his and said, "Babe, our customers are the most important people in our lives. Each one can send five new customers if they're pleased, or can stop fifteen from coming if they're not. So smile say thank you and treat each customer as if they're paying our mortgage––because collectively they are."

"New owners, new staff," Jerome said as he handed Ms. Obese her check as she arrived for work late. She was shocked; she couldn't imagine a Negro dismissing her or owning anything. Customers were delighted with Gail's friendliness; Ms. Obese was not missed. White customers when they asked about McKlosky were told he was on vacation. Negroes were "confidentially" told Jerome was De Man.

The Word spread that a colored man owned McKlosky's. Scores of Negroes came in and bought a 50 cent pack of cigarettes or a nickel pack of gum to see what a Negro business owner looked like. Some asked, "You hiring?"

Before noon, a drug addict sauntered in. He wore an oversized long sleeve nylon shirt as an outer garment; Jerome shivered for him. The razor-thin, short addict's fingers with yellowing nails and long, expertly shaped tips seemed attached to his cheek. The corners of his mouth turned downward. The junky slurred, "Say Bruz, I mean uh, what you got for a drip my man?" His dark hand with blackened knuckles left his face and grabbed his crotch. The clap stain had seeped through his rayon pants.

"Take one of these four times a day for three days. If the drip doesn't stop go to the hospital and don't even think about mentioning me. That's $5." The twelve penicillin pills cost sixty cents. The junky was surprised; McKlosky had never sold Negroes prescription drugs over the counter.

"And what you got for a––a bad habit my man?" the addict asked while scratching his shoulder.

"A headache stick," Jerome said pulling out a miniature baseball bat and pointed it toward the lost soul whose last gasp of self-esteem was tied to an emery board.

"Ok, ok, I see," the junky said through weak eyes and a knowing smile. He raised both hands in mock surrender, "Doc Holliday is up in here. That's cool."

"This is a drugstore," Jerome said as he slapped the small bat in his hand. "You got medical problems, I'll help. Anything else, go elsewhere." The Street Word went forward that the new owner will not be intimidated, but if you need legitimate help and can pay for it, this is the place.

Late afternoon a 60-ish, dark, white haired woman entered carrying a picnic basket with fresh cooked chicken and dumplings, homemade biscuits, warm blueberry cobbler, plus utensils and plates. Towels kept the food hot. "Thought you young folks might need some nourishment, decent restaurants don't exist around here. Besides," she said as she filled their plates, "owners shouldn't have to leave their place of business to eat; even I know that much."

"This sure tastes good and is truly welcomed," Jerome said after devouring the delicious meal; he gave Widow Gram a big hug. While she gathered her utensils to leave Jerome asked, "While holding several bills toward Widow Gram, can I pay you to cook one big meal a day for me and my crew?"

"Why of course," heavy-set Gram said, beaming, "as long as I can get a hug." She was delighted to have nice people to cook for, plus the income.

Within two days Jerome had hired three people from the neighborhood. The first was Josephine, a stout, friendly, middle aged woman who was working as a maid. She cherished the more dignified job and increased earnings. Agnes, an attractive single mother of two on government Aid to Dependent Children (ADC) wanted to work part-time evenings and be paid off-the-books, so her earnings would not affect her entitlements. Josephine and Agnes willingly worked each other's off day, all day.

The third employee was Henry, an amiable young man who was physically fit but mentally slow. He worked irregular, long hours, cleaned and mopped floors, busted boxes, emptied trash containers, and watched the store while Jerome worked downstairs or got off his feet for a few minutes. Henry's compensation was pocket change, Gram's delicious meals, and most important, the opportunity to belong to something.

Initially Jerome and Gail worked open to close from nine to nine. Gail, Agnes, and Josephine learned together. After a week Gail returned home because Josephine and Agnes had learned their needed skills. Gail, having watched Jerome work, had a new appreciation for his abilities. McKlosky's payroll had four employees; Jerome had two, himself and Josephine.

A week after Jerome's departure Sid tried to call the Negro hospital in Beaumont, Texas. The closest Negro hospital was in Houston and there was no patient named Martha Gerard, or any doctor named Spaulding. Calls to Jerome's home answered by "Aunt Allie" were, at best, confusing.

During the second week one of the route vendors mentioned to Sid he was surprised to see Jerome working at McKlosky's. Sid didn't understand, nor did he want to confront elderly, hard-of-hearing McKlosky, so Sid told Manny Singleton to investigate.

"Thank you for calling McKlosky's Pharmacy, how can I help you?" Jerome answered. He knew there was equity in McKlosky's name, presently.

"May I speak to Jerome Gerard?" Singleton asked.

"Yass, suh," Jerome said, "dis here is Jerome Suh, uh, what does you want?"

Singleton was dumbfounded. The ignorant-sounding Negro he gave the loan could speak intelligently. "So it is you," Singleton shouted, "you are working there. Where the hell is my money!?"

"Mr. Singleton, why are you shouting?" Jerome asked in his normal voice, "My first payment isn't due for ten weeks, right?"

"You slick, black son-of-a-bitch! You committed fraud. I'll have your family set out on the street if you don't pay me immediately. You probably lost my money shooting dice or chasing fat-ass trollops. I'm sending the police over there as soon as I hang up. Where is Mr. McKlosky? Let me talk to him!"

"Mr. McKlosky is no longer here, Sir. I now own this store," Jerome said, ignoring Singleton's insults and threats.

Singleton said, after a long silence, "Own——you own McKlosky's store?"

"Yes sir." The phone went silent again.

"Are you a registered pharmacist?"

"Yes Sir."

Again, Singleton was flabbergasted; Jerome was a college graduate? But Jerome was still a Negro, therefore automatically inferior. "If you don't pay your loan on time and we have to sue you'll pay any added expense. That's in the contract, Boy," Singleton said.

"I know, I know," Jerome said barely above a whisper, but Mr. Singleton why are we discussing a default situation? I plan to pay in a timely manner."

"You will hear from our lawyers before this day is over."

"Sir, wouldn't it make more sense and save us both money if you and I talked, then if we can't agree, involve our lawyers?" Jerome continued a conversational tone.

"Hmm, that sounds reasonable." Singleton snatched the phone from his ear, glared at it, and silently chastised himself for agreeing with a Negro. "Get your black ass in here before I change my mind!"

"Wouldn't it be better, Mr. Singleton, if you came here and let me prove how easily I will be able to repay the loan?"

"Your store; now just how in the world did that happen? When are you there, Boy?"

"I'm here all the time, Sir; all the time."

"Doesn't look like much to me," Manny Singleton said as he walked about the small drugstore, "inspecting." It was Jerome's third week. Josephine had greeted Singleton from behind a sparkling new case with a humidor; the tobacco distributor had provided it gratis if Jerome stocked fresh cigars. He also added snuff and chewing tobacco. Because the snow brought in by customers turned to slush, Henry had been constantly mopping. The hard wood floor was clean but damp.

"Welcome Mr. Singleton, glad you finally made it!" Jerome said as he rushed from behind the pharmacist's counter with his hand outstretched. Jerome's spotless, white, knee-length coat over his white shirt and tie looked very professional. Singleton ignored Jerome's greeting and gesture. Jerome moved behind Singleton and helped him out of his coat; he said, "Mr. Singleton, let me show you around. I know you are busy, so I'll be brief."

"This is my stockroom," Jerome said as they stood in the middle of his newly organized, lower level storage space. Jerome had returned $2,000 worth of outdated and damaged product for full credit to manufacturers. Other merchandise had been cleaned by Henry and displayed in full, foil covered fruit baskets that customers could reach, emblazoned, **DRASTICALLY REDUCED.**

"Direct purchases from manufacturers," Jerome explained, "yield higher profits with slower turnover. Daily orders from wholesalers that go directly on the shelves produce lower profits but faster turnover. The two sources properly balanced achieve the optimum twelve turns a year, which, with rebates and timely payment discounts, generate at least a 40% profit margin."

They went back upstairs. Jerome had convinced a small appliance vendor to install and fill a glass enclosed display case on consignment. "These watches, clocks, costume jewelry, and radios, which are slow movers, are marked up 300% and yield a 75% profit margin." Singleton mumbled agreement, but Jerome knew he didn't understand the difference between mark-ups and profit margins. Jerome, showed Singleton his prescription files. "I've already more than doubled McKlosky's prescription volume."

"That's impossible! Nobody can increase anything that much in less than a month," Singleton said as he scrutinized the documents.

"Prescriptions are marked up at 200% or more. Here is the direct line to Dr. Steinbaum's office," Jerome said pointing to the newly installed phone. He showed Singleton the prescription numbers from McKlosky's last two weeks and Jerome's first two weeks. Simple math proved Jerome right. Jerome had agreed to pay Dr. Steinbaum's rent, (less 15%) if he at least doubled his prescription volume. Now all of Dr. Steinbaum's prescriptions were filled by Jerome, unlike before when many went elsewhere.

"Look at these reports and compare the daily sales figures for our first two weeks with McKlosky's last two weeks. Don't even consider the recent cold spell which kept some customers at home."

"Well, they are up," Singleton reluctantly admitted. Singleton noticed cigarette sales were up over 100% which now included cigars and other tobacco items. Jerome's sales-oriented staff offered a sixty cent savings on each carton, a twenty-five cent savings on each half-carton, and a free four-cigarette sample pack with every three-pack cigarette purchase. Cigars were offered in threes at a 5% savings.

Sundry sales had increased as well. Josephine and Agnes were encouraged to suggest economy sizes and suggest related items as well as display case merchandise. Purchases by Dr. Steinbaum's patients' were also significant. They were encouraged to shop while awaiting their prescriptions whether they were ready or not. Neighborhood customers told friends that bargains were available at McKlosky's. Friendly, attractive Agnes persuaded older men to spend more than they intended and to become loyal customers.

"Our expenses are down with only two persons on the payroll (Singleton saw Henry working but didn't ask how he was paid or who filled in for Josephine at the end of her shift), and our rent is only $400 a month. Here is our lease." Jerome didn't mention the additional $300 a month for the next ten months he was paying for inventory.

"Even wholesalers are glad I'm here. See how full my store is?" John, with L&S Distributors, had discreetly increased "McKlosky's" available credit. The damaged returns had also allowed Jerome to increase saleable inventory without additional purchases. "And I am the real estate manager for the six nearby stores, which adds to my income and knocks 15% off my rent. Here is my written authority." Mr. Singleton nodded affirmatively; obviously impressed with all the written documents he had been shown.

"How do you like your coffee Mr. Singleton?" Jerome asked as he sat on a stool so he wouldn't tower over his short, chubby guest. "As you can see, I'll have no trouble paying my note, and if I can receive a line of credit and a business checking account I'll leave this account in your bank and send you others."

"What others? You have other accounts?" Singleton asked eager to bring new business to Avalon which could improve his chances for promotion.

"I have friends and tenants who may switch banks if they can receive credit lines and open business checking accounts. I also have favorable relationships with Mayor O'Malley and Congressman Dawson. Perhaps after you begin treating Negroes as equals I might send some city or even federal business your way."

Banks, only when encouraged by Caucasian depositors, allowed Negroes personal or business checking accounts. There was a "Gentlemen's Agreement" between all banks not to issue any credit lines to Negroes beyond their accounts' monthly average balance. Singleton knew challenging the status quo would not be possible.

"None of that means a damn," Singleton said, "You lied to me and Mr. Reis which is a felony!"

"My mother's illness is not documented; therefore, the reason for the loan is moot. All you have is a collateralized note signed by me and co-signed by Sidney Reis," Jerome said authoritatively as he stood and stepped closer to Singleton, towering over him. "No provable crime has been committed. Any bogus charges placed against me will result in a hefty suit against Avalon Bank. Payment of my loan will be the least of your worries." Jerome paused for a moment to let his comments register.

"You can't hurt me," Singleton said, bending his head backward looking up into Jerome's face as he fiddled with the chain to his vest pocket watch. Jerome heard the unstated but implied question, can you?

"Adverse publicity hurts any business, Mr. Singleton, especially banks. For instance, seventy-five percent of your depositors are Negroes, yet you hold no Negro mortgages. You have no Negro employees, not even a janitor. You have made no loans to Negro businessmen, yet Bronzeville is gradually encircling your bank." *Thank you, Buddy Laws.*

"None of which is against the law," Singleton said as he pulled out a small handkerchief and wiped his brow.

"No, but when the Negro press publishes these facts and Negro preachers blaspheme Avalon Bank from their pulpits, it could cause a run, which could-cost-you-your-job." Jerome created a pregnant pause, then said, "Why don't you and I meet with Mr. Mosel and discuss this scenario?"

"What about Sidney Reis?" Singleton said as he nervously pulled a cigarette from his pack and lit it. "He's the reason I'm here; if I don't press charges, he surely will." Mr. Singleton felt intimidated.

"If Sid agrees to forget the past, will you?" Jerome asked as he backed away from a nervous Singleton and resumed sitting.

"Why, yes, of course, and I'll have no problem opening you a business checking account. A line of credit, well, that's another matter. Can you really get Avalon some city and federal accounts?" Singleton asked in a high pitched voice as Jerome helped him into his coat.

"If you treat me and my friends equally I'll get some new accounts for Avalon and see that you get the credit." They shook hands. Neither believed the "equal treatment" day would occur soon.

As Singleton exited, Jerome called to Josephine, "Give Mr. Singleton a carton of Luckies, on the house." Singleton smiled and waved the carton as he left.

Jerome called Samuel; he now had a direct line number, as did most business owners. He went over the details and then said, "You were right again, Counselor."

"You have just learned one of America's best kept secrets," Samuel said, "which is, how dumb some White folks in responsible positions, are. I'll have a Jewish lawyer friend convince Sidney never to breathe a disparaging word against you. We have enough evidence, like the numbers on Sid's skim account from your copy of the loan contract, to have him convicted for tax evasion. He will also be told his debt of $2,200 will be forgiven if he speaks favorably about you when asked."

"Why won't you talk to him?"

"Simple. Mr. Reis will believe every word from his kindred but he would hardly listen to me."

The news of Jerome's ownership gradually spread throughout the city. Before cutting credit lines wholesalers checked Jerome's accounts and realized he was discounting his invoices which earned him the highest credit ratings and additional profit percentages. After visiting the remodeled, improved store they were confident the new corporation, Courtesy Drugs, was in competent hands.

Jerome answered the phone, he heard a familiar voice say, "is there a former silly-dilly-star-fool in the house?"

"Well, hello Louise; it's good to hear from an old friend."

"Sugar, you have graduated from 'Do Others Before They Do You, U', with honors. When Sid learned that you owned McKlosky's he repeatedly mumbled 'he can't do that. Why he was always asking me for money. How did he do that?' One day a lawyer-type Jew came in, and pointed his finger in Sid's face while lecturing him. All Sid said was 'yes sir' and 'I understand sir.'" Jerome and Louise both laughed. "And this is really strange; when he's talking to vendors he sings your praises. I've never seen anything like it. I mean here's a Jew telling other Jews what a good businessman a Negro is. You sure got over on him."

Louise waited to be enlightened, in vain. "One more thing, Sugar; If you ever need to, uh, unwind you've got my number. Of course now that you've moved up in class there may be a slight fee, but it'll be worth it."

"Thanks Louise; glad to hear about Sid's responses. Take care."

Ralph, the Plenty Good Ice Cream representative, walked in as if he were from the Board of Health. He gleaned an ice cream bar, and said, "My driver told me you couldn't afford to take delivery. Now listen Jer, if you are short of funds I'll carry you, but only for one month, and that's after you sign a non-competitive agreement." Ralph chomped down on the ice cream bar.

"You were misinformed," Jerome said. "I refused your delivery because we're going to carry Anson Ice Cream. How long will it take you to remove your freezer?"

"Mr. Gerard, the only reason," a shocked Ralph whined, "I haven't been in earlier is because——well I've been tied up, you understand. I forgot to mention you are entitled to a new owner's free fill up and I'll beat any offer Anson has made." Ralph hurried to pay Jerome the dime for the ice cream bar.

"I'm surprised you haven't learned by now, Ralph, but it's not about money. I thought you were more intelligent than that. Anson deserves this store and since your company prohibits competitors…"

Ralph said, "Su-suppose I give Anson three rows in my freezer, just between you and me. Can I keep the stop then? I've lost two stops already this month to Sealtest. If I lose another…"

"Well, if you increase our volume rebate by 5%, which is what Anson offered me and Harold Oldham maybe we will…"

"Harold too! Oh my God, if I lose him and you I'll be fired for sure."

"If you agree to give Anson three facings in each of Harold's five stores and suggest to Sid that Anson Ice Cream can have three facings in his store that may appease Anson, temporarily at least."

"Sure Mr. Gerard, anything you say, sir."

"How did you get Ralph to agree?" Harold Oldham asked when Jerome told him the news. "I've been after him for years."

"He finally listened to reason," Jerome said and then added, "Push Ralph to raise your volume discount by 5%."

"Kermit Anson? Jerome Gerard. You have just picked up seven new stops… You're more than welcome. They should have been yours all along… I didn't think you could afford to install freezers so you now have space in Plenty Good's. With the increase in sales you may want to consider starting a new business, while increasing your own… Representing manufacturers… Well, when you research the industry, you'll learn that it's not complicated. One of the best ways for us to get our products before Caucasians, is for Caucasians not to know who manufacturers them. There are a number of items made by us that are non-ethnic; leather-ized shoe strings, Soul Skins, Rex's floor wax, Cody's Bar-B-Q-Sauce, your ice cream, are just examples; there may be others. If you hire Ralph from Plenty Good, who should be interested in a better opportunity, he can represent you and the companies I just mentioned to grocery and drug stores, from a general market perspective. This would give you added distribution and profits from the companies you represent… Yeah, I thought you would like the idea. Soon you may be able to afford your own freezers, as well as non-competitive contracts.

"Oh, one more thing," Jerome added. "I have an excellent spot for a new ice cream parlor on Forty-Seventh near Lake Park… Good, I thought you might be interested." *Gail will help me construct a compatible deal for Anson and find additional tenants.*

Jerome looked over his store and envisioned it as the first of many. *Now just who was it that said I couldn't do things right?*

End of Chapter Nine

CHAPTER TEN

Within six months, Jerome's loans from Avalon Bank and Doc McKlosky had been fully paid. His raised salary included a little discretionary income. A daily skim was deposited quarterly in a numbered Cayman Island account. Thanks to Gail, his vacancies had been rented; the 15% commissions purchased tax free municipal bonds.

During his ninth month, he hired his second full time employee, young, Registered Pharmacist, Webster Henderson. They worked together until Jerome was sure Webster could; increase sales, keep Dr. Steinbaum content, eliminate or delay a doctor's visit for locals with super profitable generic remedies, and manage staff––only then, did Jerome take time off from his twelve hour, seven day schedule. Webster, noticing Jerome was taking advanced college courses, decided to do the same. Jerome agreed to reimburse him.

After three and a half years' experience, Jerome bought right, effectively merchandised and continuously taught his staff sales and people skills. Courtesy Drugs was very profitable. Gail was in the top 10% of Baxter Bridges' sales staff. He was a difficult task master but an excellent teacher.

The Gerards agreed to invest 90% of Gail's earnings in conservative mutual funds. The 10% was her "mad" money. "Don't forget Babe," Gail said over the phone, "Daddy Beau is having dinner with us tonight, so please be on time."

"I can't wait," Jerome answered.

"You're early," Gail said to her dad who had arrived by livery. Michelle and Dana almost knocked Granddaddy Beau down when they saw the miniature kitchen sets he had bought them.

"This carpet is simply beautiful; it must have been expensive," Conrad said as he removed his shoes at the front door. He sat on the couch, not in Jerome's recliner.

"We bought the carpet, including free installation and padding, for cash at a going-out-of-business sale. Looks like Hank Aaron will lead the Milwaukee Braves to the World Series," Jerome said after fixing drinks and joining Conrad in the living room. "He's the best ball player we've seen in a 100 years, White or Black."

"And it may be another century before the struggle for integrated schools ends, the way those southerners are behaving," Conrad said.

Jerome, surprised by Conrad's new Civil Rights advocacy, said, "Not much difference here. Mayor O'Malley appointed a staunch segregationist as school superintendent."

"You worked hard to get him elected, what good did it do?"

"Well not as good as we had hoped, but still it has been a definite improvement. Mayor O'Malley hired a number of Negroes in City Hall after they were blessed by the congressman and appointed a Negro as head of the Chicago Housing Authority which was a major benefit."

"How?" Conrad asked, "Most Negroes lived in public housing already, didn't they?"

"Sure you're right. But the new housing authority manager gave contracts to Negroes as movers, maintenance contractors, and exterminators, who hired scores of workers. For instance two brothers with one truck started moving Welfare recipients. They now have six trucks, one cross-country moving van, and a huge storage facility; in just two years. They will soon be a national moving chain affiliate. Their business is now mostly private sector, with 50 employees."

"That sounds great, but how did they finance their expansion?"

"They applied to our local banks and were summarily rejected. Then, they contacted Citizens Trust Bank in Atlanta who financed them immediately. Too bad we don't have a black-owned bank here."

"Dinner is ready," Gail called out to the two most important men in her life.

"This sure is some fine dining room furniture Girl. The hand carving is so detailed," Conrad said as he rubbed the expensive, Brazilian Pecan wood while taking his seat, "and the table is set so beautifully."

"We found the complete 15 piece set plus the china at an estate auction through my real estate contacts. We purchased it for one-tenth of its original value. There was hardly a scratch on it," Gail said.

"We set the table," Michelle and Dana chimed.

"Why I thought your mother had hired professional caterers. The table looks perfect!" Conrad exclaimed; his granddaughters beamed. After dinner Conrad said, "Your mother's meals aren't this delicious darling, but don't tell her I said so." Michelle and Dana excused themselves and went to play with their new toys.

"Is something troubling you Daddy Beau?" Gail asked as they lingered in the dining room over homemade sweet potato pie and coffee. Conrad was flaccid.

"Time sure brings about a change, when you kids moved here I was on top of the heap."

"What's happened?" Gail asked. She poured more coffee, and sat down.

"Integration, that's what. New York Life's first Negro agent was hired in Chicago just three years ago. He has done so well that the other major insurance companies are hiring Negro agents in most northern cities. You remember Archie Hogan? Well, he is now working for Equitable, in Detroit. In his letter of resignation he called me cantankerous. Ain't that a… something?"

Jerome camouflaged a laugh with a cough. He recalled Romanian Philosopher Emile M. Cioran's provocative quote, 'If we could see ourselves as others see us, we would vanish on the spot.'

"Negro insurance companies throughout the country are losing clients, including the five headquartered here. That's why the NIA called this emergency meeting."

"But you still have the Zanzibar complex don't you?"

"Yeah, but except for weekends we're dead as my corpses. Martin Luther King has increased self-respect, discipline, and hope. That young preacher has changed the way even I think about Negroes. People are saving money, going back to school and, as I am, supporting the Civil Rights movement. Thank the Lord my mortuaries are still profitable. We're still burying our people because White Folks aren't doing that yet," Conrad smiled.

"Good thing I started my mortgage business. I'm thinking about buying a radio station. If it works I'll buy others in Birmingham and Baton Rouge."

"Diversifying is the right move," Jerome said. "Negroes will always be buying homes, and all companies need to advertise to reach Negro consumers."

Between drinks Conrad said, "Son, this question is driving me crazy, may I?" Jerome nodded. "How did you get your own drugstore? All you had was a job that was barely paying you a living wage and you had no investment capital or assets."

"Right on all counts; first, no matter what we earned, we saved something. If government agencies could take a chunk of my wages up front, then so could we. Second, we never bought anything on credit. We saved toward purchases which were always less for cash, and without interest, right Babe?"

"Yes dear," Gail cooed. She was proud of Jerome's money management philosophy.

"Third, I had the support of a wonderful wife who stood by me during questionable times, started her own successful career, and encouraged me when I faltered." Gail was especially pleased that Jerome had mentioned her contributions.

"After seeing your store during my last visit, it had to cost––what, at least $10,000? You couldn't have saved that much so quickly, and I'm the only one who would have made you a sizeable loan, but you didn't even ask."

"I'm like the bumble bee." Jerome said. Conrad was puzzled, Jerome added, "Scientists have determined given its size, weight and short wing span a bee cannot fly. Therefore, the only reason it flies is that it never listened to those who said it couldn't."

"I hear you Son, and I deserve that. My friend Lonnie Blackman was right. I'm sure glad you didn't listen to an old foggy like me."

Courtesy Drugs was overflowing with Christmas merchandise; every crevice was profitable. Jerome was on the phone when Fred Hawkins came in. "Buy 50 shares… Sell that leach now… Hold until it goes up another 10 points… Average out our initial purchase by buying another 100 shares; it'll turn around soon. Thanks Marge, we'll talk tomorrow."

"What's going on?" Fred asked as he poured himself a cup of coffee and pulled a chocolate doughnut covered with sprinkles from his bag.

After closing his stock note book, Jerome said, "Marge is on Daniel Quibble's staff; she manages my portfolio."

"Damn man, what are you using for money? I can hardly make ends meet."

"You've been self-employed for almost ten years and, I assume, are making a reasonable profit. If you stopped picking up everybody's bar tab, drinking and lavishly tipping in Scotty's, quit shooting dice with Turkey, chasing skirts, and playing poker at the Royal Reprobates, you'd have some investment capital," Jerome said to his best friend.

"Never mind about me, just answer the damn question."

I answered the second part regarding your not having investment capital, but you didn't hear me. "Rebates," Jerome said.

"Rebates? What's that, something that replaced Welfare checks?"

"My business receives cash rebates and timely payment discounts from suppliers and manufacturers which I deposit in a separate investment account. Dan suggested I get into the market, he *told me he asked you several times but you weren't interested*, so I risked $1,000 and established a credit line of $5,000. Dan showed me how to use financial newspapers, and 10K reports to analyze stocks. I also took a home-study course from the University of Chicago to learn more about the stock market.

"I just made $652 after commissions today. My portfolio is now worth over $11,000, my investment account continues to grow, and I'm debt free. Right now I'm selling short to cover taxes. '58 ends in less than a month you know."

"This is strange," Fred said between full mouths, "There's a new investment opportunity, but I thought you were cash poor." Fred, after tasting his coffee frowned, "This mud is strong enough to box."

"What opportunity?" Jerome took a sip, shrugged, "tastes good to me."

"Corporate White Flight has created an almost vacant 20-story building on the West Side. Baxter Bridges bought it below the appraised value with a 100% mortgage after the congressman committed several federal agencies to leasing space. The Negro-owned radio station is staying, and Rachael Piernas promised to ask the governor to consider placing state agencies in his building. Walgreens wants a new lease. Baxter would rather have a brother, but I advised him not to do business with Harold Oldham, and he is the only game in town."

"That building is on the corner of Western and Madison isn't it; that's a major intersection?"

"Right. Baxter mentioned you, but I told him you were broke. I mean, you can't even afford me." Because of Jerome's accounting courses, he was handling his own books, payroll, and taxes.

"Why didn't you bother to ask me? I didn't have the cash to handle this, remember?" Jerome went into his intense thought mode.

Fred rambled on about the weather, sports, new female conquests. Jerome didn't hear a word. 15 minutes later Jerome said into the phone, "Mr. Bridges? ... Jerome Gerard, Gail's husband... Congratulations on your new acquisition... How would you like a brand new Certified Drug Store and at least three additional doctors as tenants? ... I sure can... within 60 days... Great! Can we keep this private? ... Excellent!"

"You must be taking your own hallucinates!" Fred said, "No Negro has a Certified franchise. The fee alone is $50,000 with a required net worth of at least $200,000. And that doesn't include remodeling and inventory costs. Now just how are you going to swing all that?"

"I ever tell you the story of the bumble bee?" Jerome laughed.

"Man, quit playing. If you don't deliver, you'll be out considerable up-front cash and your reputation will be ruined. Incidentally, just where are you going to get three doctors; what do you have, a physician farm?"

"I've got to get to work," Jerome said. Fred took the hint, with doughnuts in hand, he left mumbling something about idealism and pragmatism being miles apart.

Where is that Drug Store Age? Jerome asked himself. He flipped through his periodicals until he found the article stating Certified was losing significant market share to Walgreens, especially in Negro neighborhoods. A month earlier three Cuban refugee-MD's had secured office space upstairs. Jerome's prescriptions had increased, but the four doctors were not content with the patient flow.

The next day, with supporting documents in hand, Jerome said to Loan Officer Manny Singleton, "I need a credit line of $200,000. A major..."

"You know your credit line is $5,000 and you're lucky to have that."

"But I haven't explained what business opportunity is available."

"Boy, it doesn't matter. As far as your kind is concerned your credit limit is set, without upward adjustments." President Tom Mosel had criticized Singleton for authorizing a $5,000 credit line for Jerome.

"But I paid off my loan ahead of schedule. Congressman Dawson, thanks to me, authorized Avalon to hold on deposit a huge federal escrow account. Over the past year I have sent you at least 10 new customers…"

"I said no! Now get the hell out of here before I cancel your present credit line!" Singleton grabbed his newspaper, thrusting it between himself and Jerome.

No matter how valid my proposition, no matter my contribution to Avalon's growth, I'm still just another Nigger, thought Jerome. He left feeling rejected but not defeated; this was familiar territory, but with higher stakes. After intense, sustained thinking Jerome invited Buddy Laws, John T. Williamson, Rachael Piernas, and Samuel Stovall to an evening meeting at his home over fresh coffee and homemade banana cake. Gail participated and contributed.

"A lesson I've learned," Jerome said, "Is Whitey is much more concerned about losing status, assets, or money than he is about additional profit. When a loss is eminent, racism becomes too expensive and secondary." The attendees pondered his profound thoughts. Jerome outlined his plan and with input from his advisors developed the details. As the meeting ended each person knew what needed to be done in preparation for their next weekly meeting. "What will your fees be?" Jerome asked.

"Since none of us earn our livelihood as consultants," Samuel said representing the team, "there will be no charge. Just remember when the time is right, to pass the favor on."

Architect Bryan Gerard, Jerome's older brother, inspected the proposed site. He spent half a day taking photos and measurements. Bryan visited Sol Gitel's and other certified stores. He took copies of *Drug Store Age* back to Cleveland for editors' names he could call for more insight. Within two weeks Bryan sent Jerome a set of blueprints, plus a large, water-color rendering of the front of the proposed store, gratis. Jerome suggested Bryan not sign his work.

Jerome called Williamson and said, "Plant the seed."

"This is unconfirmed," Williamson said to his boss, Marvin Lepke, "Jerome may be awarded a Certified franchise." Over the last several years, three of L&S's largest accounts purchased the prestigious franchise. L&S lost major sales to McKesson-Richardson, Certified drugstores' supplier and L&S's primary competitor.

"Well, what brings you by; did one of my checks bounce?" Jerome joked with Marvin Lepke. Williamson, because Mr. Lepke's Negro secretary kept Williamson informed regarding Courtesy Drugs, and had alerted Jerome; everything was set.

"Johnny told me about this," Marvin said as he walked into Jerome's rear area and viewed the Certified rendering lying on the back counter. Jerome, feigning embarrassment, hurriedly placed the artwork in a tube, and put it under the counter.

"Damn, how did John find out? I hadn't mentioned this to him because his company, that is, your company, can't be involved. McKesson-Richardson will become my primary supplier."

"What's in those other tubes?" Marvin asked; Jerome had intentionally placed the rendering tube among them.

"Oh, nothing important; they wouldn't interest you."

"May I see?" Marvin asked as he stepped in their direction.

"Sorry, that's privileged information." Jerome blocked his distinguished guest's progress.

"How has business been lately, Jer?" Marvin asked as he retreated, poured himself a cup of coffee, and sat down.

"You know that answer; 90% of my inventory comes from you."

"You are a successful businessman Jerome, that's why we give you our deepest price-points." *Also because John insists and I discount my invoices,* Jerome thought. "What do I have to do to see what's in those tubes?"

"You're meddling now," Jerome said, slightly reprimanding Marvin. "John may have just lost a good customer."

"If I had found out after the fact I would have fired Johnny; I really need to see, Jerome."

"On one condition, you promise confidentiality."

"Of course." Jerome unrolled the blueprints. The large blue pages with white diagrams included customer traffic patterns, major fixture placements, electrical installations, material specifications, storage areas, square footage selling space, and check-out counters, all miniaturized.

"Wow!" Marvin exclaimed. "I had no idea a new store located there could be so large! Twenty thousand square feet of selling space and four check-out counters is major. That state-of-the-art cooler alone must have cost you dearly. Who did these plans for you?" Because of their quality, Marvin assumed they were done by an expensive, local, Caucasian architect who didn't want the notoriety of working for a Negro. He didn't wait for Jerome to answer. "You have to cut us in!"

"Mr. Lepke, you know as well as I that McKesson-Richardson must be our primary supplier. That will be in the contract." *Bite, Marvin.*

"So the contract hasn't been signed yet?" *You're hooked.*

"Well, no, but its firm. I wouldn't have made these investments if the deal hadn't been set. I'll sign in two weeks," Jerome lied.

"Jerome," Marvin said, insisting on eye contact, "ever since you have been in business we have given you every advantage against the advice of certain people who didn't want you to succeed. Is this our reward for supporting you?"

"But Mr. Lepke, I don't want to jeopardize my chances of getting this store. Why these blueprints, fixtures and rendering alone cost…"

"Damn the rules––and please call me Marvin. We'll loan you the money to cover all your up-front costs including these drawings, remodeling, fixtures, and inventory on a three-year interest-free loan, for a favored supplier status in both your stores. Certified will have to honor any contracts signed before theirs."

"But Marvin, I have no idea what all those costs will be," *Shades of a previous conversation with another Jew*, Jerome recalled.

"Whatever they are we'll cover them," Marvin promised. Jerome remained silent with his head down. "Additionally, we'll give you an extra 90 days after opening before your first payment is due." Jerome stared at Marvin without saying a word, "plus an additional five percent discount on all goods purchased before you open and for the first ninety days; how's that?"

"Marvin, you're right, you have been a friend during my brief time in business and that has to be worth something; put your offer in writing. I'll sign it whatever the consequences." Jerome smiled and extended his hand cementing the deal. *This is better than John had predicted.*

Benny Burns had convinced Gusto Brewery to install a state-of-the-art, gravity feed, walk-in cooler in Jerome's new store at no cost, because Buddy Laws had persuaded Congressman Dawson to speak to the head of the Alcohol, Tobacco and Firearms Agency on behalf of Gusto regarding a pending inquiry, which would have cost the brewery multiple thousands to defend. Congressman Dawson had phoned the brewery president and thanked him for his generosity toward Jerome, while informing him the inquiry had vanished. Gusto made a significant contribution to Congressman Dawson's campaign fund. Benny, commended by his brewery, offered Jerome heavily discounted beer prices for the first 30 days.

Anson Ice Cream now had 20 stops, and six ice cream parlors, most in Caucasian neighborhoods. He agreed to install two giant freezers and keep them filled, free-of-charge, for 30 days. Plenty Good's Ralph, plus a delivery man in a freezer-truck, was now working for Anson. All of Anson's brokerage clients, at his insistence, offered deep discounts on their first 30 days orders to Courtesy, Certified. Other vendors, to compete, made similar offers-including giveaways and samplings––all in writing.

Alphonso Major, President of B&W Advertising, arranged for the top soft-drink company to schedule tasting promotions and giveaways of monogrammed gifts with purchases the first four weekends. Clowns would perform the first four Saturdays for children; all paid for by Alphonso's clients. A prominent, Negro female singer would make a two-hour personal appearance, with a current hit record giveaway, on the second weekend, thanks to the building's Negro-owned radio station's influence.

Rachael Piernas persuaded Nathaniel Freeman, Executive Director, Urban League of Chicago, who wanted a sit-down with Governor Stratton, to secure an appointment for Jerome with Certified Drugs' president, William Lucich; he was on the Urban League's board. The Black community had once again come together to support Jerome Gerard.

"The first thing you need to know is how to shake hands," Samuel said to Jerome at the last of their weekly strategy sessions.

"But I thought I knew how to shake hands."

"Put your hand in his up to the base of the thumb and make eye contact; smile, but don't laugh; you will reflect confidence, like you belong there. Grip, but don't squeeze; it'll show anxiety. Shake no more than three times, then release. A longer contact and you'll appear uneasy. Keep your left hand by your side, no double hand grasps, or grabbing his arm above the elbow; that's too political." Jerome and Samuel practiced until Samuel was satisfied.

"One other thing," Samuel advised, "none of us should laugh." Everyone looked confused. "If the Certified principles say something funny, smile, even broadly, let your body languages reflect your humorous response but don't laugh out loud. If we cackle or bust a gut, we may be considered buffoons, and not taken seriously for the rest of the meeting."

"Jerome," Samuel said, "you are going to star so sit directly opposite Mr. Lucich with Rachael on your right; I'll sit on your left. Buddy, sit on my left with at least one chair between us. Then you'll be out of their line of vision so if you need to speak stridently it will be startling. I'll evaluate the meeting's progress so Jerome can stay focused.

"If things are going well, I'll interlock my fingers across my lap." Samuel demonstrated. "If the meeting is faltering I'll rest my chin in the palm of my right hand with my elbow on the table, like this. Buddy, that's your cue to get ugly."

"Oh, I know how to do that," Buddy flashed a frightening, intimidating, fierce look.

"This is most important. We will not leave without a firm commitment," Samuel said, pointing both index fingers upward. "We can't waste this high-level appointment that Rachael secured. Their suggesting they will get back to us is a kick into the abyss.

"Oh, one other thing," Samuel advised, "having liquid refreshments is acceptable but please, no foodstuffs." Jerome's posse was ready.

They walked into Certified's headquarters from the garage fifteen minutes early. Following Samuel's instructions, the men had worn dark blue suits, white cotton shirts without French cuffs or monograms, red, small diagramed, conservative ties and lace-up shined, black shoes. Rachael wore a red suit over a white, frilly blouse, with red accessories. A corner table in their conference room held push-top decanters filled with hot coffee, iced, bottled colas, chocolate Bismarcks and Danish pastries. A dial phone with five lines sat on a pedestal. An easel, requested by Jerome, stood empty.

Five-tiered, deep framed oil paintings of pharmacists, some wearing facial hair in century-old settings, compounding capsules and vivid, elixir prescriptions, with backgrounds of colorful, odd shaped glass urns, decorated the walls. It reminded Jerome of Norman Rockwell's *Post Magazine* covers. Samuel, Rachael, and Jerome had coffee. Buddy devoured a chocolate Bismarck and gulped down half a cola. Chocolate covered his teeth, crumbs stuck to his lips; morsels fell onto the thick brown carpet. Samuel glared at Buddy as he handed him a paper napkin.

Tall, overweight, President William Lucich and wiry-looking, Vice President of Operations, Don Camper, entered the room precisely at 10:00 a.m. Lucich extended his hand to Jerome and said, "Welcome to Certified's headquarters, Mr. Gerard. I've heard a lot of good things about you and have been looking forward to our meeting."

Shaking hands went well but, according to Samuel's instructions, I ignored the bull shit greeting, he wants me to behave, thought Jerome as they all took seats at the eight foot, rectangular, table. Lucich and Camper sat in the middle on one side, Jerome and his fellows sat opposite. Buddy slid his arm chair several feet back from the table. He kept on his felt hat and shades.

Jerome emphasized Buddy and Rachael's political relationships. While introducing Samuel, Jerome stressed Samuel's precedent-setting court-room victories. To further validate, Jerome presented his team's business cards. The certified executives mentioned the weather, the plight of the Chicago Bears, and how much Lucich enjoyed serving on the Urban League's board with Nate Freeman.

"Gentlemen, may I move forward?" Jerome asked ending the bland, polite gab fest.

"Of course," Lucich said, "but understand, this is just an exploratory meeting and no decisions will be made today. In fact you had better get started," Lucich checked his watch, "we only have about fifteen minutes."

"But I was told we would have thirty minutes; were the previous pleasantries a portion of my time?" Jerome brought his eyebrows together and narrowed his gaze, as had been practiced.

"I'm sure we'll have time to hear your entire story m'boy, and after we part we will ingest what you leave, so let's get into it." Lucich sounded impatient.

Jerome handed them nine by eleven folders which included a customer population grid, proposed building traffic, and household income demographics in the primary and secondary market areas, which covered two miles in all directions. Jerome used bar graphs which projected sales growth every quarter over two years for the four major departments with profit margins ranging from 200% for prescriptions and small appliances to 20% for tobacco products.

Three new physicians guaranteed by Jerome were mentioned. An advertising and promotional schedule including sketches of *Chicago Defender* full page newspaper ads, and recorded sixty second radio commercials were also presented. The sales on ice cream and beer were tremendous. Lucich and Camper said they were impressed.

"Here are the blueprints," Jerome said. Using an extendable chrome, pocket pointer he thoroughly explained each page––upside down––after which he paused for questions. The certified executives commented, "I see," and "that sounds great." With a flourish while unveiling, Jerome produced the rendering, which had been mounted on Styrofoam, and placed it on the easel.

"And this is what will attract customers to the newest Certified Drugstore from both major thoroughfares. A gleaming, pristine, permanent, horizontal, billboard-sized commercial attached to your newest and most modern location; a bright beacon, burning 24 hours a day, that will welcome its neighbors and drivers-by; an oasis to a community in need. It will be the largest certified signage in Chicagoland." Jerome's eloquent and comprehensive presentation proved he understood every aspect of his business proposal which research had indicated surpassed all Certified requirements.

"Of course the most important component is financing," Jerome said as Samuel handed Lucich and Camper a second folder of signed corporate letters pledging financial commitment and heavily discounted grand-opening offers. Documents from L&S Distributors, Gusto Brewery, Burns Distributors, Anson Ice Cream, and many others showed that Jerome could cover all initial construction and inventory costs. Jerome elaborated on each commitment, without notes.

"Your presentation was brilliant, complete, and your proposal sound," Lucich said. "We have never seen so many corporations offer such attractive terms." He stood and shook Jerome's hand. "It's obvious that you have worked hard, at great expense, and have invested considerable time. It's the best proposal we have seen in recent memory, isn't it Don?" said Lucich as he prepared to end the meeting.

"Why yes sir, it really is," Don echoed.

"We can live with L&S being your initial but hopefully, temporary, primary supplier. McKesson and Richardson should assume that role within two years, right?" Lucich said.

"But that's not a requirement, is it gentlemen?" Samuel asked, strategizing for more time.

"No, of course not, that was just a suggestion." Lucich appeared uneasy.

Camper thought Lucich was angry because Attorney Samuel Stovall had questioned obligatory purchases from McKesson-Richardson, which was illegal. Camper attacked Jerome and his associates.

"OK kiddies, what White consultants prepared you and this slick presentation? There is no way you Nig…Coloreds could do this quality of work. These manufacturers' offers and blueprints are probably bogus, as well." Camper said as he tossed the folders toward Jerome, indicating their time and preparation had been wasted.

Samuel put his chin in his right hand and his elbow on the table, as he looked passively at the two managers.

"May I enlighten you gentlemen regarding the history of derogatory, demeaning pro-nouns?" Buddy announced as he propelled himself from his chair, without touching the armrests, motioning that the executives re-take their seats. Camper and Lucich were startled. They sat back down and turned toward the angry-looking man with the satanic goatee, who had been silent since the meeting began. Buddy snatched off his hat and sunglasses and placed them on the table. He began talking.

"Since being enslaved in America, misnamed, 'The land of the free,' we have been called scores of disparaging names; none have been correct. In Africa we were content, literate, religious, family-oriented, and self-governing. You, to justify our being kidnapped, lied and said that we lived in trees, that we cooked and then ate our young, that by removing us from our homeland you saved us from annihilation. How ridiculous was that!"

Buddy strolled back and forth with his hands behind his back glaring at his audience of two, daring them to move or speak. He continued, "Millions of us died during the crossing of the Middle Passage because of barbaric, inhumane treatment. Our deaths were considered a business expense.

"As slaves, we were stripped of our religion, our languages, our history, and even our names. Our children were sold, never to be seen or held by their parents again. And because we were forbidden to write or read your language, we were called 'worthless, ignorant, a necessary evil'. These names were oxymoronic, because this nation, including our White House, was built on the backs and moistened with the blood of slaves. Cotton and tobacco enriched the South because of our centuries of free toil. To survive the sweltering, sun-up to sun-down work days, we broke our tools to delay lethal labor. Again we were misnamed dumb and careless."

"The Emancipated Proclamation freed us, then the thirteenth amendment permanently emancipated us, but without resources with which to begin being free. Immediately after the Civil War, we lived under punitive, Jim Crow laws, plus the criminal, but unpunished actions of the Ku Klux Klan which included public whip lashings and hangings, making it extremely difficult to accomplish anything.

"Southern White women and children picnicked in front of Negroes hanging from trees with their hands bound, naked. Several men had been castrated while screaming and had their bloody testicles stuffed in their mouths. Sometimes they were burned alive. Lest you forget, Black women were also hung. They were horrific sights, strange fruits, that demented Whites found entertaining." Buddy pulled from inside his suit coat a manila envelope, extracted several 8 x 10, black and white, photos of the just described, explicit scenes and flung them across the table. "These atrocities were committed thousands of times, without anyone ever being arrested or prosecuted." After glancing at the horrific replicas, Lucich and Camper rejected the photos as if a poisonous snake had been pitched toward them. Buddy continued.

"In spite of atrocities, segregation, racism, inferior primary educations, constant negative misrepresentations, and a continuous denial our unalienable right of liberty; some of us have succeeded. Sitting before you," Buddy said as he stood behind Jerome's seat and extended his arms in both directions, "are three, outstanding, educated, intelligent, Negroes, who have pushed themselves to prepare a meaningful presentation, and you dare to imply, 'you niggers could not have done this quality of work.' Mr. Camper, you not only attack our integrity by calling us the underclass and plagiarists, you insult us further by misnaming us carefree 'Kiddies,' who, without thought or purpose, aimlessly play in sand boxes, barefoot. Your racist attitude, which is manifested by your insulting remarks, is enough to make a Negro turn militant." Buddy slammed back into his seat, restoring his hat and sunglasses.

"Wha, what I meant was…" Camper stuttered.

"I think they understood what you said and what you meant, Don," Lucich interrupted as he turned the dreadful photos over while looking sternly toward Camper. "Jer," Lucich said, after an apologetic shake of his head, "You meet every qualification but two. There's a $200,000 net worth requirement which we will waive." Lucich said to Camper, "We need to be more pragmatic when dealing with Negroes."

"Yes sir, we do." Camper was pleased to be allowed to second a favorable comment.

"But," Lucich continued, "you will have to put up a $50,000 franchise fee and have two existing franchisees second your application; those are the rules. We would like to help you further, but…"

Lucich was about to, again, end the meeting. Samuel, again put his hand under his chin with his elbow on the table.

"Man, let's go!" Buddy stood, hat and glasses in place, and then shouted. "I predicted this would happen. While Mr. Gerard presented, fat Lucich and his flunky sat there like two penguins, just oohing and ahing. Afterwards, the big penguin says through a shit-eatin' grin, 'you meet every requirement but two.'" Buddy did an exaggerated interpretation of White speak, then added, "but Lucich missed one requirement: being White."

"I didn't mean…" Lucich began.

"Hell," said Buddy growing louder, "I know exactly what you meant. I even know what you were thinking and I also know how to change your racist mind!" Buddy stabbed Lucich with his most intimidating stare and loud voice.

The next series of actions took place in nanoseconds. Responding to the loud, unfamiliar voice, two armed security guards stepped into the meeting room with pistols drawn. Jerome silently told Buddy to sit down and shut up by gesturing with his fingers across his throat, twice. Samuel noticed Lucich's body language which said to the security guards, 'leave immediately.' The last thing Lucich wanted was to have their politically aligned presenters manhandled, silenced, accosted or arrested. Samuel signaled Buddy to continue. The security guards exited.

Buddy said in a lower, but still dramatic, voice while leaning closer toward the executives. "Congressman Dawson will ask on the floor of the House of Representatives, which will become a matter of public record, why, Chicago, with over a million Negroes, don't own or even manage one certified drugstore. Every newspaper will print the congressman's negative comments; including Chicago's Chronicle."

Salvo number one, bad publicity, Jerome thought.

"Perhaps," Camper said, "after we review…"

Samuel's chin continued to rest in his right hand.

"And," Buddy said, "after the *Chicago Defender* does several front page articles on your plantation-type antics, you might not have anything to review. We just might stop shopping at Certifieds, completely!"

Salvo number two, lost business.

"Just leave your proposal with us and we will…" Lucich began but was again interrupted by Buddy.

"I wasn't through talking!" Lucich hushed. "You know, I just remembered," Buddy shook the forefinger of his left hand at the two principals. "Martin Luther King was in town looking for a local cause to champion. Bus companies aren't the only businesses we can bankrupt." Buddy angrily threw on his coat, pulled his hat down, and lit a cigarette with two kitchen matches. He held the "torches" close to his face allowing them to burn long after the cigarette was glowing. The flames reflected in Buddy's sunglasses. While holding the executives' rapt attention, with protruding, tight lips, Buddy squeezed out the flaming matches with two fingers, sans pain.

Lucich and Camper shifted in their seats. They completely understood the threats of fire and mayhem.

Buddy helped Rachael with her coat as she said, "There are several shopping centers planned in Negro neighborhoods to be supplemented with government funds. They are… (Gail had identified specific vacant blocks). Walgreens is anxiously waiting what Mr. Gerard's outcome is with Certified. They would be pleased to have several new stores in Negro communities and would probably employ Negroes to run them."

Salvo number four, the competition continues to increase its market share.

Lucich glanced at Camper, who had indicated a dislike for further competitive intrusion. Samuel noted the exchange.

"Mr. Gerard," continued Rachael, "thank you for inviting me. My questions have been answered. The governor and the press will be interested in my written report."

That is the last salvo. Samuel, you're on as the good cop. Their persuasive pouch was empty. Jerome knew the end, no matter the outcome, was near.

"People please," Samuel said as he positioned his hands as if he were a priest about to bless the Host. Rachael and Buddy sat; he continued to scowl under his sunglasses and hat as he smoked his cigarette. "We came here filled with hope. We expected to accomplish significant, worthwhile goals that would benefit not only Mr. Gerard and Certified but a needy West Side community. After our appointment was granted we assumed there were two racially sensitive drugstore chains in Chicagoland, not just one.

"Obviously Mr. Gerard is qualified. You said his presentation," Samuel shifted his soft gaze directly to Lucich and then said, "and it was his presentation," Samuel allowed a pregnant pause reinforcing the presentation's authorship. "Yes, here it is. You said, 'it was brilliant, the best you've seen in recent memory.' You were being honest weren't you?"

"Well yes, but…" Samuel interrupted Camper.

"When Mr. Gerard yielded for questions there were none which indicates the two of you agreed with his projections, right?" Both men nodded, "and you made comments indicating you appreciated the time, capital, and manpower Mr. Gerard has invested to date, right?"

"Of course," Camper said.

Get Camper out and Lucich in, Samuel instructed Buddy by shifting his eyes several times, secretly. Samuel then leaned further toward Lucich, "then let us not part with retribution in our hearts or reprisals on our agenda, for once the decision to go forward with economic retaliation is made, like a huge boulder rolling down hill, it takes its own course and may cause irreparable harm before anyone can stop it. Aren't there some concessions you can make today, Sir?"

"I don't think…"

Buddy interrupted Camper while rising from his seat. "Man, why don't you be cool? The counselor was talking to the President, not you!"

"Walgreens," Lucich said more to Camper than anyone else, "already has more stores in Negro neighborhoods than we; perhaps we should modify our requirements. Call me in a week or so, after…"

Samuel's chin went back into his palm.

"Since you're here, your vice president is here, and we're here, let's do those modifications now!" Buddy said back on his feet.

"I'd like to, I really would, but I have another meeting in…"

"Hell, then cancel it!" Buddy walked over to the phone, picked it up and slammed it on the conference table in front of Lucich. "You are 'The Man,' right!"

"Ok, ok." Lucich said as he looked up at Buddy who was standing over him, glaring. "Just calm down. Let's get a few more people in here and work something out. This immediate action is only justifiable because of your exceptional proposal… and to be perfectly clear, for no other reason, right Don?"

Don slowly nodded.

Samuel's fingers interlaced in his lap; Buddy sat down, put out his cigarette and apologized for ignoring the "No Smoking" sign. He then removed his hat and sunglasses.

Two hours later Jerome issued a $10,000 check, which was the reduced franchise fee. There was no further mention of existing franchisees' endorsements.

Jerome and his crew left with a signed contract authorizing a new certified store, known as Courtesy Drugs #2, to be located on the corner of Western and Madison.

"To Jerome Gerard, who accomplished the impossible through thorough research, preparation, and sheer audacity," Samuel said as he raised his flute at Felix and Bea's, "even Harold Oldham with five stores doesn't have one."

"Amen!" The team seconded as they touched flutes.

"They know so little about building plans in our communities, or how the governor feels about Negroes," Rachael said as she sipped her champagne.

"And to Buddy Laws. That tongue lashing was tremendously effective, and those photos were the coup de grace," Samuel said as he toasted Buddy. "You need to develop some of my closing arguments."

"The disparaging names closing was something I've been working on for the congressman, the two penguins and the photos was especially developed for Certified," Buddy said, contemplating a lucrative, supplemental career. Buddy blushed and stopped eating––but only for a minute.

"The amazing thing is if Camper doesn't get stupid, Buddy doesn't get to deliver the disparaging comments, or photos, and we probably leave with nothing." Everyone agreed. Jerome continued, smiling at his upcoming pun, "Only one more bridge to cross; that's Baxter Bridges,"

"Baxter is as slick as ice going downhill," Samuel said. "I need to approve anything he asks you to sign. And that's the last free lawyering you're getting little brother. This drugstore puts you in the serious business category, so henceforth when we talk my meter will be running."

"You got that right. Ninety days after this store opens, you go on retainer." Samuel and Jerome touched glasses.

The radio station occupied the entire top floor. Baxter Bridges Real Estate occupied half of the 19th floor in his 20 story building. There were numerous desks, various sized conference rooms, and two large reception areas. There was room for 20 agents; Gail had told Jerome there were presently, only ten.

"Sure is pretty." Baxter smiled from behind his massive desk as he reviewed Jerome's collaterals and contract. "Now all we have to do is agree on your rent, my percentage of your gross sales, and we'll be in business."

"Percentage? You wouldn't get a percentage of Walgreens' gross sales!" Jerome said defiantly.

"Well boy you sure as hell ain't Charlie Walgreen, now are you?" The smile prevailed but tension filled Baxter's eyes. "According to this contract you can't put this store anywhere but in my building so that sort of makes us partners, now doesn't it?" Baxter's smile remained.

Samuel warned me; sure wish I had a couple of grains of black pepper. "Mr. Bridges," Jerome said through pleading eyes, over a smile almost as wide as Baxter's, "I'm opening this store without a pot to pee in or a window to toss it through. If my vendors and financiers communicate they will realize how little I have invested and the whole deal will probably collapse. If I get open, and that's a big if, I will be in debt up to my eyeballs and every dollar I earn early on will help pull me out of a very deep hole, so whatever help you can give me will be deeply appreciated." Jerome blinked rapidly as he maintained his smile.

"Well, that's better," Baxter said. He needed this prestigious store to enhance his building's image. "Now that we know who's sittin' in the cat bird seat, let's do some business."

"Mr. Bridges, in addition to the drugstore I'm going to need at least twenty offices, most for examining and waiting rooms, for three doctors, plus two for Courtesy Drugs."

"Twenty-two offices!" Baxter's vacancy rate was over 70%. Baxter remembered discussing doctors but had no idea they would need that much space. "And what do you think that rent will be?"

"Whatever you say, Sir, whatever you say. Of course the higher the rent the fewer doctors I'll be able to place because I'll be paying all their rent and remodeling expenses, and purchasing all their equipment. Doctors realize their value. And as I'm sure you understand, the more doctors practicing here the more desirable your building becomes to other professionals. Why you may be able to attract Caucasians who service Negroes, like legal and accounting firms, dentists, secretarial services, interior designers, advertising agencies, various consultants, even other real estate companies." Baxter's eyes sparkled as he licked his lips.

"You might want to rename your magnificent building The Bridges Professional Building or something like that. Why you might be the most prominent commercial Negro real estate owner in the nation, enhancing your reputation, which should help you sell more homes, and recruit more agents to fill this space." Jerome quit blowing smoke up Bridges' behind while he was still being effective.

"Let me think on that," several moments' later Bridges said, "twenty-two offices plus the drugstore, huh?"

"Yes Sir, and, with your cooperation, that's just the beginning."

Bridges perused the contract and the rendering on his desk, salivating over the ultra-modern store that would be located on his entrance level, and envisioning that his occupancy rate, reputation, and agent roster would increase. "OK, here's the deal. On the offices I'll give you a five-year lease at 20% below the prevailing square footage rate, giving you exclusive access to floors 15 and 16, allowing space for additional doctors. For the drugstore, I'll give you a ten percent reduction if you will give me 5% of gross sales, off the books."

Jerome smiled through soft eyes while processing the numbers. *5% of gross sales could easily represent 30% of net profits. And even as greedy as Baxter is, he couldn't knowingly be asking for that big a slice. Obviously, he doesn't understand retail.*

"Mr. Bridges, I'm sure you want to be fair and give the new store a fighting chance at staying open. Can we make your tax free income 2% of the net, excluding prescriptions? I'll be glad to pay you off the books thirty days after my rents begin." Bridges remained silent; Jerome pushed further.

"First, I should not be required to put up security deposits. Second, could the 10% discount in drugstore rent be raised to 20%, just as you so generously offered on the office space? And can all of my rents, because of my huge, initial expenditures, begin 90 days after we open? I mean, you did get this property at an unbelievable price with no down payment, and I will be your largest tenant. After five years, which is probably how long it will take me to get out of debt, I will gladly increase my rent, which will raise your profitability."

This was Bridges' first encounter with commercial and retail properties. He looked busy writing down numbers but had no idea what Jerome was suggesting. He then said, "You've done your homework, little brother. You know more about my business than I know about yours." Jerome smiled his little boy smile. Baxter continued, "Well, what the hell, you obviously respect your elders; plus your wife is an excellent agent. We've got a deal." Jerome, with Baxter's permission, asked Samuel to prepare the contract.

Cleveland's Bryan Gerard worked closely with an Atlanta Negro general contractor who hired and supervised various sized Negro construction companies. Jerome was given an immediate appointment with Mayor O'Malley, and made a contribution to his election campaign; all city inspections passed. Opening day was May 15, 1959.

The total investment exceeded a million dollars. All Jerome had invested was $20,000; a $10,000 franchise fee from his stock portfolio, and a $10,000 down payment on four state-of-the-art National cash registers, from his rebate account. Merck, Dulles, and Holmes Pharmaceutical Company, remodeled and equipped the doctors' offices gratis, for favored consideration on prescription medications.

The store, because of delayed payments, was profitable from Day One. The Cayman Island skim started immediately; Jerome reduced his salary from Courtesy Drugs #1 and received a nominal salary from #2; his total income increased slightly. He paid cash for a more current, used, Grand Prix Pontiac, as a business expense. Josephine, who had mastered inventory control, was transferred to Courtesy Drugs #2 as assistant manager. Her loyalty was proven, her judgment impeccable. Three registered, and a student pharmacist, eight cashiers, two mentally challenged porters, and a stock boy from the nearby high school became her responsibility when Jerome was absent.

Webster Henderson became manager of Courtesy Drugs #1. Agnes replaced Josephine and continued working toward her GED; she proudly removed herself from ADC. Webster hired a junior student pharmacist, and a high-school student cashier, both part-time. Webster, Agnes and Josephine were given substantial raises.

On the ninetieth day Jerome paid his rent; Bridges was delighted. Thirty days later, in addition to his rentals, Jerome handed Bridges an envelope; "Here is your two percent Mr. Bridges, as promised."

"Is that all I get!" Bridges complained while counting his cash. "Hell, I know I should be getting more than this. I want a true two percent!"

"Now Mr. Bridges," Jerome said, "I'm sure you realize if I reported all my income and expenses I wouldn't be able to pay you 'off the books' now would I? You can't have it both ways."

"Well," Bridges grinned, "you're the biggest tenant I have and you do pay on time, unlike some of my other leasees, so I guess I can live with this." Bridges' ego was hurt; he realized the young up-start had bested him, but that he didn't have a choice.

The Christmas season of '60 at both stores was super. Josephine had been promoted to manager. She recognized the need for more education and began taking under-graduate business courses. Jerome now only worked vacation shifts and spent most of his time doing what he did best: merchandising stores. Cedric, his #2 stock boy since opening had proven to be a quick learner, honest, dependable, and had, because of Jerome's encouragement, become interested in becoming a pharmacist. Jerome had promised him a full college scholarship if he graduated high school with a C or better grade average. Cedric, now a sophomore, who had never been encouraged by his teachers or parent to consider college, had improved his grades significantly.

Jerome, at store #2, was cleaning shelves and placing product strategically: small sizes to the left, large sizes to the right with broad side facing front. Black owned products were eye level and received double facings. He heard a familiar voice.

"What it be like?" The voice was raspier and weaker than it used to be, but easily identifiable.

"Damn Turkey, I haven't seen you since slavery. Where have you been, man?" They shook hands and then embraced. Jerome immediately stepped back because of Turkey's offensive body odor. He had been sleeping in the Greyhound bus station, washing in public bathrooms and eating in soup kitchens. Turkey had hocked or sold his wardrobe and jewelry. His diamond cuff links had been replaced by paper clips. His hair had reverted; he needed a conk.

"Even slavery was better than integration," Turkey quipped. "The Pershing went from sugar to shit. All we were getting were low-life transients, and not enough of those. The swells stayed wherever they wanted. When the Negro owned Moulin Rouge in Las Vegas opened, my games went west. The Pershing cut me loose about a year ago; they're just about out of business now. Since then I been keeping a low profile; gambling a little, drinking a lot." Turkey rubbed his blood shot eyes, looked ashamed, and said, "You know how it goes."

"I understand," Jerome said, not understanding Turkey's precipitous decline at all.

"Listen Man," Turkey said, through ashamed body language, "I'm on a losing streak right through here, can you spare a C note? I'll pay you back just as soon as…"

"You know better than anybody that you can't consistently win at gambling, Turkey; hell, you used to run games not gamble. You need more than a hundred," Jerome said as he steeled himself against the funky onslaught, put his arm around Turkey's shoulder and took him into the back.

Half-hour later, after Turkey had inhaled three stale doughnuts and two cups of coffee, he asked, "got anything I can do around here?"

"Sure Turkey, I was waiting for you to ask for a job instead of a stake. Clean yourself up and dry out over the weekend. Show up Monday morning at eight. You can work with Cedric; if you stay sober, in a couple of months I'll find you a better paying job."

"Hey," smiled Turkey as he pocketed ten twenties, "ain't nothin' but somethin' to do. You got my marker, man."

"You don't owe me; all I'm doing is passing the favor on.

"You just bet a double C-note on me straightening up, and you're going to win that bet––Mr. Medicine Man."

End of Chapter Ten

CHAPTER ELEVEN

Jerome's advertising consultant, Alphonso Major, persuaded international athletic celebrity, Jackson Jones, with the Muslim name of Lucius Y, to participate in a two year anniversary celebration at Courtesy Drugs #2. After greeting hundreds of fans, taking photos, and signing autographs for several hours, Lucius Y invited Jerome to his mosque.

"Sure," Jerome answered, "I might learn something."

True Muslims didn't have Caucasian friends. Fiftyish, Supreme Ruler, the Honorable Hizzy Shakur, who created his sect in Chicago in the late forties, had said, "Integration means self-destruction, death, and nothing else."

Muslim men wore dark suits, white shirts, and slim ties; women who sat on the opposite side of the crowded mosque wore white gowns. The more devout women wore headwear called hijabs that covered all but their eyes; they were nicknamed ghosts. Visitors, like Jerome, sat in the rear.

The Fruit of Islam, including Lucius Y, were the hierarchy. They wore maroon, bellmen-type uniforms with brass buttons, and round bibless hats. Scores sat on the dais behind the Honorable Shakur, who was similarly dressed. The Honorable Shakur's wife, Mother Tyri Shakur, sat next to her husband in a twin high-back chair.

Several speakers condemned using drugs, tobacco products, and alcohol, which enslaved Negroes. The addictive artifacts were presented as the Devil's contemporary chains. Speakers discouraged wasting money on bowling, shooting pool, and attending costly movies and concerts. They denounced the longer jail sentences Negroes received when convicted of similar crimes as Caucasians. The eloquent orators suggested those who were employed by the Devil quit, and support Allah. As the service ended, Hizzy Shakur, with outstretched arms, invited new converts to come forward as members chanted, "Praise the Holy Name of Allah. Praise the holy name of Allah."

Because Lucius Y had bragged about Jerome's business prowess, the Supreme Ruler invited them to his huge, Hyde Park home.

"As Salaam Alaikum," said the diminutive, soft-spoken leader as the three men relaxed in his expensively furnished library a week later. Mother Tyri welcomed the guests and then disappeared. After a prayer, the Honorable Shakur laid forth his edict, "We believe in equal justice, racial parity, and non-violence which cannot be sustained in these United States, so we long for a territory which would become our sovereign nation, free of White devils. Of course I would be Governor." Shakur said with a tight smile, continuing, "Presently so called Negroes is 11% of the population yet own less than one tenth of one percent of its wealth and are 40% of those incarcerated. This is a travesty."

As Jerome, Lucius and the Honorable Shakur talked, they were served iced tea and bean pie by three teenage girls who genuflected and bowed. They wore white gowns, and hijabs: one was pregnant.

"We own supermarkets, restaurants and bakeries in ten cities. We sell; canned goods packaged by so-called Negroes to our standards; fresh fruits, vegetables, fish, beef and chicken from our farms down South. Bean pies are our specialty. Of course we detest swine." The Honorable Shakur frowned as if he had swallowed a dose of Quinine.

"We manufacture suits, uniforms, and gowns locally, and distribute them nationally. Our tradesmen repair homes and businesses for Muslims, and outsiders. We also distribute a weekly newspaper called the *Muslim Word*. It announces our upcoming events, specifies the miscarriages of justice so-called Negroes endure, encourages daily prayer, and publicizes our enterprises. Our editorials, some written by Mother Shakur, validate why we are devoted to our religious beliefs and values. Our lives conform to the Holy Quran." Shakur picked-up a gilded copy of the Quran and caressed it.

"We have schools called Universities of Islam where we pray six times a day, teach the ways of Allah, and emphasize mathematics and science which are the universal languages."

"Won't you, as Brother Y has done, join our family? Our ultimate goal of complete separation is near." Photographs were taken of the trio which appeared in the next edition of the *Muslim Word*.

The Supreme Ruler continued, "We have millions of followers in Harlem, Atlanta, St. Louis, Watts, here and Detroit, none of whom accept Welfare. Our businesses are quite profitable because as a religious entity we don't pay The Devil any taxes. Our members volunteer their time and expertise which keep our labor costs down.

"What we don't own are drugstores. With your involvement we could open at least 20 immediately." Jerome envisioned himself managing a small, national chain.

"Of course you and your family would become Muslim, fraternize only with Muslims, and would dress as Muslims dress; your children would attend our K through 12 school. Based on acumen and devotion, further education is encouraged. Your slave names would disappear. You would sell newspapers each week. The stores you presently own would become ours. Tobacco products and alcoholic beverages could not be sold. Prescriptions that contained opiates or narcotics could not be filled.

"Of course we would pay you a reasonable management fee. You would also, as has Bother Y, be ordained, following a month's retreat, as a member of the Fruit of Islam, a cherished, prestigious position." Shakur smiled as if he had just offered knighthood to Jerome.

Well, the vision of owning my own chain didn't last long. "I'll think about it," Jerome said politely as they parted; Shakur's proposal was ridiculous. Jerome knew America could be improved, but he would not change allegiances; certainly not to a territory under the Honorable Hizzy Shakur's governance.

The Supreme Ruler was interested in building a society, as are most religious leaders, where only the principal, and his chosen few live lavishly. The men and women employed in Muslim businesses worked to support their leader's lifestyle, and accumulated no assets. Those who worked outside the religion were asked to tithe 15% of their gross income in addition to volunteering their time.

Assisting those released from prison was positive, thought Jerome; recidivism was low. But after transitioning, Jerome thought former inmates should be able to seek gainful employment, or start their own businesses, separate from the religion, which was objected to.

Becoming Muslim is ridiculous. How would the million people, activities and businesses now located and supported in various states, be moved to one territory? Would the United States allow Shakur a sovereign state; I don't think so? One day I want to be rich and famous, which would be impossible. I wonder how old that pregnant girl was, who is the father of her child, and how do her parents feel about her pregnancy? Would my beautiful daughters become servants and impregnated?

* * * *

After earning her GED, Jerome encouraged Agnes to attend a community college. Upon receiving an Associate's Degree in 1960, she was promoted to administrative assistant and further encouraged to pursue a Bachelor's business degree, part-time. Agnes studied diligently and was a fast learner. Jerome's mentoring added to her education.

"Fred called to confirm your golf date tomorrow, Mr. G," Agnes said as Jerome entered the office.

"I can't make it; Cedric is graduating from high school and I promised we would be there."

Ulysses High School's walls, inside and out, were filled with graffiti. Students were sloppy, and undisciplined. Fights and bullying were commonplace, serious assaults and murders occurred periodically. To instill some semblances of civility, gang bandanas were not allowed.

Ulysses High was built circa 1900 for 3,000 students. Because of Negro northern migration during WW II and Chicago school superintendent's determination to maintain segregation, Ulysses High now housed 6,000 mostly poor Negroes. Their books and supplies remained virtually stagnant over the years, science projects were non-existent, causing learning, and meeting pre-requisites for some majors in colleges more difficult. Most Caucasian teachers considered Ulysses Purgatory; only a precious few worked at helping students receive a first-class education. The Negro teachers, who could only work at Negro schools, were at both ends of the teaching spectrum.

It was June, 1962, graduation day. The auditorium was filled with proud families who had thoroughly groomed themselves, and dressed in their finest. Jerome had bought Cedric a dark blue suit, with accessories, for graduation.

The school's choir and orchestra performances brought prideful tears to the Gerard's eyes. Tall, handsome Cedric was an Honors graduate. He was a member of the debate team which had won statewide competition. The team's Negro, female coach, PhD Jeanette Jenkins with a doctorate in English, and extensive study in Debate Techniques and Tactics, thought they had won their last regional match against an all-white school from Indianapolis, but the Caucasian judicial panel disagreed.

After the graduation ceremony, Principal Eric Hunter said to the Gerards on the auditorium steps, "You have positively influenced Cedric. After you hired him he transformed into one of our best students; before, well that's another story. The tragedy is during his tenure almost half of his class dropped out." *Even high schools with 100% Negro student populations don't have Negro principals*, Jerome thought. "I hear you are providing him with a full scholarship plus a stipend, that's wonderful," Principal Hunter said as they talked amidst celebrating graduates.

"His scholarship will stay in place as long as he does well in college and comes home every summer to work and learn more about the drugstore business."

"In spite of peer pressure not to succeed," Hunter continued, "ten percent of our students make the honor roll, but because of economics and misplaced family values, most cannot attend college. Very few even apply for the many scholarships that go unused. If there were more people like you this neighborhood would have more professionals and fewer ex-cons. Again, thanks for all you do." Hunter was pulled away by an excited graduate anxious to introduce his family.

Jerome reflected on Hunter's comment regarding criminals. *It cost $35,000 to incarcerate one person, but only $10,000 a year to educate a public college student. What a misappropriation of funds*, Jerome thought.

The five Chambliss' hosted by the Gerards went to Felix and Bea's to celebrate. Shirley, who was raised by a single mom, on Welfare, dropped out of high school during her junior year because she was pregnant with Cedric. Shirley never received any support from any of her four children's fathers. Shirley worked in a laundry ten hours a day, five days a week and as a maid on week-ends. She spent everything she earned playing Bingo and partying; her children virtually raised themselves. Shirley's Aid to Dependent Children social worker didn't report her for not staying home. She respected Shirley for wanting to help herself; so few did.

"You are our family's hero," Shirley said while having dinner. "Cedric is the first to graduate high school; he has set a good example for his younger siblings by working hard and studying." Gail had noticed the frayed hemline in Shirley's after-five dress and that her heels were too large.

"Since he's leaving the store I'll have to replace him. Is Michael ready to go to work?" Jerome asked.

"You bet he is," Shirley smiled.

"Michael, I'll offer you a full college scholarship if over the next three years you maintain at least a C average, stay out of trouble, and become dedicated to your job." Jerome wanted to build a team of apprentices, so upon college graduation they would thoroughly know the drugstore business.

"You better not fuck up," Cedric said while giving his younger brother the evil eye.

"What a terrible thing to say," Shirley said! Jerome bowed his head and briefly closed his eyes; he had never heard Cedric curse.

"Folks," Jerome announced after lightly wrapping on his iced tea glass, "listen up. Meet Cedric Chambliss, an honors graduate from Ulysses High, heading for Xavier University and a pharmacology degree!" Jerome encouraged Cedric to stand as the patrons applauded.

After taking the Chambliss' home, Gail said, "I'm proud of us sending Cedric to college."

"Just as Willie McGhee said, 'Education is fundamental to independence for Black Folks.' Education is the lifeline needed to lift ourselves by our bootstraps from the swamps of segregation and self-indulgence. I wish we could do more to help the ten percent."

"What ten percent?" Gail asked.

"Principal Hunter mentioned ten percent of the seniors made the honor roll but could not go to college. W.E.B. Dubois identified the Talented Tenth as being successful facilitators, but those Hunter mentioned should also be thought of as the Talented Tenth who need help and inspiration."

"And look how Shirley stumbled without an education or parental guidance. But don't let your generosity gland overload your wallet; sending one boy to college is enough," Gail said.

"Don't forget our other success story, Agnes." Jerome drove while musing over missing educational opportunities for deserving, Black youth.

Agnes said over the intercom, "Mr. J., you're supposed to relieve Peter; he has to pick up turkeys from Tiny's for our employees. It's the 22nd."

"You're right as usual Agnes," Jerome said, clearing his desk. "We've been doing this for five years, since '58, and I still forget."

Midway through the day someone shouted, "Kennedy's been shot! President Kennedy's been shot!" Jerome expected to hear the punch line to a sick joke. A policeman in the front of the store was responding to his walkie-talkie. He kept yelling the refrain, turning in different directions, his hands flailing. It was no joke.

"Is the president alive?" Jerome shouted.

"All I know is that he's been severely wounded!"

"I'm going home, Josephine," Jerome said, anticipating the worst. Josephine, who was working a register, called the in-coming pharmacist and asked him to come in immediately. Agnes temporarily worked the pharmacist's counter.

"Oh Babe," Gail said from a fetal position on their couch, "Walter Cronkite just announced that President Kennedy is dead!" Jerome put Gail's head on his lap and hugged her; they cried together. "Our president was an outspoken champion for Civil Rights and peace in Viet Nam," Gail cried.

"Maybe he was too outspoken; maybe that's why he was assassinated," Jerome sobbed. They moaned in each other's arms as if one of their closest relatives had died. Jerome, exhausted and depressed, fell asleep holding Gail.

Mourning and grief engulfed the nation until after President Kennedy's funeral. Because of unheard witnesses; the sudden deaths of the outspoken; the exonerated conspirators; and the questionable investigations documented by book-writers Louisiana Attorney General Jim Garrison; Dallas, Journalist Jim Marr; and others, JFK's assassination remains an enigma.

The century old 39th Street neighborhood surrounding Felix and Bea's had substantively deteriorated. The properties were 75 years old before

Negroes could buy or rent. Banks would not make repairs and remodeling loans to the new owners; it was called redlining.

Boarded homes marred Felix's business community. The unemployed languished on front porches, door stoops, and in vacant lots on discarded sofas. Cheap wine bottles, worn tires, debris, and discarded large appliances were strewn about. Felix Long's customers were dwindling. He wanted to relocate without adding to the neighborhood's blight, so he asked his friend Baxter Bridges for assistance.

"Well, my brother, looks like you have tarried too long," Baxter quipped, "Your restaurant is in a cesspool. If it wasn't for our friendship, even I wouldn't be eating here. Tell you what, give me a six month exclusive and an additional two-point commission and I'll try to unload your millstone."

"No thanks." *He completely missed my objectives*, Felix realized. Through loose conversation, Felix mentioned his intentions to Baxter's subordinate, Gail who was having lunch with clients. After praising Felix's concerns, Gail said, "Would you give me two weeks to present an acceptable solution before seeking other alternatives?" Felix agreed.

While driving through the newest neighborhood encircled by the Black Belt, Gail noticed a store-bought For Sale sign in the window of a Veterans of Foreign Wars clubhouse. The "good ol boys" who longed for the "good ol days," i.e., without Negroes, had sold their homes, moved to all-white suburbs, and deserted their——for White veterans only——facility.

This would easily meet Felix's needs with room for expansion, Gail thought. It had a large, commercial-type kitchen, an office, a wet bar, and sufficient room for tables. The 15,000 square foot parcel was in excellent condition.

"Why did you abandon this lovely club house, Alfred?" Gail, who was passing, asked the decision-maker in white-speak after flashing her real estate license. She knew the answer.

"The reason is obvious young lady: Niggers are everywhere. Most of our members have moved, and those that haven't are trying to."

"As you know," Gail said, fueling his misguided prejudices, "the Coloreds don't have any money, especially for commercial properties. Why they can hardly afford to buy your lovely homes. That's why you are forced to sell at below market prices." Gail fed Alfred's bigotry. She knew the reason for the below market sales was whitey selling under desperate conditions because they didn't want to be the last family on their block.

Alfred agreed, he said, "You're right! When I told realtors our location they hung up. That's why that generic sign was in the window. Incidentally, which agency are you with?"

"And you know how destructive young Coloreds are, especially when the property is vacant." Gail said, ignoring Alfred's question, continuing to feed his ignorance. "Your insurance will probably cancel after the first vandalism act."

"They cancelled the minute we vacated," Alfred said, acknowledging Gail's expertise, her agency became moot. Gail frightened Alfred until he was ready to give the liability-ridden parcel away. Felix viewed the property under the guise of being Gail's handyman, determining needed repairs before listing. Felix bought the property at 40% of the appraised value, for cash; Felix and Alfred had separate closings in a Caucasian real estate office. To complete the second half of Felix's objective, Gail asked her Park Manor pastor to recommend a nearby Catholic church that would accept Felix's former restaurant as a gift. Her pastor obliged.

St. Martin de Porres Parrish, named after the Catholic Church's only Black saint, was identified. The pastor, Father Paul, refused Gail an audience until she and her family attended Sunday Mass. Jerome reluctantly attended with Gail and his daughters.

St. Martin, located in a previous furniture store, was sparse, but filled to overflowing every mass, every Sunday. Used pews and kneeling bars were available for the first one hundred; folding chairs and donated used pillows accommodated the overflow. Collections were meager. There was no organ or pulpit. Father Paul delivered inspiring sermons while standing in front of the church. The two-tier alter was built with bricks and plywood, covered by clean sheets. The choir, accompanied by a Catholic guitarist and saxophonist, sang and swayed with feeling. The Gerards were emotionally moved. Each choir member, because robes were not affordable, wore a nine inch by eight foot African swath around their shoulders.

After mass Gail asked Father Paul to accept Felix and Bea's restaurant and convert it into a haven for the hungry.

"What do you think, Jerome?" Father Paul asked. He had researched Jerome's financial status and influence in his community.

"Well, Father," Jerome responded tersely "if it's free, why not?"

"Jerome," Father Paul said as he moved closer, "You agree our 501C3 status allows the donor to receive a tax write-off well above its true market value, yes?"

"Well, yes," Jerome answered. *Oh oh, this priest has significant business sense.*

"Then you do understand why we need assistance to make this project work?"

"Of course," *I'm hooked.* "Father Paul, I guarantee you will have full financial support for your new refuge if you accept Gail's gift."

"Jerome, that's a blessed commitment!" Father Paul took Jerome's and Gail's hands in an enthusiastic embrace and said, "We accept. And I'm sure, through your efforts, Jerome, we will be made whole."

Gail was delighted to have Jerome involved. She decided to change parishes.

"Of course I'll contribute," Rudolph "Tiny" Frazier said when Gail asked for support while shopping. "Every day my stores throw out food that can be consumed within a day or two. We will also contribute fresh meat and seafood, but will need receipts to make the donations tax deductible."

"We'll furnish signed, blank receipts, you fill in the amounts," Gail said. She asked Luther Wilson, who owned a fleet of cabs, to transfer foodstuffs daily without charge. Felix, at Jerome's suggestion, paved his adjacent property to accommodate a hand car wash. The projected income would pay those working in both facilities, leaving the surplus for St. Martin. Before the paving, Father Paul called on his parishioners to help clear away the trash. Negro alderman, Kenneth Appling, insisted the city garbage collectors provide trucks. Father Paul was delighted with the conversion.

"I'll give cooking utensils, dinnerware, and trays," Samuel Stovall volunteered when Jerome told the B.S. Table of Felix's intentions and St. Martin's acceptance.

"I'll pay for all the car washing equipment and supplies needed," Rachael Piernas promised.

"Put my company down for a new steam table," Stuart Sykes said.

"I'll design and produce all of the signage for both enterprises, gratis," Alphonso Major said. Other B.S. Table regulars made contributions. The Black middle class built an uplifting oasis in Felix's old neighborhood.

Father Paul named his food bank *The Second Chance*. St. Martin's experienced business members volunteered to manage and train personnel for the two enterprises. Cooking and cafeteria food service skills were taught by Felix's staff. Expert car washing and detailing skills were quickly learned. Over time, adept workers were encouraged to seek outside employment, continuing to make room for the unemployed. Backgrounds, including jail-time, were overlooked by prospective employers; Father Paul's written recommendations were sufficient. The gainfully employed of St. Martin de Porres, plus the car wash employees increased their church donations. It was a win-win situation for all concerned. A pulpit was one of Father Paul's first purchases.

Free hot meals were served to the hungry daily. Alphonso Major issued a press release, gratis. The *Chicago Defender* published a full-page story with photos featuring Gail, Felix, and Father Paul serving dinners to mothers with children. The *Chicago Chronicle* ignored the release.

Potential real estate clients who called Bridges Real Estate wanted to be serviced by the "pretty young lady with the big heart," which increased Gail's customer base. She asked Bridges for assistance. He told her to turn over her surplus clients to other agents; she refused. Gail hired her own staffperson; Bridges reluctantly assigned him a desk.

Felix and Bea's Restaurant moved to a modern, contemporary facility on 71ˢᵗ and South Park in July of '64. Gail received a generous bonus and lavish praise from Felix for producing an optimal solution. Felix and Bea's traffic increased thanks to Alphonso Major's, B&W (for Black and White, which was never used) Enterprises. Felix hired a deejay and offered free hors d'oeuvres during Happy Hour, which attracted the young, professional crowd.

Felix's regulars ate lunch elsewhere, but enjoyed; along with players, paramours, hipsters, and partying couples, late-night steaks on sizzling platters, or, early breakfasts. Felix and Bea's delicious biscuits, cooked from Bea's original, secret recipe, were always available. Because of the After Hours crowd, Felix stayed open twenty-four, seven.

To those who questioned the visually mismatched, ten seat circular table, Felix said, "You gotta dance with those that brung ya." Every Friday, at lunch, the imposing table with the only white linen in the restaurant, filled.

The B.S. Table regulars chastised Bridges for refusing to help Felix and complimented Gail for structuring a complex deal. She became the B.S. Table's agent of choice. Bridges didn't visit Felix and Bea's for several months.

"She's gotten too big for her britches," Bridges said to his administrative assistant.

"Man it's raining as hard as times were in '29," Jerome said to Samuel as they met entering Felix and Bea's one Friday.

Samuel answered. "Be thankful my friend, when the showers end, plants will put on a show. April showers bring May flowers. Once again, Mother Nature will win, don't cha know."

"Now you're the B.S. Table's poet laureate, huh?" Both laughed as they shed their raincoats.

"Oh, oh," Bridges said as the distinguished pair took seats, "the wheeler-dealers are among us. Someone's ox is about to be gored. Who are you two ganging up on today?"

"Aw, come on my brothers," Jerome whined, "We're just two hungry Colored boys joining friends to break bread."

The murders of three young men, two White and one Black, by Money Mississippi's, arrest immune, Ku Klux Klan, was being discussed. Buddy said, "They were registering Negroes to vote; In Bronzeville too few of us vote. What's happening down South validates the importance of our voting here, which can drastically improve our lives."

Mid lunch, Leo Lafarge said while joining the table, "Brothers and sisters say hello to Lonnie Blackman."

"Mr. Blackman!" Jerome exclaimed, "It's been a long time; about eleven years!" Jerome stood, the two embraced while exchanging greetings.

"I opened my fifth office in Bronzeville; my fourth is in Los Angeles. I guess we have been missing each other. How long have you been here?"

"Long enough to buy eight stores with my money," Bridges complained. The table chuckled.

"And long enough to buy a big house in prestigious Jackson Park Highlands, with 50% down and a 15 year mortgage," Samuel said.

"And long enough to own half a block on Forty-Seventh and Lake Park," Stuart Sykes, now president of Unified Life Insurance, added.

Jerome and Gail had kept McKlosky's parcels filled with ten percent rental increases annually. McKlosky was surprised by the increased income; he died at 80, alone and forlorn. McKlosky's will sold Jerome his 47th Street holdings for one dollar. The Gerard family attended McKlosky's funeral at a retirement village in Santa Fe, NM. McKlosky's racially offensive vocabulary, but prejudice-free attitude.

"And long enough to get an MBA from the University of Chicago," Fred Hawkins contributed. U of C informed Jerome he was close to earning an MBA, via his home study courses, so he completed his required courses on site.

"Fred, how's your lovely wife, Esther?" Lonnie asked.

"Beats me; she got tired of my shit five years ago. She moved to Atlanta." Fred finished his drink, and looked for Rowena to order another.

"Jerome, Brother Beau raves about you and your family every time I see him, which is about twice a year."

"Michelle is a junior and Dana a freshman in Catholic high school. They are both honor students; here are some recent photos. As you can see Michelle is blossoming far too early." As Lonnie lavished praise over Jerome's photos, Jerome said, "Thanks to Bridges;" acknowledging him with an open palm, "Gail has a successful career in real estate; she recently received her broker's license." The news shocked Bridges. He had discouraged Gail from advancing to broker. "You know fellows," Jerome announced, "Lonnie is the reason I'm here, he encouraged me to leave New Orleans in '54.' Eleven years ago." Napkins and sarcastic comments bombarded Lonnie.

"I guess you and Harold Oldham compete for new locations, huh?" Lonnie asked. The B.S. Table stilled.

Several years earlier Harold was found in his car, outside one of his stores: murdered. The investigating detectives determined the shooting was an interrupted robbery because Harold still had his cash and jewelry. They dismissed Harold being shot twice above his left ear with hollow-point bullets through a 357 Magnum, with a silencer; their supervisor, who lived well above his salary, agreed. The investigation, like most involving Negroes being murdered, was brief and unproductive.

John T. Williamson had whispered to the B.S. Table that Harold's excessive, controlled substance purchases had been audited by the Feds just prior to his murder. The Mob's secrets died with Harold. Jerome purchased three of Harold's six stores; the remaining three were sold at Fire Sale prices. His widow and three children had moved back to Jacksonville, FL.

"Since Harold's demise," Buddy said, breaking the uncomfortable silence, "we marched on Washington, President Kennedy was assassinated, and then, praise the Lord, Texan, President Lyndon Johnson, passed the most sweeping Civil Rights legislation in history. Now we can stay, eat, sit, or study wherever we want, even in Mississippi; whether it should be a state is another question." Everyone laughed.

"There's a downside to integration," Stuart Sykes said, "our insurance companies, hotels, restaurants, and Negro colleges are disappearing fast."

"When we compete we prosper," Jerome said, "Metropolitan Assurance and Golden Community in Los Angeles are doing quite well after changing to the less costly Caucasian mortality table and began offering ordinary insurance policies. Morehouse, Howard, and Meharry are still turning away students. This restaurant and Sylvia's in Harlem are growing. The Pascal Brothers in Atlanta have a profitable mini-conglomerate, Master's and Doctorate degreed African Americans are being given significant responsibilities in major corporations." Jerome after receiving favorable nods, continued.

"If we practice sound business principles and offer excellence in product and service we can keep what's ours and gain ground in additional business disciplines. Affirmative action policies are allowing us to open retail stores on high-fashion North Michigan Boulevard, where wealthy Caucasians are our customers, and ownership is moot. Most of our Bronzeville-based retailers are more profitable because we have more discretionary income. The Black middle class is multiplying due to Affirmative Action." Jerome reminded the table of a recently visiting Black entrepreneur who had sold a better seat belt to General Motors.

"Anybody need any money just raise your hand," short, slender, Oscar Jones said as he took the last seat. Light-complexioned Oscar spent fifteen minutes each morning grooming his perfect, full mustache with a straight razor. Under close scrutiny, black eye-brow pencil could be detected. Every day, no matter the weather, Oscar wore a fresh carnation with his natty, conservative ensemble. Oscar was the special accounts manager for Second National Bank, the fifth largest bank in the city. Special accounts meant Negro accounts. His position was unique, nationally.

"Oscar," Leo said, "You've been picking up so many customers, Avalon and a few other South Side banks are hurting."

"It's simple," Oscar said, "People want to bank where they can borrow. We loan money based on a person's ability to repay; not on raced-based games. That's why Jerome and many others have become my clients."

"I overheard at lunch with O'Fay lawyers that Avalon Bank had financed a suburban shopping mall which folded. Soon, Avalon will be declared insolvent by the FDIC, so clear out your accounts ASAP," Samuel said, permitting the B.S. Table to benefit from privileged information gleaned from social integration.

"I've got a lot of work to do," Oscar mumbled.

"Now it makes sense," Rachael said after dabbing the corners of her mouth, "two downtown banks have applied for Illinois licenses as parents to new banks in Bronzeville. But, because of the new federal Affirmative Action policy, Blacks must own at least fifty-one percent. State administrators let it slip that Daniel Quibble is representing Boulevard Trust, and Bridges aren't you involved with First Security?"

"Yes," Bridges answered, "but no one is supposed to know––not yet anyway."

"This is very good news," Jerome said. "We'll be able to provide new businesses capital, increasing successes. Negro homeowners will receive low interest property improvement loans which will keep our real estate values up. Why, redlining will be eliminated!"

"Jerome," Lonnie said, "whichever bank you decide to invest in let me know. I have stock in Atlanta's Citizens Trust Bank, but I bought in kinda' late. I'd love to get in on the ground floor of a new Black-owned bank, especially here; Brother Beau will probably want in as well." Lonnie handed Jerome his business card.

"Let's see now," Buddy said with his left arm across his chest as he stroked his Vandyke beard, "a Black-owned bank. No, excuse me: two, new black owned banks. I wonder who will be Bronzeville's first Black bank president?"

"Who else is there?" Oscar asked, rising to his feet, straightening his tie, with the unread Wall Street Journal tucked under his arm, preparing to depart. "I'm the only Negro in town with banking experience plus CPA credentials. The real question is which bank will be fortunate enough to secure my services? Bridges, you're here and Daniel is not, I'm accepting bids." The table was astounded at Oscar's arrogance.

"Where is all the money coming from?" Stuart asked.

"Obviously, you have forgotten our history," Fred said. "The Binga Bank, the first Black-owned bank in the nation, located in Bronzeville, had over $100 million in mortgage holdings in 1929."

"And what happened to it?" Buddy asked.

"Well, that's another story, but there was, and still is, lots of bucks in Bronzeville." Fred, the only other CPA at the table, hoped someone would mention him as a probable bank president; no one did. "Say Jerome, when you leave, sthop by my offich; you otta hear this," Fred slurred.

"Not today man, too much to do; call Agnes, she'll hook us up." *We've been together for over an hour. Why haven't you already told me what I need to know? Jerome thought.*

"Oh, I see. I need ash appointment to talk to your black ash. Ain't that a bitch?" Jerome signaled Rowena for his check; he left hurriedly.

"Agnes, are you still here?" Jerome asked as he entered his office. It was 5:45 p.m.

"Of course," she replied cheerfully.

Agnes is great! She knew I would need her input. Agnes, now 26, was the company's bookkeeper and human relations manager for 56 employees. In May she was receiving an undergraduate degree in Business Administration.

"Any problems?" Jerome asked as he flopped down in his big chair.

"Just a few," Agnes said as she poured her boss a mug of hot coffee, then sat next to his desk. "CORE called, said Dick Gregory was arrested while picketing those portable classrooms dubbed 'Willy Wagons'. Dr. Curtis Wilson called, said he has ten doctors wanting to build a new medical center. That's about it."

Eight locked pouches containing yesterday's receipts and a manila folder full of invoices with attached checks to be signed awaited him. The portion of the day's mail which needed his attention was in another folder. "Have Samuel put up the bail for Dick Gregory, anonymously. Make sure I call Dr. Wilson, but I'm not interested in his new clinic."

"I'm scared of you, Mr. J!" Agnes said, "I thought Dr. Wilson's project would be our next major venture."

"We're going into the banking business," Jerome smiled.

"That's great; are you going to be president?"

"Now you listen here Miss Agnes," Jerome said as he paraphrased and imitated Butterfly McQueen, from *Gone With the Wind*, "I don't know nothin' 'bout runnin no bank, but then again, I didn't know nothin' 'bout runnin' no drugstore chain either," Jerome laughed.

"Seriously," Jerome said, "Owning two banks will allow Bronzeville to become the Nation's Black economic Mecca." Instructions to Agnes followed his ruminations. "Please call Daniel Quibble and Baxter Bridges for private meetings. Make sure Fred Hawkins and I meet when, and if he calls. I think I hurt his feelings today."

Agnes departed. Jerome scanned the daily reports, made notes for his monthly store managers' meetings, consolidated the stores' daily receipts, minus his skim, transferred a pre-determined percentage to his corporate account, signed checks, and wrote responses on each letter. After finishing he sipped his coffee, and reflected. He was pleased with his personal life, his business progress, his reputation in the community, and welcomed the challenges ahead.

End of Chapter Eleven

CHAPTER TWELVE

Forty ambitious and energetic Black men, with shined shoes, wearing coats and ties, thirty-five or younger, gathered in the Washington Park Field House for the monthly meeting of the volunteer, South Side Junior Chamber of Commerce, aka the Bronzeville Jaycees.

The only all-Black chapter in the Nation existed because of racial inequality in the Chicagoland Jaycees. Negroes, after years of menial assignments successfully performed, were never appointed or elected to responsible positions; in spite of professional degrees, military commissions and proven experience. The Chicagoland chapter also ignored Negro community needs. They successfully petitioned National in 1947, following WW II.

After six years of competent service, at thirty-five, Jerome's last year of eligibility, he was president. He called for order from the table top podium. "First, a belated, happy new year to all; '64 was excellent, especially with the passing of Civil Rights legislation. We now have federal law to ensure equality." Some members argued, like the 13th and 14th Constitutional Amendments, this landmark statute, also, would be severely weakened; complete racial equality would not be forthcoming. All agreed financial success and independence would come only through education, self-discipline, and hard work. Social acceptance? Well, respect was significantly more important.

"We distributed over 400 Christmas baskets to needy families, and our Big Brothers Christmas party was a huge success. Mr. Major, please present your fabulous Miss America report," Jerome requested.

Articulate, six foot three, dapper, Alphonso Major spoke like an anchor on network news; his formal education ended with a high school diploma. Alphonso had attended weekly meetings of the Washington Park YMCA Toastmasters Club, for over seven years where he improved his elocution and vocabulary. He studied biographies of successful businessmen, *Advertising Age* was his bible.

"Our chapter, for the first time, sponsored a Miss Illinois candidate; she won State, making her the first Negro in the Miss America Pageant." Positive comments and applause followed.

"Excellent work Mr. Major," Jerome said. Alphonso had persuaded a professional model and Cedric's debate coach, English PhD Jeannette Jenkins, to advise and prepare their beautiful candidate for several months—without compensation.

According to chairmen's reports; reading classes for adult illiterates, weekly shopping transportation for seniors to Hyde Park, where groceries were fresher, and cost less, and a spring barbeque fundraiser, were all on target.

"Before we adjourn I'd like to introduce a new project," Jerome said. "This is Agnes Clift, my indispensable, administrative assistant. She has been a team member for nine years and recently earned an undergraduate degree in business. Also, say hello to Cedric Chambliss, who will graduate from Xavier in 1966. He will have a pharmacist's degree, plus eight years' experience in drug store operations." Both stood and accepted applause as Jerome placed his hands on their shoulders.

"Cedric's and Agnes' scholarships and expenses each cost a little more than $20,000 a year; without which their education would have probably ended before graduating high school. Now they will earn over a lifetime a million dollars more than the average high school drop-out. "I propose we start a college scholarship fund for deserving high school students, plus offer encouragement, inspiration, and challenging jobs, like I did for these two. We should begin by raising at least $100,000 this year; I will contribute $20,000."

"What will be business owners' motivation?" a Jaycee asked.

"They will benefit, as I have, from the growth of potential, loyal managers within their companies. Racial prejudices will be eliminated by individual excellence. Every entrepreneur needs and appreciates good help,"

Jerome answered. "Each year our goal will be to raise at least $100,000 to support ten high school graduates as college freshmen. I have asked Samuel Stovall, and Fred Hawkins, both former Jaycees, to establish a tax deductible, 501C3 status.

"Mr. Chairman," Alphonso Major said, "Let's name this project the Jerome Gerard Scholarship Fund."

"Thank you, but the Bronzeville Jaycees will make it something special."

"Hmmm," Major said, "O.K., let's name it Bronzeville's Bootstraps Scholarship Fund, a positive, visual name that will encourage donations. Maybe we'll start an annual fashion show involving Greek organizations, who appreciate advanced education, as a fund raising project. Why, they might even serve as role models and tutors." Alphonso said, thinking creatively.

Jerome drafted Alphonso as acting, executive director of BBSF, with Samuel Stovall providing legal support, and Fred Hawkins as accounting consultant. Jerome also asked Dr. Jeanette Jenkins to volunteer as the college scholarship catalyst.

Making money had lost its fervor. Because both Gerards had excellent incomes, substantial savings, profitable investments, and were mortgage and debt free, generating profit had become a manifestation of efficiency and a competition between peers. With the birth of the BBSF program Jerome felt euphoric, better than when he had acquired his first drugstore nine years earlier. Jerome had a new mission; serving youth through self-help and education.

About a dozen Jaycees adjourned to Scotty's. Jerome asked Alphonso, "Do you think Survivor's Bank will make it, man?"

"Ooh yeaah!" Alphonso teased between sips of Cordon Bleu Cognac from his personal, monogrammed snifter that stayed in Scotty's, "right after you're elected Grand Dragon of the KKK."

"Why are you so pessimistic, my brother?"

"First," Alphonso held up his forefinger, "Avalon Bank failed in that same building; people won't forget that. Second," two fingers appeared under Jerome's chin as Alphonso's elbow rested on the bar, while he had difficulty holding his head erect, "moneyed Blacks don't have confidence in Black-owned anything, especially banks. They still believe if Negroes run it, something must be wrong with it. Third," another finger appeared, "We don't have enough money to make one bank successful, let alone two."

"We've only been open a year my brother; give us time."

"I didn't finish; fourth, Fred Hawkins works harder at picking up broads in bars instead of gleaning new business from decision makers."

"Wait a damn minute; Fred's my ace."

"Oh, everybody knows you're the reason he's president. I hope your friendship is worth––what did you drop––a hundred large?"

The minimum investment in preferred stock was $100,000. Jerome had once again, drained his cash reserves and stock portfolio and initially invested $60,000, leaving the seven year-old Cayman Island account intact, and growing. He borrowed $40,000 from their parent bank, payable monthly over four years without interest. Jerome also had received proxy voting privileges for Conrad Beauregard's and Lonnie Blackman's $10,000 each.

Before persuading the board, with his voting power, to select Fred as president, Jerome, during a private lunch, had said to Fred, "You will have the responsibility of protecting the life savings of our friends and neighbors. You will have to become totally committed to the bank's success which means long hours, with less drinking and womanizing."

"I will be eternally grateful if given this unusual opportunity, and will do whatever it takes to be successful, including curtailing my social life. Jerome, I will not let you down." Fred's "little brother," through self-discipline, good business decisions and planned savings, had become his sponsor, and one of his bosses. After several months because of his new, renown, position, Fred resumed and even increased his indulgences.

"Unless you can get us to believe in ourselves," Alphonso continued between cognac sips at Scotty's, "and persuade White folks to trust us with their money, two phenomenal feats indeed, both banks are doomed."

"What would it cost for you to develop that type of ad campaign?" Jerome asked.

"Man, I'm good, but I'm not God; Coca Cola doesn't spend that much." Alphonso took a sip, and then took a penetrating, long look at Jerome and said, "Did you just ask me to create an ad campaign for Survivors?"

"Hell yes, but you just said you couldn't do it!" Both men laughed. Alphonso tried to revive their earlier topic without success. Bachelor

Alphonso, dismissed the proposed ad campaign as futile, responded to a young tender sender who had sauntered by several times.

Jerome thought, *one thing Alphonso did say I found interesting: getting more White folks to invest in Survivors.*

* * * *

"Mr. G," Agnes said, "Mr. Freeman's secretary called an emergency meeting."

"What time?" Jerome asked. It was April 4th, 1968. His calendar showed a driving range outing with Samuel. Fred and Jerome no longer socialized; the bank's unprofitability had strained their friendship.

"Now," Agnes answered.

"Damn, the urban league always has some crises. Call Samuel and explain."

When Jerome arrived he approached the forty cup, stainless steel coffee maker, which was still percolating, indicated by a dim red light. Uniformed, fifth District Commander Lewis Calhoun walked in.

"I'm surprised to see you here, Lewis, what's going on?"

"I'll let Nate explain," a somber Calhoun said. As more affluent people arrived Jerome realized this was more than Urban League business.

Newly appointed Federal Appellate Judge Rachael Piernas entered. She and Jerome embraced as she said, "Isn't it terrible?"

"Isn't what terrible?" Jerome was becoming more perplexed.

Lanky, sixty-ish, Nathaniel Freeman and his petite secretary Elizabeth, entered. All conversation ceased as Nathaniel's dismal face loomed. He gathered himself emotionally and said, "Thank you for re-arranging your full schedules on such short notice. Special plaudits to Commander Calhoun who represents the mayor, and Judge Piernas, who is liaison for our governor." Freeman breathed deeply, exhaled and then said, "Reverend, Doctor Martin Luther King Junior is dead. He was shot earlier this evening in Memphis, Tennessee."

Cries soliciting the Lord's help, and utterances of disbelief, emitted from the nine men and two women. Grey-haired Nathaniel and Elizabeth stood silent.

"What did you just say!?" Jerome asked as he sat down; he felt dizzy. He hoped this tragic news was a bad dream; it wasn't.

Heavyset, Hospital administrator Rufus Harper doubled up and fell into a seat as if he had been hit in the stomach with a wrecking ball. Judge Piernas muffled a sneeze. All of her professional life she had never allowed men to see her cry. Tonight, no matter how great the grief, self-discipline would triumph.

With his cap under his right arm, the commander stood at attention. Violence and death were Lewis' forte. Several days from now; after the public's rage had subsided, and normalcy had returned to his beloved city, he would grieve over his people, the nation's, and the world's loss, but not now. Now he was motionless and emotionless, he had to help protect his city's citizens and their property.

The only sound was the coffee urn's gurgle. The red light was bright; no one bothered.

"Are you sure?" Rufus asked. "I didn't hear anything on the radio."

"Once the news reached the White House," Nathaniel said, "the feds alerted the states, who notified the cities, who then told us. It's an established procedure which gives public officials a little lead time; it's on the air now. Our president has asked all Negro civic organizations to call meetings like this to help save our cities from the expected riots."

"Ain't no doubt about that!" Six foot four, 300 plus pound, Arnold Weathers, AFL-CIO's Vice President, said, "hell, I feel like torching something myself!"

"I understand where you're coming from, my brother," Nathaniel said, "But we have to lead during times of national tragedy; not succumb to our emotions. You, our communities' leaders, are here to suggest what should be done to minimize the inevitable."

"The South Side," Commander Calhoun said, "will remain stable. Our gang control units are in touch with the Blackstone Rangers and they will remain tame, but the Devil's Disciples on the West Side are another matter."

"Why are our police coddling gangs?" Caucasian Walter Heldt, urban league board member from the Chicago based, Campbell Soup Company, asked, "Why don't you just arrest them?"

"Because they didn't shoot Martin Luther King. You did!" Arnold Weathers shouted.

"The Blackstone Rangers," Calhoun said while patting Arnold's shoulder, suggesting he suppress his anger, "have over twelve thousand members between the ages of fifteen and twenty-five. Arresting hordes of angry, young, Black, armed men, would take the National Guard in a house-to-house search. And Arnold is right; they haven't committed a crime." Arnold Weathers and Walter Heldt stared at each other, but remained silent.

"There will be broken storefront windows on the South Side tonight, perhaps calls for marches or a memorial service, but very little rioting. Our problems will be on the West Side," the commander forecasted.

"A memorial service is a good idea," Nathaniel said. "We'll hold it at Soldier's Field this Sunday and let one designated person from any organization speak for three minutes." Nathaniel turned to Elizabeth, "Clear this with New York, and then implement the plan."

"Commander Calhoun is right," Jerome said, "The West Side erupted during July of '64 and didn't cool down for three days, even after the National Guard was called in, and all over a policeman's shooting and killing a youngster who opened a fire hydrant. Martin's assassination is much worse." Jerome coughed and cried.

"Do you need a drink of water?" Elizabeth asked.

"No," Jerome replied. "I just choked on Dr. King's name. He insisted I call him Martin; I never should have been so familiar. He was too close to God for me to use his first name. We took his being with us forever as a given."

"Harry Belafonte planned for this," Nathaniel said. "He bought a million dollar term insurance policy and named Coretta King Beneficiary."

"What's so different about the West Side?" Walter Heldt asked, he still wasn't sure there was an emergency.

"Unemployment on the West Side is a major problem," Nathaniel answered. "Without jobs, young men are prime for any disruptive behavior. Commander, what do you suggest?" Calhoun was sitting at the conference table, writing.

"First, get Mayor O'Malley, Cardinal Kyle, and the well-known Reverend Marshall on television and Negro-oriented radio, broadcasting apologies every fifteen minutes. They should not ask for calm, or for order to prevail, but apologize for the Negro community's loss. They should also announce Sunday's memorial service. Alert Mr. Major, he should develop their scripts as well as layouts for the memorial service's newspaper ads. Secondly, the city's prominent clergy should walk in pairs tonight; one White, one Black, along the West Side's main thoroughfares, using bullhorns, asking people to pray for Dr. King, and to stay in their homes."

"The ministers should wear black arm bands on white shirts, and display their religious emblems," a prominent pastor added, "making it obvious they are preachers not police."

"Apologize for what?" Walter Heldt asked. "We haven't done anything wrong!"

"You killed Dr. King!" Arnold shouted through burning eyes and clinched teeth.

"What Arnold means Walter," Nathaniel interrupted, "is that Black folk know White folk killed Dr. King; the same Caucasians that won't employ us, the same Whites that refuse us apartments and mortgages, the same degenerates that shouted Nigger and threw bricks at Dr. King when he marched in Cicero. And that's why Chicago's leaders should only express sorrow for the loss that <u>we</u> have sustained." Arnold turned his back toward Walter and sat down, held his head in his hands, and sobbed.

"The world has lost one of the most impactful leaders of the 20ᵗʰ century, what will we do Lord; what, will, we, do?" Rachael asked.

"The best we can," Nathaniel said. "If we can make it through tonight the worst will be over." Nathaniel's comment was a prayer, not a forecast.

Rufus Harper called his South Side, Negro hospital, informed them of the tragedy, and declared a Code Orange, which meant all emergency-related persons should stay or come in and begin preparing to treat victims from police clubbings or worse. He also ordered that Caucasian, West Side hospitals be notified.

"To maintain civil order," Calhoun said, "Mayor O'Malley has cancelled all days off and vacations for police and firemen. Our police will make as few arrests as possible," Calhoun said, "But there are established boundaries beyond which looting will not be tolerated."

"The governor has activated two National Guard units. That's 20,000 armed troops," Rachael added. Rachael dabbed delicately at the corners of her eyes with her handkerchief, ostensibly trying to remove a stray lash. "At least they haven't been given orders to shoot plunderers on sight." Rachael was recalling the orders Mayor O'Malley issued during the '64 riot.

"You're right," Calhoun said, rising to his feet, "but that order will seem like touch football if rioters approach the Loop or North Michigan Boulevard. After the '64 riot, the boundaries for disruptive behavior and the strategy to protect the city's richest assets were drawn." No one asked to hear the plans.

"Surely other cities have similar plans," Jerome said. "How ironic it would be if a Nobel Peace prize recipient's assassination became the catalyst for national Negro genocide."

"Some psychologists have speculated," Calhoun added, "that is precisely what the perpetuators of this heinous crime hoped would happen." The silence was deafening.

"Elizabeth," Nathaniel said, "Write a summary of this meeting so that Commander Calhoun and attorney Piernas can inform their superiors. We will move quickly to get the ministers in the street and messages of tolerance on the airwaves. Tomorrow we will know just how much our profound suggestions helped our city tonight."

Everyone held crossed hands. Heads bowed, eyes closed, prayers were forwarded, mostly asking that civility would endure this night. A pastor, with a deep, bass voice, led the small, affluent group in two verses of the Civil Rights Movement's theme, "We Shall Overcome." The two Caucasians, experiencing new allegiances, slightly out of sync, held hands and hummed along.

The previous night, while speaking on behalf of the mistreated Memphis garbage collectors, Dr. King prophesied his assassination. He had said, "…I have seen the Promised Land… I may not get there with you…"

As news of Dr. King's assassination spread, African American's rioted. Looters were arrested, some beaten, several killed. National Guard troops throughout the nation restored order. Fortunately, the rioting ceased after one night, and genocide did not occur.

* * * *

The 70 x 30 foot board room over the huge vault in the rear of the bank was accessed by a steep, thirty step stairway. The wall abutting the bank was glass bricks covered with long, black drapes. Six 100 watt, light bulbs hung over a top-worn, stained rectangular table, positioned on a tattered carpet. The drab grey walls held portraits of six former Avalon Bank board chairmen. *Their portraits seem to scowl at us because we're here instead of their siblings*, Jerome imagined. Survivors' board had approved refurbishing their dingy accommodations after receiving their first positive quarterly cash flow report, which hadn't happened in four years.

Twelve board-members sat in creaky, old leather chairs, sans their original enthusiasm. Three Caucasians sat close to immense, Jewish chairman, Milton Levine. Eight blacks gathered at the opposite end of the fourteen-foot conference table. Water-filled decanters and glasses were placed appropriately: separated but equal.

"Sarah," Milton said, "This special meeting is called to order at 2:00 p.m., June 15, 1968, with everyone invited present." Bank President Fred Hawkins was not invited. Milton's crown was bald, he had dark piercing eyes. His posture commanded respect; he had never smiled during their four years of monthly board meetings. Milton and his three brothers owned Chicago's largest appliance and furniture chain. One of their stores had become encircled by the South Side's ever-expanding Black Belt. Sarah, Fred's secretary, had taken the board's minutes since the bank's inception.

Richard Thompson, president of a soaring hair care product manufacturing company was the major stock holder, but nominated Milton as chairman and himself as vice chairman when the board elected officers. "I need to learn something about banking before trying to run one," Richard had said. Jerome did not invoke Lonnie's and Conrad's preferred proxies, which would have given him the majority of voting stock.

"We'll begin with the reading of the most atrocious quarterly P&L statement I have ever seen——outside of bankruptcy court," fifty-ish Milton said. Stuart Sykes, Survivor's board secretary read the independent accountants' monthly assessment. His voice wavered, making understanding him difficult, but it didn't matter, Sarah had distributed copies.

"It's the same old story," Tiny said after Stuart's delivery. "We don't believe in ourselves." He was the only board member not wearing a tie. Tiny had trouble finding dress shirts with size twenty-two collars, so he wore XXXL, white, collared, emblemed pull-over's under size 52 sports coats over his authorized, shoulder holstered, .38 revolver. Tiny carried large cash deposits to the bank.

"Another reason…" A Caucasian board member was interrupted.

"The real reason," Milton slammed the conference table with his open hand, startling everyone, "for this bank's dire performance is its president!" Milton crinkled the report in his fist, and shook it at his board. "This is unbelievable! The payroll exceeds budget, large loans are delinquent, our overdrawn accounts ratio is excessive, and as always, there are too few new depositors."

"It's because of the competition," Jerome said, lacking sincerity. "There are two new Black banks…"

"Aw, shut up Junior Flip," Bridges said.

"You had better watch your mouth Uncle Reemus." Jerome now had ten doctors in 50 offices, and had absorbed two rental increases, but Bridges was still dissatisfied, especially with his 'under the table' 2%. Jerome threatened to build his own medical center and drugstore a block away if Bridges insisted on another rental increase. Bridges relented because Jerome was his biggest tenant. Additionally, Gail, because Bridges had "miscalculated" several of her commissions, opened her own real estate office on the South Side, and had kidnapped five of Bridges' most competent sales and support staff.

"You know what's going down," Bridges continued. "Your boy comes in late every day, hung-over, and leaves around noon. His expenses are ridiculous, and he hasn't brought in any significant business since he's been president. Why, he doesn't even give us a complete list of overdrawn accounts––does he Mr. Gerard?" Bridges stared at Jerome; his artificial smile persisted.

Over the last year, Illinois had slowed in reimbursing Courtesy Drugs for its huge number of welfare prescriptions; currently it was taking three months. Jerome, without overdrafts, couldn't discount his invoices, which would cost him profits. They were dwindling in amounts and timeframes, but still existed. Fred had left Jerome's name off the delinquency lists which were reviewed at every board meeting.

"We have two options," Richard said as he leaned back in his chair with his hands laced across his paunch. "Each of us must commit to bringing in a specific number of new depositors, or find a president who will. Doing nothing, hoping the situation will improve, is no longer acceptable."

Richard has sided with Milton and Bridges, Jerome realized.

"If we don't do something soon we will fall into receivership," Caucasian, tanned, toned, and handsome Hal Hornbeck said, "We supported the late Martin Luther King and marched against Ben Willis, but we can't continue to lose money. My daddy has said, and I agree, we cannot let Mr. Hawkins drink us into insolvency." 30-ish Hal was the youngest board member, and vice president of his family's South Side match-book manufacturing business.

"Mr. Chairman," Bridges said, standing while leaning on his cane, "I move that we terminate Fred Hawkins. Since Mr. Gerard made us hire him with his excessive votes, he should fire him!" Hal Hornbeck seconded the motion. The motion carried.

"We stand adjourned," Milton said curtly, pounding the gavel twice. Normally the two racial groups conversed separately, but not today. Suddenly Jerome was alone.

He ordered Fred's weekly check plus a generous eight weeks' severance for four years. Jerome poured a cup of coffee, and lit a cigarette, delaying his inevitable task, fighting within himself while tears escaped.

Memories over 14 years cogitated: initially meeting Fred at Felix and Bea's; Fred, in the middle of the night, inviting him to the golf course, knowing he couldn't play; Fred finding him a job and a home in one morning; Fred, who was Jerome's best friend, social facilitator, and mentor, was now his responsibility to terminate.

Should I resign rather than fire Fred? Jerome thought. *No, I can't abandon my, plus Lonnie' and Conrad's investments. Besides, someone else would execute the board's order. Fred must be replaced if we have any chance of protecting the thousands who invested their life's savings. If this bank fails, once again our investors will be set upon, or refused loans; only this time they will be several million dollars poorer.*

Jerome slowly descended the steep steps. For the first time since his discharge he summoned the military decree of "mission before man" to accomplish his repulsive task. The walk to Fred's office was the longest of Jerome's life, ending far too soon. Everyone he passed glanced away, seeming to know his mission. Sarah looked up with filled eyes. Jerome knocked on Fred's door. Without waiting for a response, he breathed deeply and entered.

Jerome recalled warning Fred during a private lunch four years ago.

"I wondered which handkerchief head that fat Jew would send." Fred's glistening wing-tipped Johnston-Murphy shoes laid crossed on his desk's secretary shelf as he leaned back and cleaned his nails with a file. His eyes were weak from excessive drinking and sleeplessness. "Man, you wouldn't even be here if I...

"You are so right," Jerome interrupted, "But over the years I've done things that worked, and you have not. You didn't keep your promises to me or yourself!"

"I know this!" Fred shouted as he swung his feet down and jumped up. Both men, with fingers spread on the desk, inches apart, stared daggers. "The board has no idea how many times I have covered your bankrupt ass. Maybe if they knew you wouldn't feel so righteous!"

"Say what you have to, man, to whomever. The bottom line is you have failed! As of now you are relieved as president. Give me your mother-fucking keys!"

Fred opened the center drawer. Jerome saw the bank keys lying in the compartmentalized tray. He also saw the handle of a .45 automatic pistol further in the drawer; a WWII souvenir. Jerome placed his fingers under the lip of the desk, to upend it if...

"Damn it!" Fred said as he pulled out––the keys. He closed his eyes, threw the ring across the desk and turned his back. Fred's shoulders convulsed as he placed his face in his hands and wept.

Jerome rushed out. He took a deep breath and then looked up; their shouting had been overheard. Employees and customers alike, frozen in place, stared at Jerome. Vice President Chauncey Adams had warily come across the bank. He was five foot seven, small boned, with meek mannerisms. Jerome said, "Mr. Adams, you are the interim president. Call our security company and change the alarm codes; here are Mr. Hawkins' keys. Employees return to work; clients please recall your reasons for being here."

"But, but what if... do I need security? Where is Bubba?" Aldophus "Bubba" Henderson, a former Chicago Bears defensive tackle, was one of two of the bank's armed security guards. "Is Mr. Hawkins going to leave calmly? I can't handle any hostility. Does he have a gun?" Chauncey placed Mr. Hawkins' keys on Sarah's desk; they were too hot to handle.

A CPA with a Yale Master's degree, Chauncey Adams had worked for a hundred person downtown accounting firm for ten years without promotion. His wife insisted that at forty he apply for a position at one of the new Black banks. "This is your golden opportunity honey; you no longer have to remain invisible." Today, Chauncey prayed for invisibility.

Security, violence, guns... "aw shit!" said Jerome as he rushed back into Fred's office. He was sitting behind his desk robotically placing personal items into a waste basket, thoroughly depressed. "Come on man, I'll get someone to drive you home, and bring your stuff over tomorrow. Put this check in your pocket." As Jerome helped Fred up, he peeped into the center drawer. The pistol was still there, removing suicide or a revengeful killing spree as an option. They walked out of the bank together, Jerome's arm around Fred's waist.

Jerome went home; at 38 he felt old and tired. *Fred sold his business to become president, now he is unemployable in any responsible position. If the bank folds it will take me years to recover my losses; I hope Conrad and Lonnie will forgive me. Thank God I still have my stores and the Cayman account. This banking business is a bitch!*

A national search revealed that no competent bank executive was interested in managing a Black-owned, failing bank. Because of a merger in Joliet, Illinois the president of the absorbed bank was available. Fortyish, partially bald, Arthur Lindquist, the lone candidate, became president of Survivor's Bank in September, 1968; three months later.

"The December, '68 meeting will come to order," Milton said. "It's been a turbulent year with the assassination of two national leaders, Bobby Kennedy and Dr. Martin Luther King."

"It seems like anyone trying to improve the Negroes' plight gets wasted," Tiny said.

"Fortunately," Milton said, "indications are White businesses are becoming more sensitive to Negroes' problems."

"Mr. Lindquist," Richard asked, "have you acquired any new business in this new, favorable environment?"

"I have tried, but without success––Oh my," Tall, scrawny Arthur said, elaborately checking his watch, "I must leave. There are some pressing issues that must be attended too, straight away."

"What companies have you approached, and what was the result, Mr. Lindquist," Hal Hornbeck asked? Arthur looked at Hal, but said nothing.

"Will your pressing issues result in new clients?" Richard yelled toward Arthur as he reached the board room door.

"If you gentlemen, per chance, make any germane decisions," Arthur said while closing the door, "I'm sure Sarah will inform me."

"Any decisions would be germane," Jerome said. "Once again Milton, Arthur has ignored questions from even a White board member."

The second Monday in April, 1969, four months later, the twelve board members plus Arthur gathered as they did every month. Chauncey was invited because insight into the banks' operation was vital, and Arthur never stayed. They sat in the same aging chairs, listening to yet another negative report. Milton suspended the minutes and began his predictable tirade, and just as predictably, Arthur excused himself because of "more pressing matters."

Jerome interrupted. "Mr. Chairman each month you scold us without results. The new business we bring in only keeps us afloat, our Caucasian counterparts, including Arthur, are even less productive. New hires from his previous bank are overpaid and placed in management positions, which negatively impacts morale. We are still losing money every month. Arthur continuously treats the Black board members as if we aren't here."

Several Blacks mumbled agreement; the Caucasians gave their silent assent. Jerome continued, "Arthur should also be held responsible, even though he's White."

"It's not Arthur," Bridges said. "He's doing the best he can; it's the Vietnam War and all."

"Yeah, sure, of course you're right, Oreo," Jerome said sarcastically. *In order to get mortgage approvals you're sharing your whore with Arthur. Sarah is not as dumb as you think.*

"I agree with you Jerome," Milton said. "He's not the man for the job. His contract ends in June, and shouldn't be renewed, but remember, it took us three months to find him. It might take us even longer to find another president."

"I'm not sure what we should do," Jerome said, "but we must do something. Every day we move toward insolvency. If our net worth drops below ten million we could fall into FDIC receivership, just like Avalon."

"Why don't you become President Jerome?" Stuart suggested. "You've attended several banking seminars at your own expense. Most of your recommendations sound excellent, but when you ask Arthur to employ them, he refuses."

"Oh no!" Jerome said, waving off Stuart's suggestion with both hands. "I've worked too hard to risk my drug stores."

"What about you Chauncey?" Hal Hornbeck asked. "You have the credentials and have been here since the bank's inception."

When Fred was terminated Chauncey, as interim President, refused to move into Fred's office; he wanted everyone to know his presidency was temporary. He had served without a major incident, or, notable performance. Presently Chauncey considered crawling under the conference table or politely refusing, but didn't have the courage to do either. He just sat there, predictably silent, twiddling his thumbs, casting his eyes downward.

"Jerome, will you at least consider leading us out of this financial quagmire?" Samuel asked. "Stuart's right, you have attended several bank-related seminars and you do have a lot of good ideas; besides, we need a Black president."

"I'm flattered gentlemen, but my stores require all my time."

"And the last thing we need," Bridges said, "is a part-time president with too many traps to check."

Milton solicited comments. The consensus was Jerome could become President, but only if he sold his stores.

"You gentlemen are ridiculous! Once again, I am not going to give up my stores! Another consideration is salary. What this bank pays its president is far less than my income, which I'm sure, is true with all of you."

"So," Milton said, "you would rather lose $120,000, than take the helm and save this bank? Tell me Jerome, why did you invest initially?"

"It sure as hell wasn't to lose everything!" Jerome looked around the room, serious stares were returned.

"Now Jerome," Samuel said with his hands apart, "you're right, it is an awesome challenge, and perhaps it might remain an enigma, even if you did devote all of your time and abilities toward its solving. All we're asking is that you keep an open mind. Just think about it, as all of us will, until our next meeting. Maybe next month we will have a suggestion that won't require a complete divestment of your stores."

"Like hell we will!" Bridges said.

Samuel's eyes grew narrow, and his lips firm. His hidden expression toward Bridges said, shut up.

"I'll remain flexible but that's all." *Did Samuel just suggest I couldn't do the job? And what was Bridges talking about? I may occasionally sleep around, but I don't keep women like he does.*

"Gentlemen, this extremely confidential subject is tabled," Milton said. "Now Sarah, please resume taking the minutes."

* * * *

"TV Host Nelson Simmons called," Agnes said as Jerome entered. "He wants you to discuss the absence of minority contractors during O'Hare Airport's expansion; it's the seven year anniversary."

"Great! I'll be there." Jerome studied the library's archives on the six year project, and others. *Now I'm prepared.*

When the director signaled Nelson Simmons, at the filming of *From the Black Perspective*, he read Jerome Gerard's, State Senator Emanuel Lofton's, and union executive Arnold Weathers' vitals over silent film footage of O'Hare under construction. The mayor had blatantly ignored the invitation.

Nelson asked, "Mr. Gerard how do you respond to the absence of black contractors on this multi-billion dollar project?"

"The mayor should be ashamed!" Jerome said, "He behaves like Black contractors don't exist. His <u>dishonor</u> also froze <u>us</u> out when building the Chicago Skyway in the late 50's. The Negro community supported his election and re-elections. We deserve better! The mayor refused to participate in this exchange because his racist policies are indefensible!"

"Our union members submitted several proposals," Arnold Weathers said, "We never saw the winning bids. We knew federal funds were involved; therefore we contacted our union reps in D.C. Washington said Mayor O'Malley approved every contractor. He has practiced plantation politics and we didn't even get what's left in the outhouse! O'Malley's boys wouldn't hire Negroes as sub-contractors or even workers. It was a barefaced insult!"

"The mayor has, on rare occasions, offered the Black community week-old breadcrumbs!" State Senator Emanuel Lofton commented, "But when the fresh bread is baked, he gives it to his friends and then snickers at the N word. He's going to have trouble getting re-elected without the Black vote!" Emanuel Lofton was the only elected Negro in Illinois who publicly criticized Mayor O'Malley.

"Gentlemen, your comments are pretty strong," the Director from the control booth said as he stopped the taping. "The mayor might find your comments offensive. We can start over if you like."

"Please let us continue," Jerome asked, and then said. "And you ain't heard nothing yet!" The hostile comments delighted Nelson Simmons. They were so inflammatory, the station pre-empted the viewing with a disclaimer. The program aired on Sunday, the city erupted on Monday.

The Urban League, Cosmopolitan Chamber of Commerce, the AFL-CIO, and the NAACP were several of the prominent organizations that wrote disparaging letters to the mayor, Democrats Governor Kerner, and President Johnson. A protest march was scheduled. The state and national political executives insisted the mayor stop the march because of the anticipated negative impact on the upcoming election. Mayor O'Malley sent his most experienced Colored alderman to persuade Jerome to halt the protest.

"Nobody has a larger ego than an elected official," Jerome had advised Agnes, "and the lesser his position the greater his ego, so escort the alderman directly into my office when he arrives." Both gentlemen were initially cordial.

"What's happened has happened," the sartorially dressed alderman said. "The mayor regrets his apparent oversight and promises you at least one large sundries store in one of O'Hare's access corridors, which will produce at least a million dollars in sales annually, at higher than normal profits." The alderman believed the huge, but fictitious, offer would impress Jerome. He continued with wide eyes and a wax smile, "His Honor remembers you fondly from his first campaign, and advises you to accept his generous gift and call off the march." The alderman offered Jerome an expensive cigar.

Jerome was insulted. He knew the mayor didn't control O'Hare's vending operations, especially seven years later. "No thank you. Oh, if the mayor has such fond memories, why isn't he here?" asked Jerome. He refused the cheroot.

"Scheduling conflicts, you understand, but," the alderman said while staring at Jerome, "if you don't call off your alley dogs, your staying in business, even staying in this town, will be extremely difficult. You think welfare prescription payments are slow now––just wait."

"You, a Black man," Jerome said slowly, "are calling our essential civic organizations, dogs. Not protective German Shepherds or intelligent Doberman Pinschers, or feisty Rottweilers, just common alley dogs?" Jerome gave the alderman a stern look. "Besides our almighty mayor, just who do you represent; certainly not your constituents? No wonder you and your Colored cohorts are known as the 'Silent Seven,' who never disagrees with His Honor."

"The mayor does not like having to explain his behavior to the governor or the president!"

"Then he should change his behavior!"

"OK, Mr. Gerard," the alderman said, "what would it take for you to call off Sunday's march? Surely you have a price. Everyone has a price."

"Build two new high schools in Negro neighborhoods, one on each side of town, the mayor should commit in writing that at least fifty percent of building contracts, equipment and supplies would be awarded to Blacks, and that the principals of both schools will be Black."

"How dare you make a hundred million dollar demand, you over-rated drugstore cowboy? You haven't made a donation to Mayor O'Malley's election campaign in years!"

"O'Hare Airport cost over four billion, so my request is nominal and timely; we have needed additional Black high schools and Negro principals for decades. And wait till you see my reaction during his next campaign!"

The alderman left, disappointed with the result. He knew he would be punished for not succeeding, maybe collared and slapped by the mayor. He might even lose his elected office.

The march took place with 200,000 participants carrying signs and chanting insults toward the mayor, the governor and the president. Jerome Gerard was in the front line. It appeared on national television, and the front pages of all the local papers.

The next week city inspectors descended on Jerome's eight stores. They identified fifty violations that must be corrected in sixty days. The century-old Baxter Bridges building needed re-wiring and the HVAC system replaced for Jerome to comply, which was impossible.

"Let's have lunch Jerome," Milton requested over the telephone. He called to make sure Jerome was properly received at the prestigious, Edgewater Yacht Club on Lake Michigan's north shore.

"We should have done this long ago," Milton said over cocktails through a smile. He was wearing a yellow golf shirt under a blue blazer; both bore the club emblem. Milton, in this relaxed environment, looked ten years younger. Jerome wore a suit and tie.

"As chairman I ordered a thorough background check; your education, net worth, and credit rating, are outstanding," Milton said.

"So this meeting is about my pedigree?"

The tuxedoed maître d' whispered in Milton's ear; he excused himself. Various sized yachts were visible through ceiling-to-floor glass walls. Casually dressed men, sans socks, in deck shoes, and young, beautiful ladies dressed in designer afternoon wear and expensive sandals, were being served lunch. Yacht hands were preparing other boats for moon-lit excursions. Jerome sipped his Rusty Nail while observing attentive service by gloved attendants, and being observed. Head waiters were standing by... just in case. *If Samuel and the guys could just see what I'm seeing; this gives a whole new meaning to expensive boy-toys.*

Jerome entered the men's room; he saw Italian marble sinks, rolled, Turkish hand towels, Venetian commode doors, an elaborate assortment of toiletries, and ice-filled urinals. The Negro attendant/shoe shiner smiled as he enthusiastically whisked Jerome's coat, pleased to see "his brother" having lunch. As Jerome departed he noticed a secluded room with an elaborate, carved oak, orange-felt covered poker table, eight leather and oak armchairs, each with a side table, and a portable bar. Jerome had had no idea how the upper crust peed or played.

When Milton returned, after apologizing, he said, "I asked this question before and was short-shifted, so I'll ask again. Why did you, your father-in-law and friend, invest in Survivors' Bank?"

"My earlier answer fit your question's tenor. My sincere answer is to have competitive loans available, so Black businesses can grow and homeowners can make improvements. A racially sensitive bank can also make college affordable for our children."

"Those are excellent reasons Jerome; they affirm the great concern you have for your people's financial station and wellbeing. Are you ready to give up on these objectives?"

"Just the opposite, I want to add even more reasons."

"And what might those be?"

"I want a few of us, after being educated and becoming successful, to enjoy <u>your</u> lifestyle, to own luxurious yachts, and afford membership in <u>your</u> club."

"I'm glad to hear that," Milton said. There were no Negro members of any of the Lake Michigan yacht clubs. After the menus were collected Milton continued. "If anybody can make Survivor's successful, Jerome, you can. You have the skills, and the energy to turn this bank around––if you will."

"But right now I have more pressing problems; Mayor O'Malley…"

"Yes, I'm aware. It wasn't very wise to publicly insult the mayor. You may want to have lunch with His Honor, probably here, and apologize. Then, my members, under threat of withholding contributions, can make your code violations disappear, that is, if you become Survivor's new president. That will allow your stores to be sold without pending violations."

"This sounds like well-planned white-mail."

"I didn't decide to lead a protest parade, you did. While considering this offer, please peruse the contract Samuel, Richard, and I forged and let us know what you think." Milton handed Jerome a blue-backed, multiple sheet proposal, and said, "Those who take risks reap rewards."

"And if I don't like what I read?" Jerome asked before reviewing the document.

"Well," Milton smiled, "it appears you have a lot of repairs to accomplish in," Milton checked his calendar-watch, "what, 47 days?"

"You're negotiating from a pretty secure position," Jerome said. "By the way, how many of your members own businesses?"

"At least a hundred, why?"

"Will they underwrite college students' education and offer jobs that may qualify them for managerial positions upon graduation?"

"Why of course, Jerome; we do that consistently. What students do you have in mind?"

"Honor roll graduates from Ulysses High."

"But all those students are Negroes!"

"I know, I know," Jerome smiled. "This is a prerequisite to my reasons you moments ago called excellent."

Milton studied Jerome. His stores had no Negro middle management personnel, yet did significant business in at least one of his stores with Negroes. He then said, "If you accept the presidency I'll put two of your students to work in each of my four stores, with scholarships in challenging positions, and then publicize my actions which will cause other members to follow suit." Negro college students in predominantly Caucasian stores would be a Chicago first.

If I accept, I have just negotiated eight of Bronzeville's Bootstraps first scholarships, and broke the retail color barrier; without spending a dime.

It was a lazy Saturday afternoon, two days before the bank's board meeting. The girls were shopping with friends, having lunch, and taking in a movie in The Loop. A nervous Jerome, while sitting on the sofa, flipping through an *Ebony* magazine, mumbled, "I'm taking over the bank, and selling my stores."

"I know I didn't hear you say what I think I just heard you say. Hurry up and deliver the funny part——please!" Gail said as she turned off the televised baseball game. Jerome stared into his magazine. Gail stood two feet in front of Jerome; hands on hips, barefoot, wide legged, livid. "After all these years of hard work and sacrifice, when we are finally enjoying a comfortable lifestyle, you want to sell everything to manage a failing bank that has ruined Fred's life!

"Then an experienced White man took over, and even he couldn't turn a profit. Now you, Mr. Smart Ass, with no experience, is going to make Survivors work!" Jerome sat with his head tilted upward, almost touching Gail's waist, dumbfounded by her intense anger. She breathed deeply, shook her head, rolled her eyes, and then said, "Obviously two Black banks was a bad idea; let's just endure our losses and walk away. Selling our stores is dumber than dirt!" Gail paced up and down, her fitted skirt pulling one way, and then the other, repeatedly glaring at Jerome in disbelief.

"But Babe, there is no way I can correct all those code violations." Jerome stood to avoid a crook in his neck. "Samuel agrees that I can't afford to fight City Hall. Besides, a successful bank can set <u>us</u> free, and the deal they're offering is exceptional. An added benefit is college educations, integrated personnel in retail stores, and challenging jobs for deserving Negro scholars. It's a very generous package, even if I do start without a salary."

"What did you just say? You're not getting paid? And that's generous? You obviously have lost your mind. Please Lord; slap some sense into this Negro!"

"But Babe it won't fail; I won't let it fail." Jerome reached out to embrace Gail; she pushed him away.

"If it does fail and you lose everything you can start over, as a salaried, underpaid pharmacist!" Gail yelled. "I will not give up our beautiful lifestyle to be set free, whatever that means, or for some strangers to go to school!" Gail, with glaring eyes, and tight jaws, rotated her neck with one hand on her hip while pointing her finger into Jerome's face. "I'm going to keep <u>all</u> my real estate earnings separate——while you work for nothing!"

"That's a great idea, Babe. There is no way we can lose everything." Jerome was thinking of the Cayman Island account and the cash he would receive from the sale of his stores. "And your real estate business will be a big help." Again Jerome reached out to embrace Gail; in vain.

"You don't hardly understand the words that are coming out of my mouth, do you Colored boy?" Gail shook her head pathetically and continued, "My money is only for me and my daughters. When the sheriff comes to evict your dumb, Colored, broke ass, who incidentally will be working as slaves used to; for nothing, the girls and I will have something to live on!

"Listen fool," Gail shouted, with both hands on her hips, as they stood, face to face. "You have had things your way ever since we got here, and I have gone along with everything——and I mean everything, which includes your philandering's. But if you don't have enough sense to keep what we have, what happens to you will be your problem, not mine!"

"Where in hell did that come from; we're talking about business, not my fidelity?!" Jerome demanded an answer as he stared into Gail's eyes; she looked away first. Jerome continued, "When we had nothing and I doubted myself, you encouraged me. Now, after I have made the most important decision in our lives, you reject me." Jerome grabbed Gail by her arms, forcefully sat her on the couch and then sat next to her.

"Further, you accuse me of being unfaithful; how do the two relate?" Gail started to answer; Jerome stopped her with a questioning stare. "First," Jerome said, "my decision to do this was not easy. I have had lengthy discussions with Samuel, Lonnie, and Daddy Beau. I have also prayed with Father Paul. Ultimately, because of the incentives and my disagreement with the mayor, they all endorsed my decision. The reason <u>we</u> haven't discussed this is no matter what happens, we will be solvent."

"And just how do you plan to do that while working for nothing?" Gail demanded.

"That's not the issue. You must believe that I will provide for us, regardless. What's puzzling is that you accuse me of sleeping around; based on what?"

"People talk!" Gail was again defiant, but without specifics.

"I have overheard talk too, about you and Paula having lunch at very nice restaurants, about White boys sending you drinks, and picking up your tabs. Should we divorce, or should I continue to trust you?"

"Honest Jerome, I haven't slept around; all Paula and I did was…"

"I never thought you have," interrupted Jerome, as he placed his finger over Gail's lips. "I mention it now to demonstrate what we hear, or think we overhear, is not gospel; people exaggerate. And if we believe the innuendo our marriage is over. We must have faith in each other." Jerome paused, as he sat closer to Gail and looked deeply into her dark green eyes, allowing his message to penetrate.

Gail nodded slightly and said, "You're right, Babe, but I'm not getting any younger and there are women out there…"

"I love you and our daughters very much, and will never put you or them in any embarrassing situations. If I ever decide to leave, you will hear it from me first," Jerome said. "But Babe, I promise, when the world ends our family will face Armageddon together," Jerome pledged.

'Decide to leave/divorce,' or, 'our marriage is over,' was words Gail could not tolerate. "I love you too Babe, I really do." Gail cried as she threw her arms around Jerome's neck. "I'm just afraid, that's all."

"Babe," Jerome said, "Welcome to the club. I'm not sure I can make the bank work, but this isn't the first time I've been unsure. Being unsure just makes me try harder." Jerome paused and then added, "During the turbulent times ahead, please keep our home a safe, restful sanctum, full of respect, love, and understanding. Don't let vicious rumors, spread by envious people, creep in. Some "friends" will lie to tear us apart, and then express amazement at our separation as they move on to destroy the next happy couple."

"Yes Babe, I understand," Gail said as she wiped away tears, and then said, "I also agree with you helping young Negroes get an education, and improving racial business relations, in spite of my thoughtless remarks. Do what you think is right, Babe, I'll stand beside you, no matter how turbulent the economic seas."

Jerome and Gail moved to their bedroom; rapture and passion prevailed for several hours. *I don't care how the B.S. Table regulars live; I'm going to change my lifestyle.*

End of Chapter Twelve

CHAPTER THIRTEEN

Courtesy Drugs' new executives, all who had pursued advanced education, knowing good would come from their efforts, were ready. Jerome had encouraged Webster, Josephine, Agnes and Cedric, to make a joint offer. Jerome, 'passed the favor on' by accepting their below market proposal with no down payment. Jerome charged two points below the prevailing bank interest rates on their ten year, 750 thousand dollar note, a third of which was interest, making Jerome a handsome profit each month.

First Security, who received the monthly payment, sent Jerome, because he was not being paid, a confidential but significant monthly stipend to cover his household and personal expenses. The bank made a quarterly deposit in Jerome's Cayman Island account, and contributed generously to St. Martin De Pores' Church monthly, per Jerome's instructions. Gail continued to invest 90% of her substantial income in money market certificates, and mutual funds.

Atty. Samuel Stovall developed the corporate papers and contracted to serve as Courtesy Drugs' legal counsel, gratis, for the first year. Its new president was Webster Henderson, a recent MBA recipient. Jerome, who had fired several thieves, advised Webster that of the 75 people he employed, all could not be honest.

CPA Agnes Clift reconciled the deposits, prepared the bi-monthly payroll, and paid the bills. Webster's and Agnes' signatures were required on $500 checks or more. Josephine, with a newly acquired Bachelor's degree in business; bought right, managed inventory, hired, and trained new personnel. Cedric, with 13 years' experience at 27, was promoted to manager of Courtesy Drugs #2; he also approved sales, advertising, and promotions, developed by B&W. Cedric had developed a fondness for education and was working toward his Doctorate in Economics. Because Jerome's salary and the secret skim had been eliminated, net profits slightly increased. The four owners gave themselves reasonable raises. Owners' bonuses would not be paid until their mortgage was eliminated.

The Bank's board, at their May, 1971 meeting, unanimously approved Jerome's incentive-laden contract; Bridges had missed the meeting.

"Here's your, ah, office, Jer," Arthur said, entering a room barely larger than a jail cell. His office was alone on the lower level. Arthur was punishing Jerome for earlier "insulting" questions during board meetings. Arthur flipped the ceiling light switch without results. He snickered, "Looks like being dark, I mean being in the dark, is your destiny," Arthur chortled as he caught snot in his handkerchief from his long, dripping nose. He patted his sparse hair strands which were anchored with a non-scented, glistening holding spray. His head sparkled like a Christmas decoration.

Dust balls and spider webs filled the cubicle; the tile floor hadn't been cleaned in years. A goose neck lamp sat on the worn, imbalanced, one pedestal desk. Jerome lighted the room. "Thank you Arthur," Jerome said. "I'm sure this will do."

"You're damn right it will, and Jer," Arthur demanded, "you must call me Mr. Lindquist! You chose to be my assistant, so please maintain the proper business etiquette. Don't you people know anything?" Arthur became irritated when any of the Black board members called him by his first name.

"Sure Mr. Lindquist. I understand."

Arthur brushed off the corner of the desk and sat. Since there was no chair, Jerome stood. "Tell me, Jer, why are you here? It's not about the money because there isn't any; you probably don't have any savings. I know; you must be escaping from your stores' violations. I heard about your troubles with the city inspectors, heh, heh, heh." Good thing your shapely wife is supporting you; does she need any mortgage or financial assistance?" He flashed a lewd look.

"Well, Mr. Lindquist, I…" Jerome was insulted by Lindquist's insinuation. He was about to explain that he and his wife were financially solvent.

"The banking business, even under my expert direction," Arthur interrupted, "won't be as easy as running a drugstore and you almost got arrested while doing that. Drug habits can be expensive."

Jerome glanced downward; the dimly lit room helped hide his disgust. *Did he just suggest sleeping with Gail, or insinuate I was a drug addict? He has no idea about my financial situation; does he think I just gave my stores away? Does he even know how many stores I had? Even he has to have more sense than that! If he wasn't so prejudiced, the reason for my being here would be obvious.*

"In a few days I'll have something for you to do; nothing too challenging of course. Until then, Jer," Arthur said as he waved a warning forefinger in Jerome's face, "Stay down here, away from the bank, which you know nothing about, heh, heh, heh."

"Ain't nothin' but somethin' to do, Boss," Jerome said melodiously, remembering the susceptible Manny Singleton.

"And they think we're equal," Arthur mumbled as he walked away with his damp handkerchief under his nose, shaking his head.

"That's better," Jerome said to himself. He took several hours cleaning his cubicle which included replacing the ceiling fluorescent bulbs, and scrounging a chair. He slipped a folded matchbook under his wooden desk's pedestal for balance. Jerome gave Sarah a list of items needed to make his office functional, including a phone.

When Arthur was around, Jerome stayed in his office and read AMA recommended banking books. When Arthur left early, which was often, Jerome reviewed the loan files which were kept in Arthur's office. He didn't approve Negroes' loan applications unless their consigned assets quadrupled the requested loan, and then at high interest rates, which was much more than competitive banks charged. Negro board members had to insist repeatedly on Arthur making loans they recommended in writing. Many of Arthur's personally approved loans made to his Joliet friends, were delinquent.

Jerome now understood why his friends had dubbed Survivors' illusionary three man loan committee, "the KKK," and why they had not made loans or opened accounts. All of Bridges' mortgage applications were approved at competitive rates.

Jerome improved his wardrobe by purchasing several suits with accessories from a wholesale clothier, getting the best value. He also bought a midnight blue Giorgio Armani ensemble from Samuel's haberdasher, anticipating that one day he would need to dress impressively for a corporate audience.

I can see why customer relations are so poor, concluded Jerome as he eavesdropped. Customers have to interrupt staff's tête-à-têtes for service. This is terrible! "Ma'am, may I assist you?" Jerome asked an elderly woman. She was standing at a service aisle, looking confused.

"Gracious me," gasped the woman, putting her hand over her heart, "you must be new here. You're the first person that's smiled at me in two years. If they hire more people like you I might transfer my savings." After explaining the difference between a money market certificate and a long-term cash deposit, Jerome said, "You're the reason we're here, Ma'am. Any time you need assistance, let me know."

During Jerome's second week he went to Chauncey's office and asked him to step into the bank's primary reception area. "This is where you should be Chauncey, completely accessible, helping clients and staff, not sitting in your office waiting for who knows what."

"Yes, Mr. Gerard." Neither Fred Hawkins nor Arthur Lindquist had given Chauncey any specific responsibilities. To avoid criticism, he cherished his secluded office.

"You know," said a well-dressed Black gentleman after thanking Chauncey for answering a question, "I asked you folks for a business loan six months ago and was refused, so I went to Westchester Bank in Hyde Park. They gave me a credit line in two days. Of course before you and Lakeside opened Westchester wouldn't even give me the correct time, but all that's changed now. Oh, I keep several accounts here just to help you brothers stay open, but this is my chump change. My serious money is at Westchester."

"May I have your business card sir?" Jerome said when Chauncey said nothing, "We'll be making some changes soon. I'll call you when we can better serve preferred clients such as yourself." His card read, *Leonard Anderson, President, Able Janitorial Service.*

"I like your attitude my brother; I'll be awaiting your call." Jerome asked Chauncey about Mr. Anderson.

"He has a credit rating in the 800's including an American Express Gold card, which is rare, especially for us. I told Mr. Lindquist we should give him at least a five figure credit line. He told me to quit wasting my time screening applications. I think he rejected Mr. Anderson because I had recommended him."

Nancy, the teller supervisor, one of Mr. Lindquist's previous employees, was perched on a chair in her cage with a phone wedged between her ear and shoulder as she filed her nails. A female customer stood before her constantly checking her watch; finally she shoved her check under the wrought iron protector. Nancy cashed it without checking the customer's signature, validating the account's current balance, or interrupting her phone conversation.

This negligent behavior has to stop! Jerome thought.

The new accounts manager, Hope Jenkins, whispered into her phone as a woman fidgeted with her purse straps while sitting at Hope's desk. The smile on hope's lovely face, her dark, penetrating eyes going from half-mast to bright and back again, her fingers playing in her long black hair, told Jerome——and the woman——Hope's call was intimate.

Hope, a twenty-one year old Afro-Asian beauty, was Bridges' private piece. He paid her rent, car note, and gave her a generous cash allowance. Their pillow talk revealed to her the board's decisions. Arthur had promoted her because of Bridges' willingness to share.

"May I help you, Ma'am?" Jerome asked Hope's ignored client.

"Well, I'd like to open a savings account, but I can't spend the rest of my life waiting for this woman to interrupt her phone sex."

"Step over here please," Jerome said as he apologized, gave her the proper forms and directed her to an empty desk. "Bring these back and I will process them immediately."

The woman while sitting at the desk glanced at Hope, who was still engrossed. She tore up the forms and handed Jerome the remnants. "If I'm having this much trouble opening an account, Lord knows how difficult it would be to handle a less important transaction." Perturbed, Jerome depressed Hope's phone cradle.

"You've got a lot of nerve; you have no idea who I was talking to." Hope's voice was as soft as the morning dew even when she was upset. It was smoky and lyrical as a flute. Men asked Hope questions just to hear her speak.

Looks like Hope's not so private a piece after all, she surely wasn't talking to Bridges. He couldn't stir that much emotion in anybody.

Hope rolled her chair back from the desk's well and crossed her shapely legs. Her firm thighs, enhanced by her tight-fitting, hiked skirt, grabbed Jerome's attention. Through moistened, full lips, and a come-hither stare, Hope said sensually, "Well hell, I guess the HNIC is entitled. Anything you see that you want, just ask."

Head Negro in Charge, huh. "Our clients need attention." Jerome replied over a cold stare.

"Maybe," Hope said, as she tucked her beige translucent blouse, into her cocoa brown skirt, revealing her tiny waist and firm, naked nipples, "We should discuss this later, perhaps in your office or over cocktails at my place."

"If you ignore another customer, serving cocktails may become your primary occupation."

"Well now, we'll just have to see about that!" Hope said.

"Your sugar-daddy already has a hard-on for me, so if you mention my reprimanding you, maybe he will bust a nut, which I'm sure he does prematurely, anyway." Hope, who was thoroughly embarrassed, busied herself.

A week later on a Friday afternoon a competent teller approached Jerome. "Here is my letter of resignation. I have accepted a position at Westchester Bank starting Monday."

"Why are you giving me this?" Jerome asked.

"Because I don't see Mr. Lindquist and Mr. Adams would probably be afraid to accept it. I told our president two weeks ago I was leaving, but he never asked why. You see, I'm not one of his pets."

We've got to stop the bleeding. Not only are we unable to keep good help, we are supplying capable Negro employees to our competitors. "Mr. Lindquist," Jerome called to Arthur, a distance away, as he left early again, "may I conduct training classes for our employees?"

"Sure! If you can teach these jungle bunnies anything, be my guest," Arthur shouted over his shoulder. Several customers looked at Jerome, anticipating his response; he had none. One said, "I thought we ran this bank." *A few more customers might bite the dust; Jungle bunnies, huh; your Momma!*

Ten of the twenty-five employees attended the meeting in the break room after the bank closed but before the work-day ended. Jerome offered fresh coffee, soft drinks, and chocolate chip cookies. Jerome insisted that Chauncey, who still spent most of the day in his office, attend.

"Thank you for being interested in your bank," Jerome said after everyone was settled. "Over the next several weeks I will arrange for job-specific workshops conducted by our parent bank, First Security's department managers, to help you become more proficient and confident. Because we are inviting presenters, attendance will be mandatory." Eyes rolled, and smirks were exchanged between attendees.

"Can anyone tell me why our morale is in the sewer?" *Questioning morale may cause a more favorable response than accusations of negligence and incompetence*, thought Jerome.

"Nobody believes Survivors will survive," young, attractive, light skinned Myrtle Hughes quipped while smacking gum, "So why should we bother? This job qualifies me for unemployment compensation—— whenever." Myrtle had been hired by Mr. Lindquist within the last six months; she was one of his pets.

"Mr. Gerard," said dark-skinned, well groomed, Helen Scott, "In order for <u>us</u> to have worked in a White bank we needed a college degree, to be light, bright, and damn near white, and have blow hair, so very few of us are experienced. I am committed to working hard and doing my best, but I can't get a question answered by any manager, and that includes Mr. Adams." Helen turned and looked at Chauncey who was seated in the rear. He smiled sheepishly. Helen continued, "It's a damn shame when your own kind won't help you improve.

"Mr. Lindquist," Helen continued, "when you can catch him, will answer a question, but makes you feel like an idiot for asking. And Miss highfaluting Nancy acts as if she is too good to work with us Colored girls." Caucasian Nancy continued doing her nails.

"Mmm humm's," and, "What's the use," were mumbled from down-turned heads. Thirty-four year old Helen concluded by saying, "We don't get raises or promotions because of what we've read, but because of who we bed." Myrtle and Nancy became uneasy.

"Tell it like it is honey," and "What you got to say about that!?" came from emboldened faces with wide eyes and tight jaws.

"OK, ok." Jerome said smiling while asking for quiet, "I hear you. First, going forward, all raises and promotions will come through me; they will be based on job performance, attitude, and attendance records. And that is all I'm interested in."

"Uh huh," and "We'll see if you can ignore Hope Jenkins' performance," was muttered. Jerome's audience had relaxed.

"Here's some more good news. If you continue your education, those who take business-related college courses will be reimbursed if you finish with a C or better." Jerome heard positive responses.

"Now here's the not-so-good news," Jerome said, "which applies to everyone so pass the word. Beginning tomorrow, all personal calls will be screened. Only emergency calls, or calls from children will be put through. Conversations between staff with clients present are no longer acceptable. Our clients should receive your undivided attention." Jerome felt resentment toward his edict.

"After all," he added, "this is a business, not just a Black business, and professional behavior must be practiced, no matter our race." Most nodded toward each other with lifted eyebrows and wide eyes. Racial pride made the restrictions more palatable. Myrtle and Nancy shared glances that indicated the new policies didn't apply to them; they had other commonalities. "Two phones will be placed in here for personal calls."

"Well, all right then," and "That's better," came forth.

"The first rule of Survivors is," Jerome took a black marker and printed on the portable easel's pad, NEVER SAY NO. "Dissatisfied clients should be referred to Mr. Adams or me. Mr. Adams will also be responsible for approving non-collateralized, or signature loans, and Small Business credit lines up to $50,000." Chauncey jerked his head up. He was anxious about being given decision making responsibilities. Jerome shook hands and thanked each for attending as they left. *This was good*, Jerome decided.

"Milton, get over here, now! Your boy has gone berserk!"

"I'll be right over," Milton answered; he immediately called Jerome and received a full accounting of yesterday's meeting.

"What's happened?" Milton asked Arthur.

"Nancy is our teller supervisor. She keeps me informed about these Nig…Negroes' subversive activities. Tell Mr. Levine what that idiot promised at that insurrection meeting."

"Well, Mr. Gerard said he was going to hold training classes, and that we couldn't talk on the phone or to each other, and that he was going to decide who got promoted, or got raises, and that we should never say no to a customer, and that he was going to pay us if we went to school, and that they should respect their race, and that pipsqueak, I mean Mr. Adams, would be responsible for approving loans up to $50,000." Nancy breathed deeply after completing her speech which had been rehearsed with Mr. Lindquist. She looked at Mr. Lindquist for approval; he winked.

"Nancy?" Mr. Levine asked, "Did Mr. Gerard say why he was assuming responsibility for raises and promotions?"

"One of the Colored girls said promotions weren't being made fairly or something like that."

"Was your promotion fair Nancy?" Mr. Levine asked.

Nancy looked at Mr. Lindquist to answer for her——he didn't. "Yes, of course. I'm the only White teller here, and I have experience, so naturally I should be in charge."

"How did you leave your previous employment, Nancy?"

"My former boss was too difficult, so because Mr. Lindquist had promised me a management position, I quit." Nancy was excused.

"There, see! Holding classes during the work day, paying these ignoramuses to go to school, giving Chauncey real responsibility, hah! You ever hear of such a thing? I'll fire him tomorrow for usurping my authority; his drugstores must have been a real mess. Thanks for coming by Milton." Arthur began shuffling papers. Moments later, noticing Milton's continued presence, Arthur asked, "Is there something else?"

"How did your last staff meeting go, Arthur?"

"Meeting! Why, I wouldn't meet with these monkeys; it would be like talking to a bunch of retards."

"You have been here almost a year and you haven't held one meeting?"

"Hell no; is that a problem?"

"I have heard you use racially derogatory terms previously, Arthur, but this is the first time I have really listened to you. You have no respect for our staff or our board, nor are you working to make this bank succeed."

"You're right on all counts! I can't get used to overdressed niggers sitting on anybody's board. I'm just waiting for my resume to hit the right desk. Whenever I get the call, I'm out of here!"

"These <u>Negro</u> board members," Milton said, "have invested all they have to achieve financial parity for their people! These are some of the finest gentlemen I have ever known, they…"

"But you're a Jew, Milton; you couldn't be a nigger lover!"

"Arthur!" Milton shouted, "If I were twenty years younger I'd knock your racist ass out of this office!" Milton took a deep breath and then said, "Your contract is up shortly, let's end it now!"

"Yeah, I wanted to talk to you about that. I deserve a raise, considering my having to run this, this poor excuse for a bank. Furthermore, you had better sweeten it, because if I resign and publicize my dissatisfactions you'll never…"

"OK Arthur, listen carefully. You and Nancy are fired!

"Fired!!! Why, you can't fire me, I've got a contract…"

"You get this week's pay. Anything else, sue me!"

Mr. Lindquist's salary went to Jerome. He stopped the monthly stipend from his First Security account. Several weeks later, while Jerome was helping a new teller reconcile an overnight deposit, he heard, "Where is the mother fuckin' president of this sad ass bank?" Jerome saw a dark, tall, barrel-chested man wearing dirty, torn, bib overalls, with one loosened shoulder strap, yelling. His muscular arms were whipping the air.

Customers stepped away; Bubba moved in the hostile man's direction.

Within seconds, Jerome stopped Bubba and signaled Helen Scott to replace him as he hurried toward the angry customer. Jerome smiled and extended his hand which the perturbed client refused. "You're not the president; you're just another token nigger. I asked for the president damn it," the customer shouted!

"Sir," Jerome said as he stood in front of the tall, furious man, his fingers interlocked under his chin, as he spoke in a soothing voice, while smiling, "you may not believe this, but right now I am in charge. Please, may we step into the president's office?" Jerome noticed Chauncey peeping from his office. He called out, "Chauncey, please join us."

"May I know your name, Sir?" Jerome asked, still smiling.

"Julian Winters," he responded cautiously.

Jerome said to Chauncey, "Mr. Winters has a problem that needs our immediate attention. Sarah," Jerome said, "Absolutely no interruptions while we're with Mr. Winters."

"Yes, Mr. Gerard."

Julian Winters was flattered when his polite and well-dressed escort called him Mister. He noticed the secretary was deferential. Julian concluded this man must be important because he is so well spoken, even if he isn't the president. And they <u>were</u> in the president's office.

"Mr. Winters, would you like some coffee?" Jerome smiled as he sat next to his mollified guest. Chauncey stood behind Jerome's chair as he said, "Sometimes, no matter how hard we try, we commit errors, and I apologize in advance for having upset you." Sarah served the three of them coffee in dainty china cups with saucers, which Mr. Winters found difficult to finger properly because of his huge hands. Jerome asked, "Mr. Winters how long have you been one of our partners?"

"Almost three years, and this shit…" Julian's anger had subsided; he was pleading to be understood. In the bank president's office with such polite gentlemen, and such elegant service, he was embarrassed by his appearance, language, and behavior. He had never considered himself a partner in this bank.

"Mr. Winters, we appreciate your business, the time you have been with us, and will do everything possible to keep you as a client; now, what can we do to make you feel better about your bank?"

Eight months had passed since Arthur's departure. Myrtle Hughes had been terminated; Helen Scott was now head teller. Chauncey Adams reluctantly accepted the added responsibility of hiring, training new personnel, and approving mid-sized loans. Hope Jenkins, responding to the winds of change, had developed a business-like attitude and was still new accounts manager.

Since the bank opened at 9:00 a.m., Jerome had greeted customers and, when needed, assisted personnel. When not busy he observed and listened; he was pleased with his staff's new professional attitude and performance. It was 10:00 a.m. Jerome called to Chauncey, "Please cover the floor."

As Jerome passed Sarah, he said, "I'll be busy until 11:30, then Mr. Levine and I are having lunch." Jerome opened a five-by-eight card file which held several indexes. The first read daily, followed by dates; the second held 12 months: the third, Suspense. He removed the cards under today's date and began dialing.

"Charlie? Jerome. How you doin', man? … Are you still looking for a car? … One of our clients has a Lincoln dealership; his name is Arnold Lovelace… No, he's Negro, worked his way up from porter… The *Wall*

Street Journal did an article on him not too long ago… Incidentally we'll finance your ride at our preferred customer rate no matter where you get it… Great. Keep me posted." Jerome noted the date, the gist of the conversation, and filed it for a next month call back.

"Arnold? Jerome. A fellow named Charlie Black is looking for a car. I directed him to you. Here's his number… You are more than welcome. Say man, thanks for those ten new car loans last month. I really appreciate it."

"Hey Gus, you and," Jerome checked his file card, "Bernice still planning a Jamaican vacation this summer? … Listen man, if you need some lettuce to make it happen, just let me know. Floyd, you're harder to catch than a trifecta… Oh I know you're busy, that's why I keep calling, heh, heh, heh. Listen, my brothah, when can we expect that account you promised at Samuel's party? … Well, will it be ok, if I stop by your office Wednesday after lunch and handle the transaction? It'll take less than ten minutes… Great, see you then." Jerome made an entry in his appointment book.

While making calls Jerome pulled a number of business cards from behind Suspense, transferred the information to eight by fives and filed them by month for follow ups. Milton knocked then entered Jerome's office. Jerome motioned him to a seat as he continued talking, "Mr. Heldt, you may not remember me, but we sat together at the Urban League luncheon several weeks ago (Jerome had arranged the seating). We originally met at the League's office the night of Dr. King's assassination… Yes, that's me, heh, heh, heh. You asked about Survivors stock availability. I sent you a prospectus. Yes… Yes… I understand. No commitment was assumed, Sir. If you have any questions, though, please call." Jerome marked his card for a thirty day call back, noting to suggest lunch, and then filed it.

"Who's interested in our stock?" Milton asked.

"Mr. Heldt is vice-president, community affairs, with Campbell's Soup. I don't expect him to buy stock; however, I do expect a sizeable deposit before the end of the year."

"And what are all those cards?" Milton was looking at Jerome's desk.

"Why, these are future clients," Jerome said. "Every morning I make calls, most afternoons I visit our larger clients, always offering an added benefit. I also call on potential clients explaining our services that would save them time and money. I pick up about ten new clients a week."

"So this is why we are growing so rapidly," Milton smiled.

"But not nearly fast enough," Jerome said. Milton looked puzzled. Without explaining, Jerome and Milton left for Felix and Bea's.

As they entered, a hush fell over the B.S. Table. Those who were not facing the door turned and glanced discreetly. Expressions of approval and amazement were exchanged. The regulars, because of Felix's suggestion, were bringing Caucasians to lunch, but rich White folk like Milton Levine dining with the brothers, was rare. The silence only lasted several seconds.

Two of the B.S. Table regulars saluted Jerome without Milton noticing. Jerome was now known as Survivors' savior, and a major striver. "The Street" had ordained Jerome as the person to contact when a business idea needed evaluating.

"Good afternoon Mr. Levine and Mr. Gerard, welcome." Felix smiled while leading them to a preferred table. He brought them water and stepped away while they perused their menus.

"Felix was a charter shareholder; we financed his recent remodeling."

"I see, or at least I'm beginning to see," Milton said as he ordered short ribs of beef, potato salad, black-eyed peas, and sweetened iced tea. The peach cobbler was a unique treat. Felix served them lunch.

"Well," Milton said between bites, "since Arthur's departure, we have increased our daily cash flow, made solid loans, have more professional employees, and have added significant numbers of new clients. You're doing a helluva job Jerome."

"Thanks Milton, but when you compare banks, our progress is less significant than a hump on a roach's back."

"But our primary customer base…"

"Milton," Jerome interrupted, "We have to expand our vision. Having lunch at your club was quite revealing."

"Did someone insult you?" Milton asked.

"Oh no, but thanks for asking. I've been thinking about the relativity between your members and us." Jerome motioned to include the room. Milton looked puzzled, Jerome continued, "We live in two different economies. Bronzeville is rich in religion, music and," as Jerome enjoyed his smothered pork chops, rice and gravy, added, "fart-producing food, but we're living in a Black bubble. We measure our financial achievements by what our clothes, cars, furniture, and homes cost. Your measurements are your yacht size, stock portfolios, and the frequency of international vacations. For instance, the 50th largest bank, nationally, has more deposits than the 26 Black banks––combined!"

"I have no idea what you're talking about Jerome. I thought…"

"Don't feel bad Milton, most Negroes don't understand what I'm saying, and most Caucasians could care less. As I said at your club, the reason for Survivors Bank is to make capital available to us at competitive rates, but we are limited by the amount of our deposits. That's why deposits from companies like Campbell Soup are so important.

"In order to serve our community adequately, we need our board to acquire more Caucasian depositors." Jerome pulled a manila folder from his attaché case. "This was suggested at one of my banking seminars. Here are lists of general market companies who do most of their business in Bronzeville. I've put companies and board members who speak the same business language together. For instance, Tiny is assigned Quality Foods Super Markets and other grocery chains, and Hal Hornbeck has Small Business manufacturers." Jerome excused himself, stopped two men who were leaving, exchanged pleasantries, collected their business cards, and then returned.

"What are these five letters?" Milton asked. They were behind the assigned lists.

"Those are form letters, developed by B&W Advertising, to save board member's time. Each should select one, add a personal paragraph, and then return it to Sarah who will mail it over the board member's name. Within a week he should call for an appointment."

"What if he is not successful?"

"In his next communication, which would be after a more strident form letter has been mailed, he will say that businesses which generate profit in our community should support Black businesses in our community, and our bank is a good place to start."

"I agree this approach should increase business; what happens next?"

"When an appointment is secured, either Chauncey or I will accompany the board member for technical support. When we acquire a new account you will lavishly praise the board member, followed by a congratulatory letter. This will give confidence to him and other board members.

"But what happens when businesses after a series of efforts don't favorably respond?"

"The member writes a detailed accounting and returns the recalcitrant client's file. I haven't decided how to handle the "leeches" yet, but I'm working on it."

"I see <u>your</u> list has major utilities, Chicago-based Fortune 500's and the feds; the big boys."

"Buddy Laws, the deceased Congressman's former legislative assistant, has become a successful, D.C. lobbyist which gives us access to 155 federal agencies with district offices in Illinois, all of whom have been encouraged by President Nixon to do business with minorities––including banks. Buddy supplements my efforts state-wide. Buddy's incentive is a one percent commission on each new federal account until we can afford to put him on a monthly retainer."

"When do you expect to see measureable results?" Milton asked.

"The private sector is already responding," Jerome answered. "Thanks to Tiny's initiative, Diamond Foods has deposit-only accounts for twenty-five Bronzeville supermarkets which have significantly increased our daily cash flow, and thanks to Buddy's contacts, we have favorably influenced several federal agencies. I'm scheduled to make a presentation to Mid-Western Bell's finance committee."

"If you had been president from the start, Jerome, we wouldn't have lost so much money."

"Thanks boss, but I needed time to learn. With your encouraging our board, Survivors will become prominent within the banking industry, and the biggest among Black banks."

"You can shove that boss bull; with the potential clients you have given me I'm working for you. You realize your commissions start with the next million in deposits?"

"I know," Jerome said over a broad smile. "I know."

"We'll eat here at least once a month, and I'll schedule some other luncheons here as well. Don't want my presence to be so startling," Milton said over a smile. He had noticed the hush when they entered, albeit ever so slight. "Besides, my club is too damn expensive." Milton was flattered with the complimentary ponies of Drambuie Felix had poured while on one knee as the prominent duo enjoyed their coffee.

"One more thing," Milton said. "Those graduates from Ulysses High are doing great. Even though their initial presence was a shock, they are contributing to our bottom line; my managers complimented my forward thinking. Their college tuition is a good investment, and its tax deductible. I don't know why we didn't think of doing this sooner."

"Maybe you, too, have been living in a bubble," Jerome said. Felix gave Milton's generous tip to Rowena.

"It's time." Jerome and Chauncey had waited in Mid-Western Bell's garage until they were only fifteen minutes early. Jerome was tense but confident; Chauncey couldn't stop shaking.

"This is your assigned meeting room, gentlemen," their amiable female guide said. "If you need anything, just ask."

The conference room's plush navy blue carpet contained various sizes of light blue, Bell logos. Sixteen high-back light blue, spring-backed, leather arm chairs surrounded a 20 x 6 foot oblong table. Solar system emblems decorated the highly polished top. Placid oil paintings of seas, skies, and ships in deep tiered frames enhanced pale blue walls. 20 blue arm chairs sat against the walls. Five obsolete telephones were positioned around the room on white Roman-styled four foot pedestals under glass domes with brass plates stating their historical data. A huge oil painting of Alexander Graham Bell hung at the far end. As Jerome moved about, the eyes of the portrait seemed to follow him. He's glad to see me here, Jerome decided.

A projectionist's booth, a pull-down screen, and a white board with various colored markers validated the importance of presentations made here. Jerome's requested easel stand was present. A slight discoloration at the end of the table indicated a pad which supported a table-top podium, and the podium, were missing. Jerome had planned to place his notes on a podium, giving him a modicum of privacy; its absence presented a dilemma.

Moments later Jerome said to Chauncey, "We will present without notes." Jerome placed his outline back in his valise. Before Chauncey could react, two women and four men entered. Jerome enthusiastically introduced him and Chauncey. A few exchanged stilted greetings with limp grasps, mumbled trite remarks, and made no eye contact; they didn't even mention the weather. The tallest man turned his back as Jerome approached.

The men's dark, blue suits were so similar in patterns they looked like uniforms. All wore red, tight patterned ties. They mumbled amongst themselves that Jerome's "Important Occasion" ensemble, like most Negroes, was excessive. The women wore beige suits over white, ruffled blouses. They conversed while consuming coffee and Danish, ignoring their guests. The coolness of the committee unnerved Chauncey. He whispered to Jerome, "Are you sure we should do this without notes?" Jerome slowly nodded yes.

At 9:58 a.m. a short, overweight gentleman entered and took his seat. The members followed their chairman's lead. At 9:59 and a half, Keith Haggerty, Mid-Western Bell's Community Affairs Vice President, entered and walked to the head of the table. He was tall with a 36 inch waist. Based on his suit coat's perfect fit, Jerome determined Keith's grey, chalk-stripe was hand tailored, probably in London.

"Whatever happened to our podium?" Keith asked. Everyone looked toward the head of the table except the tallest man who glanced downward. "Dames and gents thank you for adjusting your hectic schedules; we bloody appreciate your presence," The chairman had tried to cancel the meeting; when he couldn't he tried to move it to a less prestigious room, but Keith had insisted on the meeting and the room.

He reminded Jerome of the English actor James Mason in mannerisms and voice, but Keith was better looking. Jerome stood next to his host; they were about the same height. Chauncey passed out collaterals over a smile which was not returned. He sat opposite the committee members, avoiding eye contact and growing more nervous by the minute.

"I have known Jerome for several months," Keith began. "He serves on the Boy Scouts membership committee which I chair. Jerome is a hard working lad and the one volunteer who keeps at it." Keith patted Jerome on the back. Jerome bowed his head while sporting an, aw shucks, expression.

"When Jerome asked for this meeting I told him we were bully satisfied with our banking arrangements. To appease, I offered to deposit $100,000 in his bank, but he insisted on this meet anyway."

"Some people don't know when they're well off," The chairman said.

Keith glanced at the chairman harshly and then continued, "Jerome has promised to take no more than thirty minutes. He understands no decision will be made today, only that his presentation will be received by a polite and attentive audience." Keith stared at the finance chairman until he glanced back.

"So Jer, have at it. I have an annoyance to tend. Incidentally guy," Keith said while stroking Jerome's suit lapel with the back of his hand, "your amalgamation is exceptional, ole chap, most fellows around here wear mundane, uninspiring suits, but not you." Giorgio Armani's signature was a suit, shirt and tie with exact colors. "I wonder whatever happened to the podium," Keith mumbled as he ran his fingers through his expertly styled salt and pepper hair while leaving the conference room.

When Keith said Jerome had 30 minutes, the fifty year-plus chairman removed his wrist watch and placed it in the middle of the table. He looked sternly in Jerome's direction as he tapped his watch's dial.

Since assuming the presidency, Jerome had belabored Alphonso Major's comment regarding getting Caucasians to trust Survivors with their money. One way was to put The Board to work, as he had done. Another approach was to impress major company executives in non-pressurized environments, like volunteering for the Boy Scouts' Membership committee. Chauncey had volunteered for other, smaller but predominately Caucasian organizations; his plan was working.

"Mid-Western Bell's commitment to minority institutions has been generous," Jerome began. Practicing with Alphonso Major and his staff had produced perfect presentation mannerisms, including his cadence. "Few if any corporations match your empathy, your contributions, and your support of worthwhile minority causes."

"Then why are you taking up our time? How much support is enough?" the tall man asked. The chairman glanced at him suggesting a more polite attitude and tone.

Jerome listed three Black, not-for-profits Midwestern Bell supported; his audience was familiar with their names. "Perhaps your commitment runs deep because two Negroes, Lewis H. Latimer and Granville T. Woods, helped Mr. Bell launch his business in 1877." His audience didn't recognize the names. "By depositing significant sums in Survivors, you will increase your good work, and as an added benefit, improve your profitability without cost or risk." That sentence took B&W Advertising copywriters hours to develop.

"I'll believe that when I see it," The Chairman smiled while glancing at his subordinates.

The first four-by-six foot visual placed on the easel by Chauncey, entitled PRE-DEPRESSION, CIRCA 1925, showed a large, friendly valentine-shaped heart, wearing a wide, pink ribbon named "Bank."

Blood flowed from three smaller, happy hearts on the left named, "Small Business", "Home Owners", and "Gainfully Employed", to the big heart and back again in parallel arteries.

"Then, banks were the economic hearts of our communities." Several members smirked at Jerome's trite metaphor. The tall gentleman held his head and mumbled, "Oh no, not another one of those." The chairman leaned forward and checked his watch.

"Negroes banked some of their earnings allowing their neighbors to buy cars, homes, and do remodeling. Entrepreneurs borrowed to expand businesses. With growth they hired more neighborhood people who made more deposits. Because of increased employment and deposits <u>our</u> community grew. <u>We</u> owned the Binga Bank." Once again the members were serendipitously enlightened.

The second visual was entitled POST DEPRESSION. The committee gasped at the gory graphic. Pleasant arteries named "Deposits" went from the same three smaller valentine-shaped hearts, but the larger heart looked through glaring, menacing eyes, sans a ribbon and a valentine shape. Returning veins spurted blood from hatchet chops; none of the essential fluid reached the smaller hearts. On the right side of the Bank heart, one large, blood-filled vein named "Loans" flowed off the visual and according to the signage, to other neighborhoods. The committee was paying attention.

"After the Great Depression, the Italians, Polish, Irish, Jewish and Negro populations continued to live separately, but we no longer owned the banks in our neighborhoods. The investment capital was available, but no larger bank, by gentlemen's agreement, would become a parent for a Negro bank, which was now required by law. We made deposits into the Caucasian owned banks, but the money did not flow back again. Successful Negro entrepreneurs couldn't borrow growth capital, so their businesses stagnated. Gainfully employed Negroes with excellent credit ratings couldn't borrow home improvement loans because all of the White financial institutions practiced redlining, which was a euphemism for Negro residential and business financial genocide. Our aged homes deteriorated at an accelerated rate.

"Today Negro unemployment remains high because those who control the jobs hire us last, no matter our skill or educational levels." The next visual had two large moving vans, one named "Systematic Financial Deprivation," the other, "Institutionalized Segregation," smashing a small car named "Negro Community" from both ends.

"This accident," Jerome continued, "is an on-going tragedy for us as well as an expensive liability for Mid-Western Bell because you cannot fully market your services to an economically deprived population. Additionally, the cost of vandalism adds tens of thousands of dollars to your maintenance costs and disables your public phones for months at a time, eliminating revenue."

Chauncey displayed a cartoon of a busted public phone. The dial was a sad face; the empty coin box hung open. A sign over the phone's coin receiver read, "Out of Service for at least Thirty Days."

"There is no doubt," Ms. Heavy-set complained, "about our effort to supply you people with phone service, and no matter how hard we try, you still destroy them. There is just too much vandalism!" She glared at Jerome and shook her finger toward him; the chairman nodded his support.

"You are absolutely right!" Jerome said. His agreement confused Ms. Heavy-set. Her eyebrows came together as her attention level sharpened. "And there are even greater costs. When we are denied jobs, the more desperate among us turn to crime. Their illegal acts increase court and prison costs."

The next presentation board carried recent headlines from newspapers reporting exploding costs of the overburdened judicial system. Chauncey, encouraged by Jerome's note-free presentation, left his 5x8 cards pocketed. With an expanded pointer, he explained the enlarged graphs showing the national increase of home invasions, minor burglaries, and car thefts.

"The *Court Review* reports," Chauncey said, "that ninety percent of Negroes arrested do not have jobs. The cost of incarceration, according to the Bureau of Prisons, is $35,000 a year per prisoner. We, with your help, can reduce these numbers."

"Do you really believe our deposits in your bank will curtail phone vandalism?" asked the chairman. He said to his committee members, "Those reports are valid."

"Sir," Jerome answered, "how many busted phones do you have in middle income, Negro neighborhoods?"

"Well, none, primarily because there are so few public phones."

"You are once again correct. The first thing a family acquires when they become gainfully employed is a place to stay; the second is utilities, which includes a telephone." Jerome noticed nods of agreement between members.

"Please turn to page three of your handouts. These are the types of loans we make to working adults with good credit: first mortgages; second mortgages for remodeling and repairs; college tuition; business expansion; and automobile loans, most of which increase cash flow and jobs within our community. The children of gainfully employed parents do not break into phones to steal pocket change!"

"So," asked the tallest member, casting an intimidating look toward Jerome, "We can stop you Coloreds from committing all crimes by depositing money in your bank, right?" He glanced at his peers, head slightly bowed, wearing a sarcastic grin.

"No, Sir," Jerome answered politely, "statistics indicate the lower the unemployment rate, the fewer petty crimes. There are however, a small percentage of people regardless of ethnicity who will commit crimes, no matter their economic status: ergo Al Capone." The committee members laughed, even Mr. Tall smiled.

"What I am suggesting is you can help reduce crimes of desperation and increase your profits, not eliminate criminal activity. Hardened criminals aren't breaking into phones."

"What happens when one of your newly financed businesses fail that shouldn't have been financed in the first place?" Ms. Heavy-set asked over an "I gotcha" expression.

"Chauncey?" Jerome said. Chauncey stood and began a prepared statement. "We, like most banks, know the high risk involved with new businesses. Chamber of Commerce statistics indicate that only five percent of fledging enterprises last more than five years—and that's among general market start-ups. Therefore we don't make new business loans without applicants having more than half the collateral required, supported by a professional marketing plan. We do finance successful business growth, like cyclical loans, new equipment purchases, and facility expansion. We have had one business fail in the past six months and the bank didn't lose a dime because the loan was sufficiently collateralized."

"How do your loan criteria match that of downtown banks?" a gentleman asked who had been doodling. He realized this presentation, unlike many he had heard, was serious, and he should pay attention.

"The FDIC allows us to loan only fifty percent of our deposits. Therefore, because of our limited cash flow, our loan criteria are more conservative than Caucasian-owned banks. Of course, unlike them, we don't consider being Negro a deal breaker. That is why we need your deposits to enable us to increase the size and number of our loans." A relieved Chauncey sat back down. The last two sentences had been extensively worked on. They were the heart of the presentation; their message had to be clear, persuasive, and provocative, yet not antagonistic.

"Knowing that Negroes with college degrees are rare," the doodler asked, "how do you compete from an educational perspective for personnel in the financial world?

"Our resumes are the first two pages in your handouts," Jerome said. "I have an MBA from the University of Chicago and have attended four American Management Association banking seminars over the last two years. Chauncey has a Masters in Finance from Yale and has been our vice president since inception.

"Additionally, we encourage our employees to take evening college classes with a reimbursement program. We have an intern policy where at least one high-school student works part-time during the school year and full time during the summer to earn a full college scholarship. When the scholar graduates from college, she will have seven years banking experience. Whether we will help her continue toward a post graduate degree is yet to be determined."

The chairman was visibly impressed; Ms. Heavy-set appreciated the female reference. Mid-Western Bell didn't have as comprehensive a program for developing employees.

"But what are you doing about your welfare problem?" Mr. Tall asked, "Our information indicates welfare numbers are increasing."

"Welfare is a problem," Jerome answered. "Welfare recipients are our entrepreneurs' primary labor pool. Some recipients are talented and educated, most are trainable; all want to work…"

"That's not the way I hear it, most are shiftless, lazy good-for-nothings, and will steal the shirt off your back," Mr. Tall blared. The chairman, having been previously embarrassed, threw him another warning glance.

"And that's part of the problem," Jerome answered. "You, who only hear negative reports, or read slanted news summaries, are not receiving accurate statistics. I wanted to make this presentation to correct false information. Now, if I can continue,"

"Please go on," the Chairman said, once again silently reprimanding Mr. Tall.

"Once compatibly employed, after extended unemployment lapses, Welfare recipients become appreciative, competent, and dependable employees. Therefore the more businesses we can finance, the fewer recipients and the more telephone subscribers." This was the second closer, which was also developed laboriously.

"Survivors Bank has thirty employees. Three of our entry level positions are designated as welfare recipient positions. Once they are promoted and remove themselves from welfare, we hire another welfare recipient. We stress the concept of developing fishermen rather than offering the disadvantaged fish."

"You're training Negroes to fish in Lake Michigan?" a gentleman asked who was having trouble staying awake. The chairman bowed and shook his head.

"A Chinese proverb says, 'Give me a fish and I eat for a day, teach me to fish and I eat for a lifetime,'" Jerome answered patiently. "In summary, the added benefits to your company, available exclusively through the two Negro-owned banks, are a decrease in pay-phone installations, downtime and repair costs, an increase in home phone subscribers, and a re-direction of tax dollars because of reduced incarceration, and court costs. A tax cut would be too big a stretch." Jerome smiled as he completed his third close.

All of the members laughed, except Mr. Tall; Mr. Heavy-lids was now alert.

"So," asked Ms. Heavy-set, "you believe all welfare recipients can become competent employees?"

"No Ma'am. Unfortunately we cannot keep all the people we hire, regardless of background, just as you can't keep all the people you hire.

However, our recidivism rate among welfare recipients is lower than non-welfare new hires." Jerome checked his watch. "We are here asking you to help us help you and simultaneously help those who need help the most. My time has expired, thank you for listening."

"Not so fast," the Chairman said. "In preparation for this meeting, we investigated your bank's history. You incurred losses your first five years in business; what's changed?"

"You're right. We did get off to a non-profitable start, as do most new businesses. It took IBM fifteen years to pay investors' dividends, and Alexander Graham Bell's first company, Bell Telephone, much longer. What's changed? Chauncey and I, over the last several months, have been in charge. We will turn a profit at the end of Year Six. If you will allow me a few extra minutes." The Chairman nodded; Jerome signaled Chauncey to put up an additional graphic. Jerome used his laser beam pocket pointer for emphasis.

"During our last two quarters we increased daily cash flow 75%, reduced administrative costs from 14 to 5% and bought our bad debts ratio down from 10 to 3%. These unusual accomplishments have been validated by our independent auditing firm. Their contact numbers are in our proposal."

"I admire your honesty young man," the Chairman said. "Your early stats are precisely the same as our auditors found. Of course we didn't have access to your last two quarters."

As the Chairman replaced his watch, he stood and said, "For years I have witnessed poverty and deprivation amongst Negroes, and thought, 'why don't you people do something about that?' I didn't realize how decades of institutionalized prejudice and biased polices, that seem to Whites benign, have so negatively impacted your economic lifestyles. All we ever hear from Colored organizations is how bad things are; followed by asking how much money can you give. And I never dreamed increasing your capabilities could improve our bottom line."

"Mr. Chairman," Jerome said, "we are not asking for one thin dime. Any funds you deposit in our bank remain yours, plus the interest earned. With your anticipated deposits we will be able to make more loans to benefit those who with assistance will become productive, taxpaying, citizens." This was an additional planned close.

"Hmmm," said the Chairman, "I never thought about it like that. Another point, your presentation was very impressive, gentlemen. It was the first extensive proposal delivered by anyone, White or Black, without notes. You are quite competent. Obviously Survivor's Bank is in excellent hands. Thank you for enlightening us; we'll be in touch."

The committee promised favorable results as they shook hands with Jerome and Chauncey, this time, enthusiastically. Jerome headed toward the tall gentleman who hurried from the room.

Two weeks later, Keith Haggerty dropped by Survivors Bank. When Sarah notified Jerome, he came out of his office. "Come in Mr. Haggerty," Jerome smiled. "Have a seat." He sat next to his very important guest.

"Your presentation received plaudits from our finance committee. The Chairman suggested we establish an escrow account for first-time phone subscribers with limited credit history."

"Thank you; let me get the forms." Jerome returned to a file behind his desk. "What will your initial deposit be?"

"Oh, how about a million dollars," Keith said nonchalantly, "and that's just our starting point."

After Jerome stopped his mouth from dropping to the floor and his eyes from leaving their sockets, he said, "Relax, I'll fill out the forms!"

"That'll help you loan a few fish and chips, eh?" Keith smiled, and then added, "Just as important, our finance chairman has sent letters signed by our president to all our bloody banks, in five states, requesting quarterly reports on their loans demographically. His letter included, 'We want our business partners to make loans to all qualified applicants, regardless of race, even if that requires initiating outreach programs.' I have never seen our finance chairman so motivated. He replaced the tallest gentleman on his committee, who was determined to be a bad fit, I was told. And here's an extra morsel, we have designated one entry-level position in each of our sixty branches to be filled by a welfare recipient, and one part-time position for an above average high school minority student, eh? Scholarships are just around the corner."

"Thank you again, Keith. This check and your positive actions are much more than I had hoped for."

"One more thing," Keith asked, "how in the world did you learn about Lewis H. Latimer and Granville T. Woods? Our corporate historian had to visit the Bronzeville public library to learn that Latimer prepared the drawings for Bell's patent applications and Woods sold Bell a number of his patents, and became one of his first researchers. That bit of history will appear in our next annual report."

"Our ad agency, B&W Advertising, prepared our graphics, and uncovered that information. Their president, Alphonso Major, also directs our Bronzeville scholarship fund."

"Give me his number; we can use a fresh perspective in our annual report and some guidance managing minority scholarships."

"Incidentally," Jerome asked while filling out the new account forms, "did you ever find your missing podium?"

"Yes, it was in a broom closet just outside the conference room. Never did learn the bloody genesis of that move."

"*Hmmm*," Jerome thought, *maybe the Finance Committee Chairman did, which required the dismissal of Mr. Tall.*

The physical appearance of the bank's executive chamber was the same, but since becoming profitable, the board's mood was positive. Several of the Caucasian members congratulated Jerome on his huge single account acquisition. The Black members had celebrated with Jerome and Gail over dinner and drinks, sans Baxter Bridges, days before the meeting.

The restaurant the five Black board members had chosen to celebrate Jerome's first major deposit was one of Chicago's most elegant on the near north side. To their knowledge no African American had eaten there previously. The smiling Maître' d welcomed them and then led them to their table; Gail's napkin was spread over her lap. Menus and wine lists were distributed as each person sat down. House Menu Specials were satisfactorily explained, drink orders were taken and served; seconds were quietly suggested as glasses emptied. Appetizers were served simultaneously by seven tuxedoed staff members. Iced water glasses were kept full. The entrees were served under small domes which were all removed at the same second. A raised finger brought an immediate response. The Maitre d' checked regularly to assure complete satisfaction. Everyone was surprised and impressed. It was obvious the most elegant of Chicago's dining rooms had no problem serving upper class Blacks.

The seating arrangements in the Board Room had integrated. "The first order of business," Milton said through a smile, "will be the new accounts acquisition report presented by Stuart Sykes."

His voice was stronger; "This month seven board members have secured new business from their assigned accounts, aggregately adding over two million dollars to our deposits. Of course our president added one account for a million dollars." Everyone applauded Jerome's efforts and added positive comments, except Baxter Bridges. "That brings our level of participation to eleven."

"I'm having a problem with Quality Foods," Tiny said. "After several calls I couldn't even get an appointment."

"Generally, the program is working better than expected," Milton said. "Mr. Bridges, how can we help you bring in new business? Jerome's brilliant marketing strategy is working for everyone else."

"There's no need for me to talk to strangers until I can convince my friends to bank here, and they need more flexibility than Jerome allows."

"So you aren't even trying to acquire new business, right?" Before Bridges could answer, Milton said, "I noticed that you have moved all of your major accounts."

"Well, more flexibility was available when Arthur was here," Bridges answered. He knew Jerome had kept Milton informed. "And until I can promise my friends non-secured credit lines and at least a three-day notification before overdraft checks are returned, they might as well stay where they are, and I, at my previous bank."

"The services and privileges you want," Jerome said firmly, "are contrary to sound banking principles."

"But if I'm to operate profitably…"

"Unless this board sees things differently," Jerome interrupted Bridges by thrusting his palm toward him, "those services will remain unavailable. And if that is unacceptable perhaps you should resign from this board and sell your stock!"

Bridges smiled.

Midway on the agenda were new business opportunities. Jerome was the presenter. "Title VI, of President Johnson's '65 and '67 Civil Rights Legislation, requires that ten percent of all federal government contracts be awarded to disadvantaged citizens, which includes Blacks, American Indians, and females.

"When did women become disadvantaged?" Hal Hornbeck smiled. "Every time I'm with one she's got her hand so deep in my pocket, I'm the one who feels disadvantaged."

"I suggest," Jerome said after laughing at Hal's joke, "we form a committee that will bring Caucasians, and disadvantaged business-people together to prepare joint proposals. Buddy Laws also mentioned there's a new government agency called the Small Business Administration created by President Nixon that guarantees new business loans up to $100,000. Loans made under these two programs will not be deducted from our loan allocations."

"We should have started this effort years ago," Milton said, "and should consider putting Buddy Laws on retainer."

"You have as much chance of getting federal contracts as I have being invited to join the Nazi Party," Bridges laughed. "You know Buddy is a Democrat and the president is a Republican, or has that slipped your small, shallow minds?"

"We expect compliance with existing regulations, regardless of party affiliation," Jerome responded while staring at Bridges. The board agreed.

Bridges was incensed; he hurried from the boardroom as the meeting ended. *I remember when Jerome had one small store, and was as broke as the Ten Commandments. Now he's running a multi-million dollar bank and its board. He's become an uppity nigger that needs reigning in.*

End of Chapter Thirteen

CHAPTER FOURTEEN

"Thanks to you, this scholarship project has taken off like a brother who just stole something!" Alphonso said to Jerome while they were having lunch at the prestigious North Side Sage's East Restaurant. Negroes were acceptable in up-scale restaurants when wearing coats. Caucasians, however, without a coat would be loaned one. Negroes were not welcome in Italian, Irish, or Polish neighborhood restaurants.

"What are the specifics?" Jerome asked. He was having egg salad on lettuce and a cup of French onion soup. Weight awareness, at 41, was paramount.

"Our graduates, counting Cedric and Agnes, include 75. Presently enrolled? Including Milton's club placements, oh, we only have 700 scholars; 550 men and 150 women in 35 colleges, all who have challenging jobs and professional careers awaiting them." Alphonso bragged. "This year, our sixth, we will have over a hundred graduates. The program is booming because it is a win-win for students and sponsors alike. Jerome, this was an exceptional idea!"

"Serendipitously, at participating high schools, it has become cool to be smart, well behaved, and to dress appropriately. Violence, drugs, and gang activity have been drastically reduced. The Greeks added ten additional cities, each with two or more participating high schools. They also have an annual fashion show fund raiser that visits numerous cities. The program grew so rapidly I hired Dr. Jeanette Jenkins as National Manager with two assistants."

"What's the recidivism rate?" Jerome asked.

"It's less than 3%. First, high school students with drug or serious behavioral problems are eliminated. All scholars have at least a B average. Second, students are tested to determine where their innate interests and careers merge. Third, they are tutored by volunteer Greeks and Jaycees in weak subjects and are intellectually prepared for the companies and industries they are entering. They are visited by mentors who interview employers and students assuring compatibility. If the fit is not comfortable the student is removed. After two failed placements the student is dropped from the program."

"Do you have enough applicants?"

"We have too many. We are offering poor high school students, who work hard, a fully paid college education, compatible employment, and a professional career; why wouldn't they apply? Only 50% of students and parents pass our stringent screening, and we only have placements for half of them. Dr. Jenkins qualifies another twenty to fifty each year for special scholarships, some from professional societies, who participate in our summer programs."

"Well you have just picked up sixty vacancies, some additional cities, plus work for B&W with Midwestern Bell. Are the fashion shows producing sufficient funding?"

"In addition to the fashion shows, the alumni's 2% contribution is beginning to accumulate; last year we received $25,000. Contributing introduces the concept of giving something back early on. Some Greeks are putting our scholarship program on their annual contribution list. Each corporation covers all student costs, plus an administration fee. Additionally, most of the companies who employ our students find work for my agency. I now have offices in six cities, and have added marketing to our professional services. Now how great is that?" Alphonso said.

"Because you have worked hard, without compensation, you deserve the financial rewards. What types of companies are sponsoring our scholars?"

"All educational disciplines are included. During the summer we increase their cultural exposure by literary reading assignments, followed by discussions; art museum visitations with guided tours; and attending symphonic concerts and theatrical productions."

"We are growing so rapidly, I think we should create a board, with state managers and city supervisors where needed."

"That makes sense; I'll sit on the board, and you should become board chairman, but be sure to keep your administrative costs at no more than 5%. Managers and below should participate for only three years. It's like joining a business-oriented, African American Placement Corps. All staff should be recent college graduates, with a master's degree pending. With the contacts they develop, funding for their masters' and work at the end of their tour should be automatic. Dr. Jenkins' position should be well paid, and permanent.

"Let us," Milton said, as the January '72 Survivors Bank meeting ended, "commend our president. After six years, we are finally operating in the black!" Milton called out, "Sarah."

The board members applauded as Sarah, pushing a cart holding a cake with one burning candle, three bottles of chilled champagne, plus a special guest––Gail Gerard, entered; she was dressed to the nines. Jerome, surprised, blew out the candle, gave Gail a polite embrace and kiss, sliced his favorite chocolate-on chocolate cake, and then passed the knife to Sarah. Jerome popped a cork, followed by exaggerated cheers, and then poured the bubbly into outstretched plastic flutes.

"And to add to the significance," Milton said, "here is your first commission check. Congratulations!"

"Now just how did you get so lucky, Boy?" An envious Baxter Bridges asked as he peeped over Jerome's shoulder. The $60,000 check represented two percent of three million dollars in increased deposits in 1971. Jerome handed the check to Gail, who slipped it in her purse while smiling broadly.

Jerome's definition of luck was where opportunity and preparation meet. Bridges was insinuating Jerome had benefited from exogenous forces and had very little to do with the successful outcome. Jerome ignored Bridge's insult.

After profiting from selling his stock to invest in the bank, Jerome quit the stock market. Even though Professor Willie McGhee had been successful over decades, Jerome believed, as did Conrad Beauregard, investing in businesses where he had a major influence would be more profitable. Jerome's bank bonus would be deposited in his First Security savings account. Gail's mutual funds were growing considerably. She was now selling and managing commercial as well as residential properties. The Gerards' Investment cash was plentiful.

"The executive committee developed the incentives and the board approved them to entice Jerome to accept the presidency," Milton explained to Bridges as the celebration continued. "For the next four years Jerome will get a 2% commission on each million dollar increase in deposits, which I'll be happy to pay. Additionally, he'll also receive hefty raises, and first opportunity to buy our stock at the initially offered price. You're forgetting, Bridges, Jerome had a very successful drugstore chain prior to becoming our president."

"Yeah, that I financed," Bridges said without smiling.

"Say something, Jerome," Stuart said. Sarah and Gail poured champagne into partially empty flutes.

After reflecting, Jerome said, "Each of you worked hard to bring in new business and I thank you; a special salute to you Sarah. Without you following through on those first and second letters, we wouldn't have accomplished anything." All present raised their flutes toward Sarah; she blushed. "And plaudits to my beautiful wife, my life's partner, and best friend. Gail supported this decision, and kept our home loving and stress-free during the transition."

"That's what we all need," Stuart said, "supportive wives." His marriage after twenty years had ended.

"How are you going to get this year's increase, Jerome?" Tiny asked.

"I've been thinking about that."

"Thank you for inviting me," Gail interrupted, "but it's time for me to leave. Obviously you gentlemen have business to discuss."

The room quieted, Jerome said, "If we are to continue growing, the majority must come from Fortune 500 businesses and federal agencies, but we must still demand support from neighborhood leeches that profit from our doing business with them, but laugh in our faces when we suggest their doing business with us. It's no longer a selling situation. We need drastic action to change the hearts and minds of these insensitive bloodsuckers," Jerome said.

"A $3 million increase in one year is quite an accomplishment," Milton said, "can't we relax?"

"Oh my goodness, he's going to ruin everything," Bridges whispered to Stuart, "What's he talking about now?"

"I don't know!" Stuart said as if talking to a troublesome child. "Just shut up and listen!"

"So what's the plan, Jerome?" Samuel asked; he already knew.

"We should hire a preacher, draped in the robes of materialism, who will make callous Caucasians, and bull-headed Blacks do business with us."

"We can't do that," Bridges said, "Our depositors would desert us as if we had Lupus."

"This time you're right, Bridges, we can't do it <u>alone</u>," Jerome said, "All of Bronzeville must support the Black voice that says to non-supportive Negroes, SUPPORT YOURSELF, and to the Caucasian leeches, PUT SOMETHING BACK OR PACK."

"Why a man of the cloth?" a board member asked.

"Because ministers have been the voice of change since Jesus Christ; others were Mahatma Gandhi, Elijah Muhammad, Malcolm X, and Martin Luther King Jr."

"Sounds like a hired gun to me," Bridges said.

"Being called a robed warrior would be more appropriate, but all of these leaders were called a lot worse. Jesus was crucified, Mahatma Gandhi starved himself to death, Malcolm X and Dr. King were assassinated." Jerome continued, "Seeking our economic share can be as dangerous as walking on a greased tight rope over a swamp full of hungry alligators, gentlemen, but if we want our portion we are going to have to take the risk."

"Has anyone done this before?" Hal Hornbeck asked. He, like Bridges, disagreed with Jerome's aggressive plan.

"Yes, a reverend in Philadelphia against a bakery, among others." Debate followed. Bridges and Hal spoke against, Samuel, Jerome, and Stuart, in favor. Because of the champagne, the discord increased.

Finally, Milton rapped his gavel and said, "Jerome, you're the president, so we will continue to accept your leadership, but if this causes a financial backlash, you will be forced to resign. Because we have adjourned today, this will be voted on at our next meeting."

"I understand and agree." Jerome took a deep breath, and then said, "Another condition is we have to start leading ourselves."

"Now what dumb ass idea are you proposing," Bridges asked?

"If I'm going to risk everything again, it should be under a Black, board chairman."

Bridges laughed out loud. He believed Jerome, firing a rich White man, would end his banking career.

Everyone looked from Jerome to Milton and back again, waiting for…whatever. "Milton," Jerome said, "you have done an exceptional job leading this unwieldy, interracial gang of eleven. Without your firm and wise guidance this bank would have failed, and each of us would be at least $100 thousand poorer. But if our brethren are going to respect and support us, <u>we</u> need to prove we can manage ourselves."

Milton walked toward Jerome, flute in hand. He stared into Jerome's eyes and said, "Well, it's about time!" as he embraced Jerome and flashed a huge smile.

Bridges dropped his head; he was flabbergasted.

"I was chairman only because Richard had insisted. Please accept my resignation. The meeting is re-convened. Attorney Stovall, please assume the chair to manage an election." Richard Thompson, major stockholder, was elected chairman; he nominated Milton as vice chairman. The board unanimously agreed.

After Jerome explained the advantages, 90% of Bronzeville's moneyed citizenry agreed a militant minister could be an economic benefit. Contributions from individuals and businesses were as large as $10 thousand.

The word went forward from Bronzeville Brethren, nationally, asking help in identifying (1) an inspiring, eloquent, minister, (2) one who could debate intelligently and calmly, (3) one who had the persuasiveness, patience and energy to change the minds of biased persons, and (4) the rarest of all fusions: a minister who understood business principles.

Most of the hundreds of resumes received were tossed because of a lack of qualifications, experience, or misrepresentations. Twenty were analyzed by the five person search committee and reduced to ten through phone interviews. Miniscule infirmities reduced the ten applications to three; they were invited to Bronzeville and evaluated over two days. A week later, after hours of debate, Reverend Joshua Jones, D.D. (Doctor of Divinity), was selected.

He had delayed graduating college for a year to work with Dr. King during the Montgomery bus boycott in '56. He had attracted five hundred families to his Jackson, Mississippi church within five years while earning his master's and doctorate. He had started a credit union, which encouraged his congregation to save, and loaned money for mortgages, home repairs, appliances, and automobile purchases. With credit union funds and profits Reverend Jones had built a three story, apartment housing complex for one hundred, low income families. His credit union owned a super market. Because Caucasians considered him a hindrance to their predatory loan practices and overpriced rental units, his church was torched three times; without arrests or prosecutions. When he heard about the position in Bronzeville he was deciding where he would go to start anew.

Reverend Jones and his family were given a furnished four-bedroom Hyde Park apartment, a late model Oldsmobile, an unlisted phone, and a generous, but temporary, monthly stipend. Even the Reverend didn't know where the money was coming from.

Two weeks after moving in, after Jerome and Samuel had given Reverend Jones an overview of Bronzeville's situation, a thousand of Bronzeville's elite was invited to a Sunday soiree to meet the reverend at the Parkway Ballroom; only 125 couples RSVP'd. Samuel's eloquent introduction validated that Bronzeville's new activist was educated, had managed businesses, had often been tested and had the battle wounds and hospital stays to prove it.

Draped in a burgundy robe with a yellow lining and billowing sleeves over his large, 6'3" frame, Hershey colored Reverend Jones waved both palms over his processed hair, locked his fingers over his broad chest, dropped his head, and in a deep, James Earl Jones-type voice said, "Let us pray. Thank you Lord for blessing me with this unique challenge which includes impressing these Negroes here, because we all know, as sure as Lord is God, Bronzeville's Negroes are hard to impress." The audience chuckled.

"Thank you Jesus for bringing together those who, evidenced by their presence, will support this struggle, for they shall guide me. Jesus had only twelve apostles; I have at least two hundred. Thank you, Son of the Almighty, for authorizing me to lead these affluent folks into a more prosperous, earthly, Promised Land. Now Father, God, give me the tools, the wisdom, and the stamina to accomplish this worthy mission. Say amen."

A few of the distinguished, sophisticated, audience, unaccustomed to Baptist responsiveness, muttered a weak "Amen."

Reverend Jones detached the mike, bowed his head, stuck his left hand in the air and bellowed, "Oh omnipotent Lord, show me the way to gain the confidence of those here, mmm. The leaders of this sleeping giant, who are here to learn more about me, who have a misplaced solace in their present status, who have no concept of what a better tomorrow may bring, nooo."

"As I look into their faces, I see a curiosity, even doubt, regarding my ability to deliver a more prosperous Bronzeville." A few silently agreed. "Lord Almighty, these people need to WAKE UP and help me make Bronzeville the place where Black capitalism will reign supreme. Yesss, but I can't do it alone, Lord, nooo. I need the help of these fine folk. I need a COMMITMENT Lord, yesss. I need their SUPPORT for the hard work that lies ahead. Help me convince 'em, Lord, God and the Holy Spirit; yesss, I need the whole Holy Trinity to accomplish <u>this</u> task. Mmmm, will everybody please say amen?"

The collective amen was more fervent.

"Now I don't know the whole story," Reverend Jones said over a broad smile, pulling back thick lips to uncover his pearly white teeth, "but there is some funny stuff going on, like businesses IN OUR NEIGHBORHOOD, not doing business with us; and this is IN OUR NEIGHBORHOOD! Funny stuff, like businesses IN OUR NEIGHBORHOOD, advertising for workers, who say, when <u>we</u> show up for their publicized jobs, there is no work. And this is IN OUR NEIGHBORHOOD. Businesses," Reverend Jones pointed the microphone toward his audience,

A few said, "in our neighborhood."

"Who won't let <u>our</u> trash collectors' pick up trash, or <u>our</u> skilled tradesmen fix what's broken." Reverend pointed the mike outward; they responded loudly,

"IN OUR NEIGHBORHOOD!"

Reverend Jones nodded his approval, smiled and then said, "Mmm, and this is the funniest stuff of all. We, the Black people who live, I said, <u>live</u>," the mike went outward, the response IN OUR NEIGHBORHOOD came forth, "are not even supporting <u>our</u> own Black businesses and professionals."

The audience shouted, "IN OUR NEIGHBORHOOD!"

"Tell it like it is, Reverend J," someone shouted. The audience applauded and shouted, "Amen."

"Now, this afternoon you can relax," Reverend Jones said, holding the mike as he stepped down from the stage, asked his wife to join him, and began shaking hands. He motioned his audience toward the sumptuous buffet.

"Today, I'm not going to solicit donations or ask you to commit to anything. We are just going to enjoy the Parkway's gracious hospitality, which includes these generous offerings of fine wine; my favorite, deviled eggs; this mouth-watering, juicy, fried chicken, cooked with the condiments of love and generosity; home-made potato salad; and these delicious desserts; prepared by some of you lovely ladies standing before me. But don't eat so much that you get divine indigestion." His audience chuckled, several ladies blushed. "Just make sure all of you have signed the guest list and given me your contact information. Today I and my lovely wife are just going to get acquainted. After I have had time to do some research and pray, I'll assign some menial tasks." Reverend stepped back on the stage, and said, "So we can bring this funny stuff to an end, because IT AIN'T FUNNY WORTH A DAMN!"

The crowd roared.

During the next several weeks Reverend Jones talked with African American economic professors, lawyers, doctors, and pastors. He sought out the gainfully employed, under-employed and unemployed. He visited bars, hair salons, and pool rooms, always asking questions, making notes, listening, and collecting business cards. Some were angry, most dissatisfied, all appreciated his presence and that they were being listened to with an empathetic ear.

By appointment, Reverend Jones interviewed Bronzeville's business, entertainment, civic, and athletic notables. Gang leaders were flattered by his attention and sincerity. After completing his research Reverend Jones met with the hiring committee.

"Gentlemen, we have difficult days ahead; we are facing strange and strained circumstances. People are running businesses who don't know how to make a profit. Oh, they know their crafts; some are the hardest working people I've met, but they don't understand the fundamentals of business management. If we plan to grow by doing business with ourselves as well as White folk, our entrepreneurs must learn sound business principles. Oh yes, we have some serious work to do."

Reverend Joshua Jones' services were held on Saturday mornings in an abandoned theater on 51ˢᵗ and Calumet and were non-denominational. There was no conflict between traditional churches. The Positive Power meetings were about economic and civic issues, not righteous living. Reverend preached about Chicago's unfair politics, and stressed that we were entitled to respect, competitive pay, parity in education, and equal opportunity. Within a month he had a choir director, and a choir, supported by musicians that rocked!

Pride within Bronzeville rose like rolls waiting to be baked. People began demanding more from bureaucrats and more protection from policemen, instead of just persecution. Late night basketball, with referees, which ended for the night with any violent outbursts, was initiated at a Bronzeville high school, thereby causing gangs to curtail some of their hostile activities; Reverend Jones suggested they serve breakfast to the poor. Parents demanded more from schools, monitored their children's homework, and gave them additional reading assignments. Television viewing was limited.

Fledging Black business owners attended daily, two hour workshops, taught by experienced professionals, beginning at 6:00 a.m., before the normal business day. Signage divided the auditorium into classes: Personnel and money management; how to price goods and services; inventory control; professional sales techniques; accounting; commercial law, and composing impactful letters and contracts. Syllabuses and handouts were developed by Dr. Jeanette Jenkins. Students paid half the cost of their books so they would value them. All classes were five students or less; an expanded version of each one teach one.

Positive Power graduates who couldn't persuade significant, prospective clients were accompanied to their next appointment by "a friend of the vendor." Misunderstandings were settled and deals were negotiated, teaching businesspersons valuable lessons in the process.

Small businesses grew; unemployment and Welfare recipients were reduced. Whites and Blacks realized it was both practical and profitable to do business within Bronzeville. If businesses still resisted for prejudicial reasons, they were turned over to the Reverend.

Major consumer product companies hired Blacks as promotional/ public relations representatives. Reverend Jones explained how the alcoholic beverage and cigarette industries had successfully used Black retired athletes and celebrities as promotional persons since World War II. When one major consumer company conformed, others followed to offset the advantage. Reverend Jones also persuaded Caucasian corporations to use Bronzeville's lawyers and accountants.

A Black automobile salesman, employed by a dealer other than Arnold Lovelace's successful Lincoln franchise, was introduced at a Positive Power meeting. Afterwards, all of Bronzeville's White new and used car dealers sought Black salespeople.

Scores of underemployed college graduates were moved into better paying, more challenging jobs, creating vacancies for the unemployed. With hundreds of new jobs generated, hundreds of thousands of new dollars flowed through Bronzeville, producing even more jobs and businesses.

During Reverend Jones' first year, because of increased donations from grateful entrepreneurs, he became financially self-sufficient. During his second year, with Gail Gerard's assistance, the Positive Power purchased an abandoned synagogue, in Woodlawn, at an exceptional price. The board approved of Positive Power buying a two-hour block of radio time on the most popular Rhythm and Blues station every Saturday morning, generating income from advertisers. Alphonso Major managed the ad sales without commission. The Positive Power radio broadcast reached 300,000 listeners. Bronzeville blazed an economic trail that became the highway to prosperity.

A 30'x 5' oil cloth sign, located twenty feet over the choir, read, IMPROVE YOURSELF, YOURSELF. The message was, don't expect government to solve your problems; learn a trade or earn a degree. A second banner just beneath it read, BUY FROM THE BROTHER MAN, BYPASS THE OTHER MAN, emphasizing supporting businesses owned by Blacks, then those who employed Blacks, and to ignore companies where Negroes were not treated fairly; like Quality Foods Super Markets.

Consumer product companies who employed Negroes in managerial positions were allowed to display signs for a monthly fee. Gusto Beer, because it had a Black-owned distributorship, had a permanent streamer for a voluntary donation.

Rudolph "Tiny" Frazier was this Saturday's guest speaker. After he completed his pitch for his six supermarkets, he was asked, "Why don't you carry Anson Ice Cream my brother?"

"I'd love to, but Progressive, my co-op, won't let me."

"Reverend J. we gonna let 'em get away with that," another asked?

"Give Tiny and me some time to reflect; looks like we have some serious negotiating to do." Reverend smiled at his audience of 3,000, "but in the meantime, shop at Tiny's stores because the Other Man's supermarkets don't have Anson Ice Cream either."

Two Saturday's later six pickets appeared in front of Tiny's largest store. Their handmade signs read, BLACK PRODUCTS DESERVE DISTRIBUTION IN PROGRESSIVE STORES, BLACK PRODUCTS ARE GREAT PRODUCTS, and BLACK PEOPLE WHO SHOP AT PROGRESSIVE SHOULD BE ABLE TO BUY BLACK PRODUCTS. The *Chicago Defender* took photographs.

"If these pickets continue they are going to put me, and a lot of you, out of business." Tiny stated at the next owners meeting as he passed out the front pages of the *Chicago Defender* with negative headlines, stories, and photos. "While they picketed, my sales dropped to nothing! I was their first store, but I won't be their last. They threatened my shoppers with slashed tires when they returned to their cars. My managers were threatened with power failures which would shut us down for I don't know how long, and cause us to lose thousands of dollars in frozen foods." Tiny kept talking until he saw fear in the eyes of the White owners. He then pleaded, "All they want are a few facings for a few products."

"Tell them to come see me," The vice president of purchasing said begrudgingly. "If they meet our requirements, we'll authorize distribution."

The next day at Felix and Bea's Tiny and Reverend Jones congratulated themselves; their plan had worked. The "pickets" stayed just long enough for photos to be taken. The front pages that Tiny had passed out were counterfeits. The threats of tire-slashing's and electrical failures were figments of Tiny's imagination.

Distribution was welcomed in the fourteen Black owned Progressive stores for all Black manufactured products. The White-owned Progressive stores in Bronzeville capitulated to 'avoid pickets and economic devastation'. After a few weeks of increased sales at higher profits, they were glad they did. An unexpected benefit was their customers expressing appreciation for them carrying wanted products as well as supporting Negro businesses where family and friends worked. Reverend Jones lavished the Progressive stores with praise for being customer-sensitive, which was free advertising for 50+ stores to hundreds of thousands of consumers.

When Progressive's increased sales and profit figures were shown to competitive chains; they put in the new products. Black products that reached required volumes were warehoused which allowed stores throughout Illinois to purchase them with their regular orders. Distribution of Black-owned products had been accomplished.

Commercials were created by Alphonso Major for the Positive Power radio show for Black manufacturers, which they now could afford. Supermarket chains paid B&W Advertising to develop full page ads for the *Chicago Defender*, featuring Black products. As Black manufacturers' sales grew, employment increased. The *Chicago Defender* also added reporting and production staff.

Three months after dependability, profitability, trust, and quality-of-product, had been established Reverend Jones called on Progressive's management and persuaded them to authorize Black tradesmen to service their stores. The plumbers, carpenters and electricians who had developed their companies working for the Chicago Housing Authority repaired, improved, and remodeled Progressive's commercial buildings. Other chains acquiesced; everyone benefited. Reverend Jones encouraged trade unions, to make high school graduates not going to college, apprentices.

The only supermarket conglomerate that remained hostile was Quality Foods. The family-owned chain had thirty stores in Bronzeville with no Blacks in responsible positions, or any Black products on their shelves.

"Colored products don't deserve distribution in our stores," was their publicly stated policy.

"What we are considering may end our effectiveness," Reverend Jones said at their monthly board meeting. "Bronzeville is prospering and it has happened without confrontation––well without <u>serious</u> confrontation."

Reverend knew the threat of boycott had been frequently mentioned but never imposed. "When Quality Foods refuses me an audience our first affront will begin. If we fail, we will become a toothless tiger: all roar and no bite."

"Your accomplishments have been outstanding in your three plus years Reverend," the chairman of the board said. "Bronzeville's unemployment rate has been lowered, and our income ratio per capita is growing. If you believe we can bring Quality Foods into the fold, let's do it. If you don't, we can wait or bypass them entirely. It's your call." Reverend Jones took a three-day hiatus to pray and think. He spent time at the Bronzeville library reviewing the history of racially motivated economic boycotts throughout the country.

"I think we should move forward on Quality Foods," Reverend Jones said at his next board meeting.

"We don't know how to lose, Reverend. You show us the way, and with God on our side we'll complete the journey no matter how hot the sand!" The board chairman said.

The next open-to-buy day at Quality Foods Reverend Jones, wearing a black suit, reversed collar, and large cross around his neck, signed in. Several waiting salespersons stared as if he had entered the women's rest room. He waited patiently until several persons who had arrived after him had been seen. Reverend Jones politely mentioned the oversight to the receptionist.

"Mr. Ray don't do business with nigras," the receptionist said without ever looking up.

Reverend Jones bellowed in his deep voice, "If Mr. Billy Joe Ray won't see us here, he surely won't see us in his super markets!" The staff in their cubicles behind the frosted glass wall was startled by the Reverend's thunderous words. "Your produce will rot, your meat will spoil and your milk will curdle, while your cashiers, with nothing to do, just twiddle their thumbs!"

Two armed guards forcefully pushed Reverend Jones out the front door; he propelled himself to the ground. His large cross was clutched in his hand. Waiting photographers shot the fallen reverend, grimacing, with the armed guards man-handling him (or, helping him up), in front of Quality Foods' corporate offices. The battle had been joined.

The next Saturday morning Reverend preached, exaggerating his mistreatment, with his "sprained" arm in a sling. "It isn't right that we should feed Billy Joe Ray's family while our families hunger for jobs. Say a amen!" His congregation shouted a thunderous "a amen!" "It isn't right for Quality Foods to get fat while we endure economic starvation. Say a amen!" The radio station's sound gauge hit the maximum. Bronzeville's three Black-owned newspapers published Reverend's incisive statements along with selected photographs.

Every Friday afternoon Reverend Jones called Quality Foods; the operator always insulted him with racial epithets and then hung up. Every Saturday, after Reverend's broadcast, thirty pickets marched in front of Quality Foods' ten largest stores, chanting and singing. Onlookers shouted encouraging or disparaging comments toward the few customers entering the stores. Fights between spectators erupted, police stepped in, which added to the spectacle. Several White male employees escorted their few Black customers to and from the parking lot, until they were confronted by red, head-scarf-wearing Blackstone Rangers. When Quality Foods workers stayed inside the red head-scarves disappeared.

The Quality Foods boycott made network television news for the first three week-ends. The Black press reported that Quality Foods' Black employees said anonymously their pay envelopes were always several dollars short, and they were paid less than their White counterparts. The females were required to clean their, and the White cashiers' workstations, refill bag bins, and were thoroughly searched by at least two leering male managers in private offices before they could leave. Only the Black stock boys were required to clean the restrooms. Caucasian female cashiers were not required to do any of the menial chores, or submit to being searched prior to leaving work. The articles always ended with the truthful statement, "Quality Foods refuses comment."

The *Chicago Chronicle* quoted Quality Foods' spokesperson, "We are victims of a Communist plot. Reverend Jones is an agnostic mercenary who was run out of Jackson, Mississippi for antagonizing the Caucasian establishment. We are being blackmailed by negro (the *Chronicle* purposely used a small n) gangs." The *Chronicle's* editorial page criticized Mayor O'Malley for not protecting one of Chicago's finest family owned-businesses from the corrupt, illegal actions of hired, imported, hoodlums. Quality Foods advertised in the *Chronicle* regularly.

"The mayor disagrees with the protest. Police are always present, but cannot make arrests unless laws are broken or personal or property rights violated," read part of a statement from the mayor's office. Mayor O'Malley didn't want a confrontation with 5th District Commander Lewis Calhoun; payoffs moving up and upcoming elections may have been negatively impacted.

During the sixth week, a national weekly news magazine featured Reverend Jones and Billy Joe Ray on their cover, separated by a lightning bolt. All of the negative comments previously reported were dispelled, especially those regarding Reverend Jones' history, gangs extorting money, or there being a Communist plot.

Ninety percent of Black folks had stopped shopping at Quality Foods, but Billy Joe Ray's 30 supermarkets had shown no signs of capitulating. Seven weeks into the campaign an anonymous caller said to Reverend Jones, "St sta stay the ca ca course. Sa sales are w way da down."

Eight weeks into the crusade the excitement had waned, network television crews had vanished and volunteer pickets had dwindled. Reverend Jones knew they were hurting Quality Foods, but they still wouldn't meet with him. The ninth week Reverend Jones only had enough pickets for five stores, then, two weeks later, only three. The August heat further reduced those willing to walk the hot, energy consuming picket lines.

"You you're win winning. Ha hang in there. Th their funds a are dry drying up," the mystery caller said on the eve of the twelfth week. "An any week now; you are doing ga ga well. Th they are lay laying off em employees an and are ha having trouble me meeting th their pay payroll."

"Who are you?" Reverend Jones demanded. "Where are you getting your information? We are straining to keep the pressure on!"

"Hi hit our, I mean, their bi biggest store this Sa Saturday," The caller said then hung up.

He's on the inside, Reverend Jones concluded. *I've got to follow his advice.* Before the Saturday morning meeting Reverend Jones called the Blackstone Rangers' leader, Commander Lewis Calhoun, and Black, local TV reporter, Namon Davis.

Ending his radio broadcast, Reverend prayed, "Thank you Jesus for giving us the will to not shop at uncaring, unforgiving, unempathetic, Quality Foods. Please Lord, protect us while we picket Quality Foods largest store on 69th and Cottage Grove. Once again, that's 69th AND COTTAGE GROVE, AT NOON!"

A used Greyhound bus emblazoned with *Positive Power* on both sides parked in front of *Quality Foods Supermarket* on one of Bronzeville's busiest streets. Only twelve pickets were walking. Perspiring spectators were standing behind police barricades. When the Positive Power bus arrived the policemen left their air conditioned patrol cars and took pre-determined, strategic posts. Commander Calhoun, in civilian clothes, parked in an unmarked vehicle, surveyed the activity.

The Reverend in his maroon and yellow robe looked over the sparse gathering from his seat behind the driver. He bowed his head and prayed softly, "Some of these young people are not projecting a wholesome image, Lord, but I asked them to be here and you sent them, so I'm sure you know what you are doing, even if I don't. But Lord, is this the best we could do? I had 3,000 at our service and 300,000 radio listeners and all you and I could motivate is 12? But millenniums ago, Lord 12 were enough. I have faith in you, Lord; I see your blessings at work. It's amazing that this eclectic assemblage can walk together peacefully. To encourage them; I'm going to join the picket line."

Reverend stood, looked through his partially filled bus, and prayed aloud, "Lord God, hold your children's hands, for this may be Judgment Day." He then spoke to those on board. "Tribunes for The Cause, it's too hot to march too long. Relieve those who have been carrying the load. Point them toward our air conditioned bus."

The pickets were a mosaic. The shapely, young women wore sensuously tattered short shorts, heels, thin, white cotton socks with decorative lace tops, and halters that were too tight and too revealing. They realized it was much more difficult to walk a picket line than to work the streets.

The older ladies wore long dresses, cotton stockings, and gym shoes. They carried umbrellas to deflect the sun. Elderly men wore suit coats over soaked shirts and ties, young men wore sloppy jeans, loose fitting, too long T shirts with gang-colored bandanas hanging from their back pockets. Their immediate task was keeping their women on the picket line.

"Shout hallelujah!" The Reverend bellowed as he relieved a skimpily dressed young lady of her picket sign, gave her a hug and pointed her toward the bus; her body odor battered the Reverend. He shook a Blackstone Ranger lieutenant's hand and said loudly, "Glad to see you and yours, my young brothah." The Reverend took the lieutenant's sign gave it to a new arriver and suggested he rest. The driver, who was too heavy to walk, welcomed the relieved, tired pickets with a smile, a paper cup of iced lemonade and a bologna sandwich. Spectators encouraged by Reverend Jones' beckoning joined the line, which swelled to twenty.

Homemade signs brought on the bus read, QUIT QUALITY. QUALITY MEANS INEQUALITY. IF THIS IS QUALITY KEEP IT, and QUALITY STINKS.

The police, recognizing wanted gang members and prostitutes, headed toward the picket lines. "No arrests today," Commander Calhoun said, making himself visible. "These young people are performing a very important public service." The surprised police backed off. Noticing the police's inactions, as had been predicted by Reverend Jones, more working ladies and gang members emptied doorways and cars, and joined the picket lines. The singing and chants became louder and more enthusiastic.

Namon Davis convinced his bosses he had insider information that today was going to be decisive, possibly tumultuous; they had reluctantly agreed, and let him cover the event. He was the only camera crew on site. Namon posed the expected question, "Reverend Jones you have been boycotting Quality Foods for three months, tell us why."

Reverend turned over his sign and wiped away the perspiration with a hand towel pulled from his sleeve. He walked pass the bus' full color signage to make sure it was seen on TV, and then stood on the bus' first step to give the cameraman a better visual. He then answered, "Quality Foods refuses to stock Black products, treat Black employees fairly, use Black-owned banks, or even meet with us. Since they won't talk, we will continue to walk." The television van's public address system carried Reverend Jones' message throughout the crowd.

"May I have your microphone, son?" Namon acquiesced. Reverend, accompanied by The Spirit, in his best preacher's voice bellowed, "See all those low prices on their windows? They are selling chickens, normally forty-nine cents, for only nineteen cents a pound. They hope to WEAKEN our resolve by offering us CHEAP CHICKEN, but we're not going to trade our DIGNITY for CHEAP CHICKEN! Oh, make no mistake, we love us some chicken, especially fried chicken, or chicken and dumplings, or smothered chicken with rice and gravy." The Reverend's eyes brightened. He smiled and licked his lips as he "tasted" the delicious dishes, "and they know it, but we can't eat THEIR chicken because it is infected with CHICKEN ITUS you see, nooo. Their chicken is rancid with RACISM and BIGOTRY and DISRESPECT and INJUSTICE…"

A slightly stooped, suited, older male picketer, wearing a farmer's straw hat, started chanting, "Quality's gotten rotten, Quality's gotten rotten!" A teenage boy retrieved a five-gallon plastic pail from the nearby garbage dump, sat on the curb and began playing a marching beat with his ever-present drumsticks. The ladies of the evening strutted more explicitly. The television camera turned toward the voice, the ladies, and then the drummer. Namon, with exceptional, poetic prose, dramatically described the events over the cacophony that was heard by all. Other picketers, inspired by Namon and performing for the TV camera, started singing *When the Saints Go Marching In*, as if they were in a New Orleans funeral parade, returning from the cemetery. Onlookers joined the picket line, which now covered the entire store front. The singing grew louder. Drivers seeing the demonstration, slowed and began thumping their car doors, causing a minor traffic jam.

The White police sergeant-in-charge, noticing the increased activity, hand signaled Commander Calhoun that he wanted to call for back-up. Not yet, the commander while moving into the crowd signaled back.

Between verses a deep voice sang, "I say, oh, when the Saints!" Reverend Jones recognized the voice; it was his choir's lead baritone who had said he wouldn't be available. The picketers resting in the bus, encouraged by the surge, rejoined the line.

"Thank you Jesus!" Reverend shouted with his head back and palms stretched towards the heavens.

Suddenly, six-foot three, broad chest, Billy Joe Ray appeared in a white shirt with rolled sleeves, tight jeans, and western boots. Namon rushed to him and asked the obvious question, "Mr. Ray, how do you feel about your largest store being picketed?"

The thirty-five year old Quality Foods owner looked for a White television reporter; none was present. He grabbed Namon's microphone. "My family has served Chicago long before that jack-leg; nigger preacher ever came to my town."

"Who you calling nigger?" shouted a muscular, young Black man as he began pushing through the crowd toward Billy Joe. Several Black men fell in behind him. On a signal from Billy Joe, about 20 male Caucasians with axe handles and bats exited the back of the Quality Foods store, moving toward the rushing Negroes. Commander Calhoun signaled the police sergeant to call for back-up. Policemen moved toward the muscular Negro and his followers.

"Hey! My brothers," Reverend yelled, getting the charging Black men's attention, motioning them with both hands to stand down. He said, "Nigger ain't nothin' but a word! You all know who I am and I know what I am, and no matter what he says, he can't change that. Besides, God's on our side today." The Reverend smiled broadly. The young men thrust victorious fists into the air, and melded into the crowd. The sergeant directed the police toward the Caucasians with the clubs; there were no Black men to arrest.

"You're White; you're in charge, sergeant. Why don't you arrest all these jiggaboos?" Billy Joe's race-baiting remarks, which should have caused, at least, a fight, hadn't worked. The sergeant stared at Billy Joe but said nothing. Commander Calhoun was standing close by.

Billy Joe said, "Because the coloreds are taking over this town, and because our police," Billy Joe said staring at the sergeant with disdain, "tolerate nigra mob rule, and because our banks won't extend any more credit because of <u>him</u>," Billy Joe pointed toward Reverend Jones, "we are closing all our stores until further notice."

"Yeah! Right on! We did it! Quality Foods has quit doin' biness!" shouted a picketer.

"I have a national exclusive!" Namon said as he and his cameraman moved toward Reverend Jones. Billy Joe reached the Reverend first, grabbed him around the neck and while strangling him yelled, "You miserable Black ass hole!"

Reverend Jones grabbed Billy Joe's wrists and relieved the pressure on his neck but did not attempt to free himself. He bent backwards, looked toward Namon's cameraman with his tongue hanging out, "grimacing." Reverend Jones winked at the Blackstone Rangers' lieutenant. He understood Reverend Jones' moves and kept his followers still. In less than a minute three policemen grabbed Billy Joe, separated him from Reverend Jones, handcuffed him, and then threw him in a squad car. The Blackstone Rangers celebrated by exchanging, complex, hand, fist, and elbow bumps. They had witnessed passive resistance working. Billy Joe would never have been arrested had they intervened.

"I understand Mr. Ray's frustration," Reverend Jones said into the camera while dramatically massaging his neck and rotating his head. "His family came to Chicago from Alabama over fifty years ago and built a multi-million dollar business. We, during that timeframe, have contributed to Mr. Ray's success. To Mr. Ray, his daddy, and granddaddy, Negroes have always been the underclass, the worthless, the people whom the Rays have despised, while continuously profiting from our grocery dollars, lo these fifty years.

"We never wanted Quality Foods to go out of business. That's an affliction we wish on no man. We only want what we are entitled to: equal employment, and Black product availability." Reverend Jones shook his head, reflecting genuine sorrow. He added, "And let everyone remember, all we wanted to do was talk."

A young *Chicago Chronicle* stringer, covering the event on his own time, said, "You probably don't care about all the White people you have put out of work, Joshua, but what about all the Negroes you have robbed of their livelihood?" He stood with pad ready, prepared to write down Reverend's, hopefully angry, response to his insulting question.

"None of the now unemployed worked for me, son," Reverend said with compassion, "And I do care about all unemployed persons, no matter their race." Reverend, once again, grabbed Namon's microphone, "To all who want a job contact the Positive Power's office beginning Tuesday morning. Monday, we will call all the supermarkets and line up jobs, not just for Black people, but for all people who are willing to work in an integrated environment." The crowd cheered. "Hallelujah!" shouted the Reverend as he put both hands on his hips and shuffled with one foot in the air.

The stringer attempted to approached Reverend Jones again, but found his path blocked by the backs of men with red bandanas hanging from their pockets. The crowd crossed hands and swayed slightly. With the church choir baritone leading, they sang several verses of *We Shall Overcome.*

"Let him go, I won't press charges, he's suffered enough," Reverend Jones said to Commander Calhoun, "The Lord works in mysterious ways." Billy Joe Ray left unnoticed.

Namon's news film and commentary over the events were used by networks, nationally, ending with his name, photo, and his station's call letters. Namon's reporting was so impressive; a television network hired him as a Chicago-based, investigative reporter. Local network television affiliates, as well as independent stations, began hiring Black journalism graduates. Messages Positive Power left with previously averse businesses were quickly answered. The Positive Power's first salaried office manager was a White accountant who stuttered.

Network and independent television talk shows sought Reverend Jones as a guest. His appearances raised ratings because his comments were provocative, truthful, succinct, and quotable. Black organizations sought Reverend Jones as their keynote speaker at national conventions.

Positive Power's auditorium was filled two hours before the Saturday morning service. National media were given reserved space, managed by Alphonso Major. Arbitron, the media barometer, showed The Positive Power broadcast had an unusually high market share which meant Caucasians were also listening.

Because of the increased audience, Alphonso raised the cost of radio ads, adding to Positive Power's coiffures. Caucasian companies, impressed with Alphonso's pro bono work, commissioned him to develop television commercials to influence Black, and in rare instances, Caucasian consumers. Alphonso moved to a larger facility, hired full time staff, plus two part-time college student copywriters, and two production assistants.

All over Bronzeville, due to Reverend's constant urgings, Blacks supported black-owned businesses. Scotty's Lounge had competition from more elegant watering holes; he remodeled and expanded. Felix and Bea's became just one of many first-class restaurants in Bronzeville. Felix commissioned Gail to find a larger location.

Lakeside and Survivors Banks became the two top Black banks in the nation. The mass exodus of deposits from South Side banks caused them to hire Blacks at all levels. Oscar Jones became president of *Westchester*

Bank, with a lucrative salary, but in name only. He discarded his ego and his carnation, deciding both were excessive. He continued carrying his Wall Street Journal, occasionally reading it.

Because of increased bank loans, more Black-owned retail stores opened, offering everything. Negro entrepreneurs struggled to be competitive with the chains. When the brother's price was higher, he was made aware, but the purchase was made anyway. It was considered a required Black tax.

Retail chain stores promoted dependable, honest, conscientious Blacks who had previously been bypassed to managerial positions. Japanese auto manufacturers followed by Detroit, made concessions allowing Black dealerships to open.

Shade tree mechanics attended six week training courses, and then, with loaned investments, became owners of gas stations that also sold premium oil, tires and batteries. Fast foods restaurant management co-signed for Blacks without enough cash, so they could open new locations. Bronzeville was booming. Blacks with college educations were given entry-level, management positions in Caucasian companies. Bronzeville's African American's earnings per capita exceeded the national norm.

Negroes in other major cities renamed Bronzeville, Bucksville. They recognized the economic benefits of segregation and contacted Reverend Jones for advice on how to start Positive Power chapters. Prosperity was on the rise, nationally, Black community by Black community.

Integration and separatism, when practiced judiciously, worked.

End of Chapter Fourteen

CHAPTER FIFTEEN

Because of Survivors Bank's rapid, consistent growth, Jerome continued to receive lucrative bonuses; his salary had reached mid-six figures in two years. Baxter Bridges was envious of what he considered Jerome's rocket-like ascendency. To most, twenty years of positive business growth is not meteoric, but Baxter felt differently.

"I've had a bad night," Bridges said to Felix late one evening. Bridges didn't mention that Hope had stood him up––again. He had waited over two hours: where he was still paying the rent.

After a long day Felix was about to leave, but realized his longtime friend needed company. They had survived The Great Depression, World War II, the Italian mob Policy take-over, prejudicial unemployment and institutionalized segregation, the turbulent 50's and 60's, and were enjoying the prosperous 70's. The two successful pioneers, over drinks, recalled yester-years. The hard times were dismissed, the good times glossed over, the fun times embellished, the disagreements not even mentioned. Several drinks later, Felix said, "Life's full of peaks and valleys, don't you know."

"What are you talking about, Man?"

"About 20 years ago, then big time Turkey Stevens brought Jerome Gerard to my old place his first day in town; you were there, remember? He was looking for a job but didn't tell anyone. Now Jerome can damn near buy Bronzeville and Turkey can't change a nickel. 'Course, when the Pershing closed, Turkey's being a sportin man, ended."

"So, Turkey's in bad shape, huh?" A devious idea was germinating.

"Oh, he's working, but can't afford his habits. Turkey still dates ladies who flat back, and he gambles away every dime he gets. I've taken him on junkets to Vegas, but he never leaves winners. He manages to get ahead, but loses what he won and all he brung before we leave town. Back in the day he always quit winners, but not now. He keeps trying to break the house, and he should know better; after all, he used to be 'the house' heh, heh, heh."

"How often do you see Turkey?"

"He comes in every Friday for a free meal. You know, for old times' sake." Felix continued talking, but Bridges' mind was elsewhere.

The next Friday Bridges was having a steak dinner alone when Turkey entered. "Hey my brother, haven't seen you in a while, grab a chair and order up. How's it going?"

"You know, mutton one day, nuttin' the next. My luck's in the sewer right through here, but it'll turn around." He was pleased to have a striver show him respect. Felix was surprised to see Turkey and Bridges eating together; it meant someone else was picking up Turkey's tab tonight.

Turkey ordered a double gin and tonic, two entrees with sides, and then as an afterthought, asked permission. "Whatever you want is alright, man, you know how tight we are." As Turkey gorged himself, Bridges said, "Turkey, I've got a bothersome itch I can't scratch; know what I mean?"

"I know what you're sayin', Mr. B. Anything I can do to help?"

"Well, that depends; how are you and Jerome making it these days?"

"We're not; haven't seen him in almost a year." Turkey had written a bad check that Jerome cashed several months ago, but he had mentally erased the incident. "He got me this bullshit job. They call me the warehouse manager, but all I'm doing is countin' beer cases and loadin' trucks. He could have done better by me; I mean without me, he wouldn't even be here; am I right?" Bridges nodded. Turkey continued, "I asked him to hook me up at the bank and he laughed; that really pissed me off. I mean, I been sober for a couple of years now; shiiit, I'm smart. I ran the Pershing, right?"

"That's funny," Bridges lied, "when I suggested he repay you for the favors you did for him he laughed at me too." Turkey's frown deepened. "So you wouldn't be upset if he got busted, especially if you made a bundle in the process, right?"

"Naw, wouldn't bother me none. He's been on easy street ever since he got here. He forgot me and the others who helped him on his way up. He needs to get his come-upins." Turkey listened to Bridges', bring-Jerome-down, idea.

"Is Mr. G. in?" Turkey asked Sarah. Jerome's car was in his reserved parking space.

"Yes," Sarah said, "but he's leaving now. Perhaps if you…"

"Turkey, Turkey Stevens," Jerome said, "it's good to see you man. What's happening?" They shook hands then embraced. Turkey had not bothered to bathe; Jerome backed off a little. "It's been way too long. I'm on my way out; you need anything?" *Hope he doesn't want me to cash another check.*

"I'm having a birthday party at Louise's place next Saturday night, Mr. G., and wanted you to help me celebrate. It's my sixty-fifth and ain't too many more promised, health problems and all." Turkey exaggerated a cough. "Here's an invitation."

"I'll check my calendar and see if I can make it."

"Aw Man, I know you're always busy, but please make it, even if it's just for a little while. It'll make the whole night somethin special. My luck's turned solid, so I'm having a real bash, catered and everything. Besides, you're the only big shot I know!" Turkey laughed. He assumed a boxer's stance and threw several punches toward Jerome's chest. "I still believe we're related."

"OK, man. I'll stop by, but I won't be able to stay long."

"Great, I'll be opening presents about eleven, so if you could be there for that I'd really appreciate it, OK? Hey, how 'bout you toasting the good old days, know what I'm sayin'?"

"All that's cool." As Jerome and Turkey parted, Jerome thought, *that cough was a farce, wonder why he wants me there, and just how lucky has he been? Louise's ladies cost top dollar. I think I'll call her.*

Moments later at the corner drugstore, "Mr. B," Turkey said over the pay-phone, "everything's set; he'll be there around 10:30. Now nobody's going to get hurt, just some pictures with his pants down, right?"

"Yeah, that's the deal," Bridges answered. Unbeknownst to Turkey, Bridges had arranged through Chicago's police commander to have the party raided. He wanted Jerome photographed and arrested. The incident would end his banking career. Having the Gerards suffer through a divorce would add to their punishment––and double Bridges' pleasure.

Louise had quit her drugstore job. Now in her fifties, she had opened a classy bordello in a large Hyde Park apartment on a private street where visitors' parking was impossible, and neighbors were nosey, especially at night. To eliminate both problems, Louise had made special arrangements with a gas station several blocks away to transport her clients.

When in the drugstore business, to exercise discretion, Jerome had rented Louise's reclusive rooms with willing women. Since Gail's accusations, in spite of increased overtures, no matter how hard the B.S. Table regulars played, and bragged about it, Jerome had stopped cavorting.

"Louise, Turkey invited me to his birthday party at your place; what's up?"

"Well hello Mr. Mukity-muck. Bank presidents don't need my place, huh?

"That's a long story for another time, babe; what about this party?"

"Listen lover, you tell me! For months Turkey's dropped by and tried to hustle my girls for a lay on credit, and you know I'm too smart for that. Well, last week he gives me five large and says he wants to buy my place for the night; told me to have my whole posse in place, include drinks, a gourmet buffet, and a cake. You coming?"

"Does that matter?" *Five thousand in cash! That's much more than getting lucky; something's up.*

"Not to me, I mean," Louise said through a chuckle, "unless you had something special for the old girl." Louise paused…nothing; she continued. "He said there were going to be some VIP's in the mix, and he's bringing some friends. I don't give a damn whose here; for five large it's his party, know what I'm sayin'?"

His friends, Jerome thought, *have always operated under the radar, so who are the VIPs? Something is missing. I think I'll bring Eugene so he can see how high-on-the-hog his warehouse manager is living.*

Jerome, while having lunch, asked Felix if he had overheard anything. He recalled Bridges buying Turkey an unusually large dinner, "but I wasn't invited to a party," he sounded offended.

Bridges bribing Turkey…? thought Jerome.

"See you Saturday, Honey," Rowena whispered to Jerome while serving. *She sounds like we have a date. I'm being set-up, but why? Maybe I'm being surprised; no, not by Bridges. Well, to be absolutely sure I won't be embarrassed, I'll invite…*

"Father Paul, would you like to attend a birthday party Saturday evening?" He accepted. An evening out with the wealthy Jerome Gerard was always appreciated.

Jerome, Eugene, and Father Paul pulled into Louise's favored gas station around 10:30 p.m. Commander Lewis Calhoun exited the passenger side of an unmarked police car.

"Father Paul what are you doing with these two characters! I know you three aren't going to Louise's––not tonight! I got orders from Downtown to raid her place. There's going to be a big time drug dealer and several VIP's present, but nobody mentioned a priest!

"Just who is Louise and why are we…"

"Not now Father," Jerome said as he interrupted a confused Father Paul. Jerome said, "Then why haven't you raided it, Lewis?"

"It's scheduled for 11:00 o'clock when the prime target will be in the house. My men are in place; the press got wind of it. You three better scat. You'll be surprised to learn that Baxter Bridges is the instigator. He and his people, which includes Turkey, have get-out-of-jail passes."

"That's it!" Jerome said. "Bridges is using Turkey to set me up for a serious character assassination which would probably get me fired."

"Why did you invite me, Jerome?" Father Paul asked.

"To let those with malice in their hearts know I am no longer a sinner, Father," Jerome said.

"Well, at least we learned where the money came from," Eugene said. "I thought Turkey was your buddy. Now let's get the hell––excuse me Father––out of here!"

As they drove away, Father Paul said, "Jerome, we will have to discuss this matter, as soon time permits."

The lights were low and crimson, the music soft and bluesy, Louise's lovely ladies from eighteen to thirty in seductive lingerie and high heels were aggressively friendly. Turkey had invited some of his buddies from work. They were having a ball. Free sex, food, booze, and drugs; what could be better than this!

It was 10:30, two hours into the affair. Hope latched on to a muscular, young truck driver. Bridges was peeping out the window looking for Jerome. Having resisted sexual encounters repeatedly, he had finally succumbed to a foxy floozy's amorous attention. Bridges' photographer was being serviced by a young beauty kneeling on a pillow as he held onto his flash camera; his shirt and coat were still in place with his pants around his ankles.

"He's The Man tonight," Louise told two of her finest harlots. Turkey was thoroughly enjoying his entitlement in a king-sized, circular bed with satin sheets and ceiling mirrors. Rowena, high on weed, was being convinced by the drug pusher to inject Heroin.

Because Jerome hadn't arrived, Bridges had tried unsuccessfully to delay the raid; the police battered down the front and back doors. Rowena was found naked and dead from a heroin overdose. When notified, headquarters revoked Bridges' pass. Everybody was booked, photographed, and interrogated.

The press photographed Baxter Bridges wearing only his perennial grin. Hope, high and nude, had her arms around a vertical Bridges as she tried to hide her face. They were on the front page of all the papers. A woman's head below Bridges' waist was in the photo. The Chronicle's headline read, NEGRO ORGY BUSTED IN HYDE PARK BROTHEL. ONE WOMAN DEAD. DRUG KINGPIN AND REAL ESTATE CZAR ARRESTED.

Louise was evicted, Bridges' third wife sued for divorce, Turkey and Hope were fired. Richard called an emergency board meeting. Under cross-examination by Samuel, with Sarah taking notes, Bridges admitted giving Turkey $7,000 to entrap Jerome. Bridges was forced to resign from the board. To avoid Jerome's civil suit, Bridges sold Jerome his stock at the original price, which was less than half its current value. The decision was easy; Bridges would probably have lost it anyway in the divorce settlement.

During the next board meeting, Jerome nominated Luther Wilson to replace Bridges. Luther had repeatedly requested the prestigious position. Milton, Hal, and Norm Olberman, after reviewing Mr. Wilson's resume stood against him. Jerome argued that a man's alleged past, should not deny him board acceptance. The opposition believed Luther's questionable business activities disqualified him. Jerome argued, "I know several successful Caucasian businessmen who have survived questionable circumstances," Jerome said. The Caucasians wondered what secrets Jerome knew.

After dropping out of high school at sixteen, in the 50's, Luther Wilson drove a cab two shifts a day, seven days a week. At twenty-five he owned a fleet of cabs, a garage with a gas pump, and had hired several mechanics. His next investment was his first fifty-room transient motel. Luther later opened a ritzy night club. Several years earlier, his nightclub was closed after several customers were killed in a shoot-out. Accusations flourished regarding Luther but, thanks to Samuel, he was never convicted of any crime. Luther was now a successful multiple track home builder, still owned his fleet of cabs, his motels, a liquor super mart, plus a 300 room luxury hotel. Gail's company was Luther's exclusive real estate representative.

On the motion, the board approved Luther seven to three; Samuel Stovall abstained because of lawyer-client relationships. Milton did not vote. Luther was offered stock at the current market value with an initial investment of at least $100 thousand. He welcomed the opportunity to enhance his reputation.

"May I make two suggestions?" Jerome said, the Gerards were having dinner at the Wilsons' luxurious home celebrating his board appointment. "Improve your future management team by employing two of our high school scholars, part-time, in your organization and finance their college educations. During the next decade you will have professionally trained executives with years of experience to take your business forward. Who knows, your company might design and build Chicago's next Merchandise Mart."

"Yeah, it could happen," Luther said. "Developing talent in-house, perhaps an architect and an MBA, is an excellent idea, I should have thought of that," Luther said. "I learned how to build houses at Hard Knocks U, and there's still a lot I don't know."

"That's interesting," thought Jerome, *a Negro high school dropout who became a self-made millionaire could entertain the idea of building the world's largest building: now that's racial progress.*

The Gerards, with Bryan Gerard as the architect and Luther as the General Contractor, were planning to build a 24 story, 400 unit, residential, rental high rise with commercial stores on the first level as investment property in a middle income Bronzeville neighborhood.

"The second suggestion is to make a $10,000 contribution, annually, to Bronzeville Bootstraps Scholarship Fund to help additional young African Americans acquire college educations."

"That's done," Luther smiled. "I thought you were going to ask me to do something difficult or expensive!"

"You can always make it twenty thou a year," Jerome said. The foursome laughed.

End of Chapter Fifteen

CHAPTER SIXTEEN

"Babe, my tux is too tight," Jerome called to Gail from his dressing area in their master suite. "I think I'll wear my black suit instead." Jerome and Gail were preparing for Bronzeville's grandest, business-related, social event of the year, the 1975 Urban League of Chicago Dinner/Dance.

"You should still wear it," Gail called back from her wrought iron, cushioned seat at her ten, frosted bulb vanity. *Please don't make me elaborate*, she thought.

"A number of men will be wearing dark suits, you know," Jerome said as he sucked in his stomach and hooked his pants. *Maybe*, Jerome thought, *as Gail suggested, I should have bought a new tux*. Gail had purchased a black, silk-on-silk, contemporary bow tie and cummerbund without Jerome's permission. "Incidentally," Jerome said, "where did Dana go, and why aren't we picking up the kids?"

"Michelle and Elliot have baby-sitting problems," Gail lied through pursed lips while applying gloss, "so they will meet us at the hotel. John picked up Dana, they had an earlier stop; you know how young people move." *Please Lord, no more questions.*

"There." Jerome smiled as he fastened Gail's necklace which enhanced her cleavage. The four-karat diamond on a platinum chain was Gail's twenty-fifth wedding anniversary gift six months ago. "You look beautiful, Babe."

Valets in front of the Conrad Hilton Hotel parked luxury cars for lavish tips. Jerome parked his Mercedes Benz sedan, which was purchased used. Ladies in furs of various lengths and colors accompanied by men in vicuna and cashmere outer coats shared greetings as escalators lifted the opulent cortege to the ballroom level. Gail wore her full-length Chinchilla over a bejeweled, partially translucent, gown, which, after losing 15 pounds and three inches, she had made for the occasion; the color matched her skin. She wanted to look exceptional on this very special night. She was pleased to see uniformed, armed security in the cloakroom.

In parlors A and B, excited guests marveled over the giant U.L. of C. ice sculpture which sat above a long, double-sided buffet over an abundance of gourmet and exotic delicacies. A tuxedoed piano-led, rhythm quartet played standards in Jazz motifs. Eight complimentary cocktail bars were strategically located. Nathaniel Freeman had asked that a majority of the servers be Black.

Gail and Jerome presented their VIP invitation to the uniformed centurion. Gail whispered something Jerome didn't hear as they entered the private elevator which took them non-stop at maximum speed to the Presidential Suite, which was alone on the top floor of the world's largest hotel. *She probably wants to know where the nearest powder room is located,* Jerome surmised.

When the Gerards exited, Nathaniel greeted them. *Nate's duty station tonight must be this elevator,* Jerome thought. He was pleased he had worn his tuxedo. He had forgotten about attending the VIP reception, his first, where designer tuxedoes prevailed. Nate then introduced the Gerards to National Urban League president, DeWitt Dumas. Jerome was surprised at the brightness in Dumas' eyes, and his enthusiastic two-hand handshake. *He must be preparing to run for mayor of New York City* Jerome again concluded.

The Gerards with champagne flutes and delicious finger food, offered by polite servers from silver trays, stepped toward the substantial, double paneled, clear glass wall, and gasped at the breath-taking view of downtown Chicago. The stars, thousands of feet closer, unfettered by lights, twinkled brilliantly. The capped waves atop Lake Michigan created diamond–like tiaras before splashing against huge boulders transforming the clusters into a million drops. Buckingham Fountain, propelling rainbow colored streams fifty feet upwards and then falling into itself looked spectacular from on high. It was a dazzling view immediately beneath their feet.

"Look," Gail said, "there's *Johnson Publishing Company's* new building!" The signage atop the mini-skyscraper reading **Ebony** could be seen for miles. It was the only Black-owned building Downtown with the only driveway off Michigan Boulevard. Jerome felt proud to be part of the power structure in the third largest city in the nation, albeit only on the Black Hand side.

The bejeweled women in designer dresses, pedicured feet, painted toes, and bare evening slippers discussed upcoming benefits they would or would not support. Gail received several compliments on her anniversary gift; some privately thought the magnificent, flawless diamond was a bit ostentatious.

Most exaggerated the accomplishments of their grown children. Gail mentioned Michelle had graduated magna cum laude from Columbia, her Jamaican-born son-in-law had two masters from Yale, both were gainfully employed, and recent photos confirmed she had two of the cutest grandchildren in existence. Dana, a mid-ranking officer at Survivors, who had recently become engaged, had graduated from Howard University with a CPA degree.

Recent marriages and divorces were discussed, with equal fervor. Gail listened intently; both social events produced potential clients. Gail made mental notes; she would write memos on her pad, privately, forthwith. She would then give the leads to her associates, keeping only the most lucrative for herself.

The men discussed politics and sports. Mayor O'Malley hadn't bought a table in over five years; which was an insult. Jerome persuaded friends to introduce him to strangers. He discreetly whispered, "May we exchange cards? I have some confidential, financial information you might find valuable."

After lowering the piped-in music, the concierge played the three-bar chimes twice, ending the VIP reception. Thirty-five couples joined the 1,930 attendees in parlors A and B.

"Oh, I'm sorry—well hello Mr. Gerard," smiled the gorgeous young lady as she brushed against Jerome. Her flawless, honey-colored skin, dark brown eyes, and her perfectly proportioned 5' 8" body poured into an off-the-shoulder, embossed silk, bright blue gown made her extremely attractive. Her hair had been styled by U.L. pool designers.

Her name was Leticia; she had lunch most Fridays at Felix and Bea's, always with ladies, always fashionably dressed, often moving sensually through the restaurant. Twentyish Leticia also hung out at Scotty's occasionally. She knew who strivers were dating, and that Jerome was not involved, which made him a target…hence the bump when she was looking her best.

Gail noticed Jerome's eyes widen during the encounter. Gail caught Leticia's attention, as Jerome introduced them, and silently communicated, as only women can, "I know you now, bitch. If I ever see you with my man, I'll kick your butt."

Those enjoying free hors d'oeuvres and cocktails were awed by the VIP's as they entered A and B parlors. Many were middle management personnel invited by their employers. To be close to national and international Black celebrities, which were in abundance, was a memorable occasion.

The 40-foot high accordion doors folded, revealing 200 round tables set for ten with delicate flatware, eight utensils precisely positioned, and two stemmed glasses on spotless, white tablecloths, for seven courses. 50 tuxedoed waiters and 100 white-jacketed bus-persons stood nearby. Ten maitre'd supervisors assured superb service. The captain of the room was Black.

Four enormous ceiling chandeliers lit the great hall. Pleasant, attractive hostesses, one of which was Leticia, escorted guests to their assigned tables. The waiters and maitre'ds with gloved hands smiled graciously as they helped the ladies with their chairs and draped napkins across their laps.

A white tie and tails, 24 piece Black orchestra was playing *Sophisticated Lady*. "Our tables are closer to the dance floor this year," Jerome observed, "perhaps because we bought three." Gail knew better. The Gerards welcomed their guests, some of whom to develop the habit of 'giving something back' had contributed half the cost. Sarah and her 24 year old son were gratis, including his rented tuxedo and Sarah's new dress. After Gail was seated, Jerome found the Bronzeville Bootstraps Scholarship Fund table.

"This is your ultimate benefactor," Alphonso Major concluded as part of his lavish introduction of their program's visionary. Each of the eight scholars stood, introduced themselves, and shook hands. Jerome was impressed by their poise and comments. *These distinguished scholars will take full advantage of America's promise.* Jerome waved to friends continuously as he returned to his seat next to Gail.

The orchestra played an elaborate fanfare; the room quieted. Nathaniel Freeman and DeWitt Dumas walked onto the stage. Nate signaled the captain to cease service, and then said, "Distinguished guests, which includes all of you, thank you for your support. The proceeds from this affair finance our many outreach programs. Please applaud yourselves." Nate, with outstretched hands, led the acclamation. "This night has only two brief speeches. The first from the person selected to introduce our Man of the Year, the second from our recipient. Mr. Dumas, please introduce our first speaker."

DeWitt, through a broad smile which revealed teeth suitable for a toothpaste ad, with a touch of flirtatiousness, said, "You gorgeous ladies sure make your gowns look good, umph, umph, umph." Blushing sighs permeated the room, as if tall, physically fit, sartorially splendid, raven colored Dewitt Dumas was speaking personally to each woman present.

He then said, "Please give a warm Bronzeville welcome to a pioneer, a person who blazed a trail of prosperity through an economic wilderness filled with lynching's, overt racism, prejudice, and segregation, when being self-employed was as rare as racial equality is now. He owns a mortgage company, several radio stations, an entertainment complex, and many other enterprises. The man who started multi-state, New Orleans based Southern Fidelity Assurance Company over a half-century ago with only a dream, the consummate minority entrepreneur, Mr. CONRAD BEAUREGARD!"

Earlier, Gail said to the elevator's centurion, "Notify the Presidential Suite that Mr. and Mrs. Beauregard should be hidden, now." Nate's greeting when the elevator opened, allowed the Beauregards' to "disappear." DeWitt Dumas' exaggerated greeting validated his pleasure at meeting this year's award winner.

Conrad, after shaking hands with Dewitt and Nate on the stage looked toward Jerome, pointed a friendly finger over a broad smile, and mouthed, "Gotcha."

"What the...! Jerome turned to his daughters. Their overt innocence indicated their involvement. They had picked up their grandparents from O'Hare Airport. Gail was cheering, having successfully kept her secret. *Now I know why Gail wanted me to buy a new tuxedo. I am Man of the Year!*

"Time sure brings about a change," Conrad said into the microphone, nervously. He took too long to recall days gone by… "In the 20's, there were five of us in New Orleans who dared to be self-employed. We ate dinner together every Wednesday and shared the challenges of running businesses and meeting payrolls. Most times I had mixed greens, catfish, and fried tomatoes that cost ninety-nine cents. On good days I eliminated the fish and added two pork chops, which raised the price to $1.50. But tonight, there are so many successful Black business people in Bronzeville we can order two thousand dinners at $200 a plate and still have something left to spend foolishly!" The room erupted. Conrad warmed to the reception.

Midway through his next "Back in the Day" story, Nate gently touched Conrad's shoulder and elaborately showed him his watch. Conrad smiled, "but I was just making my third final remark!" He then said, "One of the reasons for your unusual success is Survivors Bank, one of the largest Black banks in the U. S. of A., headed by my son-in-law and your Man of the Year: Jerome Gerard!"

The coveted award was granted, in part, because of Jerome's generosity with business advice to all who asked, without cost or obligation. Those with more complex ideas were referred to Alphonso Major who offered cursory marketing information without charge. He and Alphonso repeatedly passed the favor on.

"Join me Babe," Jerome said as he stood and extended his hand. Gail waved Jerome away, and then acquiesced. After all, that was the primary reason for her beautiful gown. They embraced, shared a polite kiss and walked toward the stage. The Gerards and Conrad hugged; Jerome then turned to the audience and accepted a standing ovation.

Tears welled as Jerome bowed deeply, savoring the audience's appreciation. As he gazed into admiring faces, he waved and pointed toward those he knew. Jerome thought, *twenty one years ago I arrived here not knowing a soul. I was pushed into my first store, and then pressured into becoming Survivors' president. Daddy Beau is right: time sure does bring about a change.*

The audience sat down. Jerome, after thanking dignitaries, friends and family, said, "According to the U.S. Department of Commerce, Bronzeville has the third highest per capita income among African Americans in the nation. First is Fairbanks, Alaska, because of the new oil pipeline, and also because there are so few of us there. You know how we hate cold weather." The audience laughed. "Second is Washington, D.C., where many of us have finally been allowed to establish government and private sector careers. Third is Bronzeville because every time we exchange goods or services, a profit is generated, and every day we are doing that more and more." A standing ovation followed.

"One more major accomplishment is encouraging our next generation. Alphonso, ask your distinguished guests to stand. Please spotlight table number 34." The eight scholars stood erect, smiling slightly, looking confident. They were a dignified group, drenched in the brightest of lights, wearing tuxedoes rented by BBSF, attending their first formal dinner.

"Ladies and gentlemen meet tomorrow's leaders," Jerome said, pointing toward their table. "All are on their dean's lists, all are elected leaders on their campuses, all volunteer to help the less fortunate, all are the first college graduates in their families, and all have professional positions awaiting them upon graduation, in May, and they represent hundreds more." A standing ovation followed. "This is because of the tireless effort of Alphonso Major who directs the multi-city, Bronzeville Bootstraps Scholarship Fund. Thanks again, Al."

These seven gentlemen and one lady had come from impoverished beginnings. After years of tutoring, personal guidance, purposeful employment and broad exposure, they are now comfortable in the most sophisticated of environments. No doubt about it; A comprehensive education is the key to boundless achievement.

Jerome accepted the large plaque from the two Urban League executives; flashbulbs popped. The five on stage changed positions to accommodate the press. Afterward Jerome and Gail stood and accepted congratulations at their table. Many visited table 34, engaged the scholars, were amazed at the various academic accomplishments and majors, and then asked Alphonso how they could contribute to such a worthy cause. Alphonso passed out solicitation-oriented brochures.

Super star Nancy Wilson and her trio performed for an hour. Afterward the orchestra played topical dance music; the introduction of the Electric Slide was the hit of the evening. The attendees partied until two a.m.

* * * *

Why is Gail on the radio? Jerome's consciousness was gradually returning after being comatose in Intensive Care for four days.

"Charles Manson's disciple, Lynette "Squeaky" Fromme, attempted to assassinate President Ford," read Gail from the *Chicago Chronicle*. She saw Jerome stir, flung the newspaper, and ran into the corridor shouting, "He moved, he moved! Call Doctor Fleming, hurry! Thank you Jesus!" Sitting, Gail whispered in Jerome's ear while stroking his forehead with a cold towel, "Wake up Babe, please wake up."

An intern, a resident, and a registered nurse instantly appeared at Jerome's bedside. The resident, moving around Gail, checked the two hanging IV units. One was ingesting glucose for sustenance and Morphine for pain; the other, water. He also checked Jerome's oxygen mask. "Ingestion units' normal," he reported to the first Negro doctor-instructor at one of the best hospitals in Chicago, when he arrived. Dr. Fleming silently acknowledged the resident's report, observed the beeping screens, and then said. "He has a rapid arrhythmia. Inject one mg of Inderal, STAT, then do an EKG." The nurse handed Dr. Fleming Jerome's medical chart, he read his vitals taken two hours earlier. Jerome's heart rate was extremely weak, with a downward direction.

Damn, I don't use this much energy to pull up my garage door, thought Jerome as he forced his eyelids open. Where am I? Why are there so many bright lights? This couldn't be my bedroom. That's Gail, but what's Ralph doing here? Who are all these people dressed in green, wearing masks? What is this a Halloween party?

"What's your name?" Dr. Fleming asked.

That's a dumb-ass question. Why are these tubes in my arms? Oh, I must be in a hospital. Wow! Maybe I had a heart attack! And I don't even remember the ambulance ride! Jerome opened his mouth but couldn't say his name; he licked his lips but couldn't moisten them. He tried again, "Babe," *that doesn't sound like me,* "Ralph?" *That doesn't sound like me either but it is.* "What's going on?" *That took a lot of effort, and I still sound like I'm drunk.*

"Good!" Dr. Fleming said. "You're in intensive care at Michael Reese Hospital. What's your last recollection?"

That's another dumb question, but I'll try to answer. "I was running in the woods," Jerome slurred with his eyes closed. He rewound his memory and played it again. "It was cold. I had just felled a buck, a five pointer. I called Alphonso and Tiny as I ran toward my kill." Another rewind, new information surfaced. Leticia was in Jerome's memory bank; he erased it.

As drugged as he was, he knew better than to say Leticia's name. "It was cold," he repeated.

"That's right Jerome," Dr. Fleming said, "you were in Idlewild, Michigan on a weekend hunting trip. Nobody knows why or how but you ended up unconscious with a large, dead branch on your back. Alphonso and Tiny removed the heavy branch but didn't move you which probably saved your life. You were taken from the woods by medics and airlifted here."

"I'm right here, Babe, need anything just let me know," Gail said as she patted Jerome's head with a folded towel.

That's it. I'm dreaming. Jerome turned his head; he saw the diagnostic screens and smelled disinfectant. *No. I'm not dreaming. I'm definitely in a hospital.* Jerome moved his arm, reached for Gail's hand, they touched, and he smiled weakly through glazed eyes.

Usually, weekend hunting or sporting event trips by Jerome's peers, included playmates; but Jerome didn't have one. Tiny and Alphonso decided to surprise Jerome and had invited Leticia; she was delighted. Leticia "knew" she could hook Jerome over a weekend.

Well, I can't be angry, Jerome had decided, after the threesome reached Idlewild Friday afternoon, *after all, I have never made an issue of my morality, and they were just completing the party.* The weekend had proceeded as expected. The men went hunting, the girls stayed in the cabin planning the evenings around a warm fire, delivered meals, cool drinks, soft music, and romantic nights.

"Nothing is going to come from this," Jerome said, while accepting Leticia's passionate and amorous overtures.

"I know, I know," she responded. Jerome, without obligation, enjoyed being seduced by one of the best in the business.

The accident had happened Sunday afternoon. The three ladies, who had come separately, cleared away evidence of their presence and left before any emergency vehicles arrived. Tiny and Alphonso, after answering the medics' questions, drove back.

"Jerome, this is Dr. Kermit Mannheim," Ralph said as he introduced the last person to arrive at Jerome's bedside. "He's the best neurologist in town. I've asked him to examine you." Dr. Mannheim asked Gail to leave.

"Not now. Maybe later, but not now," Gail said. Dr. Mannheim glanced toward Dr. Fleming who, over his facial shield, approved Gail's staying.

"Mmm," Dr. Mannheim said as he examined Jerome's optical nerves with an ophthalmoscope. Then Dr. Mannheim walked to the foot of the bed and uncovered Jerome's lower limbs. "Let me know if you feel anything." Jerome, still groggy, stared at the ceiling. "Did you feel that?"

"What?"

"How about this?"

"No, I didn't feel a thing."

"Oh Lord, no!" Gail cried. She had watched Jerome being repeatedly pricked with a foot long needle in his feet, legs, and thighs, which drew blood. She ran from the room.

Dr. Mannheim said, "You're paralyzed from the waist down," in a low, slow voice with a German accent.

"Oh no, Lord. Not me, not now. I need my legs." Jerome asked, "Am I permanently paralyzed?" Then he immediately said, "Don't answer that."

"It's too soon to know," Dr. Mannheim answered. "We'll have to perform a series of tests and analyses before we can make an accurate diagnosis or prognosis."

"Ralph," Jerome said, "he sounds like I'm permanently paralyzed. Will I ever walk again?"

"There's always hope, Jerome," Dr. Fleming said, "but we're scientists; we respond to physical conditions. Right now, it's just as Kermit said; we don't know."

Jerome faded into unconsciousness as he contemplated life without legs. Tears escaped from his closed eyes.

"May I sit down?" Ralph asked as he approached Gail in the softly lit intensive care waiting room. Families were huddled together, taking cat naps, awaiting news. When Dr. Fleming entered everyone stiffened, and then relaxed when he walked toward Gail, who was sitting alone on a chrome and vinyl two-seater. She made room for her family doctor and friend.

"Paralysis is the lesser of Jerome's problems," Ralph said after placing his arm around Gail's shoulders and pulling her close to him until their heads touched. "Presently, we don't know the extent of his injuries; we can do a thorough examination now that he has regained consciousness. In addition to his paralysis, Jerome has a grave heart constriction; four of his five arteries have collapsed. His cardiovascular system is being artificially sustained." Ralph paused, tried to figure out the gentlest way to say what he had never been able to say compassionately during his twenty years of practicing medicine. "Perhaps you should ask your family priest to visit Jerome."

Gail fainted. Ralph summoned a nurse and had Gail taken to a private room. "She hasn't had a good night's sleep in four days."

Dr. Fleming mused in the doctors' lounge over a cup of coffee; *a decade ago I couldn't have practiced here, let alone teach, and Jerome wouldn't have been admitted here under any circumstance. He would have been carried from Idlewild by ambulance to a Negro Detroit hospital. The artificial heart pump hadn't been invented. In the 60's Jerome would be dead. Even though his condition is perilous; medically and racially, we are definitely moving forward.*

Dr. Fleming flushed his emotions, gathered his interns and continued making rounds.

End of Chapter Sixteen

CHAPTER SEVENTEEN

Dr. Fleming joined Gail while she was having breakfast in the hospital cafeteria. He said, "Jerome cannot know how ill he really is. His desire to want to live is essential. Your visits must be positive." Dr. Fleming then said, "Go home young lady, look better and freshen up before your husband sees you."

"Yes, you're right," Gail responded with a bashful smile as she smoothed her wrinkled, slept-in, clothes, "I do feel and look a bit tacky."

It was after lunch before Gail returned to the hospital. She had stopped by her office and suspended her real estate business involvement. She asked her office manager to drop off a daily summary of important activities at her home.

"Hey Babe, how you doing?" Jerome asked through slurred speech as he awakened. Gail was sitting at his bedside reading a book. "You sure are looking good."

"I'm doing fine," Gail, exaggerating sounding jealous, added, "these pretty nurses keep asking me if you are married; what should I tell them?"

"You know what to say," Jerome said over a weak smile. "How am I doing?"

"You're better today than you were yesterday, and I'm sure you'll improve even more tomorrow. Just concentrate on getting well and, with the Lord's help, it will happen." Gail worked at sound positive.

"It seems like you and Ralph are reading from the same page, Babe. I can take it; really, what's going on?"

"Just as I said, you're gradually getting better. Now follow your caregivers' instructions so we can continue living our lives together." Gail turned her head away; tears were flowing down her cheeks. She knew she had better leave before emotionally collapsing. "See you later, and you better be here!" Gail went to the hospital's chapel and prayed, "Lord, please leave Jerome with us a little while longer; he is just reaching his business apex, and has so much more to contribute. Amen."

On the third day of Jerome's consciousness, thin, six-foot three Father Paul visited. The IV units; nasal oxygen mask, heart stimulator, and several digital beeping monitors with red and green lines constantly moving and various sized numbers changing presented a dreadful visual. Jerome, inanimate, was breathing irregularly. Father Paul knelt next to Jerome's bed and began whispering Last Rites prayers.

"What are you doing here?" Jerome mumbled as he awakened, removing his oxygen mask.

"Gail asked me to stop by whenever I was in the neighborhood, anything I can do to improve your comfort level?"

"Is my condition that bad?" Jerome noticed Father Paul was wearing his prayer cloth around his neck, and had placed his portable sacramental kit on Jerome's night stand.

"No, no. Nothing like that, just wanted to stop and chat, to see if there were any messages you wanted me to forward to God." Father Paul decided to discontinue administering the Last Rites Sacrament.

"I Guess this is a time for honesty," Jerome said, "I don't have a lot of faith in the hereafter. Hell Father, I'm not even sure there _is_ a hereafter. And I certainly am not looking forward to living in a wheel chair, no matter what He has decided." Jerome closed his eyes and passed out.

"Just rest my son." Father Paul touched Jerome's forehead, gently made the sign of the cross with Holy Water, and prayed. He left a rosary and a small bible on Jerome's night stand.

"You still here?" Jerome noticed a rosary was wrapped around his fingers. "I know you didn't do this; didn't I ask you to leave?" Father Paul, with his personal Bible open, was whispering a prayer, kneeling next to Jerome's bed when he awakened.

"No, Jerome. I didn't, and I did. I thought you had decided to pray." Father Paul answered Jerome's first question. "I'm not, 'still here,' Jerome. It's been over 48 hours since we talked."

"Well somebody saddled me with this rosary because I sure as hell didn't pick it up. Where's Gail? She probably had something to do with this." Gail, who spent most of her day at the hospital, disappeared whenever Father Paul visited.

"You're more alert now than when we last talked," Father Paul said.

"Well, I'm a little upset." Jerome allowed the rosary to stay around his clasped fingers.

"If you're feeling anything," Father Paul said, "perhaps you might want to thank God for another day among the living by saying just one of the joyful mysteries of the rosary; not the whole rosary, you understand, just a portion. I mean the rosary is right there and you haven't bothered to remove it, have you?"

"Now listen, Father Paul, didn't I tell you how I felt about Christianity?" Jerome paused, and then asked, "How long ago was that?"

"Let's just scratch the past, my son, and thank God for today," Father Paul smiled. "I don't remember what you said; you probably don't either. As I suggested earlier, you might be grateful enough to thank the Lord with a prayer or two, just in case he has had anything to do with your improved condition. As you business-types always ask, 'what would be the downside?'"

"Ok, ok, I'll say a couple of prayers. Like you said, can't do any harm." Jerome continued to fondle the rosary. He held the crucifix between both hands. After Father Paul left Jerome prayed the Apostle's Creed.

"Did you put that rosary around my hands, Babe?" Jerome slipped the question into his conversation with Gail reducing its importance.

"Why no," Gail answered. "I saw it on the nightstand when I left, you were asleep. Maybe one of the nurses placed it there; you know how thoughtful they are. Should I ask?"

"No, that's alright. It doesn't really matter, well, not a lot anyway. If you feel like it you can ask." Whenever Jerome was alone, he prayed the Rosary. Even though he hadn't prayed in over thirty-five years, the words effortlessly returned. He recalled his earlier teachings regarding the power of prayer sometimes leading to miracles.

"His heart condition has dramatically improved, it's functioning without artificial support, and he's staying awake longer," Dr. Fleming said to Gail during their daily visit on Jerome's sixth day of consciousness. "His heart still requires monitoring, but we are moving him to the neurological ward. Now we are primarily concerned with his paralysis."

"What caused his heart to recover Doctor?" Gail asked.

"Medicine is a science, Gail," Dr. Fleming spoke slowly, "What improved Jerome's heart condition did not result from medical treatment. His arteries gradually reopened one at a time, without explanation. As they returned to normal we reduced the artificial stimuli until it was no longer needed. On occasion, even doctors have to admit that unexplained occurrences, sometimes called miracles, do happen."

As time passed and Jerome's strength grew, positive conversations with Father Paul, Gail, and Dr. Fleming caused him to look forward to returning to work––in a wheelchair. "If FDR could manage World War II, I should be able to run a non-descript, Black-owned bank," reflected his improved attitude. Dr. Fleming had ordered upper torso exercises, which included using a pull-up bar over his bed, to build the strength necessary to propel a wheelchair. Jerome insisted on lower anatomy massages––just in case. Privately, Doctors Fleming and Mannheim agreed the lower regimens were a waste of time, but if it made Jerome feel better, why not?

"Time for our workout sweetie," massage therapist Ingmar said in her deep Swedish accent.

"What <u>our</u>?" Jerome said as he looked up from *Business Week* magazine, but he really wasn't upset. For the last several weeks, every other day, Jerome had welcomed her visits. Tall, muscular Ingmar, with what must be the strongest hands in the world, took Jerome through his upper body exercises. After Ingmar completed pounding the upper arms and torso, she took a ten minute break, wiped away her perspiration, and then moved to his lower torso. Ingmar kneaded Jerome's waist and buttocks with her knuckles as if she were chiseling stone with her bare hands. "No need to be gentle down here, sweetie," Ingmar said. Jerome, as he was bounced about without feeling anything, agreed. He performed his arm strengthening exercises often when he was alone.

"Maybe we should have a personal conversation," Jerome said to Father Paul, who was now visiting every other day. They were playing a continuing game of chess.

"Anytime you're ready Jerome. Shall we call this a confession?"

"Oh, no, nothing that serious, Father. I just wanted to share some thoughts that have been on my mind for quite a while." Father Paul pulled up a chair and prepared to listen to Jerome's cogitations.

"First," Jerome began, "it was difficult becoming an agnostic; I considered it a character flaw to deny my faith. But, after considerable reading I accepted the concept." Father Paul handed Jerome his glass of water with a bent straw. Jerome looked into the priest's patient eyes, and continued.

"Second, it's pretty difficult to believe in Christianity if you believe in Science. I mean, the planet Earth is billions of years old and some form of life has been here over 600 million years. It's silly to believe God created Adam and Eve, then, after they messed up allowed them to populate the Earth with millions of people, of various physical demographics, speaking hundreds of languages, over millions of years, in every climate and terrain imaginable. Then later He drowned everybody except Noah's ark's inhabitants; and they all reproduced. By the way, where did all of the animal species come from? Then, hundreds of millions of years later, after Noah, his family and his animals had repopulated the entire Earth, God sent Jesus to die for our sins." Jerome paused, awaiting Father Paul's comment. He just stared at him.

"Third, how can Christianity be the only true religion? There are dozens, maybe hundreds of religions which worship other gods, like Jehovah, Allah, or Yahweh. Some even worship mystical leaders or idols. Some believe in the Koran, or Torah. Are they all doomed? Additionally, there are quite a few Christians that aren't Catholic; what about those?" Once again Jerome paused; Father Paul looked at Jerome with passion and understanding. "Come on Father, it's like believing in Santa Claus and the Easter Bunny."

Jerome's last comment infuriated Father Paul. "Tell me, Jerome, do you believe Jesus lived and was crucified?"

"Yes, but that Virgin Mary pregnancy bit and his rising from the dead…"

"Do you believe the air you breathe exists, without tasting or touching it?"

"Absolutely! It keeps me alive."

"If you believe the scientific fact you have just acknowledged, without proof, why not believe that which has been taught for almost two millenniums, and more recently to you by your parents and mentors, that Jesus Christ, Son of God, loves you and gave his life for you?"

"That's different, science is based on…"

"Not really," Father Paul interrupted. "You believe one because you want to, and not the other because you don't want to, and God, in his divine wisdom, gave you that right. Scientific proof of the Holy Trinity does not exist. But know this, a number of noted scientists believe in Christianity; some are even good Catholics.

"When you're ready to accept God's existence," Father Paul said as he gathered his belongings, "and you did once, my son, before you became so damn wealthy and worldly; let me know. I'll be around." Father Paul abruptly left.

"Ok, ok, I believe!" Jerome shouted after Father Paul; "See, I'm praying again."

"His heart is gradually improving," Dr. Fleming said to Gail. "His paralysis is permanent; there is nothing we can do for his damaged spine and vertebrae, they have to heal themselves––as his heart is doing." Gail and Dr. Fleming stared at each other for a long moment. "Of course we should continue the full body massage therapy, primarily because Jerome believes it is worth it. We are releasing him next week."

"How can I be happy to hear that my husband," Gail said, with tears in her eyes, "Will spend the rest of his life in a wheel chair. But thanks to you, this hospital, and of course, Jesus Christ, I am."

"Hear you're going home, Jerome, thanks be to God!" Father Paul said prior to the Monday Jerome was being released.

"A amen to God and all who He helped keep me alive," Jerome said. Father Paul was pleasantly surprised, even though Jerome's amen had an a sound as in afloat, instead of the a sound in always, and a second a syllable, like it was pronounced in Baptist congregations.

"Tomorrow is Sunday," Father Paul said. "I'd like to celebrate Mass with you and your family in the hospital chapel. Would you like that?"

"Yes I would Father, but shouldn't you hear my confession first?"

"Why that's a blessed idea, Jerome," Father Paul silently thanked Jesus for returning another prodigal son. "Then you can receive communion with your family."

"How much time do you have, Father?" Jerome asked.

"As much as we need my son, as much as we need." Father Paul prepared himself, pulled a chair with the back flush against Jerome's bed.

Jerome closed his eyes; Gail entered his room. Father Paul waved her away. "I'm ready now Jerome, we can begin."

"It's been over 30 years since my last confession…"

Gail, Michelle, her husband Claude Gustaf, their two sons, and Dana also attended the special Mass.

"Jerome, take it easy for at least two months," Dr. Fleming instructed. "We don't want you to experience a cardiac relapse. Gail told me about her preparations, and quite frankly, you'll be better off at home than here. I'll stop by periodically. If you exert yourself, its back in the hospital," Dr. Fleming said as firmly as he could to his golfing partner and friend.

"There are no diet restrictions because your weight is normal, just eat moderately. Avoid mental stress and physical excess, which means no work and no sex," Dr. Fleming smiled at Jerome and Gail. Jerome had not had an erection since his accident.

Jerome dressed in fresh clothes to leave the hospital. He put his most prized possession: his rosary from Father Paul, around his neck.

"This is Pat and Martha," Gail said at their home, "both are registered nurses who can cook; Dr. Fleming recommended them. I'm going to resume some real estate responsibilities. When they are not here, Dana, Michelle, and or I will be.

"These are your new digs, Babe," Gail said as they reached the second floor guestroom. Gail had equipped the staircase with a wheel chair lift, had installed fluorescent lights for reading and examinations, and remodeled the bathroom to accommodate a wheelchair. Their master bedroom was on the first floor.

"This is great Babe, as long as you know it's temporary."

"No doubt in my mind," Gail smiled.

"How much is all this costing?" Jerome asked.

"I've checked with the bank's personnel manager. The remodeling was on us, but its tax deductible. Pat, Martha, Ingmar, and Dr. Fleming's visitations are covered by your insurance. Your salary will be paid in full for at least the next six months. My responsibility is to get the documentation to Sarah monthly and she will do the rest."

"Thank you for these publications, Dana." She had bought her dad *Baron's, Banking Age,* and *Crain's.* He received the *Wall Street Journal,* and the *Chicago Chronicle,* daily. Dana slowed her courtship to help care for her dad.

"Tell me Honey," Jerome said to Dana as casually as he could, "what's happening at the bank?"

"Nothing out of the ordinary Daddy; everything is running smoothly."

Sarah had warned Dana, "When your father asks about bank activity, and he surely will, say only, 'everything is running smoothly.' Anything else might cause him needless stress and possibly lead to a cardiac relapse." Dana, as Personal Loans Officer, knew the bank was having problems.

Two days after Jerome's accident, Bridges, while grabbing a bite in Michael Reese's hospital cafeteria, after dropping off a client, overheard a personal conversation.

"Yeah, they brought him in yesterday––by helicopter, girl––they don't expect him to live."

"Who are you talkin' 'bout?" The practical nurse's lunch partner asked.

"Why Mr. Jerome Gerard; you know, the president of Survivors' Bank."

It had been four years since Bridges, because of his divorce, and Louise's party that had gone bad, had lost everything but his car and his broker's license. Samuel Stovall wouldn't represent him; Rachael Piernas represented Bridges' wife, pro bono. Bridges had moved into a storefront, and with one salesman started over. Bridges, on the cafeteria's phone, dialed Intensive Care. "This is Bryant Gerard calling from Detroit. I heard on the news my brother had a bad accident. What is Jerome Gerard's condition?"

"All we can say is that Mr. Gerard is in intensive care," the nurse answered.

"But I'm his brother, should I come to Chicago immediately? Does being in intensive care mean he might die?"

"Well," the nurse said, "he is in serious condition or else he wouldn't be here."

"Can't you be more specific?" Bridges said, mustering a genuine, but false, anxiety.

The nurse recalled a conversation regarding his comatose condition. She said, "If you're in Detroit and want to see your brother alive, you had better hurry," the nurse said. She immediately hung up, knowing she had violated hospital rules by giving anyone a patient prognosis over the phone. *Then he is going to die*, Bridges decided. *This may be the break I have been waiting for.*

"Yeah, that's what they said, he may die at any time," Bridges said to Oscar Jones, president of Westchester Bank, who was disappointed in not having been given Survivors' presidency, even after Fred Hawkins had been terminated. At Westchester he was President in name only; little more than a spook sitting in the president's office.

Oscar and Bridges plotted to execute a hostile take-over of Survivors' Bank. Oscar gave Bridges a seven figure credit line, far greater than he could credibly justify, and one which exceeded Oscar's authority. Bridges promised to acquire enough common stock, and with some board member support, like the Hornbeck's, would make Oscar Jones president, with stock options.

One week after Jerome's accident, a registered letter was sent to the 5,000 common stock shareholders. The message was (1) Survivors was in financial difficulty because of several large loans that were in default, (2) Jerome Gerard had incurred a life-threatening injury and his death was imminent, and (3) if any stockholders wanted to save a portion of their investment before the FDIC take over, they should contact General Acceptance Corporation (GAC), and sell their shares at fifty percent of par value, or $12.50 per share. This offer would be available for only a limited time. The letter was signed illegibly.

The letter also stated if the recipients told others, Survivor's stock value would drop further and the offer of fifty percent of par might be withdrawn, so shareholders needed to act quickly. Bridges knew the quickest way to spread news in the Negro community was to suggest that it be kept secret. The dummy corporation was established in Springfield, IL to keep Oscar's board unaware.

Some Survivor's Bank stockholders didn't know the stock's current value, which was over $50 and sold to GAC. Others, after confirming that Jerome was in the hospital, believed the rest of the story. They didn't sell their stock but withdrew their deposits from Survivor's. Several weeks into Baxter and Oscar's scheme Survivor's was experiencing a gradual but significant run.

It was over two months later; Jerome had been home two weeks. "Richard is here," Gail called from the first floor. "I told him he could have no more than fifteen minutes!"

"Man, who threw you under the bus?" Jerome asked. Richard's skin was ashen, his eyes reflected panic. "<u>You</u> need to be in the hospital. What's going on?"

"I know I shouldn't say anything, but we're having a run on the bank and nobody knows why," Richard said.

"How serious is it?"

"Very. If this continues, we will be forced into receivership. The only thing that's keeping us afloat is our chain accounts and corporate deposits."

"There's got to be a reason. Have you talked to our depositors?"

"No, but Chauncey has asked several shareholders without getting clear answers."

"Chauncey isn't chairman of the board, you are! Make some inquiries, engage our patrons, and find out what's happening. In the meantime, I'll make some phone calls."

Richard left. Gail came upstairs; Jerome's right hand was shaking terribly, stopping him from punching the phone's numbers. "Ok, that's it. No more visitors," Gail said as she unplugged Jerome's phone. She asked Pat to take his vitals, and then went downstairs to call Dr. Fleming. "Something is horribly wrong; Jerome is shaking like a leaf. How soon can you get here?" Gail asked, panicking.

"I have surgery scheduled this evening," Ralph said. "I'll be there early tomorrow morning. Let me speak to the nurse on duty. Pat, what are Jerome's vitals?" She gave him the information. "That's acceptable. Give Jerome a strong sedative. Stay overnight and monitor his heart rate every two hours. If it worsens, get him to the hospital. If he maintains his present status, I'll see him in the morning." Gail and Dana alternated, staying up with Pat. Jerome slept through the night without complications.

The next morning, "I know what the problem is!" Ralph said as he unfolded the *Chicago Chronicle* before Gail and Jerome. The headline read, "SURVIVOR'S PRESIDENT DEAD-BANK EXPERIENCING SERIOUS RUN." The story continued, it reported a confidential source and repeated what was in Bridges' letter.

"What time is it?" Jerome asked.

"It's 7:00 a.m. I came by early before hospital rounds."

"Get Chauncey on the phone," Jerome said to Dana. She glanced toward her mother who approved. Dana plugged in Jerome's phone and punched in Chauncey's home number.

"Chauncey, call Philip Hauser, and then get a copy of this morning's *Chronicle*. He'll know what to do. I'll be at the bank when it opens!"

"Oh, no you won't!" Gail screamed as she unplugged the phone again. "That trip might kill you!"

"If I don't show up at the bank this morning, after the *Chronicle's* headline, we will go into receivership. If that happens, I'd rather be dead."

"His blood pressure is up ten points, but under these conditions that's normal," Ralph said after examining Jerome, "He can withstand a brief trip."

"Oh, I see," Gail said with one hand on her hip, while pointing at Jerome, "he says he can leap tall buildings, and you," Gail's finger turned toward Ralph, "with only your stethoscope, agree! If my husband dies I'm suing your ass for malpractice!"

"In that case I had better go to the bank with him," Ralph said.

"Plug in the phone," Jerome said. "We only have an hour and forty-five minutes before the bank opens."

"Hold still," Gail said as she and Dana helped Jerome dress while he made phone calls. Pat unfolded his wheelchair. Dana got Jerome's breakfast: orange juice and toast per Dr. Fleming's instructions. At 8:00 a.m. Jerome's entourage left for the bank.

It was 8:45 when Gail pulled into Jerome's parking space. She and Pat unloaded Jerome's wheelchair and placed him in it. Pat, Dana, and Dr. Fleming, without being noticed, went into the bank's employee's access entrance. A crowd had gathered outside the bank's front door. Someone said, "There's the president; I thought he was dead!" The crowd turned toward Jerome.

Gail, forcing a smile, pushed Jerome toward the crowd. Security guard, Alfred "Bubba" Smith, rushed to meet them and cleared their path. "How is everyone?" Jerome asked as he smiled and touched fingers while rolling through the crowd. He was wearing a black, nylon Addis active wear suit, with white stripes, a black Kangol cap, and Nike white, high tops. He looked as if he had just left the Chicago Bull's stadium after a practice session. "Glad to see so many of you here; I thought we had kept my visitation this morning a secret." Jerome worked to project a strong voice and healthy physical appearance.

Short, svelte Philip Hauser, Public Relations consultant, always in a British-styled business ensemble, was inside the bank with Chauncey. Both had read the newspaper. Philip said to Jerome, "I have called the FDIC, and the press." His voice was tense but calm.

Jerome had hired Philip Hauser. He had graduated Northwestern University with a degree in Journalism, and a minor in PR. Philip had worked for Alphonso Major as a copywriter for several years and then started his own business.

"Good," Jerome answered, breathing hurriedly after his healthy, energetic entrance performance. "I called the board members and Keith Haggerty."

"Jerome, just sit there and look healthy," Philip said.

"Yeah, that's easy, just sit there and look like you're not about to die," Gail said.

"You cannot stay here," Philip said to Dr. Fleming, who was checking Jerome's heart rate. "It will make him look like he needs constant doctor's care."

"That's exactly what he needs," Gail said to Philip.

"Pat, stand near Jerome, but hide your stethoscope, and casually drop your hand over Jerome's chest," Philip said as he ignored Gail, "you will look like family." Pat was wearing jeans and a bulky sweater over her size six figure. Philip said, "Dana, go to your desk and act normal."

"I'll be in here," Dr. Fleming said, peeping through Jerome's office door. "Just signal if I'm needed."

"Gail," Philip said, "Change your expression to pleasant and confident. Stand on the right side of the wheelchair with your arm around Jerome's shoulder." After looking at the posed arrangement including Jerome, Pat and Gail, Philip said, "that's excellent."

"I'll make some opening remarks," Jerome said to Philip, "Then you can take over." Philip agreed. "Tellers," Jerome said aloud, "make no transactions until I give you the OK. Bubba, what time is it?"

"Its 9:00 o'clock, Mr. G."

"Well big fellah, let's unlock the doors."

The crowd rushed in and formed lines in front of four tellers' cages demanding to close their accounts. The tellers politely asked them to wait. Jerome, Gail, Philip, and Pat were on the opposite side of the bank. After all had entered, Jerome, through a megaphone said, "Ladies and gentlemen, I too saw this morning's Chronicle headline, and to quote a famous writer, 'the report of my demise has been greatly exaggerated.'" A murmur of laughter rippled through the crowd. The people in line relaxed a bit, and then turned to listen. Press camera crews were setting up wherever they could.

"The rest of that story is just as preposterous," Jerome continued, speaking with a robust voice and looking fit. "We haven't had any large loan defaults, and nobody is going to lose anything. Every account in our bank is insured by the FDIC." Jerome looked toward the front door as the FDIC executive was entering. "Isn't that right, Ernest?

"Take over," Jerome whispered to Philip; he then signaled Pat to slowly pull him out of sight. He was breathing deeply; his heart rate had increased. Gail started to signal for Dr. Fleming; Jerome stopped her. "I'll be alright, just need a moment…" Pat, after pressing her hand against his heart, and covertly measuring the pulse in his neck silently signaled Gail that there was no emergency.

Philip took the megaphone from Jerome, announced Earnest Frontenac's name, title and organization, motioned him to his side, and then gave him the voice amplifier. *Now*, thought Philip, *listen to the White Man*.

"Mr. Gerard is right," Ernest said, "no matter what trouble the bank has incurred, and we don't know if they have had any, your money is insured by my organization, for up to $40,000." A collective sigh of relief rose. "I have people coming here to investigate these charges. Once again, even if they are true, which we don't believe they are, your deposits are secure."

"Well, what about this letter?" shouted a shareholder as he waved Bridges' document. Philip looked over the letter, passed it to Ernest and then to Jerome.

"This letter is bogus," Philip said. "I don't recognize the name of the organization, and I can't read the signature. Jerome is alive and well, see?" Pat had pushed Jerome back toward the front; Jerome gave the crowd a vigorous two thumbs up. Philip continued, "There have been no major defaults, and before the Chronicle's headline, our stock was trading at

$55 per share on the OTC exchange. Anyone that has sold their shares at $12.50 a share has been hoodwinked; conned by crooks!"

"Mr. *Chicago Chronicle*," Philip said to the newspaper's reporter, "We know you hold us in contempt, but to print our president is dead leaves you open to libel suits. You'll be hearing from our lawyers very soon."

The *Chronicle* reporter looked for a phone.

As the board members entered the bank, each shook hands with depositors and introduced themselves. They then stood behind Jerome. Philip, through the megaphone, introduced each to the crowd. Meaningless questions continued from the press; more about the fictitious General Acceptance Corporation than the bank. The board members rephrased Philip's answers.

Keith Haggerty arrived. "Mr. Haggerty," Philip called out, "what corporation do you represent?"

"I am a vice-president with Mid-Western Bell."

"How much money does your firm have on deposit here?"

"Well over a million dollars."

"Sir, are you concerned about losing your deposits?"

"Not the least bit. Our relationship with Survivors' Bank has been excellent for several years. What I am concerned about is our relationship with the *Chicago Chronicle*. We will not continue to advertise in a newspaper that prints untruths."

The crowd moved away from the *Chronicle* reporter, who was moving toward the door. His editor, hearing that Jerome was alive had told him to "get the hell out of there".

The emergency had been dissipated. The crowd dispersed some offering apologies as they left. Positive segments regarding the bank and negative reports regarding the *Chicago Chronicle* were carried on the evening news.

"Put him in bed and keep him there for at least two days; no phone calls or visitors," Ralph said to Pat. Jerome was exhausted; the stress and strain of the morning's activities had been considerable.

Several days later Jerome sent for Chauncey Adams. "Here is my letter of resignation," Chauncey said immediately after taking a seat opposite Jerome in his study.

"If your relationship with our stockholders was more personal, they would have asked you about this letter before taking any action, then you could have brought it to the chairman's attention," Jerome said as he fingered the envelope Chauncey had given him.

"Yes sir. You're right sir," Chauncey answered as he sat erect.

"As I have repeatedly suggested, spend more time on the floor, learn our clients' first names, especially our shareholders. Do you have anything else to share?" Chauncey indicated there was nothing else of importance. "Now get back to the bank and manage things until I return," Jerome said as he tore up Chauncey's letter.

"Ye yes sir," Chauncey said while hurriedly leaving and smothering a smile.

Sarah, the day before her requested appointment, dropped off a valise full of computer printouts. Jerome had reviewed the documents; he scribbled notes on the papers and highlighted portions of loan contracts.

"Last quarter's daily cash flow was horrible. We loaned more money than was deposited; that ratio should be no more than fifty percent of deposits. Three of our middle management people quit. What the hell is going on?" Jerome sternly asked.

"That's why I asked for this meeting, Mr. G. Hal Hornbeck has assumed responsibility for approving loans. He is approving non-collateralized loans for his no-count gambling buddies who have terrible credit ratings. He also hand-carries Mr. Bridges' real estate mortgages to Chauncey and orders him to approve them. I advised Chauncey to proceed cautiously."

"Did you remind Chauncey that Bridges was no longer a board member?"

"Yes I did. He told me that Mr. Hornbeck, who was White, was, and that was good enough for him."

"And why are we losing our middle management personnel?" Jerome asked. "You know they are the linchpin to our future growth."

"As you know Mr. G., competition is searching for skilled Black people, and when someone talks to Chauncey about leaving, he quickly accepts their resignation instead of determining the level of their discontent and convincing them to stay, as I would do."

Sarah is more aware of conditions at the bank, and the remedies, than Chauncey, thought Jerome. The next day Jerome called Richard Thompson. "You and Stuart Sykes should spend more time in the bank until I return. Richard, you should assume responsibility for all personnel matters; be lavish in your praise, dissuade resignations. Talk to our parent bank about putting Chauncey in their accounting department without managerial responsibility. We should promote Sarah to vice president." Richard made notes. "Stuart should assume responsibility for approving all loans. At this juncture if equity and collateral don't cover at least seventy percent of the loan, don't make it!"

Business gradually returned to normal. Hal Hornbeck's loan requests were refused. Depositors replaced their savings after an apology was printed on the front page of the *Chicago Chronicle.* Midwestern Bell canceled all advertising in the *Chronicle* for two months. The *Chronicle*, to mollify Mid Western Bell and Keith Haggerty, became a major depositor in Survivors' Bank.

"As anticipated," Samuel Stovall reported to the chairman, "the FDIC found no discrepancies, which was reported repeatedly; Mr. Hauser saw to it. The Springfield, Illinois Company is fictitious; all they have is a mail drop and a phone answered by a secretarial service. The owner of record is a Chicago lawyer. The financing agent is Westchester Bank. They swindled fifty shareholders out of 5,000 shares, just enough to qualify for a federal grand larceny indictment."

"Will we press charges?" Richard asked.

"Before that decision is made, you and I should meet with Westchester's executives to learn what they knew. If they plead ignorant, which I think they will, we'll ask for a public apology, a return of the stock to those people who were cheated, and the termination of Oscar Jones; he's the culprit. If we find that others were involved, which I think there are, then we will probably prosecute to the fullest extent of the law."

"There are just too many people in and out of here," Gail complained to Jerome at breakfast. "Since your miraculous appearance at the bank two weeks ago, board members have been dropping by at will. This house looks like a flower shop. Sarah stops by on her way to work every damn day, and Dana won't leave without talking to you."

"Yes, but I'm still exercising, and Ingmar gives me massages three times a week, and Ralph says I'm improving," Jerome pleaded.

"Your nurses complain that they are doing more door answering's than care giving. Ingmar says she can hardly get through a massage without you checking the time for your next appointment."

"Aw Babe," Jerome smiled weakly, "each day I'm a little better than the day before," he argued.

"You can scrap your 'Aw Babe's! We're getting out of here so you can get some rest. We're taking a cruise. Now don't argue with me because I've already booked it. For the next two weeks we're going on the flagship of the Ambassador Cruise Line and sail through the Caribbean Islands." They hadn't had more than a weekend off in over fifteen years.

"Well," Jerome said, failing at sounding and looking pitiful, "if you've already put down a deposit, I guess we'll have to go."

End of Chapter Seventeen

CHAPTER EIGHTEEN

"We will need a double bed with an overhead lift bar, a special needs restroom, and daily appointments with your massage therapist," Gail had stipulated with the ship's concierge while making reservations.

"These ensembles are essential, aren't they girl?" Gail asked her personal shopper at Nordstrom's while spending several thousand dollars on she and Jerome; the commissioned salesperson ardently agreed. The Gerards were debt free, which made their rare indulgence acceptable.

The 75,000 ton, 300 yard long, ship moved effortlessly away from dockside. Tugboats, spewing 50 foot water arcs guided the vessel through the harbor. Yacht owners on various sized watercrafts waved bon voyage. The Gerards watched Miami's pristine beaches, and luxury skyscrapers fade, which was the only indication the massive ship was moving. The two lane highway and slender bridges connecting the seven Florida Keys seemed to be floating in the Gulf of Mexico. *Red Sails in the Sunset*, by Dinah Washington, resounded as two thousand vacationers put out to sea.

Smiling islanders offered tasty, rum spiked, bright blue drinks in tall, twin tennis-ball shaped glasses with generous fruit containments. Caressed by warm breezes, and slightly intoxicated, Jerome and Gail reaffirmed the intrinsic value of their cruise.

Their first day at sea, the ship's one page news digest reported Chicago had been paralyzed by a four foot snowstorm. "Your timing was perfect, Babe." Jerome reached over from his wheelchair and rested his palm on Gail's firm, smooth thigh on their private balcony, as she relaxed on a chaise in one of her new, bikini swim suits. Gail, stirred by his touch rubbed Jerome's hand with hers.

They watched whales spout tall streams alongside their ship; the exhibitionists amongst them brandished their flukes. Playful flying fish leaped out of their element, performed a Terpsichore and returned. When land disappeared, so did the graceful, gliding sea gulls.

At 8:00 a.m., the Gerards drank Mimosas and then played in their cramped, because of Jerome's wheelchair, shower. With strong, sensitive, hands he massaged Gail's soapy nakedness, and she, his. Previously ordered breakfast was served on their aerated balcony; more of everything was only moments away. After breakfast Jerome's concierge, via passenger elevators, wheeled him to the physical therapists' quarters for his hour long massage.

Delicious lunch buffets were available on the Pool Deck. Lunch in the dining room was also available for those who wanted a more formal dining atmosphere. A steel drum quartet accompanied a talented, attractive vocalist singing and dancing to reggae tunes. The exotic music transformed their voyage into a tropical delight. Honeymooners touched and kissed; their sensuousness increased which hurried them through lunch, back to their love nest. Older couples shared pleasant memories through glances and phrases. Middle-aged ladies, escaping their lonely and alone environments, conveyed interest in young, virile servers who would be available in the Disco Club late each night. Twentyish, sculpted, male and female singles aggressively flirted, realizing their dream vacation would soon end.

Gourmet delicacies served constantly threatened Gail's beautiful figure. She participated in snorkeling, shuffleboard, cooking classes, and a privileged tour, because of their oversized cabin, of the ship's inner workings. They enjoyed Bingo, trivia contests, and wine tastings. Jerome read extensively when Gail was occupied elsewhere. He catnapped in their stateroom, on their balcony, or beside the sun-drenched pool. Complete rest and mental freedom was positive therapy.

The Gerards' new ensembles gleaned repeated compliments from their peers. The beverage steward, with a large, gold plated, decorative key and chain over his maroon, mandarin jacket, suggested the proper wine to complement their selected entrees. Jerome had a rusty nail and Gail, a Bombay gin martini with extra olives before each dinner. Conversations, at the attached-to-the-deck, ten seat tables were always bland. Everyone had the same objective: to avoid stress.

During dinner the waiters, maitre'd's and busmen paraded to Caribbean music in colorful shirts, while singing and balancing flaming desserts on their heads. They also sang sentimental ballads from the grand staircase.

"Your raiment is exquisite, Mrs. Gerard," Captain Hans Dibbing said as he caressed and then bussed the back of Gail's hand; fellow passengers were astonished at the captain's rare display of affection. She was wearing her 'Man of the Year' gown. "How pleased I am to see Americans of color on board." Photographs with the captain were taken prior to being seated for their formal dinner, as was taken with every couple. Jerome found the captain's ardent attention toward Gail flattering; the captain's comment regarding Jerome and Gail being Negroes, thought provoking. After dinner, entertainment varied from renowned singers, to Las Vegas shows, to star comedians, in the ship's theater and various sized showrooms.

One day, while Gail rode a banana boat off the Cayman Islands, the ship's purser, Gunter, as was the officers' custom with alone passengers, chatted with Jerome. During a lapse, Jerome asked, "How many Black Americans take cruises?" The question resulted from the captain's 'Americans of color' comment at dinner.

"We have about one Negro couple per cruise, mate."

"Why that's virtually none! Jerome considered the small number an opportunity; he later asked, "What is your slowest period?"

"Why, the hurricane season from mid-October until December; what are you planning mate, your next cruise?"

"Oh, much more than that; may I review your most recent 10K and several of your annual corporate reports?"

"Of course; oh, I know, you're considering stock purchases, eh?"

"I just have an insatiable curiosity, Gunter. After I receive those documents, please schedule a meeting with Captain Dibbing."

"Yes sir." Gunter knew then Jerome was contemplating something important. Jerome made mental notes as they continued talking.

Gail wondered why Jerome was studying Ambassador Cruise Line collaterals, he said, "This is a very profitable business, Babe; they have ten ocean-going vessels that each net over twenty million dollars a year."

During their meeting with the captain after dinner's second seating, his personal steward served Dom Petroff caviar, wafers, and white wine in his large, reception area. Gunter was pleased to be present. "It's my home away from home," Hans said, as he proudly shared photos of his wife and four children.

"How do you get your uniforms so white?" Gail asked. "I could wash forever and never achieve that brightness."

"I don't know the laundering process," Hans smiled, "only the required result."

The Captain identified several constellations from his balcony; he explained how sailors, as early as 5000 BC navigated by observing celestial bodies, and earlier used compasses invented by the Chinese in the first century. The Gerard's vivid view of the heavens was only visible from the middle of the ocean. They had never seen so many stars at so many levels of brightness. Flaming asteroids excited Gail as they traveled at light speeds spatially. Captain Dibbing also explained how sails were positioned to capture ocean winds which, for millenniums, pushed ships in the desired direction.

"What did sailors do when there was no wind?" Gail asked.

"They drifted."

"Captain Dibbing," Jerome said, "according to your annual report your company promotes many theme cruises; sports, comedy, Broadway shows, religious, culinary, even Bridge. Obviously, there is value in special invitations to specific groups; but you promote no theme cruises for African Americans."

Hans stroked his trimmed, white beard, and said, "Since Negroes are included in the American mosaic, our theme cruises should also be appealing to them, yes?"

"But, as your passenger lists indicate, they aren't. Our American society generally ostracizes Negroes unless specifically invited; it's called segregation. The Black middle class would respond favorably to a cruise that featured our music: Jazz, and rhythm and blues."

"Maybe it would work," Hans and Gunter exchanged favorable nods. "We're always interested in attracting more customers; I'll mention your suggestion to our executives; thank you." Hans picked up his twin stem aluminum and cork pipe, and began filling it, believing the meeting had ended.

"Captain Dibbing, how much would it cost to rent this ship and crew for a week?" Gail's eyes widened; she was aghast.

"Oh, about a million dollars," Hans answered as if he were speaking to a child during a ship tour.

According to their 10K Report, that's $150,000 over fixed costs. Jerome asked, "May I rent this vessel the last week in October, for $850,000, with a five year option? I'll guarantee an 80% capacity."

"Sounds like something we might consider," Hans put down his pipe. Entertaining a prominent couple was sometimes required; but no passenger had ever mentioned a full charter rental."

"What would be your binding deposit?"

"When we agree on the terms I will wire your office $85,000. The second payment of $340,000 will be made within six months and the balance of $425,000 will be paid at least 60 days before we sail."

He's serious, Hans realized. He pulled out his pen and looked for something to write on. Gunter stumbled while getting a pad to his captain. "What are your conditions?"

"First; we would require firm dates and rental costs, five years out." Jerome pulled out a note filled paper. "Second, we would book all entertainment and passenger reservations. Third, since I am becoming a customer of yours, your company should deposit in our bank no less than five percent, or ten million dollars, of your corporation's annual profit."

Ambassador Cruise Lines, based in Australia, had deposits in banks internationally, but none in America; adding Survivors would not be a major undertaking. "You understand," Hans cautioned, "food becomes your expense; we will operate all ship's stores, bars, spas, the casino, and determine ports of call."

"I would insist on your managing your ship, your crew and your intended destinations. I would also ask that you reimburse us $4.75 per meal served to the thousand member crew, plus a surcharge for their partaking of the elaborate midnight buffet; is that acceptable?"

"Of course," Hans answered over a wry smile. *That's $150 thousand I thought he would overlook; where did he get so much information?* "There may be some slight modifications, but I think we have a deal." Hans felt as if he had landed a whale. The last week in October was their year's worst week. They seldom sailed with 400 filled cabins. 400 additional couples, spending an average of $500 on board would add $200,000 to their gross income, plus a rental fee of $850,000. "We will probably have a contract in place before noon."

"I'll wire your contract to my lawyer; with his approval, we will forward our deposit within 24 hours," Jerome smiled.

Hans summoned his steward and celebrated with a bottle of Moet and Shandon Champagne. A full charter rental during an unprofitable week would entitle Hans and Gunter to considerable bonuses. The captain returned to identifying constellations. Jerome, while being enlightened regarding the heavens, savored the expensive champagne; Gail hardly tasted it.

"Have you lost your ever-loving mind?" Gail whispered as soon as she, over a forced smile, after, with Gunter's help, clearing Jerome's wheelchair, closed the Captain's door. "You have just spent a million dollars Mr. Negro, renting a multi-hundred million dollar cruise ship!"

"Now Babe," Jerome said calmly, "let's go to the Piano Bar and talk."

"We need to go somewhere and do something! I was having a seizure listening to you spout those huge numbers! You may have just bankrupted us."

The intimate piano bar, which accommodated a white, baby grand Wurlitzer piano, with a musically gifted passenger playing standards, had three couples. Jerome ordered drinks. "Gunter was very informative when we talked. This ship has 1,000 passenger cabins, divided into seven price points. The lowest cabin is $800, a week, the most expensive, $6,000. By adding a 10% surcharge, because of our unique entertainment offering, we can average $3,000 per cabin."

"That part makes sense, but that's not what I'm…"

"Okay, Babe," Jerome said as he patted Gail's hand, "Our total investment is only $85,000, our rental cost is $850,000, add another $200,000 for food. "We'll budget $400,000 for musicians, another $100,000 for commissions and discounts. "That's a total of," Jerome added his numbers on his pad, "$1,550,000. If we sell only half the cabins we'll break even."

"Let me see those numbers," Gail said. She agreed with Jerome's math. "Now where is this huge initial down payment coming from, Mr. I-Know-What-I'm-Doing?"

"We have more than $85,000 in our parent bank account from the drug stores' mortgage payments and bank bonuses. Remaining payments will be made from reservation income. If more cash is needed we will find investors."

"So that's how bankers do it, huh?" Gail said further reviewing Jerome's numbers, as she began agreeing with his figures.

"It's called making money with a pencil, Babe. Plus Survivors' picks up a $10 million account, earning me a two percent commission!"

"That's $200,000!" Gail exclaimed, "Which more than covers our investment!" She threw her arms around Jerome's neck.

"And there's more potential income. Let's just pray there's a contract to sign in the morning."

Captain Dibbing's cable detailed Jerome's proposal, he added, "A cursory investigation revealed the Gerards are of significant, financial substance with high credit ratings, and no debt. He is president of the second largest Black bank in America. Mrs. Gerard operates a very profitable real estate business. Also, they are Negroes, which uniquely qualifies them to undertake the proposed project." It was the first time the Gerards' ethnicity was a benefit.

The Ambassador Cruise Lines' marketing vice-president had approved their proposal, requiring both signatures, but the day was even more eventful.

"Ouch!" cried Jerome. He turned and looked toward Arnold, his masseuse. They both laughed. Arnold prodded again, but with less force. Jerome felt something, albeit, ever-so-slight, which meant that the lower lumbar vertebrae, were once again sensitive. *I am going to walk again*!

Several weeks later, Richard Thompson called. "Jerome, can you stop by the bank Sunday, after Mass? We're having a special meeting and need your advice."

Damn, thought Jerome, *I told them I might be back to work soon, but they are hurrying my convalescence.* "Gail," Jerome called out, "we'll have to go by the bank Sunday; something's up."

"Can't it wait? Aren't you are still recovering?"

"Obviously not, Richard called; said it was important."

Gail opened the bank's inner doors, Jerome was surprised by a recording of *Hail to the Chief* and about a hundred well-wishers cheering and applauding. Even Father Paul, who they had just left at church, was present. A large sign across the back of the bank read, "Welcome home Mr. G."

"Please, no photos; he doesn't want his wheelchair dependency documented," Gail said. All cameras disappeared.

"You knew all along, didn't you?" Jerome asked as they stopped in the entrance. "I knew you weren't really irritated yesterday."

"Who, me!" Gail said with her hands on each side of her face, through wide eyes. Fresh flowers were everywhere. Caterers had filled one of the customer service islands with; warm, small Danish, elaborate cheese trays and wafers, chocolate dipped strawberries and fresh fruit, on white tablecloths. Carafes held cold orange juice; champagne and coffee were being served. Jerome gathered his composure, and then propelled himself further into the bank. Gail stepped behind to push; Jerome waved her off and locked his wheels. He reached down, and folded his footrests.

"Oh my God! He is going to try to stand," Gail said to Father Paul, who was close by. He made the sign of the cross and looked heavenward. Gail silently told Bubba to move in front of Jerome's wheelchair––just in case. Jerome grabbed his armrests and strained to rise as everyone watched while holding their breath. He lowered himself back into the chair, inhaled several times, then re-gripped and started up again. Each ascending inch required maximum strength. *If the pain worsens, I'll have to quit.*

Perspiration burst across Jerome's brow as he slowly moved upward. His developed muscles pulsed, expanded and strained; Jerome's hands perspired; his wheelchair's arms grew slippery. An eternity passed before Jerome was standing; his audience applauded. Jerome teetered, and then took several stiff steps. Everyone cheered as if they were at Soldiers Field and in the last ten seconds, the Chicago Bears had won.

"To the true survivor!" shouted Richard lifting his flute. The accolade echoed throughout the crowd.

"I knew you'd be surprised," Jerome said after collapsing in his wheel chair. While panting, he added, "Ingmar, Pat, Martha, and I have been practicing for over a week. Naturally I swore them to secrecy."

Father Paul bowed his head and offered a prayer of thanksgiving. He then whispered to Jerome, "Let us not test the Lord's powers any more today my son, please, just enjoy your party." Gail pushed Jerome through the bank as he shook hands and received loving embraces. He noticed a wooden ramp over his office's steps.

"That can be instantly removed," Vice President Sarah said, fighting tears.

"That's good to know Sarah, because that won't be needed in a couple of months."

"Are you sure you can return," Richard asked? "We need you but only if you're ready."

"Oh he's ready!" Gail said. "There's more bank traffic in our house than here. Besides, I've had about all the convalescing I can stand. His needs and he wanting to be spoiled are becoming indistinguishable." Jerome was looking innocent, enjoying the refreshments and attention.

Ninety minutes of accepting good wishes and hugs was enough, Gail decided. As they left, Sarah handed Gail Jerome's leather valise. "Mr. Thompson told me not to do this, but here, anyway. When are you returning, Mr. G.?"

"I'll be in tomorrow for half a day. I'll look over these documents tonight. Thanks Sarah."

That evening Jerome was shocked by an unsecured loan for $200,000. Hal Hornbeck was the co-recipient. It had Richard's initials, and Chauncey had implemented it. Jerome called Chauncey at First Security from his office.

"I'm looking at a $200,000 loan, Chauncey! You know we make no loans without a credit check; loans over $50,000 require a thorough background search, and a loan for $100,000 or more requires participation with our parent bank. This loan has no research documents, or risk sharing with First Security!" Jerome mentally re-affirmed transferring Chauncey.

Flustered, Chauncey spoke rapidly, "Mr. Hornbeck told me Mr. Thompson had OK'd the loan and that I should approve it immediately. Hell, he showed me Mr. Thompson's initials; what was I supposed to do? He's the chairman of the board! I couldn't call you and I had never communicated with anyone at First Security. I hope this job isn't in jeopardy."

"We'll see, Chauncey." Jerome, through Geneva, his new secretary, summoned Sarah.

"Sarah, payments on this loan are sixty days past due; please investigate it further."

"I already have, Mr. J., Mr. Hornbeck Jr., and Mr. Thompson approved the loan, but two weeks ago Mr. Hornbeck Senior removed his son's name from his accounts!"

"Geneva, call Mr. Thompson and set up an appointment." Jerome felt tired, he checked his watch. "Let Dana know I'm ready to leave."

The next morning Geneva said, "Mr. Thompson is out of town, so I asked his secretary to put you on his calendar as soon as he returns; was that OK?"

"Perfect," Jerome said. *Geneva is going to be just fine.* Jerome spent his half-days motivating employees, explaining new cost saving opportunities to preferred clients over the phone, and approving loans. His working, even from his new, battery powered wheelchair, was a significant confidence builder. Tuesday of the next week Richard and Jerome met. "Richard, did you approve this loan for Hal Hornbeck and Alfred Collins? All they do is engrave trophies, why would they need $200,000?"

"I did not! Hal asked me to peruse it and then distracted me the whole time. I told him this size loan could not be approved without First Security's involvement. He agreed and asked me to initial that I had seen it. I assumed he would give it to Chauncey for further evaluation."

"Well, Chauncey made the loan, and almost immediately the account was emptied; the business is fictitious. We have been swindled out of $200,000!"

"Then Hal is a thief!" Richard said.

"Yes." Jerome called the Hornbeck's company. "Hal Hornbeck, please."

"He no longer works here."

Jerome was shocked. "Is Mr. Horatio Hornbeck in?"

"Jer," Horatio said, in his heavy Texas accent, "I've been meaning to drop by, Boy." Jerome pulled the phone away, and thought, *oh no. You didn't just call me Jer and boy in the same sentence.*

"Does your son still work for you, Sir?"

"Well…no."

"So he no longer represents your company on our board?"

"Well… that's about right."

"Mr. Hornbeck, your hesitancy is troubling, we need to talk."

Horatio Hornbeck was tall with a beer gut. He was wearing a bright western shirt with pearl snaps for buttons, and a string tie held together by a silver bull's head with a large diamond between the horns. Wide, orange suspenders were clamped onto his tight Levis. He put his foot over his knee and hung his cowboy hat on his handmade boot. His smile showed more gum than teeth.

"Morning Sammy m'Boy, howdy Jer; well, let's get right to it. My son bets on any sport that moves, but he never wins. I didn't know how much he owed until two fancy suited, sour-looking sod busters came by my office a couple of months ago. I paid their wrangler $20,000 to save Hal's neck. I learned he had been siphoning from our bank accounts, so I fired him. I was trying to give him some executive experience where it really didn't matter, know what I mean?"

"This bank doesn't matter Mr. Hornbeck?" Jerome said while silently conveying to Samuel, that Horatio was a certified, racist.

"Heh, heh, heh, you know what I mean. We only had $100 thousand in this kettle. I left him one small account so that he wouldn't do something foolish. After all he's still my boy and does have a family, know what I mean?"

"He has exceeded being foolish," Jerome said. Calling him 'Sir' was no longer appropriate.

"Bless his soul, what's he gone and done now?" Horatio asked over a broad grin, as if Hal's error could be erased with a check and the trite phrase, 'boys will be boys.'

"Do you know an Alfred Collins?"

"Oh yes! That's Hal's bookie, the one I paid twenty grand to save my boy's kneecaps."

"He and Hal have stolen $200,000 from this bank!"

"Just how did you boys let that happen? What kind of president are you, anyway? Even Arthur had more sense than that; 'course he's white!"

"We know you are not liable Horatio, but your son can be charged with grand larceny. You did mention he had a family…" Samuel paused, anticipating Horatio ameliorating the problem; he didn't.

"I don't know what you boys are going to do about letting all that money get away, but I'm glad you have enough sense to know I'm not responsible. By the by, I've been thinking about selling my shares ever sense…what's his name became chairman and you became president. Never did think nig… Negroes could run a bank; this just proves it."

"His name is Mr. Richard Thompson," Jerome said, staring at Horatio Hornbeck. He looked at Jerome, wondered what his problem was, casually checked his Rolex and left.

"What's the occasion, Babe?" Jerome asked as he wheeled up to the breakfast table, seeing a Mimosa. The drink reminded him of their cruise three months ago. "Cruise!" Jerome shouted, "Damn, I've completely forgotten our commitment. I've got to get busy!"

"Not really," Gail said with a twinkle in her eye.

"What do you mean? We signed the contract last quarter; that's almost four wasted months. We only have 60 days until the second payment is due!"

"You were too busy," Gail said as she poured her second cup of coffee, and with a flourish added cream and sugar, "So I worked on the cruise."

"Now Gail," Jerome said, "just what have you done? You know you don't know anything about cruises."

"And you do, huh? Here's what's happened, you tell me if it makes sense. Samuel copywrited *Jazz and Blues Cruise* and the *J&B Cruise*, then we met with Alphonso Major and Philip Hauser. Alphonso said the copywrited names would make J&B Scotch an obvious underwriter. Philip suggested we send packets, with stateroom discounts, to *Downbeat, Billboard,* and, *Ebony/Jet,* for favorable press."

"Hmmm, I hadn't thought about publicity." Jerome sipped his Mimosa while eating his breakfast.

"I explained our cruise concept to Luther Wilson, that we had allocated $400,000 for entertainment and that he could buy a 10% share for $85,000, if he booked, scheduled and managed the talent on board. He wrote me a check. I opened an account at Lakeside Bank to avoid a conflict of interest, per Samuel's advice. I hired Chauncey as Reservations Agent, and Project Accountant; with First Security's permission.

Jerome gazed at Gail as if she was the late Madame C.J. Walker, the most successful African American business woman in America.

"Luther called known talent agents from his night club days, and presented the cruise as a week-long jazz festival for scores of musicians, annually. He hired three, nationally known stars; B.B. King, Joe Williams, and the late Duke Ellington's Orchestra; his son, Mercer Ellington, was now the bandleader. Agents said they would keep Halloween Week, '77 open until after our first cruise." Jerome had stopped eating. His chin was in his palm.

"Samuel's office wrote the contracts, Mercer Ellington's cabin demands were ridiculous, but we agreed to meet them. We used Luther's investment for deposits."

"Damn, Babe! You not only booked the talent for this cruise, you and Luther are already working on the next four!"

"After Philip's press release highlighting the main attractions, agents were pleading to get their lesser known musicians on board; gig rates went below scale. Luther booked 30 combos with 125 musicians, and a half-dozen seasoned sidemen. Luther came in under budget; he said the all-night jam sessions should be classics!" Gail's excitement level had increased.

"That's great! Now, how do we sell 1,000 cabins?" Jerome "knew" Gail had not addressed cabin sales.

"After accommodating our musicians in three bunk cabins, and our stars in suites, we had 900 to sell. We requested ship storage space for musical instruments and stands. Alphonso, Samuel, and I met with Reverend Jones' radio station. After we refused to let them book the whole cruise, the manager identified the top Black-oriented stations in ten major markets. Alphonso suggested we buy time, offer each station a 5% commission, plus their top disk jockey an upscale cabin, gratis, if they booked at least one hundred cabins in their area of dominant influence.

"J&B Scotch, has signed on for $100,000, and paid each station to tag their promos with: 'It's going to be a Jazzy-blues, J&B cruise.' Their brands will be the only scotch available, with a company rep. on board. We got special rates from Miami-based, Southern Air Lines by promoting them as our 'official air line.'"

"How are sales going?"

"We could have filled two ships. In New York City, Los Angeles and here, hundreds of cabins were sold overnight. For over a month we have been booked solid, with reservation payments in Lakeside Bank, the balances due within," Gail checked a calendar, "30 days."

"Wow, Babe, that's several months ahead of schedule!"

"You got that right! Reservations eliminated the need for additional partners. The $935,000 we owe to Ambassador Cruise Lines, which includes the cost of meals, is already in the bank. Luther Wilson owns

10%, we own 90%! We will gross over one million dollars! Alphonso wanted to do an ad book which would carry the entertainers' photos and brief bios, plus performance, and events schedule, but I told him he would have to talk to you about that."

"Are you sure I can handle that!" Jerome laughed. "You continue to speak for us, Babe. Tell Alphonso that he will receive 40% of the profit from the ad book each year. Ask him to negotiate with Cadillac to put a car and salesman on board, and to place an ad. Ask Samuel to contact a record company to purchase all taped performances, over 250 hours. Have Alphonso identify three of Bronzeville's Bootstraps senior business interns, who would enjoy a free cruise, while they sold previous recordings of the performing artists. You should also print a thousand full color, creative, 1976, J&B Cruise T shirts, for the students to sell; quadruple the sale price; the T shirts will become collectors' items.

"Be sure Alphonso, through Eugene Burns, makes Gusto our exclusive, 'official beer.' Ask Philip Hauser to compose a letter for your signature in our ad book as Cruise Director, welcoming our passengers. Chauncey will take reservations for future years at our current price; next year's rates, because of the unexpected sell through, will be 10% higher. That will give us advance cash and earned interest, which may eliminate the need for up-front capital in '78. We may consider doing two weeks after our second cruise."

"There are two more components, Reverend Joshua Jones has scheduled a Sunday morning religious songfest with an a cappella gospel sextet. Their cost was nominal, plus two upscale cabins and round-trip airfare. Reverend Jones also suggested a theme, 'An Economic Uplifting.' He wanted you two to explain how Bronzeville became the nations, Black, economic Mecca, in one hour sessions before lunch Monday through Friday."

"That's an excellent idea. We'll use sidemen to enhance the gospel group. Have Ulysses High's principal, Eric Hunter, work with Reverend Jones, and develop five program outlines including handouts. Principal Hunter should also monitor the workshops." Gail had been taking extensive notes. Jerome then said, "Babe, how did you find the time and energy to manage all of this?"

"I just imagined what you would do and did it. That which I wasn't sure of, I asked your trusted advisors."

"You do realize this will be your project for at least the next five years; with Samuel as legal advisor, Chauncey as accountant, Luther as our only partner, Alphonso handling advertising, and Philip as public relations director?"

"Rest assured, with that team, I got this!"

"You are really something special, Babe!" Jerome said as he smothered her with hugs and kisses.

End of Chapter Eighteen

CHAPTER NINETEEN

"We'll have lunch at Felix's new location on 75th Street," Samuel told Jerome over the phone.

"I'm looking forward to seeing old friends, even from a wheelchair." Almost a year had passed.

An abstract logo of F&B on a plate, etched in frosted glass on the front door surprised Jerome. Alphonso Major had also designed a full-color menu, and composed a brief, but poignant vignette highlighting Felix and Bea's 40 year history on the bottom of the inside cover. The menu was in full color in a 20" x 40" burgundy leather encasement with his logo embossed on the front. Entrées and sides were on the first page; daily specials and desserts, opposite. Felix had mounted in his office one of the carbon-copied, 8 ½" x 5" hand-written menus rubber banded on to cardboards used on 31st street, two generations ago, to remind him of earlier times.

"Well, there's 75's Man of the Year, and Bronzeville's most prominent lawyer, welcome home!" Alphonso Major said. Felix's new solid oak tables could be quickly extended to accommodate six. Leather booths lined the walls. Several strivers were seated at the B.S. Table, which still had high visibility in the larger room.

"I offered them a private room, but they insisted on staying out front where they could flirt," a slightly stooped Felix said. Those who didn't know, but knew <u>of</u> Jerome Gerard, introduced themselves. Jerome shook hands and collected business cards.

"This is the ultimate, Felix," Jerome said, waving, alluding to the recessed lighting, mahogany panels, carpeted floors, and wall mounted oil, lithograph, beautiful paintings of landscapes and waterfalls. "You have bought four star service and contemporary décor to the South Side!" Some of the paintings were emotional portrayals of Negroes in abject poverty, or suffering during slavery; others were nature scenes. Abstract paintings of Black musicians and dancers portrayed jubilation and New Orleans. Caricature portraits of famous Negroes, like Supreme Court Justice Thurgood Marshall, and Writer James Baldwin, were prominent. Sensuous Black female nudes were visually arresting. Oils in multi-tiered frames were enhanced by small spotlights. All were home sized paintings by African Americans with price tags.

"You and Gail could use some original, soulful art in your itty-bitty house," Felix teased. "I hired a Sister interior designer." The eight-seat, secluded bar was solid walnut, with a leather arm rest, and nail-head, leather-backed stools.

"What are those?" Jerome asked, referring to silhouettes of naked females in various dance positions on the bar's back, gold-gilded mirrors.

"Oh, those are *Pâttés de Mouche*," Felix announced. Jerome stared. "Well that's what she called them. Hell, I even wrote the name down!" Both men laughed. Soft music emanating through a multi CD, professionally installed sound system increased Felix and Bea's ambience.

Josephine, Rowena's replacement, wearing a blue uniform, which matched the tablecloths and napkins, began removing a seat from the B.S. table to accommodate Jerome's wheelchair. "No need Josephine, Mr. Gerard and Attorney Stovall are dining in our private room," Felix said. Its top half was partially frosted glass, installed in a four foot high oak base, and could accommodate ten.

"Well, our biggest problem is the theft," Samuel said as he finished his Jack Daniels and Coke; Jerome nursed a Rusty Nail. To assure privacy, Felix served the two notables. Samuel had ordered baked chicken with rice and gravy. Jerome was having Wednesday's special, his favorite; chitterlings, spaghetti, and coleslaw, with a side order of black-eyed peas. "I have enough evidence to file charges."

"Do we know where Hal is?" Jerome asked.

"No, but he'll surface once his father is served with obstruction warrants. Alfred Collins, with a $200,000 grift, has, like a cockroach, disappeared into the woodwork." Samuel cut his baked chicken and mouthed a healthy slice. He continued, "We'll have to buy Horatio's stock at current value, which means he will make a substantial profit. That scenario, while his son steals us blind, is ludicrous."

"Don't cut him a check just yet," Jerome said. "To digress," Jerome continued, "our bank needs to put something back into our community. "We should establish a foundation with at least five percent of our pre-tax profits. One percent should go to Reverend Jones' Positive Force U as interest-free investment loans for graduates to start their own businesses. Another percent should be donated to BBSF; Dr. Jenkins is doing a great job with her scholars. The remaining three percent will go to Black not-for-profits nominated by other board members. Of course all of this is subject to Board approval." Ambassador Cruise Lines, as promised, had deposited $10 million in Survivor's Bank in November 1976. Survivor's significantly increased profits by making many more loans.

"Those are excellent ideas," Samuel said as he made notes.

"Alphonso picked up this and all your future tabs, Jerome, so you eat here free forever," Felix said as he gave Jerome the requested duplicate of his lunch, to go. Alphonso had opened ten offices; his largest was in the world advertising Mecca: on Lexington Avenue, in New York City. He was submitting story boards for Ambassador Cruise Lines United States' advertising, which would make them his first international client.

Bubba carried Jerome into the Board Room; his wheel chair was left downstairs. Executive Vice President Sarah, wearing a St. John's suit with a new relaxed hairdo, sat away from the table.

"Let the record reflect that the July '77 special board meeting is called to order. Eleven board members, one felon and his conspiratorial father are present," Richard said; the warrants had worked.

"Now you wait a damn minute!" Hal yelled. "There are several felons here, and if these charges aren't dropped immediately, I will blow the roof off this poor-ass, colored, piggy bank!"

"Geneva, be sure you take down every word. Mr. Hal Hornbeck, would you name those felons present and their crimes?" Richard asked.

"You damn betcha. You nig…Negroes have been using this bank as your personal slush fund and these females as your whores! Loans have been made to unscrupulous characters for kickbacks, and expensive trips have been charged as business expenses. For instance, this bank paid for the Gerards' two week cruise which cost over $10,000. And I've never seen such a high-priced wheel chair. I also know who was on that fake hunting trip besides Tiny and Alphonso!" Horatio approvingly patted his son's thigh.

"You better watch your mouth, Honky!" Tiny said, glaring at Hal from his adjacent seat. Richard silently persuaded Tiny to remain calm.

"Once again, please name the felons and their crimes," Richard asked.

"Uh huh," Hal said pointing at Jerome, "You didn't think anybody knew. Well Hope knows everything and she's ready to tattle whenever I say. So these charges against me better disappear, or we are going to start a commotion that will bring this brothel masquerading as a bank to its knees!"

With Richard's approval, Samuel questioned Hal, "You still haven't mentioned any felonious criminals, but we'll table that for the time being. You mentioned Hope Jenkins; have you two been intimate?"

"Hell yes, but since she no longer works in this outhouse that's none of your damn business, now is it," Hal said.

"Were you intimate while she was working here," Samuel asked while making notes on his legal pad?"

"I just said that is no longer relevant."

"I'll take that as a yes," Samuel turned toward Horatio. "Do you support your son's accusations?"

"You damn betcha! He shared all the dirt with me; it's like the pot calling the kettle black, know what I mean? Heh, heh, heh. Why we wouldn't be here if we didn't know what we were talking about, would we Son?" Horatio, with a gummy grin, again slapped Hal's thigh.

"And have you, Mr. Horatio Hornbeck, been intimate with Hope Jenkins during her employment or since her departure?"

"As my boy just said, that's none of your damn business. There's a $200,000 loan you better erase or all hell's going to break loose, know what I mean?"

"That's the delinquent loan Hal co-signed for. Let's examine your charges individually. Samuel spoke with his hands apart and tilted upward, while reading his notes. "You mentioned felons but haven't named any; and then you accused the Black board members of making improper loans and receiving kickbacks; is that correct?"

"You're damn right. At least you boys can hear, by God!" Hal said while sneering toward his dad.

"Who received the loans, in what amounts, and when were they made?" Samuel asked in a soft, non-threatening tone. A slight smile crossed his face.

"Uh, uh, I can't say right now, but Hope knows. And she will spill the coffee if you don't do exactly what I say!"

"You can't answer any component of that question?"

"Well, not now."

"The only delinquent, signature loans on our records are those for your gambling, debt-burdened friends, you approved; were you paid kickbacks?"

"Uh, uh, I don't know anything about kickbacks," Hal muttered while looking away.

Hal's lying, but I need to stay focused. Samuel said, "Hope tends bar and turns tricks, which means she is not good at either because she does both to sustain her mediocre lifestyle. How often do you two have intercourse?"

"That's irrelevant, but her information is solid, believe you me!" Hal then asked, "Hope's a hooker?"

"You called her a whore earlier." Horatio stared at Hal, thinking, *he doesn't have any proof!* Additionally, Horatio felt violated because Hal had exposed him to a Colored prostitute he thought was "private stock," which probably infected him with several scary diseases. "So your charges, including your inability to name felons present are baseless. Another charge is that we have been sleeping with our employees, yes?"

"Hell yes!" Hal shouted. "Hope told me all about you Negroes; she's knows chapter and verse!"

"If you name one female employee who will support your charges, we will summon her before this board immediately."

"Well, I can't right now, but you boys know damn well what you've been doing." Hal had believed Hope's fabricated, exaggerated, pillow talk; the more she lied, the more cash he gave her."

Horatio was embarrassed. He thought, *Hal is sounding foolish without specifics or proof.*

"You and your daddy are the only ones who have admitted sleeping with bank employees."

"Now you wait just a damn minute, I didn't say…" Samuel interrupted Hal.

"You didn't dispute me Hal, when I declared your earlier answer as a yes. And Horatio, you have admitted sleeping with Hope. Shall we review the minutes?"

"Well no; that won't be necessary," Hal stuttered. Horatio dropped his head and closed his eyes.

"So that brings us to the Gerards' Caribbean cruise. You claim it was paid for by the bank?"

"Hell yes! The invoice was delivered to Sarah by Gail; now that's a fact!" Sarah decided to identify Hal's information source. *He is probably dating another 'chocolate drop'.*

"Did you see any checks or payment vouchers?"

"No I didn't, but why else…"

"If you had," Samuel interrupted, "you would know only the massage therapists fees off of the cruise invoice were paid because they were physician ordered. Jerome's motorized wheel chair is also insurance approved. Shall I have those documents produced?"

"Well, ah, no." Hal's voice had weakened, his eyes were shifting.

"And, a charge which has nothing to do with this bank is that you know who was on the hunting trip when Jerome was injured, yes?"

"Yes dammit; her name is Leticia!" Hal's confidence returned. "She hangs out at Scotty's and was Jerome's bitch for the week-end. He promised her a boatload of money. Tiny and Alphonso weren't sleeping alone either!" Hal said. Once again Tiny's glare toward Hal grew threatening.

"And just what does that have to do with this bank?"

"If I go public, it will send your squeaky clean president down the same road you sent Baxter Bridges, so don't mess with me, boys." Hal looked toward his dad who was regretting even being here.

"While your stealing $200,000 from this bank was a Class A felony, Jerome's personal…"

"While Gail and I were on our excursion, I told her about Leticia and others. She forgave me because she knows my life of infidelity is behind me. So you going public will have no impact on our marriage, or my relationship with Survivor's Bank."

"So let's sum up," Samuel said, re-grouping after hearing Jerome's startling admission. The code of the B.S. Table was to always and forever deny infidelities. "Of all the charges you have made, the only one that can be validated is a week-end liaison that has nothing to do with this bank, am I correct?" Samuel continued staring at Jerome.

"I can prove them all, just not right now," Hal stammered. "I know where the bodies are buried, believe you me!"

"When you have bank-related evidence, you may present it to the FDIC examiners. After which, we will respond and comply with the FDIC's ruling; do you understand the term, evidence?"

"Yeah, bu, but, wha, what about your charges against me?"

"Consider yourself under arrest. Bubba," Samuel shouted! Bubba instantly entered the Board Room's only door.

"The police are on their way," Bubba announced. Arrests had been anticipated.

"Now just a damn minute; I may have been a little hasty in my accusations, but you can't put me in jai!" Hal shouted.

"You criminals will be locked up and charges placed, pending a hearing before a judge, no sooner than tomorrow," Samuel said.

"OK fellahs, this has gone far enough," Horatio said as he slammed three checkbooks on the table. "When my boy told me what was going on I thought he had proof; obviously he doesn't. But I'm sure we can settle this amiably."

"Horatio, additional charges will be brought against you for slander, defamation of character, and extortion. You said before this board you agreed with your son's accusations."

"I said no such…" Horatio looked over at Geneva who was busy writing shorthand. "Well yes, but I didn't know he was making empty charges, know what I mean."

"Bubba, if either Hornbeck tries to leave, prevent it using all necessary force," Richard ordered.

"I understand Sir," Bubba crossed his arms and blocked the door. His stare at the Hornbeck's validated his commitment.

"Isn't there anything we can do to stop our incarceration? We came here voluntarily believing something could be worked out," Horatio said.

"That's a lie! You came here intending to blackmail this board," Samuel said. Hal's eyes were dancing, his hands were moving from his face to his lap then back again, like a frightened child.

"You can't be serious! Why I have my checkbooks right here! Just tell me how much you want! We can settle this! You gentlemen understand our dilemma!" Horatio begged the Caucasian board members for support; there was none. "What the hell is this, I gave you Nigrahs a hundred thousand dollars ––and this is the thanks I get? Why this bank wouldn't have opened if…"

"Nobody's going to take me to jail!" Hal screamed as he pushed back from the table, stood, threw his chair askance, and flashed a .22 caliber automatic pistol. He moved backward until he was flush against the wall. Several board members ducked under the table. Tiny leaned forward; his hands went under his blazer.

Geneva screamed and then peed on herself. She dropped her pad, held her breath, and squeezed her armrests until her fingers blanched. Sarah closed her eyes, bowed her head, and trembled. Jerome, immobile, placed his face in both hands, and in a low voice, prayed, "Please protect us, oh Lord."

"Boy" Horatio shouted, "What the hell are you doing; have you gone crazy? Put that damn thing away. All you're doing is making bad matters worse!"

In 1962, with a professional baseball career promised, young, fit, Hal, under requested doctor's orders, was committed to a country club type mental recovery center to avoid being drafted for the Viet Nam War. He received a deferment and was then expected to be released a short time later. During his internment three Negro male orderlies regularly sexually assaulted Hal; they made him their "girl." Under threat of reprisal Hal didn't tell a soul, which led to incoherent speech, a mental breakdown, increased internment, and ended his ability to play ball. After his eventual release, for several years he could not perform sexually. He now feared being confined more than death itself.

"Get the hell out of the way, Flubba, or whatever your name is!" Hal shouted waving his pistol in Bubba's direction. Bubba knew his bullet-resistant, chest protector would slow a .22 bullet allowing him to shoot

Hal with his .22 pistol automatic. "I said get away from that door!" Bubba stood firm, placing his pistol in his hand, while removing the safety.

"How many of us will you kill, Hal?" Samuel asked calmly from the conference table's other side. His voice was soothing, but his mind was racing. "Whenever you point a gun toward an individual the law presumes you are prepared to use it, so assault and attempted murder may be added to your charges." Hal's eyes were darting between Samuel and Bubba. His pistol with his finger on the trigger was continuously being pointed at various individuals. Hal was mumbling words no one understood.

"There are twelve of us in this room, Hal. If shooting Bubba doesn't instantly incapacitate him, he will certainly kill you. If your gun empties while shooting us, we will attack you before you can replace your clip; even if you have another. If you fire your gun, even once, our bank staff will hear it and activate the alarm. And remember, the police are already in route. If however, you drop your gun, we can solve our problems like adults," Samuel said.

The gun dropped to Hal's side then up again, his body jerked. "I said I'm not going to jail!" Hal jammed his pistol against his temple.

"Now Son, calm down, things aren't that bad, these are reasonable people. I'm sure we can work something out, can't we gentlemen?" Hal kept his finger on the trigger. His eyes squinted toward the right side of his head, gritting his teeth as he anticipated excruciating pain.

"The first thing that has to happen, is that gun has to disappear. Then anything is possible," Richard said, while staring at Hal.

"See? They understand. These gentlemen know what you are going through. They don't want you to shoot them or yourself." Horatio gradually stood next to Hal and placed his index finger behind the trigger; preventing Hal from firing his gun. Hal and Horatio sank to the floor, Hal was wringing wet, breathing hurriedly through his mouth; his finger still on the trigger.

"Please take the gun away from your head Son, before you hurt yourself!" Hal dropped the gun, placed his head over his knees and bawled. Bubba rushed over, secured the gun, threw Hal into a chair like a laundry bag, and handcuffed him around its back support.

Jerome gave thanks to the Lord. Sighs of relief were audible throughout the room. Tiny laid his .38 revolver on the conference table. With smooth, practiced movements Tiny flipped out the five-round loaded cylinder, emptied it, and then returned it. While staring at Hal, Tiny holstered his now empty weapon. The message was clear. If Hal had fired once Tiny would have instantly shot Hal several times.

"Gentlemen," Horatio pleaded with tears flowing, realizing how close Hal had come to dying, "I realize how terrible my boy's actions have been. I will do whatever it takes to instantly resolve this incident. But please don't send my boy to jail. He'll never come out alive; don't you see how frail he is?"

Hal, handcuffed in the chair, had lifted his head slightly while continuing to sob.

"Let's all think for a moment," Richard said. Everyone was recovering from various sheltered positions; some were straightening their suits while surfacing from under the table. "If any one person wants to press charges against Hal Hornbeck we will; he pointed his gun at all of us. If nobody wants to press charges, then his extreme behavior will be ignored." African American empathy prevailed; the Caucasians followed their lead. No one wanted to prosecute the mentally deranged Hal Hornbeck. Richard then responded to Horatio's plea. "You are not going to turn us into criminals! Samuel, establish the conditions under which the Hornbecks can settle their charges, and this incident without being arrested."

After several minutes Samuel said, "Mr. Hornbeck, write a check for $200,000 to cover the embezzlement, sell your stock for one dollar to the bank as punitive damages, sign a statement acknowledging Hal's behavior, and removing him from our board, exonerate all board members from any wrong doing, and we will drop all charges."

Horatio expressed relief and gratitude.

"The police are here Mr. Thompson," Geneva said holding her hand over the phone's mouthpiece.

"Tell them the emergency has been resolved and that I'll be down momentarily. Bubba, stay with Attorney Stovall until he releases this rich, white trash." Hal looked mentally imbalanced as he sat in his chair, handcuffed.

"You sick son-of-a-bitch!" Sarah said as she mightily slapped Hal; she then left the boardroom. The board members were flabbergasted. Sarah had never shown anger or frustration. Geneva, with skirt stains visible, left to prepare the documents for Horatio's signatures; there were a few snickers at Geneva's wet skirt on the bank floor, which she ignored. Samuel suggested that Bubba take the Hornbecks to Jerome's original lower level office until his documents had been signed.

"We have before us the disposition of preferred stock, valued at $193,750. How should it be disbursed?" Richard asked as he resumed the board meeting, without Bubba, Geneva, Sarah, Hal and Horatio Hornbeck.

"Mr. Chairman," Jerome said. "I move the stock be divided into twelfths and sold to board members and affiliates at its original value."

"Don't you mean into elevenths?" Richard asked.

"No Sir. I also move that the twelfth block be sold to Sarah, who has been with us since the beginning, under compatible purchasing terms."

"Without objection, so moved," Richard said.

Monday morning, Jerome rolled in with Dana pushing and Bubba close behind, carrying his walker. Each day Jerome's ability to stand and walk gradually improved. Dr. Fleming, after determining Jerome's heart was now eighty percent efficient, had extended Jerome's workday to six hours, with the stipulation that he take a half hour nap after a nutritious lunch.

"Geneva, we have a lot of work to do."

"I'm ready Mr. G." Geneva said, opening her steno pad.

"First, let's get Sarah in here." Sarah's stock purchase and her recent raise had given her a significant windfall. "What changes do you recommend as we go forward, Sarah?"

"First, we should promote Helen Scott to vice president, customer service, with a 15% raise. She is long overdue. Then we should resume our in-house training sessions that were discontinued during your absence. We have one middle-management vacancy in the loan department which I would like thirty days to fill."

"Sounds like a plan, Sarah. Geneva, contact Felix Long, get the name of his interior designer; also call Lonnie Blackman, of Blackman Interiors and Design. We have Mr. Thompson's approval to renovate our boardroom. The first rule of spending serious dollars is, 'always get at least two bids from reliable sources.' This will be your project, but keep me informed." Geneva was delighted to have additional responsibilities.

"Gail," Jerome said, over breakfast, "Please call Ambassador Cruise Lines and place a security deposit for our next cruise."

"Our profit from your first cruise exceeded projections. More than that, you have confirmed your credit worthiness. Your stated written intentions are collateral enough; your charter cruise rental payment need be paid no more than 90 days before sailing." The J&B Cruise had become investment free while generating over a $1 million profit for the Gerard's, annually.

"Would you consider a kindness?" Jerome, taking the phone, asked the cruise line executive. "In reviewing your annual report I noticed you contribute too many not-for-profits internationally, but none in the United States. Since African Americans are increasing as your customers, perhaps you might consider the Bronzeville Bootstraps Scholarship Fund for an annual contribution."

"Let me look into it; anything else?

"No sir, that's all."

It was October, '77; the second J&B Cruise was loading. Standing with his walker close by, Jerome, Gail, and Captain Dibbing, who had requested the assignment, greeted passengers as they boarded. Philip Hauser had arranged for a quartet to play up-tempo jazz while passengers boarded to put them in the right mood; it was working. African Americans, Caucasians, and Asians, riffed and boogied as they boarded. Philip had also secured dozens of vintage media jazz and blues performances. They could be played on a special TV channel in each cabin. Philip, because they would be at sea on Halloween, had secured scores of costumes for crewmembers to wear. Current headliners were; the late Count Basie's orchestra, Sarah Vaughn, and Dorothy Donnegan.

"Our public relations vice-president asked me to deliver a letter Mr. Gerard, whenever you're ready," Captain Dibbing said between greeting passengers.

"After we get underway," Jerome said.

"During your nation's history," the Australian based corporate letter began, "you fought a war to end slavery which was replaced by severe segregation and thousands of lynching's that went unpunished. We support your efforts to erase those horrific persecutions through career development and education. Beginning in January, 1978, Ambassador Cruise Lines will contribute one million dollars, each year, for ten years to the BBSF. We will also employ, during the summers, one BBSF scholar on each of our ten ships as middle management interns." Jerome mentally jumped up and clicked his heels; a new industry had been penetrated.

Late one night, while sailing through the tropics, wearing only their sheerest wraps, Jerome and Gail gazed upward from their private balcony, watching flaming meteors race through the night. They were lounging on a two-person chaise, sipping champagne. Gail had her bare leg draped over Jerome's, and her head on his shoulder. Her perfume, a gift from Captain Dibbing, awakened Jerome's senses; his loins stirred. He reached for Gail's hand and placed it in his lap; "Oh my God!" Gail exclaimed.

It had only been two years but it seemed like decades since she had even anticipated making love. She looked into Jerome's eyes; he, with an excited head shake and grin, affirmed the intercourse probability. Gail gently stroked his hardening member; she said, "Follow me." Inside, both became nude; Gail straddled Jerome in their bed.

"Let me do this Honey, you just lay there." The insertion was joyously painful. Gail's movements gradually increased as the pleasurable pain subsided and the sensual sensations flowed throughout her body.

"Oh Babe, this feels so good," Jerome moaned; his organ pulsated. He stirred precious little, much less than he wanted. Jerome's hands cupped Gail's firm, round buttocks and pulled her into him to feel her increasing gyrations. Gail placed her hands over Jerome's shoulders, bringing her closer. Jerome's grunts and groans grew louder until climax. Gail's implosion followed. Jerome fell into a deep sleep.

Gail returned to their balcony wearing only an afterglow. She stood with her legs parted, with the night's wet wind sluicing over her naked body. While their vessel parted the ocean, Gail ran her fingers through her hair and gazed heavenward. She fantasized racing through the stratosphere astride an asteroid.

End of Chapter Nineteen

CHAPTER TWENTY

While on their second J&B cruise, Jerome told Gail about the Cayman Island account. She was amazed at the accumulation of principal and interest earned over 20 years. She realized when Jerome had "risked everything" to save Survivors Bank, everything was not at risk. Gail lobbed shallow, snide barbs at Jerome criticizing his long-term skullduggery, but a striking, unique; cocktail-type diamond ring from the ship's jewelry boutique erased the affront. Captain Dibbing authorized a deep discount for Gail's gift.

Jerome's ambition to own a chain of drug stores, and his ability to successfully manage a bank were major accomplishments, but the BBSF had become Jerome's life's mission; he donated yearly. Watching poverty stricken students' graduate college and move into challenging careers made him feel born again. Jerome, seated prominently at commencement ceremonies was always introduced as the visionary of the BBSF program.

After 12 years of graduations, eight hundred, proud BBSF alumni were donating 2 percent of their take-home pay. Wealthy individuals and organizations, because of Jerome's continuous solicitations, made annual contributions to the well-funded multi-city institute.

Ambassador Cruise Line's generous contributions allowed BBSF to buy two large, empty public schools; one each in Bronzeville's and Harlem's most dire neighborhoods, for nominal amounts. With their own schools, BBSF now had the awesome responsibility of helping every student succeed.

After newly designed interiors by Architect, Bryan Gerard, reconstructed by Black general contractors, and furnished by Lonnie Blackman, BBSF's two schools accommodated students from pre kindergarten through 12th grade, at no cost. Qualified teachers were paid above average salaries with lucrative incentives based upon how many students' achieved Honor Roll status; the minimum number of Honor Roll achievers was 50 percent. Principals were ultimately responsible; they encouraged and evaluated teachers' performances.

Two hundred seventy-five students per school were selected to fill 22 classes, each with 25 students; including two levels below Kindergarten. The two 12th grades remained vacant; BBSF needed at least one year to find compatible jobs and develop above average high school graduates. Selected children would be awarded an excellent education, plus preparatory employment through high school and college, culminating with a guaranteed professional position—all free. If private education tuition had been charged, the total cost would have exceeded $500,000, per student.

Each year thereafter, only fifty, 4 year olds would be admitted to two pre-K classes. The selection process was accomplished through applicants' names being drawn from a spinning drum containing hundreds of prospects. Some fortunate parents knelt and prayed —a few passed out. Before their name was placed in the drum, each parent pledged to encourage and support their children's education, discourage gang participation and drug use, and keep them in clean and pressed uniforms.

The schools were islands of positive study and impactful instruction in seas of turmoil. High tech security systems, supplemented by armed resource officers, monitored the schools 24/7. Bronzeville's Blackstone Rangers, and Harlem's Blood Brothers, for a nominal fee, disciplined BBSF building or student molesters. There were no repeated offenses.

Gymnasiums, music rooms, and swimming pools, served as classes, recreation, and practice facilities. Music; instrumental, composition, and voice; all dance forms; drama, art, foreign languages including Asian and Arabic; were electives. The core subjects; math, English, and science were emphasized; physical education, nutrition, and money management were required, but football, and baseball were not available. Male and female Basketball was played as an intramural sport. Analytical and advanced college-credited classes were offered to above average students. Innate writers were encouraged. Country club activities, such as; bridge, chess, tennis and golf on simulated courses, were encouraged, extra-curricular activities.

Dedicated teachers, most with Master's Degrees, worked nine hour days, plus one Saturday a month. Each student was assigned an advisor for their 15 years. A psychologist and a registered nurse were available eight hours each week-day. Teachers were readily available for student and/or parent consultations. Grading papers was done at home. The schools were open from 5:30 a.m. until 7:30 p.m. Parents volunteered part-time; they learned from experts how to inspire children. Hot breakfasts, healthful lunches and snacks were provided six days a week.

Fifty minute classes were scheduled from 7:00 a.m. until 3:00 p.m. with 30 minutes for lunch. Libraries and computer labs were open after classes as study and research rooms. Saturdays, from 9:00 a.m. until 2:00 p.m., school was open for make-up work, behavioral consequences, recreation, or to accomplish extra credit assignments. Upper grade students and teachers tutored those who needed help. Expulsion, which was devastating to the family, resulted whenever the drug-free environment policies were violated, or there was repeated disruptive, or bullying misbehavior.

The school year lasted from Tuesday after Labor Day through the end of June. High school juniors and seniors, to improve their foreign language skills, lived overseas one summer month, each year. Aside from class assignments, students were required to read and write an evaluation of at least one non-fiction book a month on subjects of personal interest. The high school graduation rate was 95% with over 80% Honor Roll scholars. Because of their career selection and internships, each student's major and college were determined prior to high school graduation.

A paper, which covered BBSF's students' academic accomplishments in secondary grades, written by Dr. Jenkins, was printed in educational periodicals annually. It detailed the rankings of BBSF students in core subjects nationally and internationally. No longer could educators' claim students from underprivileged, or dysfunctional homes couldn't learn. The BBSF proved the quality of children's education is determined by the students, teachers, administrators, and parents. Conditions, if not salaries, and incentives, could be duplicated. Governing boards, who could afford to, allowed several urban city public schools to adopt some of BBSF's practices.

Corporations were encouraged by Jerome to fund BBSF college under-graduates while they earned masters and doctorates in every field including medicine and law. The only obstacle to scholars achieving the highest degrees was their ability and dedication. BBSF alumni were making outstanding contributions and achievements in all disciplines; the racial benefit was enormous.

The twelve board members of Survivors' Bank gathered for their April 1980 meeting. Fresh flowers had become the norm, thanks to Executive Vice President Sarah Marshall.

The newly painted beige walls of the board room held oil portraits of Milton Levine and Richard Thompson. Plush brown carpet supported fourteen tan spring-back leather armchairs, and an oblong, walnut table. Several chairs graced the back wall. The adjustable, florescent lighting was recessed.

Philip Hauser had recommended the boardroom wall nearest the bank become a Bronzeville historical landmark by creating a blended, one hundred-by-ten foot oil mural depicting historical and contemporary Black notables. Geneva had commissioned professional artist and teacher Amelio Cruz to manage the project. Prominent persons were recommended by a Community committee, approved by Mr. Cruz. The artists were talented Black high school and college students who vied to contribute. The mural began with Negro Revolutionary War hero Crispus Attucks; the last image on the wall was President Barack Obama. The frieze ended with space for several additional achievers. A brass plaque centered on top of the outsized painting read,

**"This mural is dedicated to
the African Americans who have made metaphorical
contributions to our nation's constant improvement."**

Enormous emotion emitted from the creative, panoramic representation. One high school teacher, while exposing his class, remarked, "This work, despite years of oppression, moves consistently forward."

In 1979, U.S. Representative John Conyers and U.S. Senator Edward Brooke, African-Americans, presented a congressional bill to honor Dr. King with a national holiday. President Ronald Reagan in 1983 signed it.

"We have several important items on our agenda, first are our plans to replace this 90 year old building. Jerome, how are they developing?" Richard asked.

"Our next meeting with Gerard and Associates is scheduled for May 15th. Construction on the new building was scheduled to start in June, but there may be a delay."

"Why?" Samuel asked.

"Thanks to our board, particularly our newest member Keith Haggerty, we are exceeding our annual growth projections. My and Bryans' calculations indicate we need at least another 50,000 square feet."

"Those are the kinds of problems we love to have," Richard said. "Have Bryan add 100,000 square feet just to be safe. Will we break ground this year?"

"Probably, but I'll confirm the starting date in no more than thirty days."

After accepting the current financial reports, Richard said, "Under the heading of New Business, Jerome has something to present."

"Personal consultations with National Bankers Association members, plus, as NBA president, my ever-increasing speaking engagements have become intrusive. Then there's my accident related reduced productivity," Jerome said, leaning heavily on his cane. "Therefore I am unable to give Survivors its deserved attention. We should begin searching for a new president." Jerome wanted to partially retire around fifty-three, which would occur on his next birthday.

The two J&B cruises generated annually for the Gerards a million dollars each; they had been extended indefinitely. Ambassador Cruise Lines, because of their compatible relationship, had given the Gerards, plus a guest couple, carte blanche to take any Ambassador cruise with top tier accommodations. The Gerards were planning to travel one week, each quarter and see the world. Jerome's mother, Martha, and her friend would be their first guests. Of course, new wardrobes would be required.

Semi-retirement would also allow the Gerards to visit Michelle, their 29 year old daughter and her family in the coastal city of Cape Town South Africa. Her husband was acquiring distribution for a group of ten African American Black hair-care manufacturers on the African continent. The Gerards couldn't visit their children and grandchildren's palatial estate often enough.

"In the interim," Jerome continued, "we should assign Sarah most of my responsibilities; give her the title of Interim President and a substantial raise.

Due to my frequent absences she has been carrying the load anyway." Sarah had agreed to stay with the new president three months, and then retire.

"I recommend that I become Chief Executive Officer, assisting Sarah, or her replacement, Harold, our senior loan vice president, and Yvonne, our new accounts vice president. I would also supervise special projects, like our new building, and manage international investments. I could then comfortably take off at least one week a month. Because of my consultation, speech fees, and net worth, I will work for a dollar a year, beginning next year. Positive Power and Bronzeville Bootstraps will also receive more of my attention."

Jerome flipped to another page, "These other personnel changes will increase efficiency, and eliminate duplication of effort," Jerome said as he displayed a new organizational chart. "Sarah and Richard agree with these recommendations. To avoid nepotism charges, others should decide Dana's direction." Dana, who had recently earned a doctorate in finance from Northwestern University, was now Human Resources Director. Jerome thought her qualified to be Survivor's chief financial officer.

"If you three have examined these changes, they are acceptable, and I agree, we need a full time president. You graciously volunteering your time and talent is commendable, and will contribute to our bank's continued growth," Samuel said. He had an office including 50 lawyers plus needed staff, specializing in defending capital murder cases.

The Gerards' net worth had reached high eight figures, without counting the Cayman Island account, which Jerome still supplemented. Gail's business and investments were flourishing as well; she too was looking forward to working less.

The following Monday morning Jerome was working the phones. Yvonne, who was pursuing an MBA, was observing. "Tiny, Jerome Gerard... There's a Pierre Francois you should meet... Naw man, he's Haitian, not French. He's preparing to import a gin, a scotch, and a vodka, from Europe and asked us to find him a partner who can guarantee distribution, initially in Chicago.... Well, think about it, man. You have six stores, and the brothers own another twenty Progressives'. Then there are fifty-some Black liquor store retailers that you could persuade... Right, and of course this will be a significant account for Survivors... Yeah, I thought you would agree.

"After you secure initial distribution you can commission Alphonso to do three advertising campaigns, and then hire a salesman to get added exposure. Within a year you should be able to penetrate the Caucasian side of town. With sufficient sales you could hire a marketing expert who could take you regional, and eventually national. Listen; remember me when you make a public offering."

"Webster, how are you doin' man? ... You have a Doctorate in Pharmacology, great! How many stores do you have? ... Eleven, outstanding, how would you like to own a generics pharmaceutical manufacturing company? ... Now wait a minute, just think about it... Of course we'll finance it."

"There's a gentleman in Dayton, Ohio who lost his family in a small plane crash over a year ago and has lost interest in running his business; he wants to sell. I met him on my last cruise; his factory is being offered at a below market price point... no, no, not just for your stores. You should get support from the National Druggist Association, who would dispense the only Black manufacture's pharmaceuticals... Caucasian druggists need not know who the new owners are. You can always increase your generic lines as patents expire."

"Long range, through research you may discover beneficial medications for our diseases like diabetes, arthritis, and high blood pressure, get your own patents, and become a national player... Here's his number, use my name when you call. If you need an outside investor let me know."

"Just a few years ago, we only financed businesses owned by Blacks to service Blacks," Jerome said to Yvonne, after hanging up the phone. "Now, we finance general market businesses that happen to be owned by Blacks." Yvonne knowingly nodded. Jerome thought, *she understands. I will encourage her and our other young guns to think creatively; they will take Survivor's to new heights.*

Sarah had become excellent at working the floor. She still occupied her Vice President's office. Jerome's replacement had been identified and was ready to move into Jerome's office. Because space was limited, Jerome and Maxine, his new secretary, would use the boardroom, until the new building was completed. Their moves would be executed in several weeks.

Jerome's son-in-law had met an African king who was interested in educating his 10,000 tribal's. This project, would challenge Jerome, Bryan, an Atlanta-based Black Construction Company, and Lonnie Blackman, with hundreds of jobs for locals. Jerome couldn't wait.

"Mr. G, its noon," Maxine said, knocking as she entered, carrying Jerome's lunch tray and medication. Maxine had replaced Geneva who had been promoted to new business loans. "It's time for your break." Maxine tuned in his favorite FM soft music station, and dimmed the lights.

"Yes ma'am." Jerome smiled as he consumed cream of mushroom soup, a half-corned beef sandwich, and a brownie with a glass of milk.

Fifteen minutes later Maxine peeped in. "Just wanted to be sure you're not in here working on something."

"Lunch was good Maxine," Jerome said as he lifted his head from a pillow on his desk, and then returned to it. Maxine eased the door closed.

End of Chapter Twenty
The End